A Warm Welcome

"A man protects what he values. Nothing is more valuable than the woman a man loves."

"How would you show a woman you loved her?" Pilar asked.

"Like this." Cade took her in his arms and kissed her.

Pilar knew that some part of her must have been wanting this, hoping for it, but a part of her was shocked to find herself in Cade's embrace. That same part was even more shocked to discover how much she wanted it, welcomed it, moved forward to meet him. Nor did she back away from the kiss when it turned from a gentle brushing of lips to an unbridled expression of pent-up emotions.

She didn't know what was responsible for the feeling that her life had suddenly turned in a new direction, had taken on a different meaning. She didn't know how to account for the emptiness inside her, or the conviction that Cade was the only one who could fill it.

She only knew she'd been swept up in Cade's powerful embrace and it was the most wonderful feeling of her whole life.

Texas Homecoming

Leigh Greenwood

sourcebooks
casablanca

Published by Sourcebooks Casablanca, an imprint of Sourcebooks,
Inc.
P.O. Box 4410, Naperville, Illinois 60567-4410
(630) 961-3900
Fax: (630) 961-2168
www.sourcebooks.com

Printed and bound in Canada.
MBP 10 9 8 7 6 5 4 3 2 1

Prologue

Shenandoah, Virginia, 1864

THE MEN FORMED A TIGHT CIRCLE AROUND A FIRE THAT was little more than glowing embers. One tossed dry moss onto the coals, and flames briefly illuminated their faces. They looked like haunted specters of the men they'd been—expressions harsh, gazes hard and unwavering, faces filmed with sweat. Ragged Confederate uniforms, the gray filthy with blood and dirt, gave no indication of the pride with which they had mounted up four days earlier. They'd spent three years protecting each other, being the family they'd left behind, but this night something less noble had drawn them together.

Revenge.

"Then it's agreed?" The man spoke with a heavy Texas drawl. As he knelt on the ground, it was impossible to tell much about his height, but he had the aura and broad shoulders of a man born to command. His intense, blue-eyed gaze moved from one man to the next around the circle. It was important that each one felt an unshakable commitment.

The men nodded their agreement.

"When do we start?" one asked.

"Where?" another wanted to know.

"They say he's dead," a third reminded them.

"He's alive," the leader said. "I can feel it."

Nobody argued with him. His *feelings* had saved their lives more than once.

"A traitor like Laveau doesn't die," their leader said. "He has to be sought out and brought to justice. Not for ourselves, but for those who aren't with us tonight."

Their troop had been betrayed by one of their own. The magnitude of the treachery, the horror of so many needless deaths, had turned the survivors into vengeful men.

"What if we don't survive the war?" one man asked. "There's only eleven of us left."

"Those who survive will carry on for the rest," their leader said.

The troop had been thirty-six strong, all young, bright, eager men, proud of their abilities and reputations, impatient to add to the growing legends surrounding the Night Riders. Then they were betrayed. They had died like defenseless animals, pinned down under lethal fire on a small farm. It was a miracle any of them had survived.

But they had, and now they had a new goal, a new reason to go on living. They would finish the war—their commitment to that came first—but afterward they would seek out the man who'd robbed them of far more than the fruits of a successful raid.

"Does anybody have a Bible?" their leader asked.

A young man got up, walked a short distance away,

and came back with a sword. "Use this," he said, his voice quavering. "It was my brother's."

The men averted their eyes. They'd all lost something that night, but nothing so impossible to replace as a brother. The leader gripped the sword in the middle. "I swear that as long as I live, I will never rest until the traitor is brought to justice."

One after another the men stood, gripped the sword, repeated the oath.

"For my brother," the boy from Arkansas said.

They continued until they named all the lost members of their troop.

"Remember," their leader said. "No matter what happens, always remember."

One

CADE WHEELER PULLED HIS HORSE TO A STOP ON THE low rise that formed the north bank of the San Antonio River. At least once a day for the last four years he'd wondered if he'd ever see this stretch of country again. He'd been born here, had grown up here. He'd come to love the harsh landscape as he could never love the more gentle, greener Shenandoah Valley, where he'd spent so much of the war. He loved the heat, the cactus, the thickets of thorn-bearing bushes where the wild longhorns hid. He loved the cedar and live oak–covered hills, the chalky soil, the blazing sky that burned a man's skin the color of tanned leather.

"Good God!" Holt Price said. "Is this the country you've been hankering after for four years?"

"This is it." Cade let his gaze wander over the hills like a loving caress. "This is home."

"It looks more like hell." Holt wiped his brow with a handkerchief. "Feels like it, too. This is September. What's it like in the summer?"

"Hotter than the hinges of hell," Owen Wheeler said. "Men have been known to die within sight of water."

"He's never set foot in Texas," Cade said, laughing at his cousin. "You can't believe anything he says."

"Doesn't look like a place friendly to a Yankee from Vermont," Holt said.

"No place in Texas is going to be friendly to a Yankee, no matter where he comes from," Owen said.

Holt was apolitical. He had volunteered as a doctor for the Confederacy because he'd been in Charlottesville, Virginia, when the war broke out.

"Don't expect anything like the big houses we saw in the valley," Cade said, prodding his horse into motion again. They headed down a worn cattle trail to the river. Cade's grandfather's ranch was on the other side.

"I wasn't expecting a mansion," Holt said.

"Cade'll be lucky if there's a cowshed left standing," Owen said. "There's been nobody to look after the place except two old men."

"My grandfather and his brother," Cade said. "My family has fought three wars since we came to Texas. There's not many of us left."

"But that's how you got your land, wasn't it?" Holt asked. "Fighting for Texas independence in 1836, then to join the United States in 1848?"

"That and a little bit of thievery."

"The spoils of war," Owen said. "You can't expect people to fight for nothing."

Cade didn't, but in this case it might have been easier if he hadn't known the people from whom his family had taken the land. It hadn't bothered his grandfather. It hadn't bothered his father either, but it had always bothered Cade. Until now.

The fourth person in the group spoke for the first time. "The strong always take from the weak."

Rafe Jerry usually contributed little to their conversations, and what he did contribute was generally gloomy. Something had made him bitter and cynical, but he didn't talk about his previous life. Not even Owen had asked. Rafe just wasn't the kind of person you asked personal questions.

"We got to go through a lot of rivers?" Holt asked as they descended the trail, dust spiraling up under their horses' hooves. Holt said people in Vermont built bridges over creeks and rivers.

"We don't believe in bridges in Texas," Cade said. "Flash floods just wash them out."

Holt's uneasiness disappeared moments later. "You call this a river?" He urged his horse into the shallow trickle that was the San Antonio River in late summer.

"If we had as much rain as you get in Vermont, this wouldn't be cow country." Cade wasn't blind to the differences between Texas and the rest of the country, but he was tired of Holt complaining about them. It had been a long ride from Virginia. "Wait until you see it after a heavy winter rain."

"Will it take that long to find Laveau?" Owen asked.

"I don't know," Cade said. "He may not have come home yet."

"He doesn't need to come home," Holt said. "Not after stealing Ivan's money."

Laveau diViere had grown up on the neighboring ranch, but he and Cade had been separated by a long-standing family quarrel. After the Texas war of independence in 1836, Cade's grandfather had carved his Wheeler 36 ranch out of land Laveau's Spanish grandmother had inherited. Cade's father had taken still more during the Mexican War, claiming the diViere grant wasn't legal under Texas law. The diVieres tried to prove their claim in court, but Texas courts rarely upheld Spanish grants.

Laveau and Cade had joined the Confederate Army when war broke out in 1861. Because of their backgrounds, they'd been chosen to be part of a mounted troop specializing in night raids, their targets primarily ammunition depots, payroll wagons, railroads, or supply trains. They rode in, struck, and rode out on the same night. They had been remarkably successful until Laveau betrayed them to the Union.

The Union casualty list showed Laveau among the dead, but no one remembered seeing him right before the attack, and afterward two horses had been missing along with Ivan's money.

"He'll come home," Cade said as his horse lunged up the opposite bank of the river. "I figure what he did is tied to getting the Union Army to recognize his grandmother's grant."

"How can they help him in Texas?"

"Once the army takes control, they'll have the power to do anything they want," Cade said.

Cade had taken a route that kept them west of the towns where troops were stationed, but the Wheeler ranch was close to San Antonio, where he was certain there would be soldiers.

"I don't see many cows," Owen said.

As they rode through the hilly, dry country west of the San Antonio River, Cade kept a careful watch for the cows that were his family's only source of income. "They prefer to bed down in the thickets during the day and graze at night."

"They're smarter than we are," Holt said. "Why don't we find us a nice, big shade tree and wait until this killing heat is gone before continuing to your hacienda in the desert?"

"I don't live on a hacienda," Cade said, "and this isn't desert."

"You couldn't prove it by me. I hope your house is close to that miserable trickle you call a river."

"It's close to a stream that empties into the river."

"Which you said is dry most of the year," Owen reminded him.

"We have a well," Cade said. "You don't have to worry you'll die of thirst."

"I'm sure I won't," Holt said. "I'll die of heat stroke first."

"This isn't half as hot as the battlefield at the Wilderness."

As tired as he was of the complaining, Cade immediately regretted mentioning that horrific battle. The smoke at the Wilderness had been so thick, soldiers on neither side could tell whether they were firing at the enemy or their own men. Dry underbrush and trees had caught fire. Cade could still hear the cries of the wounded as they perished in the smoke and flames.

The complaining ceased, and the men fell into a silence bred of long-standing companionship.

"There's the house," Cade said half an hour later.

A roofline was visible over the tops of live oaks that surrounded the ranch buildings. Cade resisted the impulse to kick his mount into a gallop. He'd been patient for four months. He could be patient a little while longer.

"I hope you've got lots of shade trees," Holt said.

"We don't believe in shade in Texas," Cade said, grinning. "Trees use up too much water."

Owen pulled up alongside Cade. "Race you to the house."

"Not on these horses. Wait until we catch up some of the old ranch stock."

The four mares they rode were Virginia and Carolina bred with some thoroughbred and Morgan blood. Cade had traded with members of the cavalry until he got the best horses he could find. They'd make poor cow ponies, but they'd be good bloodstock for the future.

They broke from the thick brush onto a trail through the range that led to the ranch.

"Anybody left at the place?" Owen asked.

"Don't know." Cade's grandfather wasn't one to write.

"Squatters?" Rafe asked.

"Could be," Cade replied. They were all silent for a moment. They knew what that could mean.

Laveau had always blamed Cade for any trouble that befell his family. When he got the letter telling him squatters had taken over his ranch, he jumped Cade. When Cade wanted to know what happened to Laveau's sister and grandmother, Laveau exploded into curses, would hardly speak to him after that.

Cade hadn't seen many signs of cows other than worn paths through the brush and trails to water, but he hadn't seen the carcasses that would be evidence of cows killed on the range, the best cuts of beef taken away, the rest left to rot. He hoped his grandfather was still alive. Cade disagreed with the old curmudgeon in just about every way possible, but he was fond of him. Cade's father had died years before, and his mother had abandoned him. His grandfather was about the only family Cade had left.

"Stop right where you are," a voice called from the post oak thicket that crowded the trail as it dipped into a dry creek bed. "One step farther, and I'll put a bullet through your brisket."

The voice didn't sound exactly like he remembered, but it was close enough to cause a smile to curve Cade's lips.

"Let's rush him," Owen half whispered.

"And if he can't, I can well enough," came a voice from the brush on their other side.

"Damnation!" Owen said. "I didn't come all the way to Texas to die in a crossfire."

The second voice was even more changed, but Cade was sure his uncle and grandfather were in the brush, determined to defend their ranch against invaders.

Cade looked over his shoulder. Holt waited, but Rafe had melted into the thick brush. Cade's grandfather obviously didn't recognize his grandson, and he'd never seen Cade's friends. As far as he knew, they were dangerous strangers.

"Gramps, it's Cade, your grandson," Cade shouted. "Come out of there before somebody gets hurt."

Cade was relieved to see the brush back along the trail stop waving. Apparently Rafe had heard and was awaiting the outcome.

"How do I know you're who you say you are? We've had lots of scallywags through here claiming to be who they wasn't."

"Stick your ugly face out of that catclaw and see for yourself, if you still can."

"I can see good enough from here to blast you to kingdom come if you ain't who you say you are," the gravelly voice announced. "And don't think to draw down on me when I step out of this here tangle. I got kin on your other side can shoot as good as me."

"You can come out, too, Uncle Jessie." Cade grinned and winked at Owen. "The old codger likes to think he's as dangerous as he remembered being forty years ago."

"My old grandpa was the same," Owen said. "Must be a Wheeler trait."

The bushes parted, and an old man stepped onto the trail about ten yards away. His clothes were thin and worn, but they appeared to be clean. He was as sinewy as a drought-hardened longhorn, his sparse hair as white as cotton, his eyes bright and alive.

"Now don't you go moving none," he said as he inched forward, his rifle held in front of him. "If you're who you claim you are, I don't suppose you'd look a lot like you did when you left here."

Cade didn't think his face had changed much, but he knew that the man inside bore little resemblance to the one who'd left this ranch four years earlier. "You haven't changed much, Gramps. Looks like you're still eating."

"Better'n most people hereabouts," the old man said.

He was about ten feet away when he came to a stop. Cade thought he saw recognition—and relief—in his eyes, but the old man didn't let down his guard. "Who's that young coyote with you?"

"Owen, your brother Harvey's grandson. There's not much left of his place, so he decided to sponge off us for a while."

Cade was certain of his grandfather's reaction this time. He lowered his rifle, and his eyes got a little brighter. "So you're one of Harvey's crowd," he said to Owen. "Who's your daddy?"

"Duane."

"I told Harvey that was a stupid name. Don't know how he could saddle one of his kids with it." He seemed to recollect himself. "Where's the other one?"

"Come on out, Rafe," Cade called. "Gramps has decided not to shoot us after all."

"Don't be too sure of that. I might change my mind yet."

Rafe rode out into the trail.

Cade's grandfather looked him over carefully. "You plan on setting up your own gang of outlaws?"

"Putting together a roundup crew," Cade said as he dismounted. "I knew an old corncob like you wouldn't be any help."

His grandfather rebuffed Cade's attempt to hug him. "None of that! I won't have a grandson of mine acting sentimental as a woman."

"Nothing sentimental," Cade said, hoping his eyes didn't glisten too much. "I just wanted to see if there was anything inside that shirt besides skin and bones."

"I got a lot of miles in me yet. Your uncle Jessie and me kept them damned squatters off our land. That's more than most people around here can say."

A man emerged from the brush behind Cade. Cade turned with a smile to greet his uncle and had to struggle hard to control his expression. He would never have recognized Jessie Wheeler. His right sleeve was empty, and he walked with a bad limp. He seemed to have aged at least twenty years.

"One of them damned gangs of scallywags caught him," his grandfather said. "Woulda killed him if I hadn't come up on them. They's all dead now, the sons of bitches. I didn't bury them neither. Let the varmints have 'em."

Cade felt guilty he hadn't been here to help his great-uncle. This wasn't Jessie Wheeler's ranch. He shouldn't have had to suffer to protect it.

His uncle also backed away from Cade's attempt to hug him. "When did you start taking up women's ways?"

"When I started losing friends faster than I could find them."

"Things aren't much better here," his grandfather said. "In the old days you could let a man sell your cattle along with his and know he'd pay you before winter set in. Now there's people here that'll steal you blind."

"Things will be better now," Cade said, turning and beginning to walk toward the house. "We'll start branding as soon as we find the horses."

"There's plenty of stock around," his grandfather said, "but I don't know if you can catch them with those skinny-rumped mares you're riding."

"They'll make good breeding stock."

"For what?"

"Riding horses."

"A mustang's the only horse a man needs for riding in this country."

"I'm not talking about men. After things settle down a bit, women will want their own horses."

His grandfather snorted. "Not decent women. They know their place."

One of the many things Cade and his grandfather disagreed on.

"What's been going on since I left?" Cade walked between his grandfather and uncle. The others followed, still mounted. "Any of the old hands still here?"

His grandfather snorted scornfully. "They couldn't stick it out. One of them got killed by the bunch of scallywags that caught Jessie, and the rest of them took off. I told them one decent Texan could handle a dozen of that trash, but they was running too fast to hear."

Cade was too happy to see the familiar outline of the house as it came into view to argue. Everything looked in need of repair, but it was all there—house, bunkhouse, corrals, even the lean-to for the milk cow and the chicken coop. He felt a tremendous sense of relief. His first concern had been his family, but his home had been in his thoughts, too. The way it had been, the way he wanted it to be. He'd told himself that when the war was over, no matter the outcome, he'd have a place to go back to, a way to provide for his grandfather and uncle if they were still alive. He'd have a way to build the kind of life he wanted for himself and the family he hoped to have.

"We lost the milk cow to one of those gangs, but I stole her back." His grandfather's dry cackle made Cade realize just how old he really was. "They never expected an old man to come after her. They attacked one of the other gangs, sure they'd took her." He laughed again. "They never did come back here looking for her."

Cade noticed some chickens around the side of the bunkhouse, wondered what had become of the garden. He didn't know why he was thinking about that. Neither of the old men could cook, at least not what most people would consider cooking. They could manage to burn some beef over an open fire or fry it hard in lard, but that was about it. Greens were another matter entirely.

"How are you taking care of yourself, Gramps?" His uncle's clothes seemed to have been recently washed, and he was fitter than many men Cade had seen.

"We got us a woman to do the cooking and washing," his uncle said. "She takes care of us pretty good."

"I didn't want her here at first," his grandfather said, "but she didn't have no place else to go."

Cade imagined there had been a lot of women displaced by the war, particularly those whose husbands hadn't come home.

"Here I've been worrying about you, and you've got some poor soul catering to your every whim," Cade teased. "I bet you even make her bring the water from the well."

"Sure as hell do," his grandfather said. "You won't see me toting water for no woman."

Some things never changed.

Cade paused when they reached the ranch yard. It felt good to be back, even better than he'd anticipated. The air was hot and dry, clean with the tangy odor of mesquite, cedar, and oak. Familiar. Friendly. No thunder of guns, scream of shells, cries of men and animals, no stench of death and rot. He couldn't put into words quite what it meant to be back on the soil of his birth, but he meant to find a way. He didn't want to forget. Ever. He wanted his children to know.

"You'd better introduce me to your housekeeper," Cade said to his grandfather. "I don't imagine she'll be happy to see us."

"She will if she's got good sense," his grandfather said.

"And she *does* have good sense," his uncle said. "Don't know how we'd have gotten along without her."

"Where's she staying?" Cade asked.

"In the house," his grandfather said. "There weren't no other place but the bunkhouse."

"Call her out," Cade said. "She might as well get the bad news."

But there was no need. The door flew open and a young woman came out of the house and started toward them. Cade's breath caught in his throat. It couldn't be. There was no way Pilar diViere would ever set foot on this ranch, much less cook and wash for his grandfather.

"What's Pilar doing here?" Cade said, turning to his grandfather.

"Squatters took over her ranch. Nobody in town wanted anything to do with her grandmother. Can't say I blame them. I never did see such a poisonous old bat."

"Do you mean Senora diViere is here, too?" Cade asked, struggling to make sense of this. At least now he understood why Laveau had been so angry.

"That's why we're living in the bunkhouse," his grandfather said. "I gotta eat, but I can't stand that woman."

Cade turned his stunned gaze back to Pilar. She had grown even more beautiful since he'd last seen her. A quarter French, she had her Spanish grandmother's black hair and eyes, her English mother's fair skin, the diViere height. Looking at her caused Cade's heart to lurch in his chest even though he knew that the years of anger and hatred between their families formed a barrier that made friendship unlikely, anything else impossible.

She looked uncertain of his reaction to her. "Where is Laveau?" she asked. "Did he come with you?"

Cade's heart thudded to a halt. She didn't know of her brother's treachery. She didn't know that seven of the eleven men who had taken an oath to bring him to justice were coming to Texas to hang him.

Two

PILAR DIDN'T KNOW WHY SHE SHOULD FEEL SO awkward. She was just asking Cade for news of her brother. The flood of eager volunteers that had flowed out of Texas had come back a trickle of disheartened veterans. Across the state, women cried for men they'd lost, prayed for those yet to come home, gave thanks for the ones who returned.

Pilar had expected that Cade would come home. Laveau had written that Cade was alive and just as conceited as ever. Laveau had hated Cade since he was old enough to understand the reason for the enmity between their families. Cade had been more defiant than hostile. Wild as a young man, full of himself, handsome in a boyish fashion, ready to do whatever caught his fancy, Cade had cut a wide swath across the county, leaving a trail of mischief that had caused her grandmother's bosom to heave with indignation that God didn't send down a plague to destroy him and every other Wheeler. She said they were common, had no respect for authority, no traditions to uphold, no fear of God.

Except for defiance, the man who faced Pilar appeared to have little in common with the boy she remembered. Age had matured his features, experience had robbed his expression of animation, and suffering had dimmed the sparkle in his blue eyes. There was a hardness about him now, a quality that said once he made up his mind to do something, he wouldn't stop until he'd done it. She also saw hostility.

"Laveau isn't with us." His voice was hard, icy.

"Do you know where he is, when he's coming home?"

"No."

"We haven't seen him in a year," one of the strangers said. "The casualty lists said he was dead."

"He's not dead," Pilar said. "I got a letter just a month ago."

"Where is he?" the man asked.

The sudden anger in the man's voice surprised Pilar.

"Let me introduce my friends," Cade said. "This is Holt Price. He's from Vermont, but he did more to keep our boys alive than most of our officers. That lanky blond is one of my Virginia cousins, Owen Wheeler. He's shiftless, much too good-looking, and you can't believe a word he says. That man astride the black mare is Rafe Jerry. No one knows where he comes from. We're afraid to ask."

Pilar couldn't imagine Cade being afraid of anything.

"What's Laveau doing now?" Cade asked. His eyes had grown colder. Owen looked angry. She wondered why.

"He's been on special assignment," Pilar said, "traveling all over the West." Her grandmother had been so proud, certain he would return home covered with honors. "His last letter was from Kentucky. He said he was headed home."

"I'm sure you'll be glad to have him back."

Laveau wrote that he'd had great success during the last year, that he'd be able to regain the whole of his grandmother's grant when he came back. Pilar wanted their land back, wanted to return home, but she didn't feel nearly so desperate as she had two years ago. She'd been humiliated when she and her grandmother had been forced to seek refuge with their enemy. She'd been ready to believe every word her grandmother said about the Wheelers. The old man's abusive attitude toward her only reinforced her prejudices.

But two years of hard work and increasing skill had altered Pilar's attitude.

She'd learned to take pride in being able to do things she would never have considered doing in the past. Learning to hold her own in the give-and-take with the old man had helped her escape the humiliation her grandmother felt.

"What was his special assignment?" Cade asked.

"Betraying someone else," Owen muttered.

Owen started to say more, but Cade cut him off. "I guess that would be his job. After all, changing sides during a war requires trading information."

Laveau's defection had shocked Pilar. She cared nothing about secession and states' rights, didn't know anybody who had slaves. But though she felt betrayed by a government that refused to recognize her mother's Spanish grant, she didn't want Laveau to be part of an army that killed people she knew.

Her grandmother thought Laveau was brilliant to put himself on the winning side. She believed it was the beginning of the family's return to power, wealth, and influence.

"Laveau said everybody could tell the Union was going to win the war," Pilar said. "He says they will make the Confederacy pay for the war. He said he could be of more help to everybody on the Union side."

"That lying, yellow-bellied son of a bitch!" Owen shouted. "Do you know what the bastard did?"

The violence of Owen's reaction caught Pilar by surprise. She wouldn't have expected Laveau's friends to like his defection, but she couldn't understand why they would be so angry. "Changing sides isn't so terrible. It's not like he hurt any of you himself."

"Owen is an idealist," Cade said, his calm voice at variance with the coldness of his eyes. He had gripped Owen's arm, dug his fingers into the flesh. There was a momentary struggle before Owen angrily jerked his arm away.

"All right," Owen said. "But I can't stand here and listen to her talk about him like he was some kind of hero."

"Why don't you unsaddle the horses? Gramps can show you where everything is."

"That gal's got to start cooking if she's gonna feed this mess of men." His grandfather cackled, his eyes alight with deviltry. "Might even have to drag the Spanish princess out of her room to help."

"My grandmother will *never* work in this house," Pilar said, anger flaring with the speed of a lightning strike to dry tinder. Pilar had come to take pride in her cooking and her ability to give the old man as good as she got, but his attempts to destroy her grandmother's pride made her angry. Her grandmother had lost everything else. Pilar intended to see that she kept her pride.

"I'm sure Miss diViere can handle everything," Cade said.

"What makes you think so?" his grandfather snapped.

"She's put up with you for two years. That's recommendation enough for me."

"I don't care who cooks," the old man said, "as long as it's hot and plentiful."

"If it's too much, one of us can help," Cade said.

"Ain't no man cooking in my house when there's a woman about," his grandfather said. "What do you think she's paid to do?"

"Whatever you pay her, I'm sure it's not enough to put up with you."

"You always did think you were smarter than anybody else."

"So you've told me." Cade smiled despite his grandfather's angry words. "I guess I haven't changed too much. Now why don't you show the boys where to put the horses?"

"I guess you're planning to take over," his grandfather said, his eyes turning angrier. "Being leader of that troop has gone to your head. As I heard tell, it got shot to pieces. Some leadership."

"Look, old man, there's a lot you don't know," Owen said. "That wasn't Cade. It was—"

"Not everybody can be right all the time," Cade said, again cutting off his impetuous cousin.

"If it hadn't been for Cade, nobody would have gotten out alive," Rafe said.

"His friends always did side with him no matter what. One of these days he'll get all of you killed."

"I figure the best chance to do that is to start them rounding up and branding our cows," Cade said, his expression tight. "Now you'd better show them where to put the horses."

"Come on." The old man turned and walked away.

"I thought Southern families stuck together," Holt said as he turned to follow the old man.

"Only against outsiders." Cade grinned. "When there's nobody else around, we don't mind sharpening our teeth on each other."

"Let's get the horses unsaddled," Owen said. "If I know Cade, he'll have us chasing mustangs first thing tomorrow."

"Sleep tight," Cade said. "You'll need all your rest."

Owen made a rude sign. Rafe and Holt followed without comment.

Pilar had never liked Earl Wheeler. Setting aside what he'd done to her family, he wasn't a likable man. He loved to criticize and humiliate people. Still, his sharp words for his grandson had surprised her. She didn't believe Cade would actually help her.

"I don't imagine it's been easy working for my grandfather," Cade said.

He couldn't know what she and her grandmother had endured.

"What made you do it? I'd have thought you'd go to Mexico."

Necessity made her do it, but she had stopped being

angry at Fate long ago. Even though the war was over and men were coming back to Texas, everything had changed. She had changed, but Cade had changed, too. She sensed he was as different from his grandfather as she was from her grandmother. Neither of them had time for the hatred and pride of the past. He might really want to know why he'd found her in the last place he would expect her to be.

She didn't like working for the Wheelers, but she had learned to take care of herself, learned from experience that loss of pride wouldn't kill her. She had grown stronger, had learned that no one had the power to destroy her belief in herself.

"Two women traveling alone would have been set upon by every bandit between here and Mexico City," she said.

"Why didn't you go to San Antonio?"

"It's been taken over by Anglos who want nothing to do with anyone who sided with Mexico." She didn't say that her grandmother's pride wouldn't allow her to live in San Antonio when her only means of support was a granddaughter who worked in a shop or the home of some rich Anglo.

"They couldn't be worse than my grandfather."

"What do you want me to cook for supper? I wasn't prepared for four extra people." She wanted to get away from his smile. It had grown warmer until she almost felt he was pleased to see her. Yet she didn't trust him. He knew something about Laveau he wasn't willing to tell her.

"We'll eat anything you fix," he said with a broad smile. "We've been cooking for ourselves for too long. I won't tell you some of the things we've been forced to eat."

She hadn't thought of that, but she should have guessed. Other men who'd come back had nothing but their rifles and the clothes on their backs. At least Cade and his friends had managed to keep their horses.

"There's some pork, but not enough to last long. We can eat the chickens, but I'd rather keep them for eggs. I'm sure you remember there are turkeys in the pecan trees along the creek. There're wild pigs, too. We couldn't feed them, so we turned them loose to forage for themselves."

"We can kill a beef now and again," Cade said, "but I'd rather keep them for market. What will you do about your place?"

"Laveau will drive the squatters off when he gets back. He said the Union Army will take over Texas. He says they'll give us our land back. *All of it.*"

His expression turned angry again. No, that wasn't exactly right. It wasn't hatred either, but the emotion she felt emanating from him was as strong as hatred.

"Do you still write Laveau?"

"He moves too often."

"Then you don't know when he'll get home?"

"He said he'd come home when the Union Army got here."

"They're here already."

"I know. General Gordon Granger landed in Galveston on the nineteenth of June. He proclaimed Texas restored to the Union, the slaves free, and all acts of the Confederacy null and void. Your grandpa told me fifty thousand more troops landed in July.

When Laveau didn't come back with them, I thought he might be with you."

Strong emotion remained in his gaze. Only now it seemed to have an element of sadness, even pain. The Cade Wheeler who rode off to defeat the Union single-handedly had been too cocky for ordinary human emotions to affect him. But that wasn't true any longer. She longed to ask what had happened.

"Laveau wouldn't be with us after changing sides. He'd have been in danger of his life."

Shock turned her stiff. "You would kill him?" She had never been allowed to forget the enmity between their two families, but it had never gone as far as killing. Her grandfather had been killed in the Texas war for independence. Her father had died ten years later. The other men in her family had been too lazy—too cowardly according to Laveau—to mount an effective counterattack against the Wheelers' depredations.

"Changing sides during a war is treason," Cade explained. "The usual punishment is death by a firing squad."

"But you wouldn't—"

"He would have received a trial before being shot."

"That doesn't matter anymore," she said. "The Confederacy is no more, and the Union Army considers him a hero. He wrote about officers he knew, even generals."

"I know nothing about what he did after he left us."

"You don't believe he knows those people," she said. "You think he's lying. Why?"

"I didn't say that."

"You're trying to hide it, but I see it in your face."

"It really doesn't matter what I believe. We'll find out for sure when he gets home. Which could be any day. I expect you'll leave as soon as he returns, so I'd better start looking around for a replacement."

It surprised Pilar that she didn't feel quite so desperate to leave as she had an hour before. Despite the family enmity, a small part of her had always liked Cade. She guessed it was the female tendency to like an outlaw or renegade, the man who would make the worst possible husband. Not that she'd ever thought of marrying Cade. But he was handsome, daring.

He used to be full of laughter.

He'd kidnapped her once and taken her for a wild ride across their ranch, outracing the ranch hands who had followed. She had been terrified—and thrilled. He hadn't hurt her. Or threatened her virtue.

She remembered his strong arms, the youthful exuberance that had caught her up despite her efforts to remain indignant, the feeling that as long as she was with him, she was safe. Which, of course, just went to show how silly a fifteen-year-old girl could be when it came to a handsome, nineteen-year-old daredevil.

"We'll leave as soon as he comes back," Pilar said. "We're anxious to return to our home."

"How many squatters are on your land?"

Far more than Laveau could handle alone. "I'm sure the army will take care of them for us."

"Let me know if you find out when he's coming back. Maybe we can work together. I probably have squatters stealing my cows, too."

"Your grandfather and uncle drove out the ones who tried to settle here. That's how your uncle got hurt."

"Who took care of him?"

"My grandmother," she said, glad that Wheelers finally owed something to the diVieres.

"I thought she wanted us all dead."

"She said she wanted him alive when the army threw you off this land. She wanted him to experience the humiliation she has lived with for so long." The anger was back. "I'll have supper ready as soon as I can."

"We'll eat whenever you have it ready."

⤷⤶

"I prayed a Yankee bullet would kill him," her grandmother said to Pilar the minute she entered the room that her grandmother hadn't left since she'd arrived at the ranch two years ago.

"Who?"

"The young one. Kill off the young, and their tribe will wither and die."

Pilar didn't like the Wheelers, but she'd never prayed for Cade's death. Except for youthful high spirits and general worthlessness, she hadn't seen anything wrong with him, though she thought it was a shame for such good looks to be wasted on a Wheeler. There were times when she had difficulty remembering she wasn't supposed to like him. "He'll be a lot nicer to work for than his grandfather."

"Men like him want only one thing. Keep away from him."

Pilar had never been able to convince her grandmother that Cade's kidnapping her had been nothing more than a prank. Her grandmother remained convinced that only the pursuit of the ranch hands had prevented his despoiling Pilar among the cactus and catclaw.

"I can't hide in this room all day like you do."

"I will not watch that vile old man enjoy his triumph. I will not come out until Laveau comes to carry me back to our hacienda."

Pilar had found it difficult to care for her grandmother and do all the other work as well, but so far she'd managed. She didn't know what she was going to do now that she had four extra men to feed.

&

"Don't let her know what her brother really did," Cade said when he rejoined his friends at the corral. His grandfather had been entertaining them with some of his stories but had stalked off in a huff when he saw Cade coming.

"Why not?" Owen asked. "She thinks that traitor is a hero."

"Everybody ought to know what he did," Holt said.

"I agree," Cade said, "but he's still writing her."

"But she can't write him," Holt reminded Cade.

"I expect that will change. He'll probably want to know if the coast is clear."

"Why should he care if he's bringing the Union Army with him?"

"I doubt he can do that. In any case, I don't want you to tell her what he did. If she thinks we're after him, she'll warn him to stay away."

"You planning on flirting with her?" Owen said, his grin mocking.

"She dislikes everyone in my family."

"She doesn't dislike you."

"Yes, she does. Her grandmother has beaten that into her very soul. It's probably why Laveau betrayed us."

"She likes you. Give me credit for knowing women."

"I'll give you credit for being the most brazen flirt I know, so stay away from her." Cade grinned at his cousin. He hadn't much liked his distant relative at first, but he'd come to see that behind all Owen's bluster and outrageous talk was a solid, responsible man who could be depended on regardless of danger. "Maybe Holt or Rafe should talk to her and see what they can learn."

"She won't like Rafe. Besides, it would take her a year to get a full sentence out of him. She won't like Holt because he's a Yankee. That leaves me and you. Want to toss a coin to see who gets her?"

Cade was certain Pilar felt nothing but dislike for him, but there was an outside chance that loneliness might cause her to misinterpret the first male attention she'd received in years. He had no intention of letting Owen trifle with her affections. He liked even less gambling over the right to do so.

"We're not tossing a coin," Cade said.

"Does that mean you're giving her to me?"

"No, it means we're not tossing a coin."

"What are you so concerned about? She's the enemy."

"Laveau is the enemy."

"Do you think she'd help him even if she knew what he did?"

"Yes."

"Then she's not innocent," Owen said, his grin

becoming more pronounced as he fished a coin out of his pocket. "You get heads. I get tails."

"I'm not gambling," Cade said, but Owen had already tossed the coin.

He let it fall on the ground. "Damn, you win."

Cade felt the muscles across his shoulders relax, was relieved he wouldn't have a confrontation with Owen. He understood the importance of undercover work—espionage, spying, anything you wanted to call it. Had this been war, he wouldn't have hesitated.

But it wasn't war, and Pilar was innocent even if she didn't like him and was loyal to her brother. It wouldn't be fair to take advantage of her. Then he remembered Laveau's treachery, and his heart hardened.

He would have revenge regardless of who suffered. Even the innocent.

But the fact that he'd always liked her made it harder. Her being young and extremely attractive made it harder still. It would be all too easy to like his task, and the more he liked it and the more successful he became, the more he would dislike himself.

"You boys had better check your equipment," he said, ready to think about something else. "We start looking for the riding stock tomorrow. They ought to be pretty wild by now."

"My mare's in heat," Holt said. "That ought to attract the attention of the stallions."

"We need the geldings," Cade said. "Stallions are no good as cow ponies."

"Then let's cut them."

Cade laughed. "You ever try to cut a wild stallion?"

"No, but I bet it would be fun."

"Only if you're trying to get yourself killed."

"I'll do it," Rafe said.

They all looked at him.

"I've done it before."

Cade wondered when and where. Though he'd known Rafe for nearly four years, he knew almost nothing about him.

"I'll hold you to that," Cade said. "If you boys need to replace any equipment, there ought to be plenty in the bunkhouse."

"What do you think you're doing?" Owen asked as Cade headed for the barn with the other men.

"I need to check my equipment, too."

"We'll do that for you. Get up to the house and convince that pretty, young thing you think the sun rises and sets on her. I expect you to know all her secrets by this time tomorrow."

Three

PILAR HURRIED TO GET DINNER ON THE TABLE. FROM her experience, men expected food to be in front of them when they were hungry, seconds to be handed to them the minute they were ready. They never seemed to understand that food didn't prepare itself or that no woman was born with eight arms so she could fulfill all their demands at once.

She grabbed plates from the cabinet while keeping an eye on the stove. The chipped and cracked plates and cups were in stark contrast to the expensive French china the squatters occupying her family's hacienda were using. She had buried the silver, but she expected that everything else in the house would be gone before they returned.

If they returned.

She pushed that thought from her mind. Laveau would be home soon. He would drive the squatters out. She grabbed a handful of forks, knives, and spoons and started putting them around the table. They were made of tin. The Wheelers didn't own anything that wasn't cheap.

She heard the door open and felt a surge of anxiety. The men were here, and she wasn't ready. The old man would have a fit.

"Need any help?"

Pilar turned around so fast that one of the knives flew out of her hands. It struck Cade on the shin and landed on his foot. She stood there, too shocked to move. Cade calmly stooped down and picked up the knife.

"I guess you need a clean one." He turned to the drawer and took out a knife. "The boys will be in any minute. I'll finish setting the table."

Pilar couldn't understand why she couldn't move. No shock should have affected her this strongly.

"I don't know what everyone wants to drink. I've got plenty of coffee, but I didn't know if anyone might want milk." She had to be losing her mind. Only farmers drank milk. A cowboy would go thirsty first.

"I can't speak for Rafe, but Holt drinks milk. He's nothing but an old farm boy. Owen will drink whatever you offer him. He's a helpless flirt around a pretty woman."

She remained paralyzed, staring at him, acting like a fool, sure her mouth was hanging open. She didn't know what was wrong with her. Maybe it was worrying about having to feed so many men. He took the forks and knives from her limp grasp.

"You'd better get the food on the table. I think I hear them coming."

He smiled, but no warmth reached his eyes. His voice sounded cold, unemotional. Pulling herself together, Pilar hurried to the stove, took a very large meat pie out of the oven, and placed it in the middle of the table.

"That smells awfully good," Cade said as he took cups from the cupboard. "Don't we have anything that's not chipped or cracked?"

"That's all I've ever seen."

He inspected one of the coffee cups, turning it from side to side. "I guess I never noticed before."

He'd grown up with cracks and chips. He probably thought that was how plates and cups were supposed to look. She wondered where he'd been and what he'd done to make him aware of the difference now. Her grandmother never stopped reminding her that the Wheelers were poor whites who didn't have any class or enough sense to know they were trash.

Cade wasn't stupid. He ought to *know* he was so poor that he was beneath the notice of a diViere. Still, she had to admire the way he brazenly forced the world to take him as he was. He didn't appear to have lost any of his self-confidence, but he clearly didn't like chipped and cracked dishes.

She couldn't afford to stand there speculating about his last four years. She put a large bowl of black-eyed peas on the table, then reached for the stewed peaches.

"Where's the milk?" he asked.

"Sweet is in the springhouse. Sour and buttermilk in the pantry."

DiVieres always drank wine with their dinner. She expected that was gone, too.

"Where are the glasses?"

"You lived here for twenty years," she snapped,

wrestling with the hot fruit to keep from burning herself. "Can't you remember where anything is?"

"It's been a long time. Besides, you've been doing the cooking for two years."

"And everything is exactly where it was when I came." She set the hot bowl on the table and turned to him. "Your grandfather said he wouldn't have any Mexican wench messing about in his house. He said everything had been put where it was by a good American woman, and I was to leave things alone if I knew what was good for me."

She turned back to put the stewed corn in a dish. She hadn't meant to say anything to Cade. She'd intended to walk away from his ranch with her head held high, but here she was about to burst into tears.

"I was in lots of houses during the war," he said. "None of them did things the same way, but it didn't seem to make any difference in getting the food on the table or making it taste good."

She didn't have time to decide whether he was trying to make her feel better or trick her. The men poured into the room as if they'd all charged the door to see who could get there first.

The old man won. "Where's the coffee, girl?" he demanded, going straight to the chair at the head of the table.

He said this every night to irritate her. Pilar set the pot next to his plate without a word.

"No wonder your ranch went bust," he said with a derisive hoot. "You with your highfalutin ancestors and you still can't count. You've set seven places. There's only six men here."

Pilar wondered if the old man was finally getting senile. She knew she'd only taken out six plates.

"I set the extra place," Cade said.

"What for?"

"Pilar."

"What's gotten into you, boy? You know the help doesn't eat at the table."

"Where does she eat?"

"I don't know. What does it matter?"

"I imagine it matters to her."

"She's not paid for it to matter."

Pilar didn't want to eat with the old man. His griping would give her indigestion, but his remark about being paid made her furious. She opened her mouth to speak, saw Cade looking at her, and closed it again. She turned back to the stove. The biscuits were ready to come out.

"How much do you pay her, Gramps?" Cade asked, an edge to his voice.

"She gets paid plenty. Now sit down before the food gets cold."

"How much?"

Pilar turned back. No one else had sat down at the table, not even Cade's uncle. The power base had shifted on the Wheeler ranch. The old man might own the place, but Cade was going to run it. He'd stepped right into the job without asking anyone's permission.

In the past she would have attributed that to his arrogance, his assumption that whatever he did was right, but there was nothing of arrogance or conceit about him now. Only confidence.

"He doesn't pay me anything," Pilar said. "I take

care of him and your uncle in exchange for his letting me and my grandmother live here."

"Sit down and eat," the old man grumbled. "I'm hungry."

"She only had to take care of two before," Cade said. "There's six of us now and more to come. I think Pilar ought to sit down with us and work out a new deal."

"You think you can come in here and tell me what to do?"

"To some degree. This is your ranch, but it's our work that'll make it worth something."

"That don't mean she can eat at my table."

Cade started taking up the plates.

"What are you doing?" his grandfather asked.

"No need for so many plates for just you and Jessie."

"We may be poor, but I won't have anybody eating out of the pots."

"The boys and I will wait and eat with Pilar."

"Are you crazy?" his grandfather asked.

"What's crazy about wanting a pretty woman across the table?" Owen winked at Pilar. "I'd eat on the steps just to look at her."

"Please, sit down," Pilar said, angry to find herself the center of this disagreement. "The food will get cold."

"We're used to cold food," Cade said. "You can't light cook fires when you're on a night raid."

"You're not raiding anybody now," the old man said. "Sit down."

"We'll be outside," Cade said to Pilar. "Let me know when he's finished."

Pilar couldn't believe her eyes when the four young men filed out of the room.

Jessie Wheeler looked from his brother to where his great-nephew had disappeared through the door.

"Stop twisting about like a sock in the wind," his brother shouted. "Sit down."

"I'll wait." Jessie turned and walked out.

Earl sat in stunned silence a moment before he turned on Pilar. "Now see what you've done, you foreign hussy. You've turned my own grandson against me."

"Don't blame me," Pilar fired right back. "I didn't make you mean and spiteful. I don't blame him for not wanting to eat with you. I'm surprised he wanted to come back at all."

Pilar knew the old man's meanness stemmed from his feeling of impotence, but it was time he learned that things had changed. The young men were coming back to Texas. Old men like him would soon be moved to the sidelines whether they liked it or not. She thought Cade would try to protect his grandfather's feelings. He seemed to have grown up and matured since he'd left, but he also had the habit of command.

"What did you do to him?" Earl demanded.

"I was too busy putting food on the table to do anything," Pilar said. "Eat your food and stop acting foolish."

She was angry that all her work had gone for naught. She had a table covered with food she'd worked hard to prepare and nobody to eat it because of this old man.

"You were trying to entice him to—"

Pilar slammed the second coffeepot down so hard it would have broken if it hadn't been metal. "I wouldn't *entice* anyone in your family if he were the last man on the earth. Do you think I don't know you've stolen my family's land?"

"You had too much," the old man said, dismissing her accusation as though it were of no consequence. "Besides, it was my protection that kept your family from losing the whole grant."

"It doesn't change the fact you're a thief. I'm a Cordoba. My grandmother can trace her family back a thousand years. We don't have anything to do with thieves."

"Your father was a diViere and your grandfather before him. They might think themselves fancy French aristocrats, but they were nothing but lazy fools. I'm not ashamed of being common, but I'd be ashamed of being a fool."

"I'm not a fool."

"No, you've got more sense than the rest of your family put together. Now go outside and tell my stiff-necked grandson to come eat his supper before it gets cold. He can't put this ranch back on its feet with a belly full of nothing but pride."

"I don't know why not. You've held it without much more."

She hated to say anything nice about the old man to his face, but he had held this ranch against a bunch of vicious and determined squatters. He'd kept her and her grandmother safe at the same time.

The old man actually grinned. "That's all I had when I came to Texas, just me, Jessie, and my young son." He stopped talking abruptly, frowned. "No sense chattering on to you. Go get those boys."

Pilar couldn't decide whether Earl was proud his grandson had stood up to him or just pretending not to care. She had to admire the old bull. And with admiration came tolerance, even a little understanding. But at times like this, it was hard not to loathe him.

"And don't forget to set yourself a place," Earl said as she went through the door. "I don't want to give that young whippersnapper an excuse to walk out on me again."

Yes, she definitely heard the pride of an old bull seeing the young bull about to take over.

❧

"Where did you learn to cook like this?" Owen asked as he passed his plate a third time. "Say the word, and I'll marry you tomorrow."

"Why not tonight?" Cade asked.

"How about it?" his irrepressible cousin asked "We could get the old man to perform the ceremony. Cade says he's a justice of the peace."

"Not anymore," Earl said.

Owen winked at Pilar again. "We can ride into San Antonio. We'll have all night to celebrate."

Cade stifled a desire to punch his cousin in his much-too-active mouth. He was surprised Pilar hadn't left the table. She had been reared by her grandmother to think herself a Spanish aristocrat. She'd been affianced to a distant cousin in Mexico since she was ten.

But then the war came, and the cousin never appeared. Cade didn't know what Pilar did after Laveau left for the army, but somewhere in her tired, aristocratic background lurked a strong determination to survive, a willingness to do whatever was necessary to stay alive. It must have been difficult for her to learn to cook. More difficult to submit to working for his grandfather.

"Be quiet, Owen," Cade said. "You're embarrassing her."

Owen appealed directly to Pilar. "Am I embarrassing you by saying you're beautiful?"

"Seems to me I heard more about her cooking," Cade said.

"That's your fault," Owen said. "If you'd been a better cook, I wouldn't be too starved to devote my full attention to her beauty."

"You cook?" Pilar asked in obvious disbelief.

"If you could call what he does to food cooking," Holt said.

"Only ones worse than Cade were Holt and me," Owen said between mouthfuls of meat pie.

"What about Rafe?" Pilar asked.

"Rafe supplied the food," Owen said. "We never asked where he found it."

Cade had been uneasy about returning to the table after his grandfather's initial refusal to allow Pilar to eat with them. He had been prepared for some sort of trick—the old man wasn't used to being told what to do—but his grandfather now paid little attention to Cade or Pilar, none at all to Owen.

Pilar had appeared reluctant to join in the conversation even when directly addressed. She'd tried to use the excuse of having to serve the meal, but the men had spent four years serving themselves. They got up to get extra coffee or refill a bowl from a pot on the stove.

"Cade was your captain," Pilar said. "I didn't think captains cooked."

"We soon learned to let every man do what he did best," Cade said.

"I hope you're good at wrangling horses," Earl said, suddenly entering the conversation. "Our riding stock is wild as antelope and peevish as mossyback steers."

"I'll leave wrangling horses to Cade," Owen said. "I'm much better at wrangling females."

Cade decided he should be the one to try to gain Pilar's confidence. He didn't think she would fall for Owen's blandishments, but women had a habit of taking a shine to the most undependable men. Owen tried to seduce practically every woman he met. Cade often wanted to tell him a little constancy wouldn't be a bad thing.

"Women like me," Owen said.

"Stop making a fool of yourself, and let's talk about finding those horses," Earl snapped.

"A beautiful woman is much more interesting than wild horses."

"I agree," Cade said, "but if you want to leave here with cash money in your saddlebags, you'd better start thinking about horses."

"What cash money?" Earl asked, his sharp gaze riveted on his grandson.

"Everybody needs a stake to get started again. I promised them half our profits on the herd if they'd help me round them up, brand them, and take them to market."

"Four men can't do all that," Earl said, his gaze going from one man to the other, "even if they do look like they'd cut a man's gizzard out."

"There're more coming," Cade said.

"How many?"

"Three or four."

"That won't be enough. Them squatters aren't going to be happy with you taking their beef. They been selling it for tallow and hides."

"That's a waste. A three-dollar steer in Texas is worth thirty dollars in St. Louis."

"What makes you so sure you can get them there?"

"If we don't, we won't have any money."

"It's hundreds of miles away, and there's Indians and farmers along the way, not to mention men who'd cut your throat for the fun of it."

"We wouldn't mind doing a little bit of that ourselves," Rafe said.

"The tanning factories are a lot closer," his grandfather said. "You could even take them to Mexico."

"We can't keep selling our stock for hides and tallow."

"Why not? It's what I've done my whole life."

"The future of Texas ranching is in selling beef to people in cities like New York, Boston, and Philadelphia. They've got money, and they're ready to spend it. All we have to do is get the cows to a railhead or the coast so they can be shipped."

"I don't want my cows on any boats," Earl said.

"And we need to upgrade our herds. The more meat we can put on our cows, the more money we'll get for them," Cade said, ignoring his grandfather's objections. "I saw bulls in Virginia bred to carry three times as much meat as a longhorn. I mean to buy several of them."

"I won't have you coming in here with all kinds of newfangled notions," Earl said. "There's nothing

wrong with longhorns. They can take care of themselves. We don't have to ride herd on them through
the winter and watch out for wolves."

"All that's going to change," Cade said. "And
the ranchers who survive will be the ones doing
the changing."

Cade spent the next twenty minutes arguing
with his grandfather, trying to show him why the
longhorn wouldn't be able to compete much longer.
He tried to convince him that everyone would soon
be upgrading like Richard King, but his grandfather
continued to object.

"I've seen bulls so heavy they can hardly walk,"
Owen said.

"A fat lot of good that'll do when a wolf comes
after them," Earl said. "You going to be sitting out
there in the brush watching over every one of those
poky critters?"

"We won't put the blooded bulls on the range,"
Cade said. "We'll keep them in a pasture and bring
the cows to them."

Earl looked at his grandson as if he'd lost his mind.
"I ain't buying no bull that don't know how to go
about his business by himself."

Cade had to laugh or get angry. He decided to laugh.

"You've been gone a long time," the old man
said. "I don't know where you got these newfangled
notions, but we're doing things just the same as always
here in Texas, and it's working just fine."

"It won't work for much longer," Cade said.
"Once the army clears the plains of Indians, there'll
be ranches from Texas to Canada. There's millions

of acres of grass out there just waiting for new herds. Somebody's going to have to provide them with stock. If we don't, somebody else will. And they'll buy from the man who can sell them stock that brings the best price at market."

"And when did you see these millions of acres of grass?" his grandfather asked. "They got some damned long telescopes back there in Virginia I don't know nothing about?"

"Of course not, but—"

"Until you've seen it, we'll keep doing things like we always did."

"I've seen the grass," Rafe said. "In places it's so high you can hardly see a man on foot. I once saw a herd of buffalo so big it stretched from horizon to horizon. There's enough grass out there for a million ranches like this."

Earl's mouth worked before he finally said, "I never heard of anything so ridiculous."

Cade felt a spurt of anger. Why was the old fool so stubborn? Why wouldn't he believe what other people had seen?

Then came understanding. His grandfather felt like he was being pushed aside, not just because he couldn't do the work any longer but because the world was expanding beyond his experience. He had been young and vigorous when he came to Texas. He had fought in two wars, claimed land from the hated Spanish, even been a local hero. Now he was feeling old and used up, and he didn't like it.

"We have to build fences," Cade said. "There's no way to improve the herds unless we can control the cattle."

His grandfather exploded. After a scathing attack on anyone foolish enough to want to fence cattle, he launched into the cost of such an operation.

"We won't fence everything," Cade said, "just enough to control the breeding. We can do a little each year."

"You think I'm gonna be dead in a year or two," the old man shouted. "You think I'm gonna leave this place to you to do with as you like."

"Things are going to change," Cade said, out of patience. "We have to change with them or be left behind."

"You've been gone from Texas too long. Wait a couple years. You'll forget all this nonsense about fat bulls and fences. You'll see the old ways are best."

Cade hadn't expected his grandfather to agree with everything he said, but he hadn't expected him to be so adamantly against change of any kind. Cade felt hemmed in. He didn't actually own the ranch. If push came to shove, he had no legal right to dictate how the ranch should be run.

Cade felt a responsibility to the men who'd come with him. He'd promised them a chance to earn money so they could start over. They had to sell their beef for more than the three or four dollars they got for tallow and hides if they were to do any of the things he'd dreamed of. One way or another, he had to bring his grandfather around, but he wanted the old man to understand. Despite the old codger's miserable temper, Cade loved him.

"Listen to Cade," Pilar said. "What he says makes a lot of sense."

Earl rounded on her, bringing his hand down on the table with a smack that reverberated off the walls. "And just what the hell do you think you know about it, missy?"

Four

"I LEARNED A LOT AFTER LAVEAU LEFT," PILAR SAID calmly. "If I hadn't, there wouldn't have been anything for the squatters to take."

"Your place wasn't nothing but a wreck when the squatters took over," Earl said.

"I also learned that men are much better at spending money than they are at making it," she fired back.

The old man's laugh was harsh, derisive. "There's not a man alive who'll believe that men waste more money than women."

"It doesn't matter what you believe about me," Pilar said. "I know about the North's fondness for beef. I know where to find bulls that carry the meat we need to make a profit. I'll see that Laveau knows, too."

Pilar swung her gaze from the old man to her plate, but she couldn't resist a quick glance to see Cade's response. She told herself she didn't trust him. That was true. She told herself she didn't like him.

That wasn't true.

He was too handsome, too charming when he chose. There weren't many young, unmarried men in south Texas, but there were none who compared to Cade. She knew that any relationship between them was impossible, wouldn't have wanted one if he had been willing, but that didn't mean she couldn't enjoy looking at him. Just because you knew a wild stallion was dangerous didn't mean you couldn't admire him.

"You and your bother can do anything you like," Earl Wheeler said. "You'll go broke, and we can buy up the rest of your land."

"You mean you're not going to take it? What's wrong? Too old, too tired, or is it because you're not on the winning side this time?"

"You'd better hurry up and marry that Mexican cousin," Earl snapped. "If your tongue gets any sharper, won't nobody have you."

"I'm not sure I want to get married. A woman has enough burdens without having to carry a husband around on her back." Pilar pushed her chair back. "Leave everything on the table. I'll wash up after you're done."

"It's too bad you didn't leave after you got the food on the table," Earl flung at her as she left the room. "Then I wouldn't have my fool grandson insisting you eat with us." The door banged shut behind her. "I won't have you falling into her clutches," Earl said, turning to Cade.

"Do you mind if I fall into them?" Owen asked.

"She's just like her grandmother, hot-blooded and poisonous. If you've got any sense, you'll steer clear of her."

"He doesn't have any sense," Holt said. "All he has to do is clap eyes on a beautiful woman, and he's lost."

"She ain't beautiful," Earl said.

Cade didn't bother to join in Holt's and Owen's efforts to convince his grandfather that Pilar was beautiful. Any male with eyes in his head could see she'd been beautiful from birth. On the outside. On the inside she was just another diViere. Maybe that wasn't exactly true. He couldn't imagine Laveau swallowing his pride and working for an enemy to protect his grandmother's pride. Laveau probably would have expected his grandmother to support him.

"We need to go over our plans for tomorrow," Cade said, breaking in on his grandfather and Owen.

"What's there to plan?" Holt asked. "We're just going to catch up your grandfather's horses."

"They might be in the next river bottom," Cade said, "or halfway across Texas. We don't have any fences to hold them back."

"Tell Pilar to put together some food for you," Earl said. "That ought to give her something to do besides flounce around the place."

"I'll see to our provisions," Cade said.

"That's what women are for."

"I'd just as soon do it. We may be gone for as much as a week."

"They won't be that far away," his grandfather said. "As long as the squatters ain't got them."

An eerie quiet fell over the kitchen after everyone had gone. Dirty dishes, cracked and mismatched, chipped mugs, tarnished utensils, and a bare wood table made Cade acutely aware of the difference between this slapped-together cabin and the gracious, sprawling hacienda Pilar had known from birth. His own family was little more than squatters from the mountains of Virginia.

Ever since he could remember, his grandpa had ridiculed the diVieres and everyone like them, called them shiftless, no-account, a rotten layer of society that should be cut away. Cade had been eager to accept his grandfather's attitude. He'd roared around the county pitting his strength, skill, and daring against the decadent aristocrats. He'd savored his victories—carrying off Pilar had been the sweetest—but he couldn't escape the nagging fear that he and his family were little more than white trash.

That was what his mother had said when she'd abandoned him.

Then he'd gone to Virginia and discovered an aristocracy that had little to do with wealth or birth. Rather it had to do with nobility of spirit, purity of goals, educated and inquiring minds. He had welcomed that eagerly, seen in it something he wanted to share.

He wanted to be part of that world.

Now looking around the kitchen, he felt scarred, chipped, and cracked himself. He didn't like that. He wanted more for himself, for his children. He could make the money. He had land, cows, and a willingness to work. He could build a house, buy the furnishings. But something was missing, something he had to have to make it all work.

A wife.

He expelled his breath in a hiss. As a child he'd felt abandoned by a father who died young and a mother who wouldn't fight to keep him. Men were loyal to death, but women were weak, and love was an untrustworthy emotion. Women had never lasted long in his family, staying only long enough to produce one or two children—always male—before running away. The Wheelers might as well have been a race of men, self-perpetuating and self-influenced.

They needed a woman like Pilar.

That thought startled him. Pilar was an aristocratic woman who represented something he could never have, a level of social refinement he could not attain, wasn't sure he *wanted* to attain. She was an ornament, beautiful and fragile, meant to belong to someone who could afford to protect her, provide her with an elegant setting. If he'd ever imagined marrying her, it had been a daydream long since forgotten. But things had changed. The woman he found in his home today bore little resemblance to the girl he remembered.

He stepped into the storeroom off the kitchen and started gathering food from the few provisions there.

"What are you doing in the storeroom?"

He looked up from the shelves. He hadn't heard her enter the kitchen. "I'm putting together some food for the next few days."

"What are you taking?"

"Some beans, flour, sugar, and coffee. We'll shoot our meat."

"I've got some dried fruit."

"I don't have time to make a pie."

Her laugh was unexpected. "Can you?"

He smiled in return. "I call it a pie. Owen doesn't."

"Where did you learn to cook?" She still didn't look convinced.

"Over a campfire. I wouldn't know what to do with a stove."

He became increasingly aware that they occupied a very small space, that her body was only inches from his. Her long-sleeve dress buttoned under her chin, but it fitted her body like a glove. The glossy surface of the black fabric—it wasn't homespun or wool, the only two kinds of cloth he knew—caught the light in a way that subtly emphasized the shape of the body underneath.

"I don't know much about armies, but I doubt that most leaders do the cooking."

"Who says I was the leader?"

"When were you anything else?"

It startled him that she would have seen him in that light. He was simply a man who was willing to do what had to be done. "Everybody did what they could. Like you."

She didn't appear to like being reminded of her present position. "Take what you want." She turned away, leaving him with the feeling he'd hurt her. He didn't understand. She should be proud of surviving on her own. He finished filling his saddlebags with dried peaches. They'd taste good stewed.

"We'll have to go to town for supplies when we get back," he said to Pilar when he closed the storeroom door. "Make a list of what you need."

She didn't look up from her work of gathering plates, scraping them, and putting them into hot, soapy water. "Do you have any money?"

"I'll ask for credit."

"You won't get it."

"Then I'll sell something."

"What do you have worth selling?"

He knew she was thinking of the ramshackle cabin, the threadbare clothes, the chipped and cracked plates. "I can sell my guns or one of the mares."

"You'll need your guns to defend this place, your horses as a foundation for a new herd."

He knew he was poor, that his family had never owned anything of value, but she didn't need to be so brutal about it. Then she left the room without explanation, returned moments later as he was about to leave, and held something out to him. "You can sell this." A small cameo surrounded by pearls lay in the palm of her hand.

"I can't. It belongs to you."

"It hasn't stopped your grandfather."

A very unpleasant feeling cannonaded the pit of his stomach. "What do you mean?"

"How do you think we've had food when so many people are starving?"

He'd assumed they lived off the land. But he knew that such things as flour, sugar, salt, coffee, and dried or canned fruit and vegetables weren't lying about ready to be picked up when they were needed.

"My grandmother and I weren't able to salvage much, but we saved our jewelry. We've been selling it piece by piece to stay alive."

Cade felt humiliated. His family might not have an illustrious background—no titled noblemen, no inherited wealth, no fancy haciendas—but they had pride. The idea of selling a woman's jewelry, especially a woman who had cooked and kept house for two years without wages, was unthinkable.

"You won't have to do that anymore," he said, trying to keep the anger and shame from his voice. "If you'll give me a list of everything you've sold, I'll buy it back as soon as I sell the herd." He had considered the possibility of selling a few steers to the tallow factories for some quick and badly needed cash, but now that was out of the question. He needed as much money as possible to pay off this debt. He couldn't hold up his head knowing his family had been supported by a woman.

Pilar set the cups on a drain board, turned, and directed a speculative look at him. She was clearly judging him, deciding whether he measured up to the job that lay ahead.

"Pride is a good thing, Cade, but don't let it stand in the way of common sense. Take the cameo. We can talk about your paying me back when your ranch is safe and your mares are all in foal." She turned back to her work. "Besides, I'll be able to buy all the jewelry I want after Laveau comes home."

Cade crossed the short distance that separated them, took her by the arm, and forced her to face him. "We both know Laveau is like your father. He enjoys being rich, but he won't do the work it takes to earn the money necessary to support his lifestyle."

She looked him straight in the eye. "He won't have to. I will."

Cade couldn't imagine the girl he remembered being strong enough to take on such a job. She didn't have the necessary knowledge. Even if she had, Texas men didn't take orders from a woman.

"I ran everything after Laveau left," Pilar said. "I

didn't want to, but I didn't have a choice. I spent two years paying off debts, getting everything straightened out, but I made one mistake. We'd always been invulnerable, so I cut our crew down to a minimum to save money. When the squatters came, we didn't have the men to hold them off."

"What happened to the men you did have?"

"They ran off."

"Because they didn't think a woman could tell them what to do?"

Her expression hardened, and she attempted to turn away. He tightened his grip.

"The cowards would have stayed for Laveau, though he didn't know any more about fighting than a puppy, but they left me without putting up a fight."

Anger flamed in her eyes. Cade couldn't tell whether it was from the loss of her heritage or the humiliation of having the men desert her. He also saw shame. He knew how that felt. The shame of losing two-thirds of his troop still cut deep.

"I'm glad you came here. My grandfather is a scrappy, hardheaded, stubborn old bastard. He can fight anything alive, but he would have starved before he could have figured out how to feed himself. Probably would have been too proud to try."

"I've noticed the Wheeler pride," she said, her eyes hard and dark, "but I've never been able to understand its source."

Cade dropped his hand from her arm. "Your ancestors were just like ours at one time—poor, ambitious, hungry for land and wealth. They took what they wanted without regard for ownership. There's no difference between your family and mine. We just got started a few hundred years later."

Pilar turned away from him. "That's a novel way of explaining your family's theft."

"Nothing stays the same for long. The strong grow weak, the weak grow strong. It's the law of nature. I'll see that you get your jewelry back. Will you be all right while we're gone?"

"We were all right for two years. I expect we'll manage for a few more days."

She wasn't giving an inch. She didn't need him, and she wasn't about to let him forget it. That was just as well. He didn't need her, either. He'd be relieved when she went back to her ranch, but he knew that couldn't happen until Laveau returned. And he intended to hang Laveau for treason.

What would she think of him then?

Did it matter? She already considered him a thief.

But Cade wanted the right to be judged for himself, to start with a clean page unblotted by the past. He wanted people to realize he was no longer a wild, reckless youth ready to do anything just because it was outrageous. He'd proved himself during four years of brutal warfare. He had come home with the intention of building a new life for himself. He wanted everyone to see him in a different light. And part of that transformation was gaining Pilar's recognition and acceptance. *She* had to look at him with new eyes.

"I'm sure you'll survive," he said, "but I mean to see that things are easier for you from now on."

She was subjecting him to that look again—measuring, calculating. Did she doubt his word, or was she unable to stop thinking of him as the wild-eyed kid and see in him the man he had become?

She turned back to her work. "The squatters haven't bothered us in some time. I doubt they'll do so now with four more men here."

"Do you think you can handle all the extra work our being here will cause?"

"It's not much different to cook for six men than two. I just cook more of everything."

Had he hoped she would admit that the job was too much for her, that she couldn't manage without him? If so, he was a fool. As she had so often told him, her grandmother was a Cordoba. They had been proud Spanish aristocrats for generations. A Cordoba would *never* ask a Wheeler for help. It would be like asking a servant—or a peasant.

"Just let me know if you need anything." He picked up his supplies. "We'll leave at dawn tomorrow."

"Breakfast will be ready an hour before you leave."

"You don't have to fix breakfast."

"It's my job. As long as I'm here, I'll do it."

Pride shot from her eyes like tiny swords intended to prick his skin and remind him who she was.

"The army taught me it doesn't matter who does the job as long as everyone's working toward the same end."

"We aren't," Pilar said. "We never will be. Breakfast will be ready an hour before you leave."

"Make sure you fix plenty," he said, his words sounding sharp even to his own ears. "Working men eat a lot."

❧

"I hope the horses have wandered very far away," Pilar's grandmother said. "I hope they will be gone a long time."

Pilar had joined her grandmother in the bedroom that had belonged to Earl and his wife. It was barely large enough for the bed, a wardrobe, a chest of drawers, and two tables. Her grandmother had removed one of the tables to make room for the chair she occupied most of the day. She had converted the other table into an altar with a small statue of the Virgin Mary, which she prayed to several times a day. A shawl and a mantilla broke the expanse of bare walls, and a heavy shawl draped over the front window gave privacy. The other window looked out on the tangle of oaks that led from the house to the nearby creek.

"The men are a lot of trouble, but I feel safer having them around."

"How can you feel safe around Cade Wheeler? He is a beast. He—"

"How many times do I have to tell you kidnapping me was just a prank?" Pilar asked, exasperation making her impatient. "He did it just to prove he could."

"They're nothing but thieving peasants. Wait until Laveau returns. Everything will be different then."

Pilar didn't bother arguing with her grandmother. She had learned long ago that no matter how much she accomplished, she would receive no credit. Laveau might succeed in driving out the squatters and getting their land back, but he would never restore the family to prosperity. She knew it would fall on her to make their ranch successful, that she was the only one with the will, grit, and perseverance, as well as an open mind capable of seeing the ways in which everything had changed. It didn't make her like Cade any more to know he had the same kind of mind.

"Whatever they are, they're all that stands between us and starvation," Pilar pointed out.

"We've paid for everything we got," her grandmother said. "A gentleman would have refused to take anything. In Spain we offered hospitality to everyone."

Pilar didn't bother reminding her grandmother that Earl Wheeler didn't believe in giving anything to anybody. He had been willing to protect them, but he expected to be paid for it.

Cade was different.

Although he had just as much stiff-necked pride as his grandfather, he didn't act as if he thought she'd been incapable of taking care of herself while he was gone. He had thanked her for taking care of his grandfather, even acknowledged that it couldn't have been easy. She didn't want to think she was silly enough to fall victim to the first man who flattered her, but no man had ever thanked her for anything. Or given her credit for being able to do anything more complicated than choose her own clothes.

"I want you to stay away from him," her grandmother said.

"Stay away from whom?"

"Cade Wheeler. Whom did you think I was talking about?"

"There are four men here. You could have meant any one of them."

"The others do not look for wives. They just want money. They will leave after that."

"How do you know?"

"I can tell."

"By looking at them?"

"I hear them talking," her grandmother said with obvious reluctance. "Men never speak softly. They think it does not matter if a woman hears what they say. This house is built with walls as thin as silk. I hear everything."

Pilar smiled to herself. Her grandmother must have stood outside the kitchen door listening to the conversation inside. "Why should you feel you have to warn me to stay away from Cade?"

"The Wheelers are very handsome men, and Manuel is slow to come."

Pilar didn't want to think of the distant cousin to whom she'd been affianced when she was ten years old. He should have come for her and her grandmother when the war started, prevented the squatters from taking over their hacienda, married her without hesitation.

Instead she had heard nothing from him for more than four years. Now that she was poor and had no dowry, she didn't expect to see him at all. "Manuel's coming has nothing to do with Cade Wheeler," Pilar said. "I talk to Cade because I have to. He doesn't like me any more than I like him."

"You are very pretty. Young men like him are subject to wild passions. He might lose control. He might—"

Pilar couldn't help laughing. The idea that Cade might fall prey to a "wild passion" was absurd. Now that he felt he was in her debt, he probably wouldn't even talk to her. "Cade would rather take a vow of celibacy than touch me."

"He must know you are far above him, but these American men think they can marry any woman they want."

"Marry!" Pilar exclaimed, her voice perilously close to a squeak. "He'd never consider marrying me."

"I am sure he has thought much about it. You are beautiful, young, rich—"

"Not anymore."

"—and much too good for him. That is enough to make a Wheeler determined to have you."

"It won't do him any good if I refuse."

"He is very handsome. Have you never wondered what it would be like to be his wife?"

Five

PILAR COULDN'T QUITE DESCRIBE THE FEELING THAT meandered its way through her body, leaving pockets of warmth in one place, causing shivers in the next, as she considered her grandmother's question. She'd never felt like this—except the time Cade kidnapped her. She'd been frightened by the speed of the horse, the suddenness of the attack, and the uncertainty of its ending. Yet she'd also been excited. She'd never before sat behind a man on a horse, her arms wrapped tightly around him for safety, her body pushing hard against his. No man except her father and brother had ever touched her. She'd never been alone with a man. She had never been the center of attention. In her family, men held the stage practically from the moment of birth.

"How could I when you always said he was the offspring of the devil?"

"Sometimes young girls cannot see that such a man is a great danger to them. I did not want you to be dazzled by his looks."

"I'm not."

"Never forget you are of noble blood."

"It's unfortunate our *noble blood* can't keep us from being dependent on Cade and his grandfather for our safety."

"Adversity comes to everyone, but we will rise again."

"With the help of the Wheelers."

"It is the destiny of such people to be useful. If they had not been thieves, we would have shown our gratitude. As it is, Laveau must destroy them."

Pilar didn't bother pointing out that the Wheelers were the ones in a position of power. Maybe being in the army had taught Laveau responsibility, planning, perseverance. The land and the cows already belonged to him. If only he had acquired the knowledge and determination to work. Cade had those things. "In the meantime we're dependent on them."

"We have more than paid them for their services. I do not hold myself in their debt."

In her grandmother's eyes, people were her social equals or servants. As servants, anything they did could be compensated for and therefore left her under no obligation. Pilar believed that was part of the reason her grandmother stayed in her room. She couldn't command Earl Wheeler as a servant in his own home. If she came out, she would have to speak to him as an equal, and her grandmother would never do that.

Pilar stood. Though this was Earl Wheeler's house, entering this bedroom was like entering a different world, one a little bit like the world she had left. It offered her comfort. She could be certain that Earl would never bring his sour face and insults in here.

But now there was work to be done. She didn't

think Cade and the others would get back tonight, but she had to be ready to feed them if they did. She hoped they wouldn't come back for at least two more days. Tomorrow she had to do the washing, and she had no intention of washing for all those men. She didn't know what Cade would say when he discovered that.

"It's about time you did some work," Earl said as she stepped out of the house. He was sitting on the porch, rocking, his rifle across his lap, eyeing the trail down which Cade had disappeared. "I could use some supper about now."

"You'll eat when I get it ready." He didn't expect to eat now. He'd said that to irritate her. She guessed it came from knowing she paid for the food he ate. Treating her like a servant made him feel less beholden. He was like her grandmother. She shuddered at the heresy of that thought.

"If you didn't hide in that room yapping with *that woman,* you'd have time to do your work."

He refused to call her by name, always referred to her grandmother as *that woman.*

"I hide there so I won't have to put up with your complaints or see your scowling expression. It's hard to cook with a sour stomach."

"You can't cook no matter what your stomach's doing."

"I'll be happy to turn the stove over to you," she said, taking down the egg basket and grabbing the milk pail.

"I'm not doing all your work for you."

She hurried down the steps and across the yard,

ignoring his reply. They indulged in the same sparring each day. He couldn't stop criticizing and complaining about everything she did any more than she could stop replying in kind. It had been going on for so long, neither of them got upset by what the other said. She was beginning to wonder if they could ever learn to converse differently. Not that there was any need. She would leave this ranch the moment Laveau returned.

It didn't take long to collect the eggs. The hens were kept penned up to protect them from varmints. It seemed virtually everything that walked on four legs liked the taste of chicken. Earl's hound dog kept coyotes away from the house, but he'd kill any chicken that managed to get out of the pen. Pilar didn't complain. The dog had twice warned them of squatters.

Milking the cow took longer, but Pilar enjoyed the company of the large, dun-colored animal. She was surprised the cow had had the patience to endure her learning how to milk, but the placid bovine merely turned a curious eye as she chewed her cud. Pilar had fallen into the habit of talking to the cow while she did the milking. Earl thought she was crazy, but she didn't care what Earl thought.

"I don't know whether I need butter, cream, or milk," she said. "Four new men to feed, and I don't know a thing about them." Long streams of warm milk pinged against the bottom and sides of the metal bucket, the sounds becoming muted as milk covered the bottom.

The cow turned her head and focused her large, brown eyes on Pilar.

"I shouldn't care what they want. They're just like

Cade, convinced no woman is half as smart as they are. I wonder how they think we got through the war without them. They probably don't notice that farms are still producing, ranches still running, and San Antonio is as busy as ever." As her agitation increased, she milked harder and harder, driving the milk into the bucket with such force that foam began to form on the surface.

A particularly vigorous pull on the cow's teat caused her to shake her head and stamp her foot. Part of the milk missed the bucket.

"If you don't want that, I'd rather you aim it at my mouth."

Pilar started so badly she nearly turned the bucket over. She turned to find herself facing a total stranger. The man's tattered Confederate uniform gave her hope that he was friendly, but Earl had filled her ears with many tales of soldiers who preyed on helpless women. "Who are you?" she managed to ask, hoping her voice didn't betray the extent of her fear.

"Broc Kincaid, ma'am. I'm looking for Cade Wheeler's ranch."

"What do you want him for?" She couldn't take her eyes off his face.

"Do you know him?"

"Yes."

"Then could you tell me how to find him?"

"As soon as I know why you want him."

She didn't know why she was trying to protect Cade. He could take care of himself, even with a man as fierce-looking as Mr. Kincaid.

"I served under him during the war," Broc said.

"I've come to help him hang the bastard who betrayed us. In the meantime, he offered me work. I could do with a grubstake."

Pilar's fears receded. Cade had said more men would be coming, but he hadn't mentioned that one of them would have such a badly scarred face. Pilar knew he knew she was staring at his face, but he stood his ground.

She'd been startled at first—no, frightened—but she had herself under control now. Once she realized that the other side of Broc's face was exceptionally handsome, she felt a great rush of pity. It must be horribly difficult for such a good-looking man to know that, for the rest of his life, people would recoil at the sight of him.

"I hope you'll forgive me for being so suspicious. A woman can't be too careful these days. You never know who might come up when your husband isn't about."

"Is Cade married? Are you his wife?" He sounded shocked.

"No, I'm not Cade's wife, and he's not married. I'm Pilar diViere. My grandmother and I are staying here until my brother comes home."

Even before she'd finished her explanation, she sensed a stiffening in Broc's posture, a coldness in his attitude. He'd been stiff at first, prepared for her reaction to his scar, but this was different. Now he was angry, and his anger was directed at her.

"Is your brother Laveau diViere?"

"Yes." She could feel the condemnation in his voice.

"Do you know what he did?"

"I know he changed sides during the war." She

rushed ahead, unable to stop defending her brother. "The Texas courts have let Americans steal our land and will do nothing about it. You can't blame him for not feeling loyal to such a government."

"Your brother hasn't come home yet." It was a statement rather than a question.

"No. I'm hoping to hear from him any day now."

"So am I," Broc said, his expression grim. "I have a lot to say to him."

"I won't have anybody on my place taking up with the diVieres," Earl announced as he rounded the corner of the shed, his rifle pointed at Broc, his hound dancing about his heels, growling, teeth bared, but keeping his distance. "You look like one of Cade's bunch of lean and hungry jackals come to fatten on my ranch. Well, you needn't think I'm going to allow it. I say who stays and who goes."

"I gather you're Cade's grandpa." Broc stuck out his hand. "I'm Broc Kincaid. Served under your grandson the whole time I was in the army."

"Lot of good that did you," Earl said, keeping his distance and his rifle raised. "Looks like he let you get your face blowed off."

Much to Pilar's surprise, Broc didn't seem upset at the mention of his scar. "Our troop was betrayed. This scar is a small price to pay for being alive. If it hadn't been for Cade's hunches, none of us would have made it."

"He's been having them *hunches* all his life," Earl said. "Didn't keep him from turning up with the shabbiest bunch of friends I ever saw, and you look worse than the others. How am I supposed to know who you are?"

"He said he was in Cade's troop," Pilar said.

"Well, he can say anything he wants, can't he? Then he can cut our throats, rob us in our sleep." He grinned at Pilar. "You got any notion what he could do to you?"

Pilar squeezed a few more streams of milk from the cow before standing. "I have a very good notion. Supper will be ready in about an hour," she said to Broc. "Why don't you unsaddle your horse and put your stuff in the bunkhouse?"

"What makes you think you make the rules around here?" Earl shouted at Pilar. "I ain't bedding down with no man I've never seen before."

"I'll sleep out, if you don't mind," Broc said, to all appearances not the least ruffled by Earl's lack of hospitality. "Cade said you were as prickly as a cocklebur."

"I'll leave you to get acquainted," Pilar said. "Don't worry about the dog. He acts fierce, but he won't bite."

"He'll tear your throat out if you make a wrong move," Earl said.

"Then I hope you lock him up tonight. I'd hate to die in my sleep."

"Bullet ain't never locked up. Twice he's warned us of squatters. Drove them off both times."

"Glad to meet you, Mr. Kincaid," Pilar said. "I hope you'll excuse me while I start supper."

"Call me Broc."

"You don't have to act fancy with her," Earl said. "She ain't nothing but hired help."

Pilar bit her tongue, turned, and headed for the house. Would she ever stop getting riled when Earl referred to her as *the help*? He did it just to provoke her. And she did cook, clean, and wash—the usual tasks for *hired help*. She scolded herself for her pride. She had watched pride turn her grandmother into a dissatisfied old woman who spent her life trying to recapture a past that had ceased to exist. Laveau was too proud to work, to acquire the knowledge necessary to rebuild the family fortune. A man should take pride in his own accomplishments, not look to the past to provide him with respect. The past would not help her now.

Broc said he had come to Texas to help Cade hang a traitor. Pilar had the terrifying suspicion that traitor might be her brother.

❧

Pilar couldn't sleep. The uneasy feeling that had settled over her when Broc arrived wouldn't go away. Broc had stayed outside until it was time for supper, then left the kitchen immediately afterward. He had talked easily with Earl and Jessie during the meal, but the whole time he kept glancing at Pilar as though she were a coiled snake about to strike.

His string of jokes and stories had put Earl in such a good mood he'd invited Broc to bed down in the bunkhouse. Broc said he was so used to sleeping outdoors he expected it would take him some time to get used to sleeping under a roof again. He then proceeded to tell more stories, but he never again mentioned the traitor or what they planned to do to him.

Pilar grew even more suspicious when Broc pretended to have had only a slight acquaintance with Laveau and no interest in his present whereabouts.

He'd asked if she knew when he was coming home but appeared to be unaffected when she said she hadn't heard from him in more than a month.

"Something is going on," she had said to her grandmother. "I need to find out what it is."

"How do you propose to do that?" her grandmother asked, uninterested in the appearance of another of Cade's fellow soldiers.

"I'll have to try to get friendly with one of them."

Her grandmother's attention became sharply focused then. "I order you to stay away from Cade."

"I didn't mean Cade. He and Holt are too clever, Rafe doesn't say anything, and Broc watches me with suspicion. I was thinking of Owen."

"That one is not serious about anything."

"I don't know about that, but he is interested in me."

"He's interested in a *woman*. Besides, he is more clever than he looks. You will never get him to talk about anything but women."

"Then maybe I should try Cade."

"I do not trust him."

"I don't trust him either, but they know something about Laveau. I think they believe he betrayed them. If so, they mean to hang him."

That had set her grandmother off on a long tirade about the unfairness of a world where people like the Wheelers were allowed to take land from a family like the diVieres. She had ended with a pronouncement that Laveau was smarter than Cade and all his friends put together, that Pilar was not to think of getting friendly with Cade. He would see through her immediately.

Pilar was too used to having her abilities under-rated to be upset. She spent several hours that night trying to decide which of the men might be the most susceptible to her.

She kept coming back to Cade.

The fact that they had known each other since childhood might cause him to be more relaxed around her than men who didn't know her and were suspicious. Cade had gone out of his way to be helpful. Maybe he felt guilty that a Wheeler had had to depend on a diViere. That ought to make him more anxious to please her, maybe anxious enough to tell her what she needed to know.

But there was the fact that he was extremely attractive. From what her grandmother said, all handsome men—unless they were diVieres or Cordobas—were untrustworthy, a veritable collection of snakes in the grass who specialized in using their looks and charm to dupe unwary females. Her grandmother hadn't explained just what had happened to these unfortunate women, but Pilar believed they'd probably been forced to marry someone of less than noble birth or suitable fortune. In her grandmother's estimation, a woman couldn't suffer a worse fate.

But Pilar was in no danger of being forced to marry Cade, even if she flirted outrageously. Their relationship as enemies was so well defined and of such long standing, nothing could change it. She could be reckless in perfect safety.

She'd just decided that Cade would be her target when she heard a mournful howl from Bullet, followed quickly by a couple of rifle shots. She snatched up a shawl, threw it over her shoulders, and ran out of her bedroom to the kitchen. She looked through the windows.

Moonlight enabled her to see the bunkhouse. Bullet was still howling, but she couldn't see him. She saw the bunkhouse door open and a rifle barrel appear, followed soon after by Earl in his long johns. Despite the potential danger, she smiled at the sight of his spider-thin shanks as he scurried across the yard in the direction of the shots.

"What is it?" her grandmother asked from the doorway of her bedroom.

"I don't know. I'll find out."

"Stay inside. It could be squatters."

"It could also be Cade coming back."

"In the middle of the night?"

"He said they rode during the night for most of the war. Working at night is probably normal for him."

"That may be, but it's even more reason for you to remain out of sight." Her grandmother started in on her litany of Wheeler sins, but Pilar opened the door and slipped onto the porch, ignoring the fact that only a shawl covered her bare shoulders.

Jessie emerged from the bunkhouse carrying a rifle.

"Is it Cade?" she called out.

"It could be anybody," he replied in a loud whisper. "Stay at the house." Then he disappeared.

The ranch yard looked bleached and colorless in the moonlight, shadows deep black, everything else milky pale. The silence felt deeper, bigger, stronger than usual. The night seemed to reach out and wrap itself around her, welcoming yet ominous. What should have been a familiar landscape had become strange, its features nearly unrecognizable.

Bullet was getting closer all the time. His howls changed into a series of yelps that progressed to a whine. Finally he burst forth with an agitated "yip-yip" that caused Pilar to fear he'd been injured by one of the shots.

"What the hell are you doing to my dog!" Earl's angry voice carried easily through the night as Broc came into view down the trail. He strode openly, clearly not worried about hidden danger. Behind him, a rope around his neck, trotted a dispirited and reluctant Bullet.

"I'm bringing this damned hound dog to you," Broc replied, clearly irritated. "You ought to lock him up in the bunkhouse."

"I'm not locking him up anywhere," Earl said, darting from behind the bunkhouse. "He's the best watchdog in Texas."

Broc dragged Bullet into the ranch yard before taking the rope from his neck. "He might have heard the squatters before you did, but he wasn't warning you. He was begging you to protect him. That dog is yella!"

Pilar thought Earl would have a seizure right there. He charged Broc like a longhorn cow in defense of her calf, waving his rifle at him like a pointed finger.

"If you wasn't a guest in my house, I'd put a bullet in you. There's not a better dog in Texas."

"Then God help Texas." Broc pushed a cringing Bullet toward Earl. "There was somebody in one of those dry creek beds. I heard him without the help of your *watchdog*. I was about to try to get behind him when that *animal* started howling like he'd stepped on a cactus."

"He was trying to warn you, you fool," Earl shouted.

"The cowardly bag of bones poked his nose in my belly and practically crawled under me."

"That's his way of waking you up," Earl said.

"Believe what you want. Just keep him away from me."

Earl had launched into a scurrilous depiction of the history of Broc's family, past and present, with some pointed observations on the circumstances of his birth, when Bullet started to whine. Earl only shouted louder. Even Pilar could tell that someone was coming and wasn't trying to be quiet about it.

"Look at your dog now," Broc said. "You can't tell me he's not a coward."

Bullet had taken up a position behind Earl and set up a mournful howl. He was pushing up behind Earl, his head between Earl's legs.

"He's trying to get me to go after the damned sneaks," Earl argued.

"That's nobody trying to sneak in. They're riding in making plenty of noise. I suspect it's Cade. He always did like night better than day. You can tell your dog to stop sticking his nose up your butt. There's nobody going to hurt him this time."

Earl started shouting at Broc again. Pilar focused her attention on the patch of silvery landscape to the west. She made out moving shapes in the distance. Lots of shapes. Horses. As they got closer, she heard shouts, yells, and calls of the men driving them.

Pilar experienced an unexpected feeling of excitement. She moved a few steps from the door, reached out for a rail post, leaned against it. She told herself it was relief that the men were safe, that they had found the horses, that they would be able to round up and sell their cows, that somehow this would lead to her and her grandmother going home and everything being all right again. She told herself it was relief that whoever was out in the brush was gone, that they wouldn't come back, with so many men at the ranch.

But the moment the riders came close enough for her to identify individual men, she knew it was all a lie. She knew that every bit of her excitement was for Cade's return.

Pilar sagged against the rail post, needing the support to keep her from sinking to the floor. How could this be? Cade had been her enemy her whole life.

Just looking at him caused her heart to beat faster. The moonlight was incapable of turning him into a ghostly image. He looked as vibrantly alive, as smilingly handsome as ever. All the men were in high spirits, but his good humor leapt the distance between them. She could almost believe he was reaching out to her, pulling her into the aura of high spirits that surrounded him. When he looked at her and let out a whoop, she was certain of it. When he separated from the group and rode toward her, she felt her strength drain away.

He leaned out of his saddle to shake hands with Broc, spoke to his grandfather, then brought his horse right up to the steps. He looked down at her with a look that hurtled her back to the day he'd swept her up on his horse for that impossible ride, a juggernaut driving all before him.

That's how he looked tonight—happy, confident, successful, and so handsome it was impossible not to smile back.

"We brought back more than fifty horses and we're starved," he said. "If I help, do you think you could rustle up something for us to eat?"

Six

As HE BREATHED DEEPLY TO SAVOR THE AROMA OF stewed beef, a smile of contentment spread over Cade's whole face. "You can't know how often I've dreamed of this," he said to Pilar. "A man can get awfully tired of his own cooking."

"Especially when he's no good at it," Owen said.

Pilar had been a little angry that Cade's first words to her had concerned food. Consequently she didn't understand why she didn't mind cooking so late at night or why she was actually cheerful. She should have been furious.

"Sit still until I finish sewing up this wound," Holt said to Owen. "You're lucky that mare didn't kick you. Not even your hard head could withstand such a blow."

A mustang had charged Owen's mount, knocked him out of the saddle, and caused him to cut his head on a rock. Holt cleaned and stitched Owen's wound while Cade helped Pilar. Rafe and Broc had gone with Earl and Jessie to inspect the aqueduct used to carry water from the creek to the garden. Fifty horses would use up all the water in the well before morning.

"He's not seriously hurt," Cade said to Pilar, giving her a wink. "He just pretended so he could get to the kitchen before anyone else."

"I'm starved. I couldn't swallow a mouthful of that stuff you burned," Owen said.

"I don't recall having to stuff it down your throat," Cade said.

"Or you offering to cook," Holt pointed out to Owen as he wound the bandage around his head.

"We'd have starved if he'd tried to cook," Cade said. "We let him try once. It was so bad we used it to poison the bluecoats. General Sherman sent out an order that nobody was to eat anything they didn't cook themselves. He said he couldn't afford to have his entire army down with diarrhea."

"Don't believe him," Owen said to Pilar. "He's just jealous I'm more successful with the girls than he is."

Cade leaned close to Pilar, whispered in her ear. "They were only trying to keep him away from a stove."

"What lie is he telling?" Owen demanded.

"Would I lie?"

"Yes."

Even after he moved way, Pilar felt Cade's closeness, the warmth of his breath on her ear as he whispered to her. It shook her concentration so badly she put sugar in the stewed tomatoes instead of the peaches. She hoped the men would be too hungry to notice.

Cade had been as good as his word. He'd built the fire in the stove, brought in more wood, set the table, fixed the coffee, even helped peel the potatoes. He'd opened cans, got pots off shelves, took cold food out of the storeroom. But none of this had had the effect of that whispered comment in her ear. Or the smile and wink that followed it. Cade had looked straight at her. *At her and no one else*. The implied intimacy excited her.

It also frightened her.

She wasn't supposed to be excited about being close to Cade, working with him, brushing against him more than a dozen times. She should have been incensed that he would have the impertinence to whisper in her ear, the effrontery to believe she would tolerate such a show of familiarity, much less welcome it. She should have turned on him immediately, frozen him with a look, blistered him with her words.

Instead she struggled not to blush, not to yield to the giddiness that threatened to swallow her strength. "Everything is ready," she said, forcing herself to concentrate on ladling the stew into a bowl. "See if the others have gotten back."

Earl must have been coming up the steps as she spoke. He shoved open the door, nearly obliterating her last words. "I don't know why the hell you didn't leave these boys in Virginia. They don't know a damned thing about nothing."

"You couldn't fix the aqueduct?" Cade asked.

"Rafe fixed it just fine," Broc said. "It just wasn't the way your grandfather thought it ought to be fixed."

"What do you know about aqueducts?" Owen asked Rafe.

"That water flows downhill." Rafe pulled up a chair and sat down at the table.

"I'm going to bed," Earl said. "There'll be plenty of

work to do in the morning while you boys are lying in bed."

"Sit down and have a bite," Cade said.

"I don't eat in the middle of the night," Earl said. "It ruins my digestion."

"Maybe Jessie wants to eat."

"It ruins his digestion, too."

"It doesn't ruin mine," Broc said, "but Pilar already fed me. I'll see you boys in the morning."

"You don't have to go to bed now," Pilar said.

"Sure I do," Broc said, grinning. It was disheartening to Pilar to see that his smile made the scar even more unsightly. "Your grandfather won't have any fun complaining if there isn't somebody there to hear him."

"I'd sleep out if I were you," Cade said.

"I've already tried that. His dog tried to hide under me when he heard somebody sneaking down the wash."

The lighthearted atmosphere disappeared in an instant.

"Did you see who it was?"

"Not a chance with that dratted hound making enough racket to be heard all the way to San Antonio."

By the time Broc had finished telling Cade about the intruders, he'd forgotten about going to bed early. Pilar poured coffee for him.

"Join us," Owen said to Pilar, obviously tired of talking about intruders.

"I've already eaten," Pilar said.

"You can't stand," Cade said. "It'll make us too nervous to eat."

"Not me," Holt said. Rafe had already served himself.

"Okay," Pilar said.

Cade pulled a chair up next to Broc. "You'd better sit here. If you sit next to Owen, he's liable to get a brain fever."

"Cade will bore you to death," Owen said. "He can't think of two consecutive sentences that don't have to do with horses, cows, or war."

"This will give me a chance to practice," Cade said, beckoning Pilar to sit.

She did. "I suggest you all concentrate on eating," she said. "If you sleep late, Earl will never let you hear the end of it."

She didn't know why she was talking about Earl. She couldn't think of anybody except Cade, that he was next to her, speaking to her, smiling at her. She tried to withdraw inside herself, but no matter what she did, he remained close. Too close.

She tried to tell herself she would get used to being close to him, that being close to him didn't matter, that before long it wouldn't be any different from being close to Owen, Holt, or the others. They were handsome young men in the prime of their lives, charming, energetic, vibrant, masculine enough to arouse feelings in any woman. Maybe it wasn't just Cade. Maybe it was being around so many men. After all, she hadn't seen any men except Earl and Jessie for nearly two years.

She had been too young when the men of Texas left for the war to feel the animal attraction she was experiencing now. The energy was palpable, more than enough to disorient her.

It was okay to feel this way as long as it was caused

by all four men. It was only dangerous if she felt the same way when she was alone with Cade.

But she had to be alone with him. If she wasn't, she would never learn if Laveau was the traitor they meant to hang.

◆

Cade knew he wasn't the cleverest man in the world when it came to women. He'd made some mistakes due to ignorance. He'd made even more due to lack of interest, but he was no longer ignorant, and he certainly wasn't uninterested. But he kept getting conflicting signals from Pilar. One moment he was certain he had her full attention; the next she was doing her best to ignore him.

He had spent a good deal of time over the last few days trying to decide how best to gain her confidence. He'd reached the conclusion that the best way was to make her think he no longer felt the animosity that had kept their families at odds for nearly thirty years. The only way to do that was to be around her as much as possible.

That was partly why he'd offered to help her fix supper. It was also why he'd made certain she sat next to him at the table, why he winked or smiled at her when they shared a joke. But she was acting like a nervous filly being bred for the first time, willing to give it a try but pulling back anxiously just the same.

"I wasn't sure you were coming, Broc," Owen said. "I figured you'd be on a stage somewhere."

Cade's glance swung to Owen, worried his remarks might have offended, but Owen was watching Broc, intent on his reaction.

"People don't pay to see anything ugly."

"Does that mean you're giving up the stage?" Holt asked.

"Only being on it myself. After being on stage since I was able to walk, I figure I know enough to put together a show of my own. I'd like to take one out West. There's lots of men in mining towns who'd pay just about anything to watch a pretty woman sing a song and do a little dance."

"Does it take a lot of money to put together a show?" Holt asked.

"A lot more than I have."

"I thought that's why you went back to Memphis."

"They took one look at my face and told me they had no place for me."

"Good," Cade said. "If the cows need singing to, you're our man."

Broc's amusement didn't mask his bitterness. "My cousins would sure get a laugh out of that."

"They'll be laughing out of the other side of their mouths when you have the most famous traveling show in the country," Owen said.

"Maybe I should hire you as my leading man," Broc said. "You're good-looking, charming, and you can lie with a straight face."

Everyone laughed. "He's got your number, Cousin," Cade said.

"I don't think I'm cut out for the stage. I was thinking about being a lawman—you know, being able to shoot people in the name of justice. Seems like a good way to get rid of everybody I don't like."

"Could he be talking about you, Cade?" Broc asked.

"He's too dull to be annoying." Owen turned to Rafe. "What are you going to do with your share of the money?"

"Maybe I'll stay here."

There was something dark and bitter in that man's past. Even knowing so little about Rafe, Cade was certain he wouldn't stay in Texas.

"That just leaves you," Owen said to Holt.

"I need money to set up a practice," Holt said.

"You won't make any money here," Owen said. "Cows aren't very good about paying their bills."

"I might go West with Broc. Maybe folks there won't care about my accent."

Cade was relieved that Owen didn't question Holt further. They all knew he'd come to Texas to find the woman he fell in love with during medical school. "Time to pack it in, boys," Cade said, getting to his feet. "We've got fifty horses that need to be reminded what it's like to have a man on their backs. After four years, I expect they've forgotten altogether."

"I got that dappled gray stallion," Rafe said.

"He'll stomp your guts out," Owen said.

"I'm hoping he'll try," Rafe said with what was the closest thing to a grin Cade had ever seen on his face.

"You can have all my ornery ones," Owen said.

"We'll help you clear away and wash up," Holt said to Pilar. "We don't want you to be up all night."

"I'll do it," Cade said. "You make sure the horses are settled. It's been a long time since Gramps has had to worry about anything but a lazy old gelding. And don't stay up bragging about how many horses you're going to break tomorrow. I'd rather you be awake enough to do something worth bragging about."

"We're all waiting to see you on a horse," Holt said. "We want to see what a *real* Texas cowboy can do."

"I'm betting the first nag will have him picking cactus out of his bottom," Owen said.

"If I never had any doubt you were a true Wheeler, I don't anymore," Cade said. "You're too good-looking for your own good, charming as a snake, and mean as sin."

"What happened to you, Cousin?"

"Took after my mama's side, I guess."

The quiet the men left behind felt even deeper by contrast, being alone with Pilar more intimate. Pretending to like Pilar to gain information about Laveau was proving unexpectedly difficult. Even dangerous.

He was starting to like her, and it was hard to remember she was the enemy.

When Cade had rolled in at ten o'clock with a herd of horses and four hungry men, she hadn't complained about his thoughtlessness or fallen into a fit of temper at having to fix a second supper. She didn't drag her feet or make things difficult. She didn't say it in so many words, but he could even believe she was glad they were back.

She wasn't mean-spirited, aggressive, or always looking for ways to make trouble. She was pleasant, cooperative, more than willing to do her share of the work, and she got along with all the men. She seemed the perfect woman for this ranch and this situation.

And he liked having her there. He could barely remember living in a household with a woman. His grandmother had left thirty years before to go back to her family in North Carolina. His mother had left when he was six. His grandfather had always hired men to do the cooking, cleaning, and washing. Having a woman around gave the place an entirely different feeling.

But the stirring deep in his groin had nothing to do with beautiful china, clean clothes, or some feminine style of furnishing a room. It had to do with the fact that Pilar was a beautiful woman to whom he was discovering he had a very strong physical attraction.

"I think you're just as good-looking as Owen," Pilar said.

"What?" He had been so deep in thought, he spoke before he realized he had heard what she said.

"I said—"

"Thanks, but everybody knows Owen is the best-looking Wheeler."

Pilar didn't look up from the pan of dishes she was washing. "Men can be good-looking in different ways. Owen is *pretty* attractive. You're *ruggedly* attractive."

Cade had spent most of his youth getting by on his looks and high spirits, but coming face-to-face with the same traits in Owen had caused him to stand back, look at himself, and discover he didn't like what he saw. Being around a man as truly handsome as Broc had been before he was wounded had convinced Cade he'd been considered handsome only because everybody else was as homely as his grandfather's hound dog.

Knowing Pilar thought he was ruggedly handsome caused the stirring in his groin to intensify. He carried the last of the dirty plates to the sink. "I doubt you'll find anyone who'll agree with you."

"A woman makes her own judgment about a man. It doesn't matter if no one else agrees with her."

He wondered if men could be so independent, but it didn't matter in this case. Everyone agreed Pilar was beautiful.

"There's more to being handsome than a pretty face." Pilar kept her gaze on her work. "There's character. A man can have a truly handsome face and be cruel and self-indulgent. A plain man's face can be transformed by honesty, generosity of spirit, and courage."

Was she saying he was honest and generous of spirit when all the time he was pretending to like her so he could hang her brother?

Decency required him to leave immediately, but he couldn't. Laveau was a traitor responsible for the deaths of twenty-four innocent men. Cade had made a vow on the sword of a dead comrade that he wouldn't rest until the traitor had been brought to justice. His duty to his fallen companions was greater than his desire to appear decent and honorable in Pilar's eyes.

She would hate him in the end, but he had known that from the first.

It hadn't mattered then. Why should it begin to matter now? And why wouldn't the stirring in his groin die down?

"You don't have to stay," Pilar said. "I'm almost done."

He looked at the pots still on the stove, bowls on the table with food to be put away, cups and plates that had to be dried, forks and knives still in the hot, soapy water. "You're much too pretty to be telling such bald-faced lies. I'll wash while you put away the food. I don't know where anything goes."

She looked at him as if he'd gone mad.

"Haven't you ever seen a man wash dishes?"

"No."

He hadn't realized until he saw the expression of disbelief on her face how much the war had changed him. Maybe other men would return home and fall back into old habits, but he couldn't.

"Every man in my troop cooked or washed dishes at one time or another. Washed his own clothes, too." Pilar hadn't taken her eyes off him, but her hands kept washing forks and knives. "Move over. It's my turn."

He lifted her hands out of the water and dried them. It should have been a simple task, but Pilar stared down at her hands, then gazed up at him with a look that caused his insides to knot. It wasn't the surprise that got him. It was the look that said he was a minor god and she could hardly believe she had been so fortunate as to have him turn his attention on her, if only for a few minutes.

He was a fool. No woman thought that of a man, even when she was madly in love with him.

But the feeling wouldn't go away. Nor did it diminish as he dried her hands, one finger at a time.

"I could just as easily have dried them on my apron," Pilar said. "They'll be back in the water soon."

She held her hands in front of her, fingers spread, looking at them as though they had changed somehow. He'd never really looked at a person's hands before, never realized they could be attractive, even beautiful.

"You shouldn't have to wash dishes."

She started, as though coming out of a trance. "They won't wash themselves. Neither will the pots."

"We should get someone to do the washing for you."

"I'm not fragile, Cade. Thousands of women all over Texas wash dishes every day. Besides, you have no money to pay anyone."

Cade wondered why the lack of money had never bothered him before. His grandfather was much more interested in acquiring land than in doing anything with it. He was a fighter, not a rancher. Cade had known for some time it would be up to him to make something of the ranch.

"I'll have money as soon as I sell the herd."

"If you don't start washing, I'll be through before you get your hands wet."

She had kept working while she talked. He had followed her as she moved about the kitchen, emptying pots and bowls. He turned to the sink and plunged his hands into the water. His finger encountered the sharp point of a fork. He stifled a sharp intake of breath, told himself to be more careful.

"You've promised to share your profit with your friends. And there're a lot of things that need doing around the ranch. Then there's your intention to buy blooded bulls to upgrade the herd."

"I don't have to do all of that at once."

"Probably not, but you don't have to do anything for me. When Laveau comes back, he'll clear out the squatters and I'll go home."

Cade forced himself to focus on his work. He didn't know why he should be so worried about the amount of work Pilar did. She hadn't complained or asked for help. He'd planned to wiggle his way into her confidence by any means possible, but this was a genuine concern, one that indicated a potentially fatal weakness in his plan. He'd better get himself under control before he messed everything up.

"A few more men may show up," he said. "I don't know how many."

"That's your business, not mine."

"What I'm getting at is it may be too much work for one person. Let me know if that happens. I know you didn't expect to have this many settle on you."

"I didn't expect to be thrown out of my own home by thieving vagrants, but I survived. I expect I'll survive you and your friends."

It must have been devastating to have to beg to be taken in by a man she considered her worst enemy. Her grandmother had drummed it into her head that she was too far above the Wheelers to even speak to them. Having to cook and clean for them must have come close to destroying her. Now he was implying that she couldn't do the work. One more instance to support Owen's claim that Cade didn't know anything about women.

"I don't want you to feel we're taking advantage of you. After all, you are helping to support us. In all fairness, you and your grandmother deserve part of the profits from the sale of the herd."

"You'd do that?" She finally stopped working and stared at him in disbelief.

"I'll talk to my grandfather."

Her mood changed abruptly, and she went back to work. "He won't agree."

"My grandfather isn't above taking advantage of anyone when he can, but he's got just as much pride as you. He hates feeling unable to take care of himself. The world has changed, and he doesn't know how to change with it. He strikes out at you because you offer him money he doesn't have. He strikes out at me because I have youth and strength he doesn't have, new ideas he can't understand."

"You've changed, Cade Wheeler. You aren't the same man who left here four years ago, bragging he was going to beat the Yankees single-handed."

"I hope you think it's for the better." What the hell was he doing asking her a question like that?

Well, actually it was exactly the kind of thing that would convince a woman that her opinion of him mattered.

Only what Pilar thought of him *did* matter.

Her girlish smile caught him by surprise. "Girls are silly creatures. We tend to admire the most unsuitable boys. We dream about them, make up all sorts of stories about being carried away by a handsome young man."

"Did you ever dream about me?"

She turned back to her work but not before smiling once again. "Many times. I thought you were romantic." She looked at him again, her expression serious now. "But girls grow up. They might sigh and regret the passing of their dreams—might even weep over them—but they put aside their youthful daredevils to look for someone they can depend on, someone who will care for them and keep them safe. I think you've turned into such a man. Some young woman is going to be very fortunate."

Cade didn't know why he said what he said next. He could only assume that Pilar's words had knocked every bit of sense out of his head.

"We'll need to take baths tomorrow. You'll have to heat lots of water."

Seven

NOTHING HAD GONE AS PILAR EXPECTED. SHE HAD been prepared to fix a large breakfast. Instead, the men nibbled all day and washed what they ate down with endless cups of black coffee.

"You can't ride a bucking horse with a full stomach," Cade told her. "You'll throw up on yourself before you hit the ground."

She couldn't understand why the endless cups of coffee didn't bother them.

"We sweat it out as fast as we drink it," Cade said. "There's nothing like the hot Texas sun to make you thirsty."

Pilar had expected to have no part in what the men were doing. But finding herself outside, she became spellbound by the drama in the corrals. At home she'd rarely been allowed beyond the hacienda courtyard. Every time she expressed curiosity about the work done on the ranch, her grandmother told her that work involving men, horses, and cows was coarse, unsuitable for a young woman to know anything about. Her job was to look beautiful, marry well, and provide her husband with children.

Pilar had seen a lot in the two years she ran the rancho, but none of it had prepared her for this exhausting, brutal, dangerous work.

"You can't call yourself a real cowboy until you've been thrown at least a dozen times," Cade had said earlier that morning after being unceremoniously dumped by a pinto mare. "It keeps you limber."

"Or breaks all your bones," Pilar replied. But the most unpleasant part of the day had been gelding the colts and young stallions.

"I don't mind telling you, I'm glad Rafe volunteered for this job," Cade said.

She spent most of her time during the afternoon heating water in a huge copper bathtub. The tub had been ordered by Laveau but had remained in the stables in a wagon. Pilar and her grandmother had hidden their clothes and jewelry in it. When they made their escape, it was easier to harness a horse to the wagon and bring the tub filled with everything they could carry away. It had remained behind the Wheeler bunkhouse ever since. Holt pounced on it the minute he saw it. "At home we didn't have a tub like this," he said. "We took a cloth bath. In the summer we went in the lake." He gazed at the tub with a smile of anticipation. "Sinking in water up my neck will be a wonderful pleasure."

For most Texans, taking a bath on a regular basis wasn't of primary importance. Water had to be carried inside by hand and heated with scarce fuel. As for bathing outside, no sensible man dived into a river in south Texas without first checking for poisonous snakes—and the water level. Most rivers went dry in the summer.

Women *never* bathed in public.

Owen and Jessie had volunteered to gather firewood. Earl spent the day at the corral, criticizing everything Cade and his friends did.

"You going to work the kinks out of that buckskin?" he asked Cade when it came down to the last horse. It was late in the afternoon, and all the men were tired. Holt was looking longingly at the bath. Tendrils of steam had begun to rise from the surface of the water. "You can't keep expecting your friends to do all the work for you. You could learn a few things from that Rafe fella, though. I don't much like outsiders, but he knows how to handle a horse."

Pilar didn't see that Rafe was any better than Cade. They were both tall and slim waisted with powerful shoulders. They both walked like they'd been born in boots and rode a horse like they didn't know any other way to get from place to place. Rafe had been thrown one time more than Cade, even though they'd ridden the same number of horses.

She had been counting.

"Well, you'd better get on that horse if you're going to," Earl said. "I'm getting hungry for my supper. Ain't it about time you start bustling about in the kitchen?" he asked Pilar.

"It'll be ready as soon as the men finish their baths."

"Baths!" Earl said with disgust, as though being clean was something to be ashamed of. "I can't see why you want to go taking a bath. You'll just get dirty all over again tomorrow."

"Then we'll have to take another bath," Cade said.

"There's not enough wood between here and Mexico for that many baths. What do you think that girl will use to cook your supper?"

"You won't starve, old man. Now I'd better climb on that buckskin. I don't want him to feel left out."

"You're the one's going to be left out when he pitches you tail first over the corral fence."

Cade had called his grandfather *old man* most of the day. She figured it was a sign of affection. He had been careful to make sure Earl didn't get on any of the bad horses, but he'd also tried to make sure he didn't feel left out. He asked his advice on which horses they ought to keep, which they might consider selling. He even asked whether Earl thought he should breed any of the Virginia mares to a young sorrel stallion he decided not to geld.

"You won't get nothing you can use," Earl had said. "Those mares are too long-legged and skinny-rumped. Look at the hindquarters on that buck-skin. He's got enough power to throw you from here to San Antonio, then chase down a half dozen ornery steers."

Cade had pointed out advantages to be gained from the mares' height and streamlined conformation. As testimony to his grandson's persuasiveness, Earl had agreed it might be an interesting experiment.

Cade had discarded his Confederate uniform for some old clothes, but his body had filled out during the last four years. Watching him move about in pants that fit him like a second skin kept Pilar in a state of constant turmoil. She couldn't tell whether the heat in her face came from the fire or the internal flame ignited by the sight of Cade's muscled thighs gripping the sides of a horse, his hand brushing dirt from his bottom after he landed in the dust. He had a habit of sliding his hands into his back pockets when he stopped to talk with one of the men. Pilar wondered what it would be like to put *her* hands on his bottom.

Even when she wasn't looking at him, she could visualize his hands pressed tightly against the curve of his buttocks. Until today, no thought even remotely similar to that had ever disturbed the serenity of her mind. Now tremors shook her body, an unfamiliar heat coiled and uncoiled in her belly. Maybe this was why her grandmother said a lady should keep herself separate from men on all but formal occasions.

For most of her life, Pilar had chafed against her grandmother's tight restrictions, but she'd never rebelled. Then Laveau had gone off to war, leaving no one to run the ranch. Her grandmother had insisted they hire an overseer, but they didn't even have the money to pay their servants. Despite her grandmother's objections and continual predictions of failure, Pilar assumed management of their ranch.

The last four years had gradually turned her into a different woman. She knew she could never return to being the biddable girl she used to be. She also knew she could never be the silent, obedient wife her Mexican fiancé expected. She felt confident of her ability to make decisions, to act on them.

But this newfound sense of physical awareness,

this unforeseen and unmanageable fascination with Cade—especially his body—was something she was neither confident about nor able to control. She'd never felt anything like it before.

Except when Cade kidnapped you.

She refused to take that comparison seriously. She had been a virtual child then, frightened, thrilled, fascinated by the whole experience. It had been the single most exciting event of her life.

But she was a woman now. How could she explain her reaction today?

"I'll hold him while you mount up."

Pilar came out of her self-absorption to see Rafe holding the bridle of the buckskin and Cade preparing to climb into the saddle.

"Better stand back," Earl said to Rafe. "I give Cade five seconds before that buckskin tosses him."

Despite having been hobbled, the horse had fought the lasso over his head, the bridle, blanket, and saddle. He should have been exhausted by now, but Pilar could tell from the wildness in his eyes that he had neither exhausted his energy nor given up the fight. He watched Cade's approach with fearful expectancy, sidling away when Cade reached for the saddle horn. Rafe held the horse's head tight against the hitching post. A single powerful leap, and Cade was in the saddle. Rafe let go of the bridle and jumped back.

Pilar had watched the men break horses all day, watched the horses expend every available ounce of energy to get rid of the men on their backs. But watching Cade ride the buckskin was like seeing it all for the first time.

The horse came alive with incredible energy, jumped straight into the air, came down on stiff legs, spun to the right, reversed to the left, spun to the right again, bucking furiously as it turned rapidly.

With a swiftness she didn't think possible, the buckskin broke into a run, stopped dead in its tracks, thrust its head between its legs, and threw its hindquarters into the air.

Cade left the saddle, sailed over the horse's head, and landed in the cut-up dirt. Rafe ran to grab the buckskin's bridle. When Cade didn't move immediately, Pilar waited, breath suspended.

"Damn, that's one fine horse," Cade said, still lying on the ground. "I'm claiming him."

"You'll have a damned hard time doing that with your face in the dirt," his grandfather said.

Cade pushed himself into a sitting position. "Just trying to make him think he hurt me."

"You fooled me," Broc said. "I thought he knocked the wind out of you."

Feeling as though he'd knocked the wind out of her at the same time, Pilar finally relaxed enough to take a full breath. Cade got to his feet and brushed the sand from his shirt and pants.

"How can he be thrown like that and not get hurt?" she asked Broc. It was a foolish question. She'd seen it happen all day. She'd been shocked and surprised at first. Now she felt worried and fearful.

What had changed?

Maybe she'd begun to realize some part of the real danger a man faced when he pitted his strength against an animal's. She understood how to manage a ranch, what it took to keep one going, but she knew very little about the actual work it took to support the luxurious life she and her grandmother enjoyed.

She'd begun to doubt that Laveau could ever do this work even if he tried, that his return wouldn't restore the life she had known.

"The secret is to relax, just let your body fall naturally," Broc said.

Pilar couldn't imagine how anybody could *fall naturally,* but it was obvious that Cade was unhurt. He didn't even limp.

"I'm ready to go again," he said.

The buckskin eyed him fearfully and attempted to back away, but Rafe twisted his ear and the horse stood still long enough for Cade to mount.

The moment Cade's boots were in the stirrups, he shouted, "Stand back!"

Rafe ducked toward the rail, and the buckskin turned his mind to bucking.

Pilar couldn't begin to remember the names of all the jumps, twists, turns, stops, starts, and feints Earl called out as the buckskin did his level best to get rid of Cade, but Cade stayed on. He actually seemed to be enjoying himself. He smiled, even laughed as he dared the buckskin to try something more dangerous, bragging that the animal was his from this moment.

The buckskin finally came to a halt, its trembling legs spread wide, white lather flecking its neck and shoulders, its breath coming in huge gulps, its sides heaving. But unlike the other horses, the buckskin didn't hang his head in submission when Cade dismounted. He stared back at Cade, momentarily defeated but still defiant.

"That horse will go after you the minute you turn your back," his grandfather said.

"He's the best of the bunch," Cade said as he unbuckled the cinch and pulled off the saddle and bridle. "One of these days he's going to save my life."

"Right now he wants to take it," Holt said.

"He won't try now," Rafe said, speaking for one of the few times that day. "He's rethinking the situation, trying to figure out what to do next time."

Cade laughed. "You boys trying to spook me?"

"Naw, just keeping you on your toes," Broc said. "Seeing as how you were the last man to get thrown into the dirt, I suppose you ought to be the first one to get a bath."

Holt tried to argue his own case, but after Earl refused to have anything to do with submerging his body in hot water, it was unanimously decided that Cade should go first.

Pilar stopped breathing the moment Cade released the second button and a small patch of chest hair came into view. His nimble fingers didn't stop until all the buttons were undone. He pulled his shirttail out of his pants and took off the shirt.

Pilar felt her heart lurch into her throat. Her limbs felt as shaky as those of the buckskin, her breath just as labored. She had never seen a man's body. The sight mesmerized her.

"You going to strip naked in front of this girl?" his grandfather asked.

Cade turned to Pilar, his eyes sparkling with mischief. "If that's what she wants."

Cade was laughing at her. Pilar refused to let him see just how strongly he'd affected her. She managed to pull herself together. "It's time I started supper. Put your dirty clothes in the wash pot, but wait until *after* I get inside."

"Doesn't sound like you've made a very good impression on the lady," Owen crowed. "Maybe she'd like it better if I undressed first."

"I don't want to see anybody undress," Pilar said, able to speak more decisively now that she had herself in hand. "I'm not one of your camp followers."

"So you've heard about them, have you?" Owen said, his eyes alight with devilment. "None of them were as lovely as you."

Pilar headed to the house, spurred on by laughter and whispered comments. She didn't know what all their comments meant—her grandmother said love was vulgar, sex a necessary evil, and that a woman should remain ignorant of what happened between her and her husband until the wedding night—but she knew enough to blush. She jerked open the door. But rather than find the solitude she needed to regain her equilibrium, she nearly ran into her grandmother.

"That's disgraceful. If we were in Spain, he would be whipped."

"What are you doing out of your room?" Pilar was so shocked, she momentarily forgot Cade's bare chest. Her grandmother had been adamant that she wouldn't leave her room as long as strangers were about.

"You haven't been in the house all day," her

grandmother said, the disapproval in her voice nearly as heavy as that in her expression. "I've been worried what those men might do to you."

"I took them coffee and heated their bathwater."

"You should have let them get their own coffee."

"Everybody was busy. It didn't seem right that I should sit back and do nothing." Pilar headed toward the stove to light her fire and begin preparations for dinner.

"Do you call cooking and cleaning for all those men *nothing*?"

"I don't clean for them. We're the only ones staying in the house. You could come out anytime you want."

"I don't *want* to come out."

Pilar didn't bother interrupting as her grandmother ran through her litany. She had learned that the best thing to do was to let her finish.

Pilar tried to forget that Cade and the others were taking baths, that they were naked in the ranch yard, but she couldn't. Despite her determination to stay away from the window, she couldn't resist taking a look. She got a brief glance of Cade's bare shoulders above the rim of the bath before someone blocked her view.

"Stay away from that window!" her grandmother ordered. "Earl Wheeler is the lowest and most vile of God's creatures, but I didn't think even he would allow his grandson to bathe in full view of a lady so far above him."

"I don't think Cade and his grandfather consider us above them," Pilar said as she sliced a ham. "I think they believe they're as good as anybody else."

"Which shows how ignorant and uncivilized they are. Even wild animals recognize their leaders."

"Cade's been a leader since he was a boy. You used to say it was a shame how every boy in the county followed him wherever he went."

"I also said he would come to a sad end."

"We're the ones who've come to a sad end. The only way we'll get back any of our money is if Cade sells his cows."

"Laveau will return soon. Everything will be as it was."

"Maybe," Pilar said, unwilling to argue. "But until then we're dependent on Cade and his grandfather."

"I do not like all those strange men. Maybe we should go into San Antonio."

"Maybe a few people have stopped hating us for being Spanish, but now a lot more will hate us because Laveau's a traitor."

"Laveau is not—"

A burst of laughter from the yard caused her grandmother to stop, glance through the window, swell with indignation. "I would not have believed it, not even of the Wheelers. They are chasing one of the men half-naked around the yard."

"It has to be Owen," Pilar said without pausing in her work. "He's probably hoping I'll see him and be impressed."

But Pilar's thoughts were on Laveau.

Her brother was handsome, charming, aristocratic, everything her grandmother wanted in a grandson. He could preside over a wealthy estate with style and grace, but austerity wasn't in his temperament.

Nor was it in her grandmother's. She had been unable to understand that figures in a ledger could actually represent the money they did—or didn't—have. She could only understand what she saw, and many servants, the best food, and premium wine indicated they had money. Pilar feared Laveau would be the same.

Cade was different. He understood what represented real wealth. He understood what it took to get and keep it. She had learned a lot about how to run a ranch, but she didn't know as much as she needed to help Laveau restore their fortune. She knew only one person who could help her learn.

Cade.

"What do you think of Cade?" she asked her grandmother.

"He's as bad as his grandfather."

"I mean as a businessman."

"He's nothing but a cowhand."

"That's exactly what Laveau will be when he comes home."

"How can you compare that man to your brother?"

"I wasn't comparing them. I was asking what you thought of Cade."

Her grandmother launched into another tirade about the injustices of a world that allowed people like the Wheelers to rise above the level of peasants. But Pilar had learned that being aristocratic had not endowed her family with business sense. She had also learned that even a family used to wealth and position could lose everything overnight. A patrician birth guaranteed nothing. If they were to regain their wealth, they'd have to work for it.

She had also learned that intelligence, skill, character, even physical beauty, could come from humble
sources. As Cade had said, at one time her ancestors
were probably exactly like the Wheelers. Talent and
ambition, combined with luck, had enabled them to
rise above their station. The Wheelers had used luck
and skill to acquire their land. It looked like Cade had
the talent and ambition to turn it into an empire.

"I think we ought to ask Cade to help us."

"Help us!" her grandmother said, her voice rising
nearly two octaves from her normal contralto. "No
diViere needs the help of a Wheeler!" She pronounced
the name as through it were unclean. "Earl Wheeler
stole his first land from us nearly thirty years ago, and
he is still poor. I am in disbelief that you would think
he has anything to teach us."

"I said Cade."

"He knows nothing."

"He's got plans. I heard him explain them to his
grandfather. They're good."

"I doubt it, and I forbid you to speak to him about
it. Even if he were one of our class, it is not a suitable
topic for a lady."

The shattering of Pilar's lifelong habit of obedience
was almost audible.

Tired of being told what she couldn't do, angry at
having her accomplishments dismissed and Laveau's
shortcomings ignored, sick of her grandmother's refusal
to realize that her aristocratic heritage wouldn't put
food in their mouths or a roof over their heads, she was
beyond weary of stepping back, dutifully waiting for
some man to make all the decisions that affected her life.

"Being poor and having to cook for half a dozen men isn't suitable for a lady, either. I mean to ask Cade to teach me how to run a ranch. I mean to ask him as soon as he gets out of that bathtub."

Eight

"ARE YOU SURE YOU WANT THE MEN TO GIVE YOU their dirty clothes?" Cade asked, sticking his head into the kitchen. The first to finish his bath, he felt a thousand times better. Even his bruises didn't hurt as much, but the mounting pile of clothes bothered him.

"They won't get clean unless the men put them in the wash pot," Pilar answered without turning away from her work.

"You're talking about clothes for seven men."

Pilar turned to face him. "Do you want to wash them?"

"No."

She turned back to the pot she was stirring. "Then you'd better leave them to me. How much longer before the men will be ready to eat?"

"We'll eat when you're ready."

"That's not what I asked."

"Twenty minutes. I'll help."

"You don't have to."

"And you don't have to wash our clothes."

"I'd rather you didn't smell like a barnyard when you came to the table."

She turned, and her smile sent nearly every thought except one catapulting from his brain. He'd never realized what a truly beautiful woman she was, never been able to see past the hacienda, the money, the diViere name. It had been like looking at a portrait.

But the woman standing across the room from him now was wonderfully real. In a plain dress, her raven hair caught under a kerchief, her skin moist with perspiration, she looked very human. Very reachable. Very touchable. And Cade realized he very much wanted to touch her.

A small part of his brain screamed this wasn't part of the plan. He was to show interest, not *be* interested. That way lay frustration, trouble, disaster. He forced himself to retrieve the threads of their conversation.

"Do we really smell that bad?" His grandfather had told him to get downwind on occasion, but that had never been accompanied by an order to take a bath.

Baths had been impossible during the war. The men would sometimes go weeks without changing their underwear, but that didn't matter when they slept outdoors in camps that were stink holes at best, cesspools when the rain turned everything to mud that caught and held all the waste of the human and animal population. He had forgotten how ordinary human beings lived. He'd never known how people like Pilar lived. She must think him akin to a barn-yard animal.

"I guess we did," he said, not waiting for her answer. "You can set the plates out, if you want to help."

He felt like an idiot, standing immobile by the door, drinking in her beauty, feeling unworthy of being in the same room with her. The change staggered him. He'd never felt like this before, but there was a quality about Pilar he'd seen in only two women during the war.

The first woman had been the mistress of a small farm in the Shenandoah Valley. She had a large family to care for, but she hadn't hesitated to give the soldiers all the food she had. She turned her family out of doors so the soldiers could sleep in beds. Her ancestors came from nearly every great family in Virginia, but she and her daughters had waited on the soldiers themselves.

Another woman had been the mistress of a huge plantation before the war, but her house had been burned, her crops destroyed during the Battle of Fredericksburg. The woman and her family had been reduced to living in a modest house given to them by one of their relatives. The woman had never lost her graciousness, nor did she complain about what she had lost. She had set to work acquiring skills she'd never needed before, doing everything necessary to take care of her family.

Their circumstances had changed, but these women hadn't. That was how Cade felt about Pilar, which made him feel even worse about using her to get to Laveau. But he only had to think of the wives, parents, and children deprived of loved ones forever, and his resolution hardened.

"Was that your grandmother I saw at the window?" Cade asked as he crossed to the cabinet and began taking out plates. "I thought she never left her room."

"Your friends upset her. She wants to leave."

"Where would you go?"

"We have nowhere to go until Laveau comes home." She set ham and butter on the table.

"Have you heard from him again?"

"No. Move those cups so I can set this bowl down. It's hot."

He watched her closely. She didn't appear to be lying. She'd probably never had to learn to lie. But then neither had Laveau, and he'd fooled everybody.

"I would have thought he'd have written at least."

"So would I, but he hasn't." She was busy at the stove again. "My grandmother is getting very anxious about him."

"Aren't you?"

She turned toward him. "It doesn't do any good to worry when I don't know what to worry about. I'm more worried about our ranch."

She checked the biscuits. He finished with the plates and cups and started on the silverware. Tinware, he ought to say.

"I thought you said Laveau would come home and magically put everything back the way it was." He couldn't keep the sarcasm from his voice, but she didn't appear to resent his tone.

"He'll get rid of the squatters, but I'm worried about the rest. Laveau isn't good at thinking through a problem or sticking to a plan."

Her candid evaluation surprised him. Even in San Antonio where the diVieres were still distrusted and disliked because of their opposition in both the Texas wars, women thought Laveau could do no wrong. Which went to show what looks, money, charm, and a long pedigree could do.

"You need to tell him to come home soon. All over Texas, men will soon be rounding up and branding cattle that are running loose. If he doesn't get his brand on his cows soon, somebody else will."

"Why can't I do it?"

Good thing Cade had finished with the cups and plates. He dropped the knife he was about to put beside his grandfather's plate.

"You don't have to be so shocked. How do you think Texas got along during the war if it wasn't for the women taking over where the men left off?"

Cade bent down to pick up the knife. "I thought women in your family left everything up to the men."

Pilar wiped her hands on her apron and turned toward the window, away from Cade's gaze. "My grandmother wanted me to do that, but it didn't take me long to realize we were deeply in debt. I think the old manager took what little money we had."

"You could prosecute him."

She shook her head. "What matters is I was able to put the ranch back on a solid footing in two years." She turned to look at him. "Laveau doesn't know how to run the ranch. I want you to teach me everything you know, so I can help him." She heaved a sigh, as though having rid herself of a great burden. "There, I've admitted the Wheelers can do something better than the diVieres. That ought to make you happy."

It did, but not in the way she intended, or in the way he wanted. It excited him that she would turn to him, but he wasn't thinking about revenge. He was thinking about Pilar, about her beautiful hair, skin as fair as her hair was dark, a body that had just reached the full ripeness of womanhood. He was thinking like a man who'd been without a woman for so long he'd forgotten what it was like.

He was thinking like a man who realized he'd discovered a treasure and wanted her for himself.

He told himself he was crazy, that he was letting lust cloud his thinking. Her family had hated his family her whole life. She would marry a goat farmer before she'd marry him. If he hanged her brother, there wouldn't be enough money in the world to induce her to speak to him. He had to proceed with his original plan, not let physical desires get in his way.

"What do you want to know?" He looked out the window. Holt and Broc were emptying the water out of the bathtub. They would be ready to eat soon.

"How do I go about hiring men?"

Good. She'd hit a roadblock with her first question. "You can't."

"As long as I have the money—"

"It's not a matter of money. Texas men won't work for a woman, especially *vaqueros*."

"Why not?"

"Such a man couldn't call himself a man. He wouldn't be respected by other men."

"But men *do* work for women. My grandmother told me—"

"Maybe in other places, but not in Texas."

"So what am I to do?"

"Get a man to do the hiring for you."

"But wouldn't I have to hire him first?"

"You could get someone to take the job if you gave him complete control."

"I can't do that."

"Then you'll have to wait for Laveau."

"Would you hire them for me?"

Cade had considered the possibility that Pilar might want him to drive off her squatters, but not that she would want him to hire her crew. "It wouldn't do any good. The men wouldn't take orders from you."

"I could give them to you, and you could give them to the men."

It was time he brought this conversation to a close. "I've got my own ranch to run. I can't be here and at your place at the same time."

"But I need someone to run my ranch for me," she said as the first of the men entered the kitchen.

"How about me?" Owen said with one of his brightest smiles.

Cade couldn't think of anyone he less wanted close to Pilar. Owen wouldn't deviate from their plan to hang Laveau, but he would think nothing of seducing Pilar in the process. Cade didn't have many scruples in a situation like this, but he balked at ravishing virgins. Lost innocence was gone forever. "Fortunately, she doesn't have a ranch for you to run."

"I doubt Pilar considers that fortunate."

"She would if she had to put up with you for long." When it came to women, there was some demon inside Owen that seemed to goad him.

"Sit down before the food gets cold," Pilar said. "You can argue after the blessing."

"Are you looking for a foreman?" Broc asked Pilar after they had said the blessing and taken the edge off their appetites.

"I thought squatters had taken over your ranch," Holt said.

"I was thinking ahead to when my brother comes home."

"I expect he'll do the hiring," Broc said. "I can't imagine any man letting a woman do something like that."

"I know a woman who runs a farm back in Vermont," Holt said.

"There's no accounting for Yankees," Earl said. "They're nothing but a bunch of heathens."

Cade nearly choked on his food. As far as he could remember, his grandfather saw every Christian virtue as a weakness to be exploited. Fortunately for the peace of the meal, Holt didn't feel impelled to defend the honor of his home state.

"Women don't do that in Tennessee," Broc said. "Their menfolk won't let them. What about where you come from?" he asked Rafe.

Rafe forked a piece of ham into his mouth, answered by shaking his head.

"There you have it," Earl said, giving Pilar a satisfied smile. "It ain't fittin' for a woman to do any such thing."

"It *ain't fittin'* for women to starve or be forced to marry men who beat them, but it happens all the same."

"A man's got a right to beat his wife if she needs it," Earl insisted.

"Is that why your wife left you?" Pilar asked.

"She was a weak woman," Earl said, anger turning his cheeks a mottled red. "She couldn't stand up to the work."

"Not every woman is as strong as a plow horse," Pilar said.

"You sure as hell look a lot better than any horse I ever saw," Owen said.

"If that's your idea of a compliment," Cade said, "maybe you should be quiet."

"I didn't hear you saying anything."

"I don't need compliments from Wheelers," Pilar said.

"Maybe you don't want any, but I don't mind saying this is a fine meal," Cade said. "I don't know where you learned to cook, but you were taught well."

"I taught myself," Pilar said.

"She learned on Jessie and me," Earl said. "Nearly died a couple of times."

"That didn't stop you from eating enough for two people," Pilar said.

"A man's got to eat to stay alive."

"There's no law saying you have to stay alive."

Cade wondered if they had been going at each other like this for the last two years.

"What is your ranch like?" Broc asked Pilar.

"She doesn't have a ranch," Earl said spitefully.

Broc rephrased his question. "What was it like before the squatters took it?"

"We lived in a big hacienda built by my great-grandfather," Pilar said. "My grandmother's father. We had a land grant given to us by the Spanish king."

"Not that anybody in your family was able to hold on to it."

"We held on to it until you came along."

She sounded more tired than angry. Cade supposed she'd faced that particular truth too often for it to generate great anger.

"Our house was filled with beautiful things collected through several generations. We had wines from Spain and Italy, laces from Brussels, silver serving dishes from Germany and England. We had servants, and guests came to stay for days at a time."

"They were a useless, spoiled lot," Earl said, "incapable of doing anything except eating too much and spending too much money."

"It must have been hard to lose all that," Broc said.

"I was bored a lot of the time," Pilar said. "I hated having nothing to do, being told a proper lady didn't *want* to do anything with her time. But while I would be lying if I didn't say I still miss my old life very much, I don't mind working. I actually enjoyed running the ranch after my brother left."

"We'll get it back for you," Owen said.

Everyone looked at him in surprise.

"Laveau will do that," Pilar said. "I've had enough of being made to feel like a leech." She got up from the table. "The second pan of biscuits should be about ready."

Cade didn't know why he hadn't offered to run off the squatters. Having them that close was bound to be a source of trouble.

But his first responsibility was to his own ranch, to the men he'd promised a grubstake. It would take every bit of their time and energy to round up his cows, brand them, and take the steers to market. With only five able-bodied men—he didn't count his grandfather and uncle—they might have to hire help. Next spring, or maybe during the winter after he'd sold the herd, he might see what he could do.

Of course, that would depend on whether the others stayed around. They might not.

Then there was the matter of casualties. The squatters would fight hard to keep what they had. Cade didn't know how many had settled on the diViere ranch, but he was certain it was more than five. He and his friends would be outnumbered. While Cade was certain his five were equal to any ten squatters, the men were tired of war. Tired of being injured. Tired of seeing their friends die. Their desire for revenge was the only thing that held them together.

There wasn't a single logical reason why he should attempt to retake the diViere ranch.

And that might have been the precise reason that he made up his mind to do just that.

"I want to start the roundup tomorrow," he said, breaking in on a conversation about how living in Texas differed from Virginia, Tennessee, and Vermont.

He grinned at the groans from around the table. He was always full of energy when he was preparing for battle, and anyone who'd ever been on a roundup knew that trying to round up and brand longhorns that had run free for four years would be a battle of enormous proportions.

❧

Pilar didn't know how they did it. From sunup to sundown they rode in the saddle with no letup except to drink gallons of coffee and gulp down the food she brought to them. They had to be exhausted, but they didn't slow down. They joked with each other, making light of everything from bruises to cuts to narrow escapes from the horns and hooves of animals determined to kill them.

The men had been gone for a week. At supper Pilar sat down to the table with her grandmother. They talked about how nice it was to be by themselves, what it would be like when Laveau returned, but never once did Pilar forget that the men were miles from the ranch, pitting their strength against cattle who knew the brush, canyons, and low hills far better than the men who hunted them.

"I wish I could have gone with them," Pilar said for the hundredth time.

"There is no need for you to concern yourself with anything those men do."

"Laveau's never rounded up cows before. If I knew what to do, I could help him."

"Laveau *will not* round up cows." Her grandmother looked as shocked as if Pilar had uttered a blasphemy. "He will hire men to do the work for him. A diViere does not soil his hands with labor."

"How can he hire men without money?"

"Laveau will know what to do."

It was futile to try to explain being broke to her grandmother. She had never had money, had probably never held a coin in her own hands, might not have any idea what one looked like. For her, and for generations of women before her, wanting something had been enough.

Her grandmother believed that Laveau's absence was the only reason money wasn't as plentiful as ever. Once he returned—being a man and capable of solving any problem and handling any difficulty—everything would return to normal. But the more Pilar learned, the more certain she became that Laveau wouldn't live up to her grandmother's expectations.

Pilar was relieved when the men staggered in late one night with an urgent request that a full meal be on the table within an hour. They had more than two thousand cattle held a short distance from the house. They were going to fill the bathtub and clean up for the first time in a week. It would be midnight before the water got hot.

They were in such good spirits she enjoyed having them back. She hadn't realized how much she had come to relish their company. She even felt some of their enthusiasm when Cade announced they were going to start branding first thing in the morning.

But after she saw what they did, her whole attitude toward cows and branding did a complete turnabout.

Pilar had never really looked at a longhorn. She'd seen them from a distance, but she'd never been curious enough to want to see one up close. Until now, they had just been something her family used to support the way of life she took for granted.

Brought face-to-face with hundreds and hundreds of bawling cows, Pilar realized that longhorns were extremely unattractive animals that didn't smell good. Some were spotted, as if they wore old fur coats with enormous bald patches. Some had black streaks going down their legs or backs. Others had black around their eyes that gave them a particularly evil look. They held their heads low, swung them from side to side, always looking for a chance to escape. But nothing about them looked as evil and threatening as the horns that extended several feet on either side of their heads and curved forward in lethal hooks.

Pilar knew that brands were necessary to identify an owner's cattle. It wasn't so difficult with the calves. The mamas bellowed and tried to break away while their little ones were being branded, but the calves were too small to have any great strength. Nor did they have horns. The men could wrestle them to the ground, brand, and castrate them if necessary—she closed her eyes and turned her head away when they did that—without danger.

That wasn't true when it came to bulls that had been running wild for three or four years and weighed more than a thousand pounds. Pilar didn't need anyone to tell her that branding and castrating these animals was extremely dangerous work. Nor was she surprised to find Cade in the middle of it.

"Why doesn't he let someone help him?" Pilar asked Owen after Cade and Rafe had branded and castrated three bulls in succession.

"Cade says they're his cattle, so he ought to take the risks," Owen replied. He grinned broadly at Pilar. "I think he's showing off for you."

"Me!" Pilar drew a deep breath to tell Owen exactly why he was wrong, then realized he was teasing her. She let the air out, feeling unaccountably let down. She didn't want Cade to show any interest in her, but she didn't want the possibility to be so remote it was a laughing matter. "He always was a show-off," she said, trying to sound casual. "He used to race across the countryside doing crazy things. Every boy his age would do practically anything he wanted."

"They still do, but he's got two left feet when it comes to women. Take you, for instance."

"He probably can't wait until I leave his house," Pilar said. "I know his grandfather is counting the minutes."

"A man should never let a family disagreement get in the way of his appreciation of a beautiful woman."

"I have no difficulty appreciating beautiful women," Cade said, coming up to them, "but I try not to let it interfere with my work."

"No work is more important than a beautiful woman."

"That's as may be, but right now it's your turn. Broc has just put his rope around a young heifer. Think you can handle that *beautiful female*? I need a few minutes to catch my breath."

"Cade should have invited me to Texas years ago," Owen said to Pilar. "The poor boy can't do anything without my help."

"Get going," Cade said. "You're holding everybody up."

"Is he always like that?" Pilar asked as Owen strutted toward the heifer being dragged toward him.

"Ever since I've known him," Cade replied.

She wondered if Cade would be as charming when he met a woman he could love. He was certainly handsome enough to turn a woman's head, but he never seemed interested. He'd been too busy causing mischief when he was young; now his entire concentration was on making his ranch successful.

"Thanks for bringing fresh coffee," Cade said. "The men really appreciate it."

"I stopped *bringing* it hours ago. It's easier to make it over the fire."

Earl still complained about having to share the fire he used to heat the branding irons, but she didn't see any sense in going back and forth to the house when she could make the coffee right here. She was debating cooking their meals here as well.

"You don't have to do this," Cade said.

"I agreed to take care of the men on this ranch as long as I'm here. I intend to be as good as my word."

"You've never had to cook for a roundup crew, much less been present during the branding and castrating."

She didn't mind the branding too much, but she wished he'd stop reminding her of the other. "I don't mind working. I refuse to accept charity."

Cade laughed. "I can't imagine anyone describing working for my grandfather—even living in the same house with him—as receiving charity. Just keeping your temper must have been a full-time job."

"Your grandfather is difficult, but he's not—"

A shout drew their attention to the knot of activity. Owen lay on the ground, a steer doing its best to open his rib cage with its hooked horn.

Nine

CADE CUSSED EVERY STEP OF THE WAY TO THE HOUSE. He had no business leaving the branding site. With Owen hurt, they were shorthanded, but that didn't make any difference. Owen had been virtually alone with Pilar for a whole day, and Cade had to know what was going on between them. According to Broc, he'd gotten hurt because he'd been more interested in attracting Pilar's attention than in his work.

Owen's wound wasn't severe. The heifer hadn't given him any problem, but the young bull he'd castrated next was in a very bad temper. When he staggered to his feet and saw the human responsible for the indignity a short distance away, he'd decided to get even. The only serious injury was to Owen's pride, but the gash in his side had required stitches. Pilar had moved in with her grandmother so Owen could have the only other bedroom in the house. Cade meant to see that Owen moved to the bunkhouse after dinner.

Cade stepped into the kitchen in time to hear Pilar call out, "Are you feeling strong enough to come in here?"

"I hate to be such a bother, but I'm too weak to

leave the bedroom," Owen replied, his voice sounding remarkable vigorous for his weakened condition.

"How's he doing?" Cade asked when Pilar turned toward him.

"Fine, but I think I'll change his bandage. He says it itches."

It would do more than itch when Cade got his hands on him. "I'll take care of the bandages. The men could use some fresh coffee."

"I've got a pot on the stove right now. It'll be ready in a few minutes."

"They're hungry, too. I was hoping you could slice some ham. You don't have to heat it up. Cold will do."

"I don't mind cooking."

"How's your mother taking having Owen in the house?" Cade asked when she disappeared into the storeroom.

"She's not happy about that, or about my being at the branding site. She doesn't think it's suitable for a lady."

"It's not."

"I'll survive."

She emerged from the storeroom with strips of cloth, pins, a tin of salve, and lint. "You sure you want to do this?"

"I took care of hundreds of wounds during the war. I'm probably better at it than you are."

"I watched Holt. I'm sure I can do it again."

"I'm sure you could, but there's no need."

"It's itching real bad," Owen called out. "I don't know how much longer I can stand it."

"Then you'd better come into the kitchen," Cade

called, smiling as he thought of the irritation Owen
must be feeling at hearing Cade's voice.

"Should he be out of bed yet?" Pilar asked.

"If we were still with the troop, he'd have been in
the saddle as soon as Holt finished stitching him up."

Pilar seemed doubtful. "I suppose that would be
necessary in time of war, but he really was hurt."

"We'll all get hurt before we're done."

"That's a callous attitude."

"Commanding officers never show compassion,"
Owen said. He hobbled into the room rather melo-
dramatically, holding his side and glaring at Cade. "If
they did, the poor common soldier might think they
were human."

"It's malingerers like you that use up all our sympathy." Cade pulled out a chair and pushed Owen down
into it. "You take advantage of us any chance you get."

"There were precious few."

"If I'd known you better, there wouldn't have been
that many. Now stop trying to make Pilar think you're
about to die and let me change your bandage."

"I want Pilar to do it."

"She's busy fixing something to eat. You'll have to
do with me."

Owen groaned. "I'd rather put up with the itch."

In other words, he didn't itch at all. He had been
trying to engage Pilar's sympathy. "I can't have you
uncomfortable. I want you in the saddle tomorrow."

"He can't throw a rope yet," Pilar said. "He'll rip
the stitches out."

"I'll give him Jessie's job. All he has to do is circle
the herd. Even a child could do that."

"I'd rather take my chances on ripping out the stitches than get so bored I fall asleep."

"It's up to you, Cousin, but I'd hate to overtax your strength."

"I'll let you know when I'm too weak to carry on."

"Don't let him bully you," Pilar said, throwing Cade an indignant look.

"I don't want him giving you trouble," Cade said.

"He's no trouble."

"You sure you're talking about Owen? Ask Broc how many times we had to pull his rear end out of trouble."

"How about the times I've saved yours?" Owen shot back.

"He had a brilliant plan," Cade said. "I just couldn't convince him to direct it toward the enemy rather than the nearest female."

"You're jealous," Owen said.

"I know when it's time to put personal interests aside."

"You think I'm sitting in here when I should be working?"

"That's not what he means," Pilar said.

"Ask him," Owen said.

Cade didn't know what drove Owen to try to impress every female he met, but he knew why he wanted to captivate Pilar, and he wasn't going to let it happen.

"I'll ask Holt to take a look at him," Cade said. "Nobody can argue with a trained medical opinion."

Owen got to his feet with a curse. "You can't take the opinion of a man who amputated enough arms and legs to supply a whole battalion. I'd have to be holding my guts in my lap before he'd recommend I stay in bed."

"You can take over the branding irons. Gramps is itching to throw his leg over a horse."

"I'll be damned if I'll be treated like an old man," Owen said. "I'll see you at the herd. I'll be in the saddle when you get there." He stormed out of the kitchen.

"You can't let him go," Pilar said to Cade. "Those cows look like they can't wait to kill somebody."

"I imagine that's pretty much how they feel."

"Some of them are very big. And they've got those horns!"

"Those horns keep them from getting killed by wolves. The fact that they're fast and mean doesn't hurt either. Rafe told me he once saw a steer take on a grizzly bear. The steer got so roughed up they had to shoot him, but he killed the bear."

"How can you send an injured man to face animals like that?"

"I'll make sure he doesn't get hurt."

"Like you made sure before?"

"He was showing off for you."

Cade had been angry that Owen's thoughtless behavior had caused the other men to have to work harder to make up for his absence. And all because he wanted to show off for a woman he didn't even care about.

Cade wasn't certain Owen even liked women. He never mentioned his mother without going white about the mouth. Cade had decided long ago that what Owen did was none of his business, but he wasn't going to let him play his tricks on Pilar. She was a strong, proud woman, but she was alone and vulnerable. Circumstances had been cruel to her, but she'd swallowed her pride and risen above them. Cade was determined she wouldn't have to pay the still greater penalty of being punished for her brother's sins.

"I can't believe he was showing off for me," Pilar said.

"He can't help himself."

"Then it's up to you to take care of him. You're the leader."

"That's what I'm doing."

"By sending him back out there where that steer can get at him again?"

"That steer is headed back to his old grazing territory. Another steer will be after him."

"I don't see how you can laugh."

"I'm trying to protect you."

"From what?"

"Owen. He's handsome and very charming. I've seen him—"

"You think that I, a Cordoba, would fall for a Wheeler!"

Cade still didn't know Pilar really well, but he was certain she wasn't as arrogant as she sounded. Anger had caused her to repeat her grandmother's words.

"You're no different from dozens of women who have fallen for him already. I've seen him work."

"I don't need your protection."

Cade knew he had more on his mind than protection. Try as hard as he would to deny it, he was jealous of Pilar's possible interest in Owen. He knew what it was like to feel the pull of a physical attraction so strong it woke him out of an exhausted sleep, his body tense and hard. He would have sympathized if Owen felt that, but he was certain Pilar was only another potential conquest for him.

It was different with Cade.

In the short time since he'd been back at the ranch, he'd been struck by her quality of mind, her strength of character. She had been reared to live a pampered and useless life, but when circumstances turned against her, she didn't blame others for what had happened. She had done what she had to do to survive with class and dignity.

She was a spirited woman who didn't cling and was optimistic. She had put up with his grandfather's belittling her without getting bitter, and she had accepted the arrival of five men without complaining. She was not only a beautiful woman who aroused powerful desire and lust within him, she was a woman of character he liked being around.

"Maybe you don't need it, but I feel responsible for you as long as you're on our ranch. I didn't protect my men as I should have. I don't mean to fail you."

He hadn't meant for that to slip out. He hoped she wouldn't want an explanation he couldn't give her.

"I can take care of myself," she said, her ruffled feathers a little smoothed. "You concentrate on your work. I only want to watch."

He could feel some of his inner tension relax. "Only if you'll let me feel protective."

"Like a sister?"

He thought he could see humor in the back of her eyes. "I may not be a lady's man like Owen, but I'm not immune to a beautiful woman." He was pleased to see her blush. Even the slightest change of color was evident in her porcelain-like skin.

"A Wheeler shouldn't think I'm beautiful."

"Wheelers have many faults, but we've never been blind."

"If I didn't know you hated me, I'd say Owen needed to protect me from you."

"I don't hate you. I like you." The words came out so quickly, he was sure she couldn't doubt that he meant them. He felt relieved to have said them without pretense.

Pilar didn't appear to know whether to pursue the subject or run to her grandmother. "But you've hated me for years."

"I never hated you, but I don't like being swept up like so much dirt with every other Wheeler who's ever lived. I don't want to be judged by the aristocratic nonsense your grandmother has fed you all your life."

She looked bewildered, as if his liking her altered the only way she could think of him.

"You have lots of reasons to dislike and resent my grandfather, but you have none to hate me. I've never done anything to you."

But he was setting her up to help him hang her brother. She'd have reason then to hate him.

"What about the time you kidnapped me?"

"You remember that?" It had been a prank, a stupid stunt. He'd almost forgotten it.

"How could I forget it? You scared me half to death."

"You didn't sound frightened. You spent the entire time telling me in great detail what you hoped Laveau would do to me."

Color once again tinged Pilar's cheeks. She didn't

seem angry. She didn't even seem upset. She seemed... Was it possible she treasured that memory? His gaze narrowed, and she actually blushed.

Well, he was damned for a double fool. She *did* like remembering it. "Confess, it was exciting."

"If you think frightening her is a suitable way to excite a woman."

"I can think of much more suitable ways, but I don't think you'd have let me demonstrate them back then."

Color flamed in her cheeks. "I hope you don't think I would now."

"We're grown up now. There are grown-up games to play."

"It's just like you to think of life as one big game where there are no rules."

"That's my grandfather," Cade said, more convinced than ever that Pilar's attitude toward him had undergone a change. "I used to be thoughtless and irresponsible, but the war changed all that. Life is still a game I want to win, but I know there are rules. That's something else I learned in the war. You can win and be ashamed of yourself. You can lose and stand proud. It all depends on how you play the game."

How had he ended up preaching a sermon? No wonder he never got anywhere with women. "Sorry to get on my high horse. I'll take the coffee and go."

Her quarrelsome posture relaxed at once. "Since Owen's gone, I'll come with you."

They walked in silence for a few minutes, Cade carrying the coffeepot, Pilar almost trotting to keep up with his long stride.

"How long will it take you to finish branding?"

"About a week."

"What will you do then?"

"Round up some more cows. We've got thousands out there without brands. If I don't get brands on them, anybody can claim them."

"They can do the same with our cows, can't they?"

"Yes. You ought to urge Laveau to come home as soon as possible."

She didn't look up from trying to keep her skirts from getting caught on the dozens of cactus and other thorny plants that crowded in on the narrow path. She pulled her skirt to one side, then looked up. "I'm worried about him. Do you think he's all right?"

Cade hoped so. He wanted the pleasure of watching Laveau's face as the tightening rope squeezed the breath out of his body. "I'm sure he is. Laveau has always had the ability to come out on top no matter what kind of trouble he runs into."

"That's what Grandmother says."

"Just tell him to come home soon. If he doesn't, I'll brand my brand on all his mavericks after I finish with mine."

"Would you do that?"

"Would you rather somebody else steal your family's cows?"

"I don't want anybody to steal them."

"Somebody will if Laveau doesn't get back soon."

"But I can't tell him that if I can't write him."

Her distress was genuine. He was certain now she hadn't received another letter. "Did he say where he was in Kentucky?"

"No. He said somebody else might see the letter."

"Did he tell you why it was so important to keep his location a secret?"

"Just that people might be angry with him about the war. You know, because he changed sides."

"That's all he said?"

"Should there have been more?"

"I don't know. I didn't see him after he changed sides. The official report said he'd been killed."

"He said he didn't get a scratch the whole time."

Cade thought of his twenty-four comrades dead because of Laveau's treachery. The rage he kept banked inside flared up so hot he couldn't answer Pilar.

They reached the camp. "Get ready for a stampede," Cade said. "Every man out there will want the first cup of coffee."

∽

They worked like dogs for the next four days. The cows were wild, strong, and determined to avoid the branding iron and the knife. All the men were fine horsemen, but their work during the war had been very different from this. Staying in the saddle continuously for three days might have driven them to the point of numbing exhaustion, but it hadn't been the brutal, muscle-tearing, sinew-straining work of wrestling full-grown cows and bulls to the ground one after another, day after day. The work took a savage toll on their bodies. Their bruises got bruised. Dirt and sweat worked their way into small cuts, making them sting and burn under the hot sun until tempers turned savage. It seemed every living plant in the desert had poisonous thorns that punctured their skin, causing swelling, cussing, a lot of groans, and a few yells when Holt removed them. At night they fell into bed too tired to care that they were filthy and fit only to be in the company of each other.

Cade decided they would take a few days off before rounding up more cattle. Tempers as well as bodies needed rest. They had been working most of the morning without uttering an unnecessary word to each other. To the cows, however, their conservation had been steady, loud, filled with precise descriptions of how they'd like to cut the offending animals apart, bit by bit. Cade would have sworn Rafe actually enjoyed wielding the knife.

The situation had become so strained and the working conditions so uncomfortable due to the heat, flies, and smell that Pilar had taken to staying at the house, only appearing to bring fresh coffee at regular intervals. Cade could tell she'd redoubled her efforts to cook meals that would nourish their exhausted bodies. What they needed was more hands.

Ivan Nikoli had arrived two days earlier. A Polish nobleman who'd served in the war as a mercenary rather than a partisan, he didn't know anything about cattle, but he was a genius on a horse. He'd quickly learned how to cut an animal from the herd. Owen's wound was healing rapidly, but his temper was getting worse. Cade kept him away from Pilar, which made him even angrier.

"Time to saddle some fresh horses," Cade called to Owen, Holt, Broc, and Rafe when he saw Pilar approaching with a fresh pot of coffee. After they changed horses, one of them would take some coffee to Jessie and Ivan. Even though the herd was smaller now—they turned the newly branded animals loose to return to the open range—they never left it unattended.

Cade retreated to the spotty shade of a live oak, their only relief from the sun, sat down, and stretched to loosen the shoulder muscles that had got tight from wrestling cattle. His grandfather sat down on one of the oak limbs that rested on the ground.

"You won't get these cows done by sitting down every hour."

He said that every time they took a break, but Cade noticed he was the first to retreat to the shade and the first in line for coffee.

Cade turned to Pilar, giving her a welcoming smile. "You didn't have to come out here. I'd have sent someone after the coffee."

"You say that every time," his grandfather complained. "It's the girl's job to bring the coffee."

"It's not her job to put up with the noise and the stench." She never said a word about it, but he could tell she found it unpleasant. How could she not? "Now stop complaining and drink your coffee."

"I don't want a woman nosing about," his grandfather said. "No telling what she's up to."

"What could I be doing?" Pilar asked, pouring a cup of coffee and handing it to the old man.

"Women are cunning. You can't trust them."

"You can trust me not to want anything to do with branding cows," Pilar said. "I'd rather spend the whole day washing clothes."

Cade didn't know if that was a hint. At the end of the day, nobody had enough energy to haul the wood nd water necessary for baths or washing clothes. Too tired even to change their clothes, they fell into bed as they were. He was certain their smell was ripe enough to be detected a mile off. "We'll wash our own clothes," Cade with. "Ivan makes eight."

"Trying to turn her up sweet?"

Cade turned to see Owen approaching the tree, massaging his side. Holt had taken the stitches out last night. Cade imagined the scar itched.

"Where's your horse?"

"Holt volunteered to look after it for me. He was worried about his patient. Which is more than I can say for my cousin." He turned to Pilar, his ugly mood vanishing. "It's a relief to feast my eyes on you. It's not fair of Cade to keep you all to himself."

"Nobody's been keeping me anywhere," Pilar said. She poured a cup of coffee and handed to Owen. "How is your side? You really shouldn't be using a rope."

"I won't be accused of being a slacker," he said, eyeing Cade. "I intend to earn every penny of my share."

"I'm sure Cade doesn't want you working so hard."

"My cousin may be paying a little too much attention to you to know what I'm doing."

Cade knew Owen thought he'd be better than Cade at discovering Pilar's secrets, but he didn't know why Owen's temper had turned so sour. Maybe it was because Pilar seemed to show more interest in him than in Owen. Owen had always competed with Cade for leadership. He'd been angry when Cade was chosen to command the Night Riders. His consolation had been that women always preferred him to Cade. Maybe his pride couldn't stand Cade besting him in both areas. Cade doubted that had ever happened before.

"Maybe he's trying to learn from you," Pilar said, "trying to be more gallant."

"Calling Cade gallant would be like calling a mule a thoroughbred."

"You got a burr under your saddle?" Earl asked.

"I sure as hell do."

"Then pull it out," Earl said. "I won't have a man sulking around like a woman."

Cade wasn't certain it was a good idea for Owen to get his gripe out in the open. A man might be ashamed of his feelings, but once he'd stated them, he'd feel obliged to defend them. That often caused men to do things they really didn't want to do.

"Maybe you'd better go see to your horse," Cade said. "I expect Holt is wanting his coffee about now."

"That's one of the burrs under my saddle," Owen said, turning on Cade. "You always thinking you know what's going on in a man's mind. Like you're a whole lot better and smarter than the rest of us."

It had never been difficult to know what was on Owen's mind. He was either thinking of how to do the most damage to the enemy, win a point against Cade, or seduce some girl. He'd never appeared to care if he was hungry or soaked to the skin, lips blue, body shivering, as long as he had one of the three to occupy his mind.

"What are you getting at?" Cade asked.

"I'm tired of you giving all the orders around here like you're the only one who can think."

"Somebody's got to give the orders." Rafe Jerry

walked up to Pilar to get his coffee without looking at Owen or Cade. "It makes sense it should be Cade since this is his place."

"It's my ranch," Earl stated furiously.

Rafe ignored Earl, took his coffee, and withdrew to the far edge of the shade, his part in the conversation obviously finished.

"He doesn't own Pilar," Owen said.

"What?" Pilar turned so quickly, she spilled some of the coffee intended for Broc's cup. The rest of the men had come up behind Rafe.

"He's protecting her from me." Owen's laugh was harsh. "He thinks I'll steal her honor."

"That's ridiculous," Pilar protested.

"When a man starts protecting a woman from another man, it's a sign she'll soon have more influence over him than his friends, men with whom he shares a *vow*."

Cade didn't like the looks the men were giving him. They were questioning, wondering if he might be thinking of backing out of his vow.

"Why don't you go to the bunkhouse and lie down?" Cade said. "The herd's small enough that Jessie or Ivan can look after it."

"You never have thought I was as good as you," Owen said, anger twisting his handsome face.

"That's not what I meant."

"What else could you mean when you think an old man or a Polish count who's never seen a cow can do my job better than I can?"

"Owen, I'm not—"

Cade got no warning before Owen jumped him, and they went down in a tangle of arms and legs.

Ten

PILAR COULDN'T BELIEVE THAT OWEN WOULD FIGHT Cade over her. She could never have, and didn't *want* to have, any influence on Cade. Anyone could tell he was the kind of man who made up his mind what he wanted to do and did it regardless of opposition.

As she watched the men rolling about on the ground, she realized she had thought of Cade as her enemy, but she didn't feel that way about him now. There was none of the evil she expected of an enemy. He worked harder than anyone and remained cheerful under his grandfather's gibes. She had come to respect his sense of responsibility as well as his even temper.

Who wouldn't admire a man like that?

But that wasn't what surprised her. Even though she knew Owen was wounded, she found herself hoping Cade would be the one to land the telling blow.

The other men watched in silence, but Earl Wheeler's sentiments were never in doubt. "Knock the son of a bitch's teeth out!" he called to Cade. "That'll teach him to bite the hand that feeds him."

"Shouldn't you stop them?" Pilar asked Holt. "Owen is hurt."

"Owen's got something under his skin he needs to work out. Besides, Cade's going easy on him."

Pilar couldn't see anything easy about the fight. Each man punched the other relentlessly. Cade appeared to be trying to pin Owen to the ground, but that only made Owen madder.

"Don't treat me like a baby!" he yelled. "Fight like you mean it, dammit!"

"Do what he says," Earl called. "Beat the—"

"You got some more coffee in that pot?" Broc asked.

Pilar nodded, unable to take her eyes off the two men. It had taken a fight to make her realize that her feelings for Cade had undergone a change. No, that was too mild. Setting aside respect and the fact that he was a very attractive man, she *really* liked him. Maybe it was because he saw her as a person, not as a pawn. He had acknowledged her abilities, understood some of her feelings. He'd even admitted his family was in debt to her.

She heard a sound over the noise of the fight, saw Cade and Owen freeze.

"It was a gunshot," Holt said.

Rafe had already dropped his coffee and set off for his horse at a run. Broc followed close on his heels.

"What—"

Pilar's question was drowned out by a burst of gunfire.

"That's too damned close," Cade said, surging to his feet.

"My grandmother!" Pilar cried.

"It's not coming from that direction," Cade said. "It's coming from the trail in from San Antonio."

Broc and Rafe galloped by, dropping off two horses. Owen sprang up from the ground and threw himself on one of the horses. "You stay here with Pilar. At least *this* is something I can do."

Holt mounted up and followed him.

"I'm going, too," Earl said.

"Stay here," Cade said. "I don't know what's going on, but it's possible they're trying to pull us away so they can steal the herd."

"Why? There's only a few hundred left."

"I don't know," Cade said. "None of this makes sense."

"I'm worried about my grandmother," Pilar said. She'd never forget the fear, confusion, and desperation she and her grandmother had felt when they'd fled the squatters' attack on their ranch.

"Go find Jessie and Ivan," Cade said to his grandfather. "I'm taking Pilar up to the house."

"You can't tell me what to do on my own place," Earl said.

Without replying, Cade took Pilar by the hand and headed toward the house at a fast walk. She had to trot to keep up with him.

"Do you think it could be Laveau?" he asked.

"Why would he be shooting?" Thorns grabbed at her skirt, but she didn't have time to worry about possible tears. It was all she could do to keep up with Cade. They hadn't heard any more shots, but none of the men had come back, either.

"Laveau never liked me," Cade said. "He didn't want to belong to our troop when he found I had been given the command."

She would have been surprised if he had, but the war was over now. Laveau would be grateful to the Wheelers for taking his grandmother and sister in; he wouldn't come riding in shooting.

The house came into view. Pilar was relieved to see no one around. "I expect my grandmother has locked herself in her room," Pilar said. "I'd better go see that she's all right."

But Senora diViere surprised her granddaughter by meeting her at the door. "Where do those shots come from?" She glanced at Cade, her expression hard to interpret.

"I don't know," Cade answered. "The men have gone to find out."

"Squatters," Senora diViere spat out.

"Why should they attack us?" Pilar asked.

"Because he steals their cows."

"I'm only branding my cows."

"You should know about squatters," Senora diViere spat at him. "They are like your grandfather. They come in and take what belongs to someone else. When you try to take it back, they kill you."

The embarrassment that flooded through Pilar surprised her. Her grandmother spoke the truth, so why did she wish the old woman hadn't thrown it in Cade's face?

"We don't have to worry about the squatters," she said to her grandmother. "Cade will protect us."

"Considering the jewelry I have given his despicable grandfather, he should treat us as honored guests, not make you cook for so many men." With that, her grandmother shot Cade a look meant to convey to him that even though she depended on him for her safety, she considered him no better than a rat.

She took Pilar by the wrist. "Come inside. You," she said, returning her eagle-like gaze to Cade, "make certain whoever fired those shots does not come near the house." She pulled Pilar inside and closed the door.

"Grandmother, you can't—"

"What possessed you to let that man hold your hand?"

"I'm sure he didn't think. I know I didn't. We were hurrying to the house to make sure you were safe. I could barely keep up. I guess he took my hand to make sure I didn't lag behind."

"That's exactly the kind of story a Wheeler would tell."

"I doubt he was even aware of what he was doing."

"Wheelers *always* know what they do. How do you think they managed to hold on to our land for nearly thirty years?"

Pilar didn't want to think about anything that had happened so long ago. She wanted to know what had caused the shooting. She wanted to know what had caused her feelings for Cade to change, when they had changed, what it meant. She hoped he would no longer consider her his enemy.

"Has he been asking you questions about when Laveau will come back?" her grandmother asked.

"No more than usual."

"Did he seem worried? Frightened?"

Pilar laughed. "Cade Wheeler has never been frightened of anything in his life. I'm not sure he has that much sense." That wasn't true. She knew him better now. Anyone expecting the old Cade Wheeler back from the war was in for a big surprise. "Cade's concerned about getting his cattle branded before anybody can steal them, about getting them to a market that will give him a good price, but he's not worried."

"You keep away from him. I do not like what I am seeing." Her grandmother's gaze narrowed.

Pilar's defenses went up instantly. "What do you mean?"

"You sound like you admire him."

"I do. He's—"

"I forbid it. He is a Wheeler. He is not worthy of your admiration."

Pilar tried once more. "Admiring him doesn't mean I like him, not the way you mean. He's smart and he's willing to work hard. His friends are smart and hardworking. It's a credit to Cade that they're willing to take orders from him."

"He has cows. They do not."

"It's more than that. People followed Cade even before the war."

"Foolish boys."

"Maybe, but these are not foolish men. I plan to get Cade to teach me as much as possible."

"I forbid it. Laveau will not need your help. He is a man."

Pilar gave up trying to explain anything to her grandmother. She didn't know whether tradition, fear, or hatred kept the old woman from opening her mind, but she was not willing to change, to accept that things had changed. Most of all, she was not willing to accept that a Cordoba should know anything about work. It was out of the question that Pilar should attempt to run a ranch when there was a man available to do it. Her grandmother had complained about every economy Pilar instituted, insisting that Laveau wouldn't have done anything so absurd. Her grandmother didn't feel obliged to settle debts, especially with people she didn't know or considered inferior.

"You should be thinking of your fiancé, not this running of ranches. Manuel will not want a wife who tells him what to do, what to think."

"If he's so concerned about me, why didn't he help us when the squatters attacked?"

"He did not know."

"He's had two years to find out."

"Maybe he has squatters of his own?"

"Cade wouldn't have left his fiancée alone for two years."

The words were no sooner out of her mouth than she felt the shock she saw in her grandmother's expression. She didn't know what Cade would have done—war forced people to do all manner of things they wouldn't have done under normal circumstances—but she felt certain he would have found a way to protect the woman he loved.

Loved! What was she thinking? Love had never been a consideration for marriage in her family. A man married a woman who could bring him a dowry, an influential family, bear him children, and be a credit to his position in society. A woman married the man her family picked out for her. It didn't matter if he was ugly or cruel, or if they hated each other.

Even though Manuel was neither ugly nor cruel,

she didn't love him. But a woman had duties, responsibilities, loyalties, a position to maintain. According to her grandmother, love was a vulgar emotion that would cause her to cast all this aside, thereby endangering herself and her family. No, love had never been part of Pilar's thinking, but she was certain it was part of Cade's.

"What makes you think you know Cade so well?" her grandmother demanded, her gaze piercing, her brows furrowed.

"He offered to share the money he gets for his cows with anybody who needed money to start over again. If he would do that for his men, surely he'd do even more for the woman he loved."

She'd said that word again! What was wrong with her?

"You might know a Wheeler would do something as vulgar as fall in love."

"I don't know that he has."

"You think too much about this man."

"I'm living in his house, cooking his meals, and washing his clothes. We both depend on him for protection."

Her grandmother's expression grew stern. "You are with this man too much by yourself. I will come out of my room. I will watch."

Pilar was stunned. "But you despise Earl Wheeler."

"He is a barbarian, but I like that new boy."

Her grandmother had been caught out of her room when Ivan arrived. An aristocrat himself, Ivan had immediately recognized one of his own kind. He'd paid court to her grandmother, rolling out his family's titles, names and sizes of their lost estates, the positions at court they'd once occupied. Much to

Pilar's surprise, her grandmother had accepted Ivan as an equal.

"You and Earl hate each other," Pilar said. She could just imagine the war of words that would fly between her grandmother and Earl.

Her grandmother drew herself up. "I do not let my passions rule me. I will refuse to recognize his presence."

"But what will you do?" She knew her grandmother would plunge a dagger into her own heart before she would serve Earl Wheeler. Or sit down at his table while he was present.

"I will watch."

Pilar didn't trust her grandmother to be able to *watch* anybody she disapproved of without speaking her mind.

"If you're doing this because you think I'm falling in love with Cade, you're completely wrong."

"I would never believe you could do anything so vulgar, and certainly not with Cade Wheeler."

"Cade will make some woman a very good husband," Pilar said. "He's steady, dependable, honorable, hardworking, and is going to be a rich man one of these days."

"I knew you were falling under his influence."

"I'm not falling under anybody's influence, but I can see we have nothing. No hacienda. No cows. No *vaqueros*. In a few more weeks, we will have no more jewelry."

"Laveau will get everything back. He will—"

"Laveau doesn't want to learn how to make money. He just wants it to be there. Well, I found out it doesn't happen that way. You've got to be willing to work, to fight, if necessary. When somebody tries to take what belongs to you, you can't sit back and wait for the courts to fix it. If we'd tried to take Earl Wheeler's land, he wouldn't have stopped trying to get it back until he was dead."

"Your father and grandfather are dead."

"They died in a war, not fighting Earl Wheeler. You don't have to like Cade to realize he'll hold on to everything he's got. Then he'll double it, triple it, make it worth a dozen times more. He's going to buy up people like us, people who've gone for years without paying our debts, expecting to receive credit because we've always received credit. Well, I don't want to be bought up. I want to do the buying. And if Cade can teach me, I'm going to learn."

"I would never have spoken to my grandmother in that manner."

"You never had to cook and wash clothes for eight men to survive. I will never have to live like this again, do you hear me? Never!"

Pilar took a deep breath and tried to calm her nerves. She didn't know what had caused her to lose her temper with her grandmother. "Be careful what you say to Cade. I doubt he's willing to be treated as a common laborer in his own home. If you anger him, he could force us to leave."

"You like him."

"Yes, I do. He treats me like a real person. If I do something well, he even thanks me."

"I think Laveau had better come home quickly."

"You don't have to worry. Even if I liked Cade that way, he doesn't like me. He doesn't even trust me. He knows something about Laveau he won't tell me."

"What?"

"I don't know, but that's another reason I have to keep close to him."

"Do you think they mean to hurt Laveau?"

"I don't know. They didn't like his changing sides."

"Cade Wheeler has always hated my grandson."

"You forget they fought together."

"War changes nothing. We will always hate each other."

But Pilar didn't hate Cade. In fact, she was realizing more and more that her feelings were of a quite different nature.

❧

Cade didn't like the silence that hung over the ranch like an ominous threat. Even the birds had fallen silent. He glanced over his shoulder as he headed toward the bunkhouse. He ought to be out there with his men, but he couldn't leave the ranch house undefended.

He was convinced this was an attack of some kind, but couldn't decide whether the objective was the ranch buildings, the women, or the herd. There was nothing in the buildings that hadn't been there for the last four years. Why wait until it was defended by six extra men? The same was true of the women. And if they'd been after the herd—to rustle or scatter it—why wait until most of the cows had been turned back onto the range?

He entered the bunkhouse and took down his rifle. As he let his hands run over it, he was flooded with memories of the war, of depending on his wits more than his weapons. But his wits hadn't been proof against Laveau's treachery. He'd asked his commanding officer not to assign Laveau to their troop, but they needed expert riders. He'd watched Laveau closely at first, questioning every move, every statement. But after two years, with the battles becoming more desperate, he'd had less time and attention to give Laveau.

That had been his fatal mistake, and two-thirds of his troop had died because of it.

He couldn't discount the possibility that Laveau might be behind the attack, but he wouldn't want to attack the ranch while his mother and sister were still here. He'd wait until they'd left.

I don't want Pilar to leave.

Cade couldn't decide whether he'd spoken the words aloud or merely thought them, but they sounded in his brain with the impact of a shout. There could be no doubt. He didn't want Pilar to leave the ranch. It had nothing to do with her cooking. Well, not much. He would miss her. And he couldn't deny the physical attraction he felt for her.

That was normal. Expected. She was a beautiful, desirable woman, and he was a normal adult male with normal appetites, none of which were being satisfied. He imagined all of the men had dreamed of her on more than one occasion.

To his surprise, that made him angry. He didn't want anybody dreaming of her in that way. He was the only one allowed to think of her as a desirable woman who might have the same physical appetites he did, who might be just as anxious to relieve a need growing more insistent each day.

Cade reined in his thoughts. He had enough on his mind without worrying about rampaging lust. If he allowed himself to start thinking of ways to seduce her, he wouldn't be giving the proper attention to his objective of capturing her brother. Besides, it would violate his own personal code. He could become friendly, gain her confidence, encourage her to confide in him, and then seize her brother, but he could not do her any permanent damage.

Cade reached for a box of shells, started putting them into his Spencer rifle, a trophy he'd captured from a Union supply train. He was counting on this rifle to help him defend his land. He didn't have as many men as the scavengers, but he hoped that being better armed would give him an advantage. But they would need more ammunition.

He emerged from the bunkhouse. The silence remained oppressive. Why hadn't at least one of the men come back? He didn't like being left out of the action. He liked being in the middle of whatever was happening.

The faint clink of metal on stone caught his ear. Someone on horseback was out there. He strained his ears, waiting for another sound, anything to give him a more accurate idea of the direction of the sound. South Texas had enough trees and thorny shrubs to provide cover for anyone wishing to approach the ranch unseen.

He caught a brief glimpse of a horse's ears. The rider had dismounted a couple of hundred yards away from the trail, was leading his horse in. Whoever was coming didn't appear to expect trouble. The horse, a big, black animal, approached at a steady pace. Something about those big, mule-like ears seemed familiar. Almost immediately the picture connected with a memory in his brain, and Cade stepped away from the bunkhouse, raised his rifle, and took careful aim.

Eleven

"Come from behind that tree, or I'll put a bullet between your eyes."

The branches of a post oak quivered, the black, mule-like ears appeared, but no man came into sight.

"This is my last warning," Cade said. The click of the rifle hammer sounded loud in the silence.

"This is a damned poor way to welcome a fella who's come to sponge off you as long as he can." A tall, long-limbed man with a narrow face, piercing, blue eyes, and lank, brown hair stepped into the open, his black horse following more than twenty yards behind. "And me expecting a band and a couple of dancing girls to make me feel welcome."

Cade lowered his rifle and grinned broadly at Nate Dolan, a skinny razorback from Arkansas. "You old coon dog. You probably fired those shots yourself just to get everybody in a lather."

"Wish I'd thought of it," Nate said, taking his friend's hand into his powerful grip and giving it an enthusiastic shake. "Somebody else thought of it for me. Caught them sneaking along one of those dry creek beds. I figured they were up to no good, so I took a shot at one of them just to shake him up a mite. Must have done more than that. They started shooting at everything in sight before hightailing it out. I decided to come in sorta quiet like in case Rafe's about. Anybody showed up yet?"

"Rafe, Ivan, Owen, Holt, and Broc are out there looking for you right now."

Nate grinned broadly. "I always said an Arkansas coon hunter could get past anybody born east of the Mississippi."

Cade noticed Pilar looking through the window. "Let me introduce you to the woman who does the cooking and tries to make us take a bath more than once a week."

"What is she, some sort of fanatic?"

"Just has a highly developed sense of smell."

Nate laughed. "Poor woman. Must have been hell growing up on a dirt-poor ranch like this."

"She didn't. She grew up in a large hacienda with servants. She's here because squatters overran her place."

"She the one at the window?"

"Yes."

"How do I send thanks to the squatters? Is she married? Anybody staked a claim on her?"

"She's Laveau's sister."

Nate's attitude changed so dramatically, he looked like a different person. His eyes became hard as granite. His mouth pressed into a hard knot. His shoulders drooped slightly and his hair seemed to cover his face. "Where is the son of a bitch?"

"I don't know. She doesn't know what he did, so pretend nothing is wrong."

"How the hell am I supposed to do that?"

"The same way the rest of us do."

Pain filled Nate's eyes, twisted his handsome features. Cade was certain that not even hanging Laveau would relieve Nate of the guilt, grief, and anger that tortured him.

"The rest of you don't have to explain to your mother and sisters how you let their son and adored little brother get killed while you, their not so adored big brother, didn't get a scratch."

Cade was relieved to see the other men returning. Nate would soon be engulfed in a rough but hearty welcome that would brush aside some of the bitterness.

The greeting ritual didn't last long. Nate had hardly had time to shake hands with his old comrades before Owen turned to Cade. "Let's go to the bunkhouse. We want to talk to you."

"What did you find?" Cade asked.

"Just some tracks," Owen replied. "Probably the same guy Broc saw that night."

"Nate said he saw several men."

"So the guy has friends. It doesn't matter. They're gone."

"It does matter. Who are they? Where did they come from? What were they doing here?"

"We'll find out if they come back."

This wasn't like Owen. He liked fighting. He liked planning strategy. In fact, he would have stayed in the army if the Confederacy had won. Neither did Cade understand the sober, almost grim mood that had settled over his friends. Nate was one of the best-liked members of their old troop. They should have been laughing and enjoying themselves. Yet after a short greeting, all trooped to the bunkhouse without waiting for him to follow.

"What's going on?" Nate asked as he fell in alongside Cade.

"I don't know."

"How'd you get those bruises on your face?"

In the confusion over the gunshots, Cade had temporarily forgotten the fight with Owen. "A difference of opinion over a woman."

Nate nodded his head over his shoulder. "That woman?"

"She's the only one here except her grandmother."

"Owen?"

"Who else?"

"What about?"

"I expect I'm about to find out."

The men gathered in the bunkhouse looked more like judges than friends. No one sat. Holt didn't appear comfortable with the situation. Cade couldn't read Rafe's expression, but he had no difficulty telling that Owen, Broc, and Ivan were dead serious about something.

"What's up?" Cade asked as casually as he could.

"We want to talk about Pilar," Broc said.

"She's doing about as much work as we can expect."

"It's not that," Ivan said.

"Then what?"

"You're going soft on her," Owen said. "You're supposed to pump her for information, not fall in love with her."

Cade felt his tension ease. "I'm not in love with her."

"You're protecting her from me."

"I doubt she'd be very cooperative if you seduced her."

"She's the enemy."

"She's also my neighbor."

"She'll get married and move away."

"Not if you seduce her. Aristocrats are very particular about that," Cade said.

"Why should you care?" Nate's voice had lost the friendliness of moments before.

"It's a matter of ethics. I can't use Pilar without regard for what will happen to her."

"Why not?" Owen asked. "Her brother used us."

"He did much worse," Nate said.

There was nothing Cade could say that would ease Nate's pain, but he couldn't let them punish Pilar for her brother's treason. "Both sides fought the war for principles we believed in. They had our women behind their lines, and we had theirs. We fought like hell, but we never took it out on innocent bystanders. If men in the midst of war, in the heat of battle, can remember that, we have no excuse for forgetting it in time of peace."

"If you're too gutless to do what has to be done, I'll do it," Owen said. "I—"

"No, Cade's right," Broc said.

"Her brother is a traitor," Nate said, his voice raised to a shout.

"He's still right," Holt said.

"But if she's withholding information—"

"She's not," Cade said. "She hasn't heard from him."

"How do you know?" Owen asked.

"She's worried something might have happened to him. She knows that a lot of people might want to get back at him for changing sides during the war."

"They'll have to get in line," Nate said.

"I doubt she'll come running to me when the letter comes, but I can tell if she gets one."

"I don't see why we have to be so secretive about it," Nate said. "We can all watch her."

"We might know when she gets a letter, but that doesn't mean she'll tell us what's in it."

"We can take it from her."

"You forget Pilar is living with us. If she wanted, she could become a spy in our midst."

"We either have to trust Cade to gain her confidence or send her away," Holt said.

"I say we send her away," Nate said.

Cade felt his stomach clench. He couldn't send Pilar away. If it came to a choice, he would make the men leave. Shock that he would even think of choosing Pilar over his friends shook Cade to his toes. What had come over him?

"We can't afford to do that," Cade pointed out. "If you want to know the grim truth, we are dependent on the sale of her jewelry for our supplies. Do any of you have money?"

Adding up all their resources, they had barely more than a hundred dollars among them.

"We need ammunition," Cade said. "I think those people we keep seeing are squatters and they're planning to attack us. We also need supplies for the cattle drive. It's a long way to St. Louis."

"When are we going?" Broc asked.

"As soon as we can get supplies."

"But Texas is as brown as a berry."

"We won't take a large herd, but we've got to have some money now."

"Have you thought of shipping them to New Orleans?" Owen asked.

"I'll take them anywhere as long as I can get more than three dollars a head. I need to tell Pilar everyone is safe, that Nate was just trying to make a spectacular entrance."

Cade didn't wait for anyone to disagree. It had been all he could do to remain calm, to all outward appearances unruffled by their discussion. In truth, he was angry they would consider harming Pilar.

Owen was right to some extent. Cade was getting soft on her, but not just because she was beautiful and seductive. Though no one but him seemed to realize it, she was a remarkable woman. Many Texas women had stepped into the traces after their husbands left for the war, women who had worked alongside their husbands, been bred to trouble and hard work. Pilar had been shielded from the knowledge that it took hard work to produce the wealth she took for granted. Yet she had learned the difference between earning money and spending it.

Everyone would have expected her to collapse into hysterics when the squatters drove her from her home. Instead, she'd gone to where she knew she'd be safe—even though she hated being there. She'd learned to cook and clean, things she'd never had to do in her life. Most remarkable, she hadn't lost one bit of her dignity. The men might not understand what an amazing journey the last two years represented, but he did, and his respect for Pilar grew a little each day.

But his *liking* her seemed to be growing even more quickly. He couldn't admit to himself that Owen might have understood more of what was happening between them than either he or Pilar. They'd hardly done more than brush against each other.

But he had held her hand earlier. He hadn't been so worried about a possible attack that he hadn't been affected by the feel of her fingers pressed into his own.

He'd better get himself under control. That wouldn't be easy when he was supposed to give the impression he was falling for Pilar. *That* was getting easier every day.

❧

"You must take the place of honor at our table," Ivan said to Pilar's grandmother.

Senora diViere had emerged from her bedroom looking like a dowager Spanish queen. Dressed in black from her mantilla to her shoes, trailing a fortune in lace, and wearing all her remaining jewelry, she seemed jarringly out of place in the rustic kitchen.

Pilar was so tense, her nerves so on edge, she could hardly concentrate on her work. She would be greatly surprised if she didn't burn something before she got supper on the table. Despite Pilar's efforts to change her mind, her grandmother had decided to make her first appearance at the supper table. Ivan was trying to convince her to sit at the head of the table—in Earl's place.

Pilar couldn't imagine anything more certain to end in disaster.

"My grandmother doesn't like to eat with strangers," Pilar said. It was just like her grandmother to do the opposite of what Pilar wanted. "Besides, Earl Wheeler sits at the head of the table."

"I'm sure he'll be happy to vacate it for your grandmother," Ivan said. "He must be aware of the honor bestowed on his table by her presence."

Pilar wanted to shake him, tell him to stop remembering that he had grown up in a formal Polish court and realize he'd landed in the middle of southern Texas. Nobody here cared how many counts or princesses someone had in his pedigree. Most Texans didn't know what a pedigree was and wouldn't care if they did. What counted was how many cows you could put your brand on, how many sons you could father, how well you could fight, cuss, ride a horse, and throw a rope. If you could drink enough whiskey to make six ordinary men fall down drunk, you might be considered a real man.

"Earl Wheeler is a foul-tempered, sour-faced, mean-spirited, dried-up husk of a man," Pilar said. "He doesn't even like his own grandson. You won't be able to stop him from saying the most horrible things imaginable to my grandmother."

"I'm sure your grandmother is too large-minded to pay attention to anything Mr. Wheeler might say," Ivan said. "A woman such as your grandmother knows how to handle people like him."

Pilar didn't know anything about the Earl Wheeler types in Poland, but she was bone certain they had nothing in common with the Texas variety.

"Please have your dinner in your room as usual," Pilar pleaded. "You can invite Ivan to join you."

"I can't dine with your grandmother in her private chamber," Ivan said, as if Earl Wheeler's ranch house were some sort of palace. "It wouldn't be proper."

"Neither is ruining supper for everyone," Pilar said.

"You underestimate me," her grandmother said, preening under Ivan's adulation. "I am more than equal to Earl Wheeler."

Pilar gave up arguing but made up her mind to warn Cade. She watched for him through the window. He always came in early to help set the table.

Something had been bothering him when he came to tell her of Nate's arrival. He'd tried to shrug it off, said it had nothing to do with the shots, that it was something personal. She wasn't sure she believed him, but she didn't feel she could push for an explanation. Their relationship had become much more friendly, more relaxed, but they hadn't reached the point of sharing confidences, even minor ones.

Ivan said there was trouble in the bunkhouse, but he wouldn't say any more. She couldn't imagine what could have gone wrong.

"Was Cade telling the truth when he said we weren't in danger of being attacked?" she asked Ivan.

"We do not know who Nate saw, but it was nobody to frighten you. They ran off when Nate shot at them."

Pilar imagined that anybody would run away if someone started shooting at them. That didn't mean they weren't squatters or that they didn't mean to attack the ranch at the first opportunity. Just thinking about it brought back memories of the horrors of the attacks on the hacienda.

But Cade was here. He wouldn't let anything happen to her.

Pilar realized she had started to take his protection for granted. She didn't know when it had started, but there was something about him that seemed so solid and dependable, she didn't need to question whether she would be safe. Cade's physical presence had become her guarantee of safety. At the thought of danger, she looked to him. In fear, she turned to him. Just knowing he was within reach enabled her to sleep soundly even though she knew that danger lurked all around.

More than that, she'd started to like having him there. Not just because he made her feel safe. Not just because he was the only man to give her credit for having brains or being able to accomplish something without a man's help. It wasn't even his being a very attractive man who had made several disturbing appearances in her dreams. She just plain liked him. He didn't act toward her the way Laveau or even Manuel did. She couldn't pinpoint all the differences, but he made her feel better about herself. Maybe it was the fact that he helped with the supper preparations, that he didn't consider her work beneath him. Maybe it was the fact that he didn't automatically turn to someone else when he asked a question.

Maybe it was the fact he seemed to like her, too.

"Are you sure they won't come back?" she asked Ivan. Her other thoughts were too dangerous to pursue. She had to put them out of her mind.

"Do not be afraid. Nate can shoot a fly off a mule's ear at a hundred yards. He was only playing today."

"But if there are more of them?"

"I am sure Ivan knows what he is talking about," her grandmother said. "You had better check that big pot. I see white clouds coming out." Steam always escaped from the pot when Pilar boiled potatoes.

She saw Cade come out of the bunkhouse. "I've got to talk to Cade," she said and ran out of the kitchen before her grandmother could order her to remain where she was.

It took only a few seconds for Pilar to reach the front porch, but the series of emotions that flooded through her had ample time to shock her by their nature and intensity. She looked forward to talking to Cade alone, away from her grandmother or anyone else. She valued their privacy, had resented the presence of her grandmother and Ivan, which would prevent it tonight.

Cade smiled when he saw her appear on the porch, and knowing he smiled at the sight of her sent her heart hurtling over some dangerous precipice. With no hope of retrieving it. She wasn't sure she wanted to.

"I hope you're not going to tell me supper is burned and we have to cook our own," he said, his smile growing warmer, more welcoming.

"No," she said, feeling more relaxed and even a little ashamed of her worries. "But Ivan has persuaded my grandmother to sit at the head of the table for supper."

She'd never before heard the curse he let out.

"And he's told her that your grandfather would insist upon bestowing that honor upon her."

"You haven't given him any vodka, have you?"

"I don't know what that is."

"Ivan is peculiar all the time, but he becomes positively dangerous when he drinks vodka."

"You may not care about your grandfather, but my grandmother is an old woman," she said, annoyed he was taking things so casually. "It's not good for her to be upset. You know your grandfather will insult her. He says something mean every time anybody mentions her name."

"Why should she want to eat supper with us?" Cade asked. "She's never even been in the same room with us before."

"Ivan has flattered her, gotten her to thinking she'll be doing everybody an *honor* by eating with us."

Another new curse.

"She'll be expecting you to practically bow and scrape," Pilar said, relieved he had finally started taking her seriously. "She would never have done anything like this if Ivan hadn't talked her silly."

"Ivan is very friendly. Everybody likes him."

"So do I, but I'm going to be very angry if he causes my grandmother to be upset. I know she hasn't been very nice—okay, she's been horrible sometimes—but she doesn't understand what's happening. She's scared. It's too late for her to start over again."

"But not too late for you."

She could tell he meant that as a compliment. She felt herself blush. "I guess I was always something of a rebel. I wanted to learn how to ride a horse rather than ride in a carriage. I outraged her greatly when I took over the ranch. She'd have allowed herself to starve to death before she would have done that."

"I can just see her now," Cade said, "head held high, her aristocratic heritage wrapped securely around her as she wasted away."

Pilar tried not to smile, but it was so like her grandmother, she couldn't help it. "Please don't make fun of her. She's the only family I have."

"There's Laveau. And don't you have a fiancé in Mexico?"

She didn't know why Cade's mentioning her fiancé should cause her such deep embarrassment. "I haven't heard from Manuel in years. I expect he's married somebody else and already has a family."

"Foolish man."

"Manuel wouldn't marry anyone without a dowry, and I don't have one anymore. But I don't want to talk about Manuel," she said when Earl came out of the bunkhouse. "You've got to do something. Maybe your grandfather will agree to eat later. We can barely fit so many people around the table."

"Then my friends and I will eat later. This is my grandfather's home. I know it looks like I've taken over, but I only boss him around when I know more than he does. He's as ornery as a stomped-on rattlesnake, but—"

"But you love him."

"Yeah. Like you, he's all I've got left."

"What are you standing out here for?" Earl asked Pilar as he approached them. "You ought to be watching out for my supper."

"In a way she is," Cade said. "Her grandmother wants to join us for supper tonight."

Earl looked shocked, didn't say a word.

"I was hoping you could say something nice to her," Cade said.

"Be nice to that battle-ax!" Earl thundered, regaining control of his vocal powers. "You wait until I get my teeth into her. She'll wish those squatters had captured her instead of letting her come here," he said, turning and striding purposefully toward the house. "They probably let her get away so they wouldn't have to put up with her. Any sane man would have done the same."

Twelve

CADE DIDN'T UNDERSTAND WHY SOME PEOPLE SEEMED determined to court danger. He could have understood if Senora diViere had become so desperate for company, she had decided to join them regardless of the consequences. He could have understood if she'd wanted to upset his grandfather. He could even have understood if she'd wanted to pump them for information about Laveau. But he absolutely couldn't understand how she could believe Earl Wheeler would feel honored to have her at his table. Having the two of them at the table would be uncomfortable at best.

At worst, it could be a bloodbath.

"Wait up, Gramps. I need to talk to you." Cade turned to Pilar once he was certain his grandfather wasn't going to march straight into the kitchen and take the bull…uh, the senora, by the horns. "Can you talk her out of it?"

"I tried, but your silver-tongued friend countered everything I said."

"Ivan worships any female he considers a true aristocrat."

"And my grandmother drank in every word. I have a few words to say to your friend, and he's not going to like them." She turned and headed to the house.

"If anything's burned, I'll take it out of your wages," Earl called after Pilar.

"You'll have to start paying them first," Cade said.

His grandfather's expression changed. "I could pay wages if I wanted."

"Nobody's taking Confederate money, Gramps."

"I never did take that stuff. I'm talking about gold."

"What did you do? Rob a stage?"

"I sold cattle."

"To whom? The rustlers?"

"I'm not as helpless as you think. Jessie stayed here while I took a few head at a time. Didn't lose a single steer to squatters."

Cade's amusement vanished. "You've been taking that old woman's jewelry when you had money all the time?" His grandfather actually looked proud of himself. "You selfish old bastard!"

"They been eating, too. I don't see why I should be expected to pay for everything."

"Because Pilar worked…" He broke off. It was a waste of time to try to make his grandfather understand what he had done. "How much do you have? We need supplies."

"More than enough to take us through the winter."

"Enough for a cattle drive next spring?"

"That, too."

Cade didn't know whether to hit the old man or hug him. He didn't have to sell any steers for tallow. He could take all of them to St. Louis.

"Now what did you want to talk about?" his grandfather asked. "Make it snappy. I'm hungry."

Devilment sparkled in Earl's eyes. Cade figured he was more hungry for a piece of Senora diViere's hide than for his supper. "You've got to promise you won't say anything to upset Pilar's grandmother."

His grandfather looked at him as if he'd lost his mind.

"I know there's bad blood between you two," Cade said, "but think of Pilar. If you upset her too much, she might leave."

"And just where do you think she'll go?"

"I don't know, but I'd have to make sure she was safe."

"You'd side with *that woman* against your own grandfather?"

"This isn't about Senora diViere. It's about Pilar. She's worked hard since she's been here, and you've been hateful to her every chance you got."

"I didn't notice her holding her tongue."

"No, she's got spunk, but she never once refused to cook your dinner or wash your clothes. Since I've been here, she hasn't said anything mean to you unless you've been a stinker to her first."

"So you're taking that young hussy's side."

"That's just what I mean. You've got no reason to call her a hussy."

Earl regarded his grandson with narrowed eyes. "You developing a hankering for that gal?"

"Would it make any difference if I was?"

"You're damned right. I'd lock you in the bunkhouse until you got some sense. I noticed you been sidling up to her, but Owen told me you was trying to get some information out of her about Laveau. I was hoping you was trying to figure out how to get the rest of their land."

Cade couldn't decide which of their grandparents was more stubborn. He supposed it didn't make any difference.

"If you've said all you got to say, I'm going inside. I see your friends headed this way. You'd better get in front of those boys, Jessie, if you want anything to eat," Earl called to his brother.

"What's up?" Holt asked when he reached Cade. "You look worried enough to be delivering twin calves."

"Ivan has talked Pilar's grandmother into eating supper with us. She and my grandfather can't wait to rip each other's throats out."

"Sounds like fun," Owen said. "Things have been too quiet lately."

A tenuous quiet reigned when Cade entered the kitchen. Ivan had seated the two formidable grandparents at opposite ends of the table. Pilar looked white about the mouth. Cade glanced from Senora diViere to his grandfather. The two would-be potentates appeared to be weighing each other up, trying to determine the best method of attack.

"Do you need any help with the food?" Cade asked Pilar.

"No," she hissed. "Just see if you can keep him quiet."

"Why don't we let them have at each other, crown the winner, and bury the loser?" he said quietly.

"How can you joke about this?"

"I don't see how we can do anything else. I'll agree

to drag my grandfather from the kitchen if you'll haul your grandmother back to her room."

"You know I can't."

"Neither can I. Hand me those potatoes. Come sit down. I promise to stop them before they draw blood."

Cade was relieved to see that Holt had passed the word. Half his friends were keeping Earl so busy answering questions, he didn't have time to overhear what was being said at the other end of the table, where Ivan and Rafe were doing a masterful job of distracting Senora diViere.

"I bet you never had any food like this at your fancy hacienda," Earl Wheeler suddenly shouted at Senora diViere from his end of the table. She ignored him, continuing her conversation with Rafe.

"See anything you recognize? We don't have any armadillo or rattlesnake," Earl said. "I don't much like it myself, but I hear Frenchies like that sort of stuff."

"French chefs, they do wonderful things with food," Ivan said. "*Huîtres à la Florentine*"—Ivan kissed his fingertips—"they are *magnifique. Escargot à la Bourguignonne* was my mama's favorite. Papa, he liked *Gras-double de boeuf à la poulette.*"

"Can't say I care for snails or the inside of a cow, but I won't say no to a good oyster," Earl said. "But I don't want it messed up with your fancy sauces," he said, looking straight at Senora diViere. "I like them raw."

Cade didn't know what his grandfather and Ivan were talking about, but from Ivan's brilliant smile, he gathered his grandfather knew a lot more than anyone had given him credit for.

"How do you know about French food?" Ivan asked.

"I lived next to a Frenchie when I first came to Texas. Never would let us throw away anything. Let me tell you some of the things that man would eat."

"My stomach is already feeling queasy," Cade said before his grandfather could elaborate. "No point in putting us off Pilar's good supper."

"I am familiar with your beef and your vegetables," Senora diViere said, her voice deliberate, her expression frosty. "They are so-so. My granddaughter could do more, but with such a kitchen…" She shrugged her shoulders and turned back to Ivan.

As she let the sentence trail off, Cade realized she was caught on the horns of a dilemma. She couldn't criticize the food without criticizing Pilar. He was positive she would eat her meal in the corral with the horses before she criticized Pilar in front of a Wheeler.

"Tell me about your kitchen," Earl said with feigned politeness. "I want Cade to know what to buy when we get rich and build us a grand place like yours."

Earl must know that Senora diViere had never set foot in a kitchen. "You don't have to worry about that," Cade told his grandfather. "My wife will do all the choosing."

"Are you planning to be married soon?" Senora diViere asked.

Cade was aware of a sudden tension in Pilar's body. She continued eating, but she had started so badly, a piece of stewed fruit fell off her fork.

"Cade's gonna wait until we're rich so he can marry himself a fine, young society lady," Earl said. "Can't have a rich man marrying a poor woman. She wouldn't know how to get on with all his new friends."

Cade was furious at his grandfather. The old man was so intent on picking at Senora diViere, he didn't notice he was upsetting Pilar. He didn't know she hadn't heard from her fiancé in four years, but he probably wouldn't care. Cade knew the rejection had to cut deeply into her self-esteem. No woman wanted to think she was valued only for her dowry.

"A true aristocrat would not marry a common laborer," Senora diViere said.

"In this country, a rich man's not common, and a poor aristocrat isn't worth a damn."

"They are not worth much in Poland, either," Ivan said.

"I'm not getting married anytime soon," Cade said. "But when I do choose a wife, it won't be because of her daddy's money or her ancestors. She'll be strong enough to stand by my side, intelligent enough to share in planning our future, courageous enough—"

"He got those crazy ideas from you," Earl said, turning to Owen. "I always said half the people in Virginia were crazy. Too much inbreeding. That's why I left."

"You left so you could steal our land," Senora diViere said, dragging into the open what everybody knew was the driving force behind the Wheeler and diViere hatred. "You have nothing of your own, so you take what belongs to others."

"You ought to be glad I did," Earl said, proud rather than apologetic. "My protection is the only reason you have anything left."

"Your *protection* did not work against the squatters."

"It saved your hide, though I don't know why I

bothered. It was bad enough when you stayed locked in the bedroom, but seeing you at the other end of the table, staring at me with those black eyes like some kind of vulture, nearly ruins my appetite."

Senora diViere laid down her napkin and pushed back her chair. "It is you who is the vulture. You come to Texas from your inbreeding Virginia to tear the heart out of our beautiful country. Then, before your victim is dead, you pick the bones clean."

"Coyotes wouldn't touch your bones. Hell, you'd poison a rattlesnake if it bit you."

A second chair slid back from the table with a screech. Pilar jumped to her feet, her flushed face turned toward Earl. "Can't you go five minutes without being hateful? I don't ask you to like me. I don't even want you to, but just once you could show some appreciation for what I've done. My grandmother comes out of her room for the first time in two years, a room she has remained in because of you, and you can't stop jabbing at her. I don't know why you hate yourself so much, but I assure you I hate you even more. I'm surprised Cade wanted to come home. I'd have gone as far away from you as I could."

"That's because you're a Frenchie," Earl called after Pilar as she followed her grandmother from the room. "You don't have any sense of loyalty."

"*You* don't have any sense of fairness," Cade said, getting to his feet. "DiViere jewelry has kept you fed for the last two years. Instead of being man enough to admit you owe them a debt, you take your spite out on two defenseless and homeless women. I don't suppose being a Wheeler means very much, but I'm ashamed of you for bringing our family lower."

"You've put your foot right in it," Cade heard Owen say as Cade followed Pilar out of the kitchen. "Now you got everybody thinking you're a silly old fool."

Pilar had run out the front door, down the steps, and across the yard to an old post oak that must have sprouted a hundred years ago. She lost herself among the low-slung limbs, but nothing could hide the sound of her sobs. Cade was too big to follow into the depths of the tree's branches.

"I want to apologize for my grandfather," he said.

The crying stopped abruptly. "Go away."

"You have every right never to want to set eyes on a Wheeler again."

"He's an old bastard."

Cade chuckled. "I see his language has infected you, too."

Pilar charged out from among the branches. "Don't make fun of me. I hate him. I hate you. I hate all your friends."

"I'm sorry to hear that. I rather like you." He didn't know what made him hold out his arms to Pilar. But the moment he did, she stepped forward, fell against his chest, and burst into tears.

As his arms closed around her body, he felt himself being deluged by a multitude of unfamiliar and unnamable feelings. He hadn't held many women in his arms, never one who threw her arms around him and then proceeded to sob her heart out. He felt as if he'd become the strongest man in the world and it was his job to protect this fragile woman.

He couldn't help being aware of the difference in their sizes, of the smallness of her bones, the fragility of her body. He had never realized that her head barely reached above his shoulders. His arms fit around her with many inches to spare. She felt so tiny, so vulnerable, he had a need to hold her tight, to make sure nothing could hurt her.

She was alone with no one to turn to. Her brother was a traitor, and her fiancé was nowhere in sight. She had turned to Cade not as an officer but as a man.

It made him feel all-powerful and totally helpless at the same time. There was no man or beast he wouldn't have faced for her, but he didn't know what to do to ease the hurt, stop the tears, so he held her tighter.

Pilar pulled away. "I'm sorry," she said. "I don't know what got into me. My grandmother would—"

"Your grandmother wouldn't understand," Cade said. "I do."

"But I'm engaged. I shouldn't be—"

"You never gave your consent, and your fiancé has made no claim on you. You can consider yourself free."

"If Manuel doesn't want me, who will marry me?"

"You're a beautiful woman. Lots of men will want to marry you."

"They may *want* me, but they won't marry me."

Cade felt her statement as an accusation against him. "Everything will be different after Laveau comes home. You'll see; everything will be like it was before." He didn't know why he was saying those things. After he hanged Laveau, nothing would ever be the same again.

"But when is he coming home?" Pilar asked. "Every day I hope for a letter, but nothing comes."

"He'll write you soon. I'm sure of it."

She had stepped farther away from him, as if increasing the distance would disavow the emotion she'd revealed in a moment of weakness. "Where can I go until then? I can't face your grandfather."

"Of course you can. Give him the rough side of your tongue like you always do."

"I can't—"

"You've survived far worse than my grandfather's ill humor. You're stronger than he is."

It wasn't easy to read her expression in the twilight, but he had no difficulty seeing that she regarded him with a kind of disbelief. "Why are you trying to make me feel better?"

"I learned a bitter lesson during the war. Life is short. Sometimes cruelly so. We don't have time for pretense. My grandfather and your grandmother have an argument they will never settle, but that doesn't involve you and me. We're in each other's debt, but my debt is far greater than yours."

"Why are you being so generous?"

She had recovered from her moment of weakness. She didn't sound helpless or afraid. She sounded suspicious. Was he doing all of this simply to gain information? He didn't want to ask himself that question. It had been just a few hours since he'd assured his friends he had no other purpose in pretending to be interested in Pilar. And he had meant it, hadn't he?

He didn't know anymore. His original goal hadn't changed, but his feelings for Pilar had. No man could be around her and not fall under her spell.

"I'm not being generous, just facing facts. That's

something else I learned in the war. Fooling yourself just gets people hurt."

"Did everybody come out of the war as wise as you?"

He laughed. "My grandfather thinks I'm a fool."

"Your grandfather is afraid. He knows his time is past."

Cade knew that, and he felt guilty, but his grandfather still thought of Texas as an empty, lawless place to be claimed by the strongest. That was still true in some places, but more and more wealth and success would come to the man who knew how to use the laws to make the most of the natural resources. And the most plentiful natural resource was cattle.

"And your grandmother can't understand that the days of the Spanish aristocrat are past."

"What are we going to do?"

"Continue to round up and brand cows. You're going to wait for Laveau."

She seemed disappointed with his answer. It didn't satisfy him, either. Laveau's return would mean that Pilar would leave their ranch. Hanging Laveau would mean he'd never see her again.

Pilar sighed. "I'd better go back inside. They'll have finished eating by now."

He reached out and took her by the hand when she started to walk past him. "You don't have to. We can hire someone else."

"I have to work for our living. In spite of your grandfather, this is the best situation I could hope for."

The fact that what she said was probably true made him feel even worse. He ought to do something, but he didn't want her to leave. The present situation was perfect for him. He couldn't achieve his objective if she left.

"I'll talk to him," Cade said.

"Don't bother. I don't know what got into me tonight, but I'm all right now."

"Are you sure?"

"You would take my side against your grandfather?"

"It's not a matter of taking sides. It's being fair."

That was true in one sense, but it was a lie in another. A necessary lie if he was to achieve his goal—punishing a man who'd been responsible for the deaths of two dozen innocent men. That justified anything he did.

That rationale didn't satisfy him as it once had. Intellectually he still believed it. An eye for an eye, a tooth for a tooth. His men had been betrayed by one of their own. Every law of civilization said he had the right to bring that man to justice. In another corner of his soul he knew he was lying to himself, but he refused to listen. He had many more strident voices demanding his attention. Maybe after they hanged Laveau…

"Did you ever think of going somewhere else?" Pilar asked. "Did you ever want to be something besides a rancher?"

No one had ever asked him that question. He hadn't asked it of himself. "Texas is my home. I can't imagine living anywhere else."

"But you're a natural leader. Men follow you anywhere. You could have done practically anything."

Odd, he'd never considered himself a leader. He'd just done what needed to be done. And he'd always wanted to come home. Much to his surprise, he realized that Pilar had always been part of that vision. Not as his wife, but she'd always been there. Tantalizing. Tempting.

"Your grandmother will tell you that being a leader involves a certain amount of willingness to court danger. I've had enough of that. I want something more solid now. Glory turned out to be very hollow."

"Did losing the war hurt that much?"

"The loss of my men hurt more." He wouldn't explain if she asked; she might figure out what he was doing. "It's time to go back inside. Hold your head up high, stick your chin out. Gramps likes to pinch and poke at everybody around him, but he respects anyone who has the gumption to poke right back."

"Then he ought to respect me."

"He does. We all do."

But what he felt was much more than respect. The extent of it frightened him. "I want you to make a list of everything you need before you go to bed tonight."

"Why?"

"We're going to town tomorrow."

Thirteen

"ARE THE WOMEN IN SAN ANTONIO FRIENDLY?" OWEN asked Cade.

"Women are always friendly to a handsome rogue like you."

"Good. Tell me where I can meet you when it's time to return."

"You aren't going with us?" Broc asked.

"You don't need me to decide on bullets and flour. And I *do* need to see something besides your ugly faces. Not that your face is ugly," Owen said, flashing his patented smile at Pilar, "but I'm in the mood for some dancing. And maybe a little moonlight."

"And a lot of mayhem," Holt said.

"If I'm lucky," Owen said.

Pilar thought his laugh was almost relaxed and natural. He was a strange man, driven by some inner demon she didn't understand. But she didn't want to ruin this day by trying to make sense of Owen's moods. She was so excited she could barely sit still. After two years of being stuck on a ranch, she was going to town. She would see people, new clothes, maybe even hear some music.

They reached the town at sunset from the south, along the mission trail. She'd wanted to stop at one of the missions to offer a prayer for Laveau's safe return, but Cade said they could stop on their way home. When they came to one of the irrigation canals the priests had built a hundred years ago, Ivan said he would build a better one at the ranch. Cade said he wanted a windmill but didn't have the money for the equipment.

The sight of limestone buildings, wide streets, buggies, wagons, and carriages added to Pilar's excitement. She felt as though she were waking out of a kind of trance that she'd been in ever since the war started. San Antonio looked alive, happy, and colorful. She felt better just being there. Some buildings of stone and iron rose as much as four stories above the ground. She couldn't imagine going inside. She was certain she'd be dizzy just knowing she was at such a height.

"What do you want to do?" Cade asked her.

"Go shopping." She'd just look. Nobody had to tell her she didn't have money to buy anything.

"Do you have any friends you want to visit?"

"Maybe next time."

She had no friends. Since her family, at her grandmother's insistence, had sided with Mexico in both Texas wars, they were disliked and distrusted by everyone.

"They don't have much in the windows to tempt you," Broc observed.

"I guess they're still getting over the blockade," Cade said.

"What blockade?" she asked.

"Union ships blockaded Confederate ports to keep them from shipping cotton to England," Cade said.

"They tried to stop commerce altogether," Broc said.

Everything looked new to Pilar.

"I was wondering if the Union soldiers had reached San Antonio," Cade said.

"I guess you've got your answer," Broc said.

Pilar turned to see a group of several men in blue uniforms walking in a loose group along the other side of the street.

"It's a good thing we're not wearing our uniforms," Nate said. "They'd probably arrest us on sight."

"They can't arrest every man who fought in the war."

"No, but they can arrest us if we give them the slightest pretext."

But Pilar wasn't thinking about arrests. The soldiers might be able to tell her something about Laveau. She opened her mouth to ask Cade to stop, then closed it. She was certain none of the men would be happy that she wanted to talk to Union soldiers. If nothing else, it would bring them attention they didn't want. She decided to wait for a chance to speak to the soldiers alone.

They found a room for Pilar in a modest hotel on the edge of the business district. The men decided to sleep outside of town to save money.

"I haven't slept in a bed in so long, I'm still not used to the bunkhouse," Nate said.

Pilar felt guilty for having to spend money so she could spend the night in a hotel. "Consider this your reward for faithful service," Cade said.

Everybody except Cade went off to find some "entertainment" for the evening.

"You're the designated chaperon," Broc said. "You always said a good leader should take the jobs nobody else wants."

Pilar felt sorry for Cade. He couldn't say he didn't want to spend his evening entertaining her without being unpardonably rude.

"I prefer Pilar's company to yours," Cade said good-naturedly. "At least I won't have to put her to bed drunk."

"I'm going to bed early," she said. "I plan to go into every store in town tomorrow. It's been years since I've seen a new dress or a bolt of cloth."

The men wandered away, all wondering aloud how a woman could spend a whole day just looking. By the time Pilar got settled in her room, it was almost time for dinner. Cade didn't act as if they were doing anything out of the ordinary, but Pilar bubbled with excitement. She was having dinner alone with Cade, a meal she didn't have to prepare, serve, or clear away. It was almost like a romantic assignation.

She told herself not to be foolish. Cade had only brought her because he needed her help to buy supplies. But when she descended the stairs and found him waiting for her, she felt anything but ordinary. She saw in this man the embodiment of just about everything she wanted in a husband. She hadn't known what that was until now because she'd always expected to marry Manuel, so there'd been no point in thinking about what she could never have.

"They're having some kind of festival tonight," Cade said. "Would you like to go after we eat?"

Music! Dancing! Laughter! Pilar thought her heart would burst with anticipation.

"Where do you want to eat?" Cade asked.

"I don't care as long as it's not beans and bacon."

Cade found a tiny restaurant that served French food exactly like her family used to have. "How did you know what I wanted?" she asked.

"I thought you might miss some of the things you used to have."

Manuel wouldn't have considered what she wanted. She'd come to expect Cade to be more thoughtful than the men in her family, but the variety and depth of his thoughtfulness continued to surprise her.

But nothing surprised her as much as his choice of the correct wine to go with the meal.

"I learned in Virginia," he said, aware of what she wanted to know but didn't dare ask. "We spent a winter working out of one area. The local gentlemen insisted that I dine at their homes every night. We protected them from attack. They considered it repayment."

Over dinner she encouraged him to talk about the war, about the years that changed the wild boy she had known into the responsible adult. Even though she asked, he wouldn't tell her anything about Laveau. She sensed his anger. She supposed she couldn't expect anything else. Her grandmother might think Laveau was wise to change sides, but she had an uneasy feeling it showed a lack of character.

But what could a man do when the government didn't protect his property?

She couldn't answer that question.

"Are you ready to go to the festival?" Cade asked.

The meal had gone by too quickly. Even though worry continued to buzz in the back of her consciousness, she had enjoyed listening to Cade's stories about the people he'd fought alongside. She felt she knew the six men who'd come to help him a little better now. "I haven't been to a party or danced and laughed in so long, I've almost forgotten how," Pilar said.

"Then consider this a new beginning. I'll make sure you have a chance to do all this again soon."

Pilar refused to let herself speculate on what his statement could mean. She was certain that what he had in mind wasn't at all what she was thinking. She didn't ask. She wanted to pretend for just a little while.

It was easy to pretend she was with the man of her dreams. He had been charming, fun, and a pleasant companion. Even though other women had cast glances in his direction all evening, she'd been the sole focus of his attention. That made her feel important, pretty, desired. She was certain he'd rather be with his friends, yet he hadn't shown any sign of irritation. If she hadn't known better, she'd have sworn he *wanted* to stay with her.

They walked side by side, talking easily until they reached a small plaza where a band played and people had gathered to sing and dance. Cade put his arm around Pilar's waist to guide her through the press of people. She was certain it was an instinctive act, but it caused the tension in her body to increase tenfold, her awareness of his nearness to skyrocket. When he took her by the hand and guided her to an open spot, she felt a kind of closeness she'd never experienced before.

A small band of six people—two trumpets, two

guitars, and two women who sang and played the castanets and maracas—played a familiar tune. It made her think of a time when she was innocent of all the dangers that lay just beyond the hacienda walls.

She started to hum the tune, then sang the words softly. Cade joined in.

"You know this song?" she asked, surprised.

"I used to go to every fiesta I could find," he said, his face appearing wonderfully different in the flickering light of the torches scattered round the plaza. "I considered myself a great Lothario, irresistible to women."

She imagined he had been. Some of the couples started dancing to the energetic rhythm of the song. The music was infectious, and Pilar's foot started tapping. Within moments she was swaying to the rhythm.

"Do you want to dance?" Cade asked.

If she'd been surprised he could sing, she was stunned he could dance.

"You can't be a successful Lothario unless you can dance," he said, his eyes dancing with laughter. "All the senoritas expect it."

"And do you always try to fulfill a senorita's expectations?"

"Whenever I can."

She couldn't believe how flirtatious she sounded, but something inside her had burst loose. Maybe it was relief from four years of worry and fear. Maybe it was the natural reaction of a young woman in the company of a handsome young man. Maybe it was a desperate attempt to have a little fun while the opportunity lasted. She didn't waste time trying to validate the impulse. She would behave tomorrow. She wanted to enjoy herself tonight.

"Can you teach me this dance?" she asked. "Grandmother disapproved of dancing."

Cade pulled her into the open.

"Not where everybody can see me."

"They won't pay us any attention. Just do what I do."

He demonstrated one four-beat pattern. She copied it. He demonstrated another. She copied that, then put them together. The steps weren't difficult to do, but as Cade added more, the sequence got harder to remember. She concentrated so hard, she was unaware of her surroundings until Cade started to chuckle.

"Don't laugh at me," she said, looking up slightly irritated. "I'm doing the best I can."

"I'm not laughing at you," he said. "I'm laughing at them."

Following his gaze, Pilar discovered they were surrounded by a cordon of interested spectators encouraging her with smiles and occasional supplements to Cade's instructions.

"They're rooting for you. Come on, show them what you've learned."

Some strange demon must have taken over her body. She opened her mouth to say she wanted to go back to the hotel, but the only word that came out was, "Okay."

Even the band appeared to have taken an interest in her progress. They started the next song slowly. When it became clear that Pilar had mastered the steps, they picked up the tempo. Other couples joined in until the plaza was filled with couples whirling, shouting, and encouraging each other. The music built until it came to a climax that left everyone breathless.

"I've got to sit down," Pilar said as she clung to Cade. He didn't act winded. Apparently wrestling full-grown cows to the ground was good conditioning for dancing. Cooking and washing dishes weren't.

Cade led her to a bench under a tree. "I'll find us something to drink." Moments later he handed her a richly colored red drink.

"What is this?"

"I don't know, but the woman who made it said it would give you energy to dance all night."

Considering the way she felt, Pilar doubted that. The drink, a medley of fruit flavors, was delicious.

"Don't drink it too fast," Cade warned. "I'm sure they put something alcoholic in it. I don't want anybody saying I tried to get you drunk."

"I've drunk wine all my life," Pilar said.

"Just take it easy. Fruit juices can disguise practically anything. I expect it's made with tequila instead of wine."

Pilar had never had tequila. Her grandmother said it was a drink for common people. "Is anybody else drinking tequila?"

"I imagine everybody is."

Nobody around her seemed drunk. They were all talking, dancing, laughing, and having fun. If it didn't bother them, it wouldn't bother her. "I'll be careful, but it's very good. What are you drinking?"

"Beer."

Laveau had let her taste his beer years ago. She thought it was awful. She was glad Cade had brought her the fruit drink even if it did contain tequila. The music started again, but this time the tune was slow and mournful. Pilar looked to see what steps the dancers were using, only to find it didn't seem to matter. That the men held the women in their arms seemed much more important.

"Are you rested?" Cade asked.

Immediately her heart started to hammer in her chest. She'd never danced like that with a man. French dances were all pattern dances with couples doing little more than touching hands. The Spanish dances her grandmother approved were even more formal. A married woman could go through an entire evening and barely touch her husband's hand. Unmarried women had been known to quiver and quake from fear of any contact.

But none of the women here tonight appeared the least bit upset by being held close. Rather, they seemed quite pleased. Pilar took a swallow of her drink. "I'm ready."

She wasn't, but a diViere never admitted fear. And of course all Cordobas reaching back into the mists of time had been fearless warriors. Pilar wondered what unacknowledged ancestor she could blame for her shaking knees.

They shook even more when Cade pulled her into what could only be described as an embrace. He didn't force her, just gently guided her into the crook of his arm. A big, strong arm that wrapped around her with the solidity of stone. She knew without asking that he would be here tomorrow, the day after, and all the days after that.

Inside, the cocoon she had built when Laveau left began to unravel. So, too, the walls she'd built to keep out the knowledge that danger lurked all around, the feeling that she would never return to her home, the fear that no man would want her now that she was poor. This feeling of safety could only last an evening, for one dance, maybe even a moment, but Pilar wanted to treasure it.

But her thoughts couldn't long remain focused inward when she was in the arms of a man who pressed her body close to his. She became aware of Cade in a manner that was entirely different from anything she'd experienced before. She remembered the night when he'd held her, comforted her as she cried, but this had nothing to do with comfort. It had nothing to do with his appreciation for what she'd been able to accomplish on her own. He was a man and she was a woman, and she'd never been more aware of it than in that moment.

She looked around, certain she was the center of attention, that everyone was directing disapproving frowns at her. To her relief, all the couples appeared to have thoughts only for themselves.

Pilar let her muscles relax, let herself lean in. There was no danger that either of them would misinterpret these movements. Their relationship had been defined long ago.

Now, instead of acting as a barrier, their enmity served as a release. She could follow her inclinations without fear that anything would come of her actions. With a huge inward sigh, she allowed herself to feel swallowed in Cade's embrace. It felt absolutely marvelous. For the first time in years, she didn't feel the weight of the world on her shoulders. She only had to think of herself, there, in that moment. Cade would take care of everything else.

"Why don't they play something faster?" she asked, suddenly bursting with the desire to express this new-found sense of freedom.

"They will in a little while."

"But I want it now." She pulled Cade in the direction of the band. "Faster!" she called out. "This is a fiesta, not a funeral."

The band didn't need to be asked a second time. Without missing a beat, they shifted into a version of the same melody that had the dancers gasping for breath moments later.

"For someone who just learned the steps, you sure are a zealous convert."

Pilar felt marvelous. She intended to pack as much fun as she could into this one night. She wanted to dance until she couldn't stand up. Then she wanted another of those fruit drinks. Tomorrow they would buy their supplies and head back to the ranch.

An hour later, Pilar had finished her third fruit drink and danced a fandango that left her so exhausted she had to lean on Cade as they left the dance area.

"I think it's time to go," he said. "You need to get to bed."

"I don't want to go to bed," Pilar said. "I want to dance some more." She had the feeling that her desire to lean on Cade wasn't entirely the result of fatigue, but she refused to feel guilty.

"Let's go for a walk instead."

"I don't want to walk," she said, angry he'd forced her to leave the fiesta. "I can do that anytime."

"We can walk along the river. The moonlight on the water makes it look like a river of silver."

A walk sounded awfully dull compared to dancing, but she'd never seen a river in the moonlight. Young ladies of aristocratic lineage weren't supposed to be interested in such things. Cade made it sound very pretty. "Okay, but if I don't like it, I want to go back to the fiesta."

The fruit drinks had undoubtedly contained more tequila than she'd suspected. She had never felt so uninhibited, so unfettered by tradition, so unrestrained by her grandmother's strictures. It felt absolutely marvelous.

"Have you walked along rivers in the moonlight with a lot of girls?" she asked.

Cade chuckled softly. "You should ask Owen that question."

"I'm not interested in Owen. I'm interested in you." She didn't mean it quite the way it sounded, but it was too much trouble to explain.

"No one seemed particularly interested," Cade said.

Pilar couldn't understand that. To her, Cade seemed like exactly the kind of man a woman would want to walk with in the moonlight. He was strong, handsome, and dependable, everything a young woman would look for in a man.

"I can't believe the young women you knew were so silly."

"Young ladies want excitement, clever words, flattery," he said.

"They'd want something very different if they'd been

driven out of their home and forced to cook for a living." She hadn't meant to mention that, but what he said seemed so frivolous, she couldn't help herself.

"Some lost more than you. They just wanted to forget."

She would *never* forget. "Let's not talk about the war. Pretend I'm one of those silly women who pant after Owen. Tell me I'm pretty and you get lost in my eyes."

Pilar felt herself flush with embarrassment. She didn't know where those words had come from. She'd never even thought anything so foolish in her entire life.

"You're not pretty," Cade said.

That's what she got for putting words into a man's mouth.

"You're beautiful. Any man would give his right arm to be able to drown himself in your eyes."

Pilar didn't know what more those Virginia beauties could want. Manuel had never said anything half so poetic.

"Your fiancé should be cut into small pieces and fed to the coyotes for leaving you unprotected. If I had been your fiancé, not even loyalty to my country could have been enough to make me leave you."

Pilar was wise enough to know that no man ever valued his wife above his loyalty to his country—his money or his children perhaps, but never his wife. But the effect on her was the same as if it had been the truth. She'd never felt so important in her life, and she liked it.

"Would you really have stayed in Texas if I'd been your fiancée?"

"Maybe not, but I'd have made sure you were safe before I left."

"Why?"

"A man protects what he values. Nothing is more valuable than the woman a man loves."

Pilar had never expected to be loved by her husband, but when she was alone and faced with the future, she couldn't help dreaming about it. Respect and all that stuff about lineage and money didn't seem enough in a world that could turn cold and cruel at any moment.

"How would you show a woman you loved her?" Pilar asked.

"Like this." Cade took her in his arms and kissed her.

Pilar knew that some part of her must have been wanting this, hoping for it, but a part of her was shocked to find herself in Cade's embrace. That same part was even more shocked to discover how much she wanted it, welcomed it, moved forward to meet him. Nor did she back away from the kiss when it turned from a gentle brushing of lips to an unbridled expression of pent-up emotions.

She didn't know what was responsible for the feeling that her life had suddenly turned in a new direction, had taken on a different meaning. She didn't know how to account for the emptiness inside her, or the conviction that Cade was the only one who could fill it.

She only knew she'd been swept up in Cade's powerful embrace and it was the most wonderful feeling of her whole life.

She'd never imagined that anything could feel as

wonderful as this kiss. His lips were full, his mouth soft. His tongue darted between her teeth before she knew what was happening. But even as her conscious mind started to reject the idea, her body's response was the opposite—and enthusiastic. Her own tongue rose to duel with Cade's, entwining sinuously around his, plunging deep into his mouth.

Gradually Pilar became aware that other parts of her body were reacting to Cade's embrace. Her breasts—pressed hard against his chest—had become extremely sensitive, her nipples swollen. A feeling unlike anything she'd ever experienced uncoiled deep in her belly, then began to spread through her limbs, causing her muscles to go limp. Instinctively she clung still more tightly to Cade.

Without warning, Cade broke the kiss, took her by the shoulders, and thrust her away from him.

The shock was total.

"We have to go back to the hotel before I forget you're a lady I've promised to protect," Cade said.

Pilar's brain refused to function. She couldn't understand what Cole was saying. She could only understand that all comfort had suddenly been torn from her. "What would you do if I weren't a lady, if we didn't have to go back to the hotel?"

Fourteen

PILAR DIDN'T KNOW HOW SHE COULD FACE CADE after what she'd asked him last night. How could she have asked such a question? She knew what men did with willing women. Cade had had every reason to think she was asking him to do the same with her. Just the memory caused her to flush with embarrassment.

It's impossible to think of you as anyone but yourself. It's my duty to keep you safe until Laveau comes back.

His answer had sounded so high-minded and admirable, it had taken her half the night to figure out why it made her so miserable. She didn't want Cade to think of protecting her as a duty. She wanted him to think of her as a woman so desirable he would forget duty and honor and spirit her away to some secret hideaway where they could…

Another flush of heated embarrassment prevented her from finishing that thought. She had to stop acting like she was falling in love with Cade. That was impossible. She had to stop acting like she wanted him to make love to her. She knew *that* was absurd. She didn't feel like that about him, and he certainly didn't feel that way about her. Just as important, she had to stop having dreams like the one she'd had last night.

More embarrassment overwhelmed her. In her dream he'd carried her back to the hotel and made passionate love to her all night long. And not once had she uttered a single word of protest.

At least Cade had no way of knowing about that dream, and she had a whole day to put it out of her mind. If she could just survive that first moment of meeting. She prayed all his friends would be there.

When she reached the lobby, Cade was alone.

Her instinctive reaction was to turn around, but Cade had seen her. He started toward her, his warm smile of welcome brightening up the dismal morning. "Where is everybody?" she asked before he could say anything about last night.

"Nate, Holt, and Broc went off to visit as many saloons as possible," Cade said. "We need information on who's buying cattle and what prices they're paying. Owen took Ivan and went off on his own. Rafe and I are planning to go to the Menger Hotel to see what we can find out about trailing cattle north or shipping them to New Orleans."

Pilar felt disappointed but immensely relieved. "I want to do some shopping."

"We can go with you," Cade said.

"No, *we* can't," Rafe said, emerging from a tobacco shop in time to hear Cade's offer. "Do you know what women do when they shop?"

"No, but—"

"They look," Rafe said as though it were some loathsome practice. "They look and they examine, they try things on, and they discuss in detail. Then they go to another store and start the whole process over again."

"Is that true?" Cade asked Pilar.

She didn't know. Merchants had always brought their merchandise to the hacienda, but this gave her the excuse she needed. "I'm probably worse. You two go on."

"How long will your shopping take?"

She had never shopped, but not even the shortage of merchandise would deter her now. "I could look for days."

"That'll be too long."

She laughed. "Okay, I'll meet you for lunch. How about the Menger Hotel?"

"Okay," Cade said, "but if you're not there by noon, I'll come looking for you."

"I don't know where I'll be."

"I'll find you."

Cade was being very circumspect, but his gaze settled on her more frequently than before and stayed longer. And not even a novice could miss the warmth in those azure eyes. Today it was a caress that reached out and wrapped her in its warmth.

The only way Pilar could stop thinking about him, stop wanting to pick up where they'd left off last night, was to think of Laveau. She had noticed a group of Union Army soldiers on the far side of the plaza. If she could talk with them, maybe they could tell her something about Laveau. She hated to deceive Cade, but she couldn't pass up this chance. As soon as Cade and Rafe disappeared, she set out at a brisk pace in the direction the soldiers had taken.

It didn't take her long to catch up. They were strolling leisurely down the street, ogling all the young women. Pilar was shocked to see that quite a few young women ogled them back. She didn't want to know what her grandmother would have to say about that, or about Pilar walking unescorted through a public street to approach several strange men.

"Excuse me," she said as she touched the sleeve of one young man's uniform.

"Women don't need no excuses," the soldier replied as he spun around to face her, "not when they're as young and pretty as you."

He appeared a little unsteady.

"Why don't you talk to me?" one of the others said. "Clyde is not himself today."

Clyde giggled. "If I'm not myself, who am I?"

"You're a drunken fool." The speaker looked older but not reluctant to stare directly at her bosom. "A single woman shouldn't be without an escort," he said.

"I'm here with my...employer." She nearly choked on the word. "I'm looking for information about my brother. He hasn't come home from the war yet."

"We don't know anything about the Johnny Rebs," the soldier said, his welcome suddenly gone cold.

"My brother was in the Union Army," Pilar said. "His name is Laveau diViere. Have you heard of him?"

All the soldiers shook their heads. "You ought to speak to our commanding officer," one suggested. "If anybody would know, he would."

"Where can I find him?"

"I'll show you," the inebriated soldier offered.

"We'll all show you," the older man said. "It's not far."

Pilar wondered what people thought when they saw her walking with seven Union soldiers, all but the oldest one pushing and shoving to walk next to her. If she could learn anything that would help her find her brother, she wouldn't care.

Except Cade. She didn't want him to see her with these men. She didn't like doing this behind his back, but she was uncertain how he would react. She'd talk to the officer first. If she thought what she learned wouldn't make Cade angry, she'd tell him.

The Union Army was headquartered in the Alamo, a building closer to the Menger Hotel than she liked. She just hoped Cade didn't come out the same time she did.

"Scott tells me you're looking for your brother," Major Kramer said to Pilar after he'd ushered her into his office and invited her to be seated.

"Yes. I haven't heard from him in more than a month, and I'm worried." Pilar didn't like the way he was looking at her, as though he had bad news and was trying to decide what to say. "Is anything wrong? Has something happened to him?"

"Not that I know of," the major said, "but I haven't heard anything about him in several months."

Pilar sank back into her chair.

"Are you aware that your brother turned traitor during the war?"

"He wrote he would be coming home with the Union Army." *Traitor* was such an ugly word.

"You've been here for months. He still isn't home."

"There are several groups of troops coming to Texas. Most of them haven't arrived yet."

She could sense he was still holding something back. "You know something, don't you? Something you don't want to tell me."

"No, but I feel I must give you a warning. It may not be safe for your brother to return to Texas."

She'd never considered that Laveau wouldn't come home. "Do you mean because he changed sides?"

"Miss diViere, where are you living now?"

Pilar felt herself flush. "Squatters took over my home. My grandmother and I are staying with a neighbor."

"Are there any men in that family who fought for the Confederacy?"

"Yes."

"How many?"

"One. But he has six friends who've come to help him round up and brand his cattle."

"You have seven ex-Confederate soldiers staying at one ranch?"

"Yes."

"Did they lose friends, relatives, their homes?"

She didn't know anything specific, but she knew they'd all lost comrades. "Yes."

"What kind of men are they? Tough, strong, determined, unafraid?"

"All that. Especially unafraid."

"Do you think these men will be happy to have a traitor turn up in their midst?"

"He's not a traitor. He just changed sides."

"People who change sides are traitors," the major said. "The Confederates shoot them. So do we."

Pilar felt as if she were going to faint. "You shot my brother?"

"No, miss. We shoot our own men who turn traitor. We welcomed Confederate turncoats, but we didn't respect them. Traitors are despised by both sides."

Pilar felt so weak, she wasn't sure she could draw in a breath. "He said the Union Army would protect him."

"We will as far as we are able. But anyone in his troop might want revenge."

"What will they do if they find him?"

"Probably kill him."

Pilar was certain she couldn't breathe. Laveau had been in the troop with Cade and his friends. If anyone wanted to kill him, they would be the ones.

"Are you all right?" the major asked.

Of course she wasn't. She'd just learned that the man she liked far too well for her own good probably wanted to kill her brother. And if Cade didn't, it was almost certain that one of his friends did.

"I'm fine. Just shocked to learn that my brother is in such danger. He's all the family my grandmother and I have."

"Maybe your neighbor's son will be willing to let bygones be bygones."

Cade was a man who took responsibility seriously, but she couldn't imagine him shooting Laveau. He was stern, but he wasn't a murderer. Pilar struggled to her feet. "Thank you. You've been most helpful."

"Your brother might come back with his own command," the major said. "If so, he would be reasonably safe."

But if he came home alone, his life would be in danger.

"Let me have one of my men escort you back to your employer," the major offered.

"Thank you, but that won't be necessary."

"It won't be a problem. That's what they're here for."

"I'd rather be alone." She had to have some time to herself to think, to figure out what to do.

She was so upset, she walked blindly, unaware of people until she bumped into a man who apologized. Realizing it was her fault rather than his, she entered a store. She reemerged moments later and started down the street again, stopping to stare into windows for long periods of time but seeing nothing.

She had been a very foolish woman. She didn't merely like Cade. She was well on her way to falling in love with him. The man she wanted to trust with her heart could want her brother dead. While her heart rebelled at the idea, her head insisted it was possible, even probable. If Laveau wrote her, she would have to find a way to warn him that Cade and his friends were at the Wheeler ranch.

Pilar had been so absorbed in her thoughts, she had nearly come abreast of a man before she noticed him speaking animatedly to his two companions and pointing at her.

He appeared to recognize her, but Pilar didn't remember having seen him before. There was a tattered, unkempt aspect to his appearance. His clothes appeared dirty and unmatched, as though chosen at random. A torn pocket and missing buttons supported the assumption that he was without a wife to mend and wash his clothes.

The man grinned, nudged his two companions, pointed directly at her, and said something that caused the three of them to burst out laughing. He spat a stream of tobacco juice into the street and grinned broadly as they came toward her.

"We was wondering where you'd got to," he said to Pilar.

Pilar froze, unsure what to do. "I don't know you."

"Didn't expect you'd remember us, but we remember you. I been sleeping in your bed for two years."

Squatters! These were three of the men who'd driven her out of her home.

"I never knowed a bed could be so soft," the man said. "Pretty sheets, but my boots got them so muddy, I had to throw them out."

She'd slept on silk sheets. Her grandmother wouldn't settle for anything else.

"Me and Costa here don't care nothing about sheets," one of the other men said, "but we sure did like that wine your grandma hid in the cellar. You ain't got no more hid somewhere, do you?"

Pilar didn't want to think what Laveau would say when he discovered his prized wine collection had disappeared down the throats of squatters. Nor her grandmother when she learned what had happened to her sheets.

"We sure do like eating your beef," the first man said. "We ain't been hungry a day yet." He patted his stomach. "Only eat the best cuts. Throw away the rest."

Pilar was so angry she wanted to do something, *anything,* to hurt these men, but she was alone. "Let me past," she said. "I have to rejoin my employers."

The first man laughed. "So that's what you call them. I would have called them something else."

Pilar was becoming more and more nervous. She

didn't think she was in any danger on a public street, but these men didn't seem the least concerned about people passing around them.

"There weren't no need to run away. We woulda let you stay. You coulda slept in you own bed."

Pilar didn't need his leering gaze at her bosom to know she wouldn't have been allowed to sleep alone. "You're nothing but cowardly thieves who wait until the men are gone, then attack defenseless women."

"I wouldn't be acting so high and mighty," the first man said. "I seen where you run to. I seen you come into town with all those men."

"Then you'd better get away from me. If they find you're bothering me, you'll be sorry."

"I always thought you'd be good in bed," the first man said, "but you've got to be mighty good to keep that many men satisfied."

"Come back with us," one of the other men said. "We won't make you cook or nothing else."

"Not as long as you treat us good."

"If you don't leave me alone, I'll scream," Pilar said.

"Won't do you no good," the first man said. "Everybody knows women like you ain't nothing but sluts. You jump from bed to bed like any whore."

He reached out, attempting to grab her by the wrist. Pilar backed away, but the three men closed around her. She looked to passersby for help, but there was no one close. The people she did see—walking along the boardwalk, talking or staring in windows, or driving buggies and wagons through the streets—appeared unaware of her plight. The hotel where Cade and Rafe had gone was far away.

She was on her own.

"Come with us," the man said, his smile more of a leer now. "If you're real good to us, we'll buy you some new sheets. There's lots of cows about. Won't be no trouble to round up a bunch."

"You have no right to those cows," Pilar said, her back against the storefront. "They belong to my brother. If you take them, you'll be stealing."

"We can't steal what we already took," the man said. Abruptly his wheedling grin turned to something cold and ugly. "Now you come along. There's no use screaming. Ain't nobody gives a damn what happens to a woman like you."

He reached for her once again. Pilar put her hands behind her to keep him from dragging her off. She looked frantically for help, but the three men had formed a tight circle around her, cutting off her view. She couldn't believe this was happening to her in San Antonio. Women couldn't be attacked on the street and dragged off to be raped by a gang of thieves.

One man pulled her arm from behind her back, gripped her by the wrist, and started to drag her behind him. She opened her mouth to scream, prepared to fight him as best she could, when a body burst into the tight circle around her.

Cade's fist connected with the face of her would-be abductor and sent him flying through the air to land nearly a dozen feet away. Showing remarkable resilience, the man scrambled to his feet and barreled into Cade. He didn't fight with his fists. He kicked, scratched, even tried to bite Cade, all the while screaming obscenities at Pilar.

A particularly powerful blow to his jaw sent the man stumbling from the boardwalk into the street, where he collapsed almost under the hooves of a mule tethered to a post. Cade started toward the man, fists raised. Pilar opened her mouth to call him back. Her first words were drowned out by two explosions.

Someone had fired a gun.

She whirled around to see one of the other men crumple to the ground, a second stagger against the wall, his hand grabbing at his side.

"That one pulled a gun on Cade," Rafe said, pointing to the man who now lay still. "That one has a knife." The weapon lay at the man's feet. "The cowards were going to attack him from behind."

The sound of the shots had caused Cade to turn back to Pilar. "Did they hurt you?"

"No."

"But he had his hands on you."

"Only for a moment."

A crowd had gathered drawn by the sound of the shots.

"I saw it," announced a young man in a white shirt and suspenders. "I saw everything."

"What happened?" an older man asked. He looked like he was used to being in command.

"I saw everything," the young man announced again. "I was inside," he said, pointing to the window of the store right behind them, "stacking cans of peas. Those men attempted to abduct this woman."

"Do you know them?" the stranger asked Pilar.

She shook her head.

"Why should they want to abduct you?"

"They wanted to use her as a sex slave," the young man said. "I heard them. They said they would buy her anything she wanted as long as she treated them good."

Pilar felt heat flood her body. She was certain her face had turned crimson. Cade moved next to her, providing a partial shield from the curious gazes all around.

"Are you sure you're all right?" he asked.

"I'm fine," she whispered. "Just get me away from here."

"I'm taking her to the Menger Hotel," he said to the older man, who appeared to have taken command of the situation. "She needs rest and a doctor."

"I'll need to talk to her," the man said.

"Who are you?" Cade asked.

"I'm Preston Wilcox," the man replied. "I'm a member of the mayor's council. We'll need this young woman to tell us exactly what happened."

"I saw everything," the young man repeated. "I can tell you anything you want to know."

"You can find us at the hotel," Cade told the man.

Cade took her by the arm and started toward the hotel without waiting for the man to answer. "Find Holt," he said to Rafe when they were clear of the crowd. "Now tell me exactly what happened," he said to Pilar.

"They're three of the squatters who took our hacienda. They think I'm your...that I'm...that all of you—"

"I can imagine what they think. Go on."

"They tried to get me to go back to the hacienda with them."

"I shouldn't have left you," Cade said.

"You couldn't know what was going to happen. It's over. I just want to forget it."

"You'll be able to lie down in just a few minutes. Rafe will bring Holt to your room as soon as he finds him."

"I don't want a room, and I don't need a doctor. I'm fine." At least physically. Mentally and emotionally she wasn't doing as well. She wanted to go home, to surround herself with the familiar and the safe. It shocked her badly when she realized she was thinking of the ranch, not the diViere hacienda.

She made no objection when Cade propelled her inside the hotel, made arrangements for a room she could occupy immediately, and escorted her to the second floor.

The room was light and airy, decorated in a style wholly foreign to Pilar, who was used to the heavy Spanish style of the hacienda. The wallpaper was white with thin trellises of tiny, pink flowers. All the furniture was painted white and covered in near-white fabric. The bedspread was white with touches of the same pink used on the wall. Even the pitcher and basin were white. The window looked out on a quiet inner courtyard.

Pilar felt safe.

"Lock the door behind me," Cade said. "I'll bring Holt up the minute he gets here."

"I'm all right. Really. I don't need—"

"Maybe, but I intend to make sure. Now lie down. You've had a bad scare."

"Okay, but you tell Holt I'm neither hurt nor hysterical. If he's got any bad-tasting medicine, I refuse to take it."

Cade smiled. "I'll tell him. By the way, I don't intend to let you out of my sight again."

The door closed. Pilar listened unmoving, unbreathing, until she heard his footsteps disappear down the hallway. She let her breath out with a rush, clasped her arms tightly around herself.

Cade *liked* her. Not just as a cook or in appreciation of what she'd done for his grandfather. He liked her for herself. He'd kept asking if she was all right. He'd spent some of his precious hoard of money on an expensive hotel room for her—he hadn't even asked the clerk the cost of the room—and now he wanted Holt to attend to her.

She'd been left to manage a whole ranch by herself, had been attacked and driven from her home by squatters, and had learned to cook for an old man who constantly belittled her. She was as tough as any one of Cade's precious Night Riders.

She smiled broadly as she looked up at the white ceiling. It was absolutely wonderful to have someone determined to take care of her. She didn't mind being treated as though she were so fragile the slightest upset might break her. It was a welcome change.

But it wasn't Cade's treatment of her that caused her to continue smiling as she closed her eyes. It was the look in his eyes. No one had ever looked at her like that, made her feel as if she were the most important person in the world, that he'd lay down life and limb for her.

Not Manuel. The most emotion she'd seen in his eyes was when the cook served up a particularly rich dessert. She couldn't imagine him flinging himself into any fight. Yet Cade hadn't hesitated. He would prob-ably have beaten the man even worse if Rafe hadn't shot his companions.

That memory caused her happiness to wane for just a moment, but nothing was powerful enough to dislodge the euphoria of knowing that Cade felt as strongly about her as she did about him. She didn't worry about the fact that their families were enemies, that neither one could possibly love the other, that any thought of marriage would be insanity. She blocked out all thoughts of the future. She wanted to enjoy the knowledge that a man was willing to fight to defend her. She wanted to savor the look in his eyes, the sound of worry in his voice, the tenderness of his touch as he brought her to safety.

She felt herself begin to grow drowsy. She tried to stay awake. She didn't want to lose one precious minute of this day, but before long she felt herself falling deeper and deeper into a wonderful daydream.

She was dressed in a white gown of such diaphanous material it billowed around her like sheer curtains at an open window. Somewhere apple blossoms scented the air with their heady perfume. The sky was so blue it seemed like a solid canopy overhead. The air was soft with the warmth of spring, moist with the promise of life. It was her wedding day.

Her groom awaited her at an altar built with branches of apple blossoms. Relatives from both sides of her family—some of them long dead—lined the path between her and the altar. Ahead her grandmother detached herself from the crowd of well-wishers.

"You must be happy. This is your wedding day."

She said it over and over again until it became a singsong

...ant. *Pilar's feet carried her forward until she reached the altar and her groom turned toward her.*

Manuel. She cried out, but no sound came from her throat.

"You must be happy. This is your wedding day."

No one listened to her protests. The guests started applauding, softly at first, then louder, until it sounded like the pounding of a drum. The priest called her name, asked her to take this man as her husband. She shook her head, but he kept calling her name over and over as the clapping grew louder and louder.

Terror pulled Pilar from her dream. A fine film of perspiration caused her clothes to stick to her body. She unclenched her hands, tried to still the rapid pounding of her heart. It was only a dream. It was—

The sound of knocking, a voice calling her name over and over. It wasn't part of her dream. Someone was pounding on the door and calling her name. She sat up, struggled to bring herself fully awake.

"Pilar, open the door."

It was Owen. She got up, crossed to the door, and fumbled with the lock before getting it open. "Sorry, I fell asleep. Where is Holt?"

"Forget Holt. Cade and Rafe have been arrested for murder."

Fifteen

THEY HURRIED ALONG THE BOARDWALK, PILAR HAVING
to trot to keep up with Owen. "When did it happen?"
she asked. "I just lay down a few minutes ago."

"You slept two hours."

"Why didn't Holt tell me?"

"Maybe he doesn't know. I only found out when
I went looking for Cade. The clerk said when Broc,
Ivan, and Nate tried to stop the soldiers from taking
Cade and Rafe, everybody ended up in a fight. The
soldiers called in reinforcements and carried all of them
off to jail."

"But why?"

"The men who tried to abduct you said ex-
Confederate soldiers had attacked them and taken
their woman. Once the soldiers heard they were
Johnny Rebs, they didn't listen to anybody else."

"It was self-defense."

"That's not what those men said."

"But they're thieves."

"Can you prove it?"

"Yes."

'Good. You may have to." Owen's gaze narrowed. There was nothing of the flirtatious, carefree young man about him now. Pilar could easily imagine this man going on a dangerous night raid. "Cade always said your family and his were enemies. Is that true?"

"Y-yes."

"He also said you'd do anything to get back at the Wheelers for the land they stole."

His words shocked her. She hadn't felt that way for so long, she'd almost forgotten that she ever had.

"What are you going to say when you talk to the major?" Owen asked.

"I don't know. I—"

"You can't say anything about stealing. If you do, they'll never let him go."

"I wasn't—"

"I don't care what anybody did in the past."

Pilar could hardly believe the undercurrent of menace in Owen's voice. "But you got into a fight with him. I'd think you'd be happy he's in jail."

"That has nothing to do with this. Cade's the only reason any of us survived that…that surprise attack. I owe him my life," Owen said.

"I didn't know—"

"Cade would never tell you. I've got to know you'll do everything you can to convince them to let him go."

"And if I don't?" She didn't know why she asked that question. She wouldn't hesitate to do anything she could to obtain Cade's release, but a macabre fascination with the change in Owen made her want to see what he might do.

Owen's eyes grew even harder. "You can lose people you love just as easily as others have."

Pilar's blood ran cold. She had no doubt that he was talking about her grandmother. "I can't believe you would do something like that."

"I wouldn't have five years ago."

"Did the war change you that much?"

"Not just the war."

"What?"

"We don't have time to discuss it. The longer they keep Cade, the harder it'll be to convince them to let him go."

Moments later, Owen touched her arm and came to a stop. "The commander's office is just around that corner. I can't go with you. If they lock me up, too, we're lost."

"But surely—"

"It'll be up to you to convince the commander. If you don't succeed, we'll have to think of something else."

Pilar entered the building, her thoughts in such disorder she didn't know how she was going to marshal an argument. She wanted to know what had happened to turn Owen into a different man. She wanted to know how Cade had saved so many lives, what had happened to the ones he wasn't able to save. She didn't want to think of what would happen if she failed to gain Cade's release. It shocked her to realize she'd already begun to take his presence for granted, begun to assume he would always be around.

The young officer remembered her. He ushered her into Major Kramer's office immediately.

"Courtney says you're here to ask for the release of

several ex-Confederate soldiers," Kramer said without waiting for her to be seated.

"I'm here to speak on behalf of Cade Wheeler and his friends," she replied, disconcerted by the major's changed demeanor. The switch reminded her uncomfortably of the change in Owen.

"Do you know they tried to steal a man's woman, that they killed one of his companions and wounded the other?"

"I'm the woman they tried to steal."

She let that piece of information sink in while she took a seat. When she looked up again, his expression was different, though still not as friendly as earlier.

"You'll have to explain that."

The major remained silent while Pilar related what had happened.

"Didn't anyone stop to inquire about what was going on?"

"They didn't threaten me at first. Later there wasn't anybody near. They were trying to drag me away when Cade arrived. Rafe shot them to protect Cade. I saw the gun and the knife. So did the young man who works in the store."

"He told us substantially the same story."

"Then why didn't you arrest those men instead of Cade?"

"Cade and his men got into a fight with half the regiment. I have half a dozen men in the infirmary this very minute, and that many more nursing bruises and contusions. They came very close to overpowering the whole regiment."

Pilar tried hard not to look pleased, certain that

would cost her any sympathy the major might feel for her.

"They've been very protective of my grandmother and me," Pilar said. "Ivan Nikoli is some kind of Polish count. He treats my grandmother like a queen."

"I'm sure the young lieutenant whose head he nearly cracked open will be delighted to hear that."

"They were defending a lady, Major, something that's very important to Texans. I'm sure you appreciate how they must have felt."

"I also know how my men feel."

It appeared the major might have been willing to let them go if it hadn't been for the fight. Now he had to save face.

"Have you considered how these men might feel toward your brother? He's a traitor to their cause. They probably want him dead."

"The Confederate courts have been disbanded. There's no one to convict him."

"I expect they'll hold their own trial, then hang him."

She couldn't imagine Cade or his friends hanging Laveau, but the Owen she'd seen today could have done anything. Would Cade feel that way under similar circumstances?

"Cade Wheeler was the leader of a group of raiders who were nearly wiped out in a surprise attack. He might hold your brother responsible."

"Laveau couldn't be responsible," Pilar said, shocked at the thought. "He's known Cade all his life. We're neighbors."

"But he's still a traitor to the Confederate cause. You might want to reconsider getting these men out."

"But you can't keep them in jail more than a few days for fighting."

"If you support Clarence Odum's story—he's the man who you say tried to rape you—I can try them for murder. They'd be sentenced to hang. That way it would be safe for your brother to come home."

Pilar couldn't believe her ears. This man whom she'd thought so considerate was calmly asking her to lie to allow him to save face by hanging innocent men.

"Even if I believed that Cade or his friends would harm my brother, I couldn't lie so you could hang them. Clarence Odum is a thief and a murderer. He and his friends brutally murdered three old men, faithful and trusted servants. They would have carried me off with them today if Cade hadn't stopped them. They would have shot Cade in the back if Rafe hadn't stopped them. I'm sorry your men got hurt, but you shouldn't have believed a man like Clarence Odum."

"My men are reluctant to believe anything an ex-Confederate says."

"How would you feel if people refused to believe you even though you had witnesses to support your story?"

The major didn't appear gratified to find himself facing a woman who had the courage to turn the mirror of prejudice back on him.

"Even if I dropped the charges filed by Mr. Odum, I couldn't let them go. They resisted arrest."

"Wouldn't you resist an unfair arrest, especially when you doubted you'd be treated fairly in prison?"

"Are you saying I abuse my prisoners?"

"You seem to think Cade would have abused you if

the circumstances were reversed. Why should I think you'd act differently?"

"Ma'am, I'm an officer in the United States Army."

"Then it's your responsibility to protect honest citizens."

"We do."

"You didn't protect me. I was assaulted in the middle of San Antonio."

"The fact remains I can't release these men. They'll have to stand trial for—"

Pilar got to her feet. "I want to see them."

The major looked startled. "Women aren't allowed in the prison area."

"Why not? Don't you trust your men to treat a lady with respect?"

"Ma'am, you seem determined to disparage the character of my men."

"And you seem determined to punish five men merely because they're better fighters than your soldiers."

"Six."

"Five. Holt is a doctor. I insist on being allowed to see Cade."

"I can allow only family into the prison."

"I'm family. I'm engaged to marry him."

❧

Pilar's knees felt so weak she worried that her strength wouldn't last until she reached the home of Preston Wilcox. He was an ex-state senator. She hoped he could do something to help Cade.

She didn't know what had possessed her to say she was engaged to Cade. The words had popped out of er mouth before she'd even thought of them. Maybe she'd been thinking them for a long time but couldn't admit it, unable to face the fact that she wanted to be the wife of a man her family hated and despised.

No, she couldn't have done anything so preposterous, not even subconsciously. She'd been upset, not thinking clearly. She'd said that because she'd hoped she could see Cade to make certain he was okay. She owed him too much to balk at such a small lie.

But she would very much like to be married to a man *like* Cade.

Not that her lie had helped—Major Kramer had still refused to let her see Cade.

She had tried to get Owen to come with her to see the ex-senator, but Owen said he'd better start working on their backup plan.

Finding the correct number on an iron gate, Pilar stared at the house, her heart in her throat. Preston Wilcox was obviously a wealthy man. The three-story house of brick with its limestone columns and tile roof intimidated her. She told herself not to be foolish, that her family's hacienda was just as impressive. But she was aware that her dusty and wrinkled appearance didn't reflect her background. Taking a deep breath, she opened the gate and walked in.

Mr. Wilcox was in. A maid whose glance indicated that she thought Pilar wasn't entirely respectable instructed her to wait in the parlor. Unused to such treatment, Pilar nearly spoke sharply to the young woman but held her tongue. Just a few years earlier she would have made the same evaluation. Mr. Wilcox's entrance didn't relieve her tension.

"Do I know you?" he asked.

"My name is Pilar diViere. We met earlier today. A man was trying to abduct me. Cade Wheeler stopped them. When two others tried to attack him from behind, one of Cade's friends shot the men."

"I remember now." The senator's brow grew dark. "We have too many men like that in Texas, robbing and stealing with no one to stop them."

"The man went to the commander of the army troop here and told him that ex-Confederate soldiers stole his woman and shot two of his friends. The major sent troops to arrest Cade and his friends. The soldiers wouldn't believe Cade or the witness. When they tried to arrest Cade, they got into a fight. Now Cade and his friends are in jail, and the major won't let me see Cade. I'm afraid he means to make an example of him."

"Nobody wanted to see the Yankees in Texas," Mr. Wilcox said, "but if they had to come, we hoped they'd do something about rustlers and squatters. I can't do anything tonight. By the time I see the people I need to talk to, it'll be too late. Meet me here in the morning. We'll go down to the Alamo together."

The Union Army had commandeered the old mission site for its headquarters.

"Can you get Cade out?" Pilar asked.

"I'll do my best."

What if his best wasn't good enough?

Then she'd have to depend on their backup plan. She hoped she hadn't misjudged the men of Texas.

❧

should have left town while we had the chance,"
de said to no one in particular.

"I never thought that piece of trash had the brains
to turn his own story around so it would frame us,"
Rafe said.

"They're smart enough to have seen an opportunity and taken advantage of it. The question is
whether they have enough discipline to hold on to
their stolen property."

"Your grandfather did," Nate said.

Cade's belly tightened. He didn't like being lumped
with squatters, but his grandfather's methods hadn't
been all that different. At least he didn't abuse women.
The tightness in his belly grew more acute. What did
he call trying to make Pilar think he liked her so he
could get information about her brother?

He was trying to rationalize what couldn't be
justified, but if he couldn't figure a way out of jail, it
wouldn't matter. None of their arguments had swayed
the major.

"What do we do next?" Holt asked.

"Let Cade figure it out," Nate said. "He got us into
this mess."

"He told you to stay out of it," Broc said.

"Hell, you can't expect me to stand by and watch a
bunch of slimy Yankees arrest Cade. Damnation, man,
I couldn't look myself in the face if I did that."

"Then stop blaming Cade and think of a way out
of this."

"I'm going to sleep," Nate said. "Thinking makes
me tired."

"You haven't thought much."

"We don't have to in Arkansas."

"We should all go to sleep," Cade said. "Maybe we'll get some ideas during the night."

"All I'll get are nightmares of having my neck stretched," Nate said.

"They're not going to hang us. We're more likely to get hard labor."

"I don't like that any better," Broc said.

"We'll have a better chance of escape," Holt said.

"I will not do hard labor," Rafe announced. Then he pulled up his knees, rested his head on them, and went to sleep.

They didn't have beds. Not even pallets. They'd been thrown into what had once been a convent on the grounds of the Alamo, a group of buildings that had begun life as a mission for the local Indians. It had long ago been turned to other uses, most recently by the Confederate forces during the war.

"We do not treat our prisoners like this in Poland," Ivan said.

"Then it's a shame we didn't get arrested in Poland," Nate snapped.

"They may treat ex-noblemen well, but peasants like us get thrown in with the rats," Holt said.

"I'm not a peasant," Nate protested.

"We would be in Poland."

"You can argue all night if you want, but I'm going to sleep," Cade said. "I'll have thought of something by tomorrow."

"You'd better," Nate said. "I got a date with a rope and a traitor's neck, and I don't want to miss it."

Cade rolled up his jacket and put it under his head.

He didn't want to think that he had failed his men again, but he couldn't escape it. Nate had started the fight—ever since his brother's death, he'd hated Yankees too much to listen to reason—but Cade felt responsible. He had spent much of the afternoon trying to think, but the constant bickering destroyed his concentration. He'd go to sleep. When he woke up, he'd be rested and things would be quiet. He'd figure out a solution then.

He hated to think that his defense of Pilar was responsible for his arrest. He couldn't have done anything less, even if she had been a perfect stranger. He hoped things hadn't come to such a pass in Texas that riffraff were allowed to accost honest women on the street. Just the thought made Cade want to fight the man all over again.

Cade forced himself to clear his mind. He needed sleep. He would have to be mighty sharp to find a way around Major Kramer.

But as he drifted off to sleep, the image of the man trying to drag Pilar off came into his mind. And he knew as well as he knew his name that he'd had no choice but to stop him, even if he had to hang for it.

❦

Cade couldn't sleep. He was uneasy about the raid, but he had no reason. The Union Army was more than fifty miles away. His troop was famous for its speed and the horses that carried them spectacular distances to raid unsuspecting trains, supply wagons, and munitions factories. They had conducted so many night raids they were called the Night Riders.

No, this was a different kind of uneasiness. He kept having

bad dreams. In one, his favorite mare had lost a new foal to wolves, which made no sense. He had no favorite mare and his grandfather's ranch wasn't plagued by wolves. The others had been more fantastic than realistic—mythical beasts attacking princesses, an earthquake splitting the crust of Texas and swallowing the San Antonio River whole.

None of it made any sense except that he was certain there was danger ahead.

Cade sat up on the blanket that was his bed on the hard ground. Because of the stifling heat, he and his men slept outside. The morning was very still and the humidity oppressive. They would raid a payroll wagon tomorrow. It carried a gold shipment, bullion the Confederacy needed to pay its bills to countries unwilling to extend credit to the Confederate government. Everything had been planned down to the last detail, but he couldn't sleep.

Something somewhere was wrong.

They rode at night, spent the day sleeping in the woods or wherever they could find a sympathetic farmer. Today his men were scattered through an apple orchard, some sleeping under the grapevine, others on the shady side of a wall or building. They would all move when the sun changed direction in the afternoon.

Suddenly the sense of impending danger was so great, Cade threw aside his blanket. "Get up!" he shouted as he got to his feet. "We've got to move. Now!" he shouted when no one moved. "We can't stay in the open."

"It's too damned hot inside," one man grumbled. "Even the ground is hot."

But even as the men complained and rolled over to go back to sleep, Cade's sense of danger grew stronger, more urgent. "We've got to find cover. We're not safe here."

"Is this an example of your famous sixth sense?" Nate asked.

"I don't know," Cade replied. *"I've just got a feeling something's wrong."*

"Come on," Ivan said to Holt, who was sleeping close by. *"Cade's sixth sense is good enough for me."*

"Where's Owen?" Cade asked.

"Probably trying to find a way inside the farmhouse to the daughter's bedroom," Holt said. *"That man can't think of anything else when there's a woman around."* Holt stood and rolled up his blanket.

"Tell everybody to get inside one of the buildings," Cade said.

"I don't know why you're so worried," one of the men said. *"We got a sentry posted. Nobody knows we're within a hundred miles of this place."*

This place wasn't even on most maps. It was a farm very much like thousands of others in the Shenandoah Valley.

"Just get inside," Cade said. *"I'll see if anybody's sleeping on the other side of those barns. And don't leave your weapons behind."*

They had to guard their horses just as carefully. Good horses were in even greater demand than good soldiers.

Cade didn't find any of his men sleeping beyond the barn, but he did find Owen having a late-morning tryst with the oldest daughter of the family. It angered him, but didn't surprise him. His Virginia cousin was addicted to females of any description. *"You're supposed to be resting up for our ride tonight."*

The girl blushed and tried to pull away from Owen. He held on to her, his face tight with anger.

"I'm always ready to do my part. You don't have to worry about me."

"I have to worry whether we'll be less welcome than the Yankees if you don't keep your hands off every woman in the valley."

The girl succeeded in breaking away and ran toward the house, her laugh as joyous as her eyes were bright. Owen tried to call her back, but Cade stopped him.

"Leave her alone. You're not good enough for her."

"I don't need your sanctimonious preachings. I'm your cousin, not your brother."

"You're part of my command, and as such—"

Cade never finished that statement. At that moment, a cannonade of gunfire broke out all around them. Men on horseback came crashing through the orchard. He looked up in time to see the girl throw up her hands and fall to the ground.

"You son of a bitch!" he shouted as he and Owen both ran for the cover of the barn. "You got that girl killed."

Less than half of the troop had followed Cade's orders. Many of them had been caught in the open, defenseless, as Union cavalry swept into the open areas around the house and buildings, shooting down sleeping and running men like ducks on a pond. Even those who escaped the first assault barely had time to bring their weapons into play before they, too, came under intense fire.

Cade could do nothing more for his men than run for cover himself. Just stay alive for the survivors, he told himself. He had to know what had gone wrong, had to know if he was to blame.

Just stay alive.

Cade woke to find Holt shaking him awake. "Get up. Pilar has come to get us out. And she's brought a senator to help."

Sixteen

"YOU HAVE NO AUTHORITY TO KEEP THESE MEN IN prison," Mr. Wilcox was saying.

"They got into a fight with Union Army soldiers," Major Kramer said.

"They wouldn't have if you hadn't ignored the testimony of eyewitnesses."

"I had an eyewitness who testified to the opposite."

"Did you attempt to learn the character of that witness?"

"That's not my job."

"Neither is locking up citizens. You have no authority bestowed on you by this town or by Texas."

"I don't need—"

"Not even the army is above the law," the senator stated.

Mr. Wilcox's intervention seemed to have hardened the major's determination to try Cade and his friends before an Army court.

They had been in his office for more than an hour. Mr. Wilcox had advanced several arguments. Voices had been raised, threats had been uttered, but the major remained adamant.

"I intend to make an example of these me said. "The Union Army will not allow its soldi be abused by rabble."

"Does the Union Army ordinarily consider har working men of property to be rabble, or are they rabble because they were Confederate soldiers?"

Owen's entry into the office prevented the major from answering.

"I'm in conference," the major barked. "The sergeant wasn't supposed to let anyone in."

"I didn't see a sergeant," Owen said, his expression blank.

"He's at the desk in the outer office."

"There's nobody there," Owen said. "I didn't see any soldiers at all."

The major headed for the door, went outside. The senator turned to Owen. "Who are you?"

"He's Cade's cousin," Pilar explained. "He's helping me get Cade out."

"I intend to speak to the mayor and the city council," the senator said. "Major Kramer intends to use every soldier at his disposal to defy local authority."

"He may find he has less manpower than he thinks." Owen winked at Pilar, then retreated to a corner when he heard the major's bootheels ringing on the flagstones of the outer room.

"Where are my men? Where are the prisoners?"

Everyone turned to Owen. They sensed that his coming into the room hadn't been the accident it seemed at first.

"There weren't any soldiers around to ask, so I let Cade and my friends out."

s heart started to beat so rapidly it hurt. Cade
ee! She wouldn't have to feel guilty for being the
on he was in prison. But the extent of her happi-
ss went far beyond relief from guilt.

This was personal. She wanted him free for herself.

"Where are my men?" the major thundered. "What
have you done with them?"

Owen's laugh was low and easy. Pilar thought it
sounded evil. "Are you accusing me of having overpowered more than twenty soldiers? If I'd been able to do
that, the Confederate Army would be in Washington,
D.C., rather than the Union Army in Texas."

Wilcox looked from Owen to the major, back to
Owen, then back to the major. A slow smile spread
over his face. "If I understand the situation correctly,
you're alone here."

"If you've so much as lifted a finger against a single
soldier of the Union Army—"

"You keep saying *Union*," Owen pointed out. "I
thought it was the United States Army. Since we're
part of the United States, that means it's our army. It's
supposed to protect us, too."

"The young man is right," Wilcox said. "It's
your responsibility to protect every citizen of Texas,
and the most immediate protection we need is from
Cortina and his bandits coming up from Mexico to
steal our cattle, and from squatters taking over farms
and ranches."

The murmurs of assent were drowned out by the
major's loudly stated intention to lay the entire situation before General Phil Sheridan, and his threats to
bring in a whole division to take over the town.

"I doubt that the general will be anxious to trust a division to a man who has lost a whole troop," Owen said. He pushed off from the wall. "If you'll excuse us, Miss diViere and I need to get home before her grandmother begins to worry. Squatters drove Miss diViere and her grandmother off their property. So far, the United States Army hasn't shown any interest in getting it back for her. I guess she'll have to see if there are any ex-Confederate soldiers who feel obliged to come to the rescue of a couple of honest citizens unable to defend themselves against outlaws the United States Army seems incapable of, or uninterested in, pursuing."

"Where are my men?" the major demanded.

"I don't know," Owen said, "but I do recall hearing someone say he saw some soldiers headed toward Victoria."

�ැ

"It worked!" Pilar exclaimed as they left the Alamo.

"You were right," Owen said. "Texas men hate being sneered at and threatened by a handful of rowdy soldiers. They didn't need much urging to get the soldiers drunk and bundle them off one by one."

"Won't they just come back?" she asked as they hurried along the boardwalk.

"I doubt it. The major didn't have any authority to bring them here. He was never under orders to come this far west."

"What will happen to Cade and the others?"

"Nothing as long as they keep out of sight. No general will like what happened to his troops. He can't prosecute the whole town, but he could start with us. Let's hope Cortina's bandits give him something else to do."

"Where is Cade?"

"Waiting for us outside of town. I tried to get him to go ahead, but he had to make sure both of us made it out. I tried to tell him the major couldn't do anything to you, but he had to see for himself." Owen eyed her closely. "He didn't seem to be half as worried about me."

"You're a soldier," Pilar said. "I'm not." She said that as much to convince Owen as herself. She didn't want to believe that Cade had any special feeling for her. If she did, she wouldn't be able to hold her own feelings in check any longer.

She didn't like the look Owen gave her, couldn't decide whether he was jealous or just angry. She didn't know how she could have given him reason to be either.

Pilar asked Owen to tell her how he'd convinced so many strangers to help him get the soldiers drunk, but rather than listen to his explanation, she tried to sort out her own feelings. So much had happened, she didn't know where to begin. But the way her heart leapt into her throat when she finally saw Cade convinced her that she had to start all over from the beginning.

❧

Cade couldn't understand why he should feel so proud of Pilar. He could understand feeling grateful. She and Owen had gotten them out of jail. She'd even talked the ex-senator into helping her. Admiration was acceptable, but pride? That implied there was something more to their relationship than friendship.

"You should have suggested to the major that he try running the squatters off your land," he said to Pilar. "That would be one way to curry favor with the locals."

"He wasn't interested in anybody liking him," Pilar said.

Cade sensed that a different kind of relationship had developed between them. He had tried to tell himself it was his imagination, but he knew it was there, knew he wanted it to remain. Because he felt connected to her in a special way, he felt proud of what she'd done. Not many women would have had the courage to face down an army major, not even with an ex-senator's support. Few if any would have thought of how to make use of the natural dislike of Texans for outside authority.

Pilar deserved more than an arranged marriage to a man who still believed women were chattel. She deserved—

"What was the major doing in San Antonio?" Cade asked Pilar.

"He didn't say."

"You should have asked him about Laveau."

"Why? He can't know everybody in the Union Army."

Cade didn't understand why she seemed uneasy whenever he mentioned the major. She wouldn't even look at him after he mentioned Laveau. She started talking to Holt, who was riding next to the wagon. Cade could understand modesty, but this felt like evasion.

He wished she hadn't turned away from him. He didn't mind rejection—he expected that—but her pose left him free to concentrate on her profile, the nearness of her body. He did mind that.

He'd become accustomed to her face. He'd kept her image in his mind all during the war. Her jet-black hair and magnolia-petal-white skin. Her enormous black eyes, alive with curiosity and excitement, served as a window into an uncomplicated mind. They bespoke innocence, openness, an eagerness to explore life.

But she had the lush body of a woman of the world.

During the war, Cade hadn't had much time to think about women. Despite the certain knowledge that Pilar was beyond his reach—or maybe because of it—he had used her as a standard against which to measure the women he met. As a girl, she could stand comparison with any woman.

As a woman, she was matchless.

Despite the modesty of her dress, nothing could hide the outlines of a body that caused his body to become hard in seconds. He longed to see her shoulders, to be able to touch skin he was certain was as soft and white as a gardenia blossom. Her throat rose from the ruffles around the collar of her dress like a white marble column, thin, supple, elegant. Her white skin was taut over jaw and chin, only to yield to the generous abundance of her lips, full, soft, and pink. Thick brows arched over prominent eyes fringed by inky lashes.

But he was more intrigued by the curve of her breasts. He had felt them press against his chest two nights ago. Everything between then and now seemed compressed into a few seconds. He felt as if nothing of importance had happened since the night they kissed, and he realized he wanted to go on kissing her—her mouth, her eyes, her throat, and all the rest of her. Even now, he had to grip the reins to keep from reaching out to touch her.

He tried to put it all down to lust and long absti- nence, but he had an increasingly uneasy feeling that something else had muscled its way into the equation. Every time he became physically aware of Pilar, and that happened more and more frequently, he realized his friends were looking at her in the same way. Each time he admired the swell of her breasts or the neatness of her waist, he knew Owen or Rafe was doing the same. Whenever he woke up uncomfortable because he'd dreamed of her, he figured Ivan and Broc had probably done the same.

That made him angry. He didn't want *anybody* to think of her like that. It was one of the reasons he'd nearly killed the squatter. And though he hadn't real- ized it until now, his feelings for Pilar were responsible for his growing impatience with the men. They were irritated because he was being very slow to press her for information, considering her feelings too much. Now he realized he'd become seriously interested in Pilar, and he wouldn't allow—

A distant sound scattered his thoughts. It was faint, almost lost amid conversations, squeaking saddles, the rasp of the wagon wheels.

"Stop!" he called out, bringing the wagon to a halt. "Don't anybody talk!" he said when Pilar turned back to him, a question in her eyes. The men had brought their mounts to a standstill. Not a single bridle jingled. The sound didn't come again.

"What was it?" Owen asked after a moment.

"A rifle shot." Cade wondered if he'd actually heard it.

"You hear that out here all the time," Pilar said.

"Let me have your horse," Cade said to Holt as he climbed down from the wagon. "Stay with Pilar. I think someone's attacking the ranch."

The men reacted as they would have a few months earlier. They took out their weapons, checked their ammunition, and waited for Cade's orders.

"Holt, take the wagon up to the ranch as quickly as you can. Ivan, stay with him. I don't want to take a chance on anyone kidnapping Pilar. Rafe, scout around. The rest of you come with me."

The four men rode down the trail at a fast canter.

"It could have been a hunter or a cowhand," Owen said.

Cade didn't answer. He was listening intently for any sound he could catch over the sound of sixteen hooves.

"Maybe you just thought you heard a rifle shot," Owen said.

"Cade never hears wrong," Nate said.

"Nor is his instinct wrong," Broc added.

Cade hoped this was one time his ears and instincts were wrong. He hoped it would turn out to be the single shot of a hunter, even a hunter killing one of his own cows. All ranchers expected to lose a few cows to poachers. They lost even more with the drift south each winter.

A single shot could mean so many things, too many of them bad. If it was an attack, there ought to be more shots. The only reason for a single shot was if it was the last shot, if someone was finishing off the last pocket of opposition.

The last defender.

A burst of gunfire erupted, and Cade felt himself shudder with relief. Without waiting for an order, the men spurred their horses into a gallop.

"Make as much noise as you can," Cade said. "Let's hope we can drive them off before anyone gets hurt. We can worry about capturing them later." He pulled out his pistol and started firing into the air. The others followed his example.

"How many do you think there are?" Broc shouted over the noise.

"I hope no more than four or five," Cade shouted back. "They probably think it'll be easy to overpower two old men."

"Not if they're the same ones who tried before," Owen yelled.

Cade dug his heels into the sturdy gelding's sides and let out a rebel yell he hoped would strike terror into the hearts of the attackers. Nate let loose a yell that sounded more like a Comanche war cry.

"Hold your fire for a moment," Cade called out. They couldn't hear any more shots. "Let's hope we broke the attack. Owen, you and Broc check the horses. We can't afford to lose them. Nate, check for dead cows. I'll check the house."

"How about Pilar?" Owen asked.

"Holt and Ivan will look after her."

"What do we do if we catch one of them?" Broc asked.

"Capture him alive," Cade said. "I'd like to know who he's working with and what their plans are."

The men separated, the powerful quarters of their horses bunching and gathering as they rode off in different directions, shod hooves sending occasional sparks when they struck stone. Cade turned his mount toward the house, both reassured and unnerved by the continued silence.

The ranch yard was wrapped in silence when he rode in. That unnerved him more than a rifle shot. His grandfather wouldn't allow anyone to approach the house unchallenged. The fact that he didn't see any bodies or any sign of blood didn't reassure Cade. His grandfather was too wily to be caught in the open.

Cade raced to the bunkhouse, found it empty, the rifles gone. A quick look at the corrals showed that the attackers had run off the horses, but he had no clue as to what had happened to Earl or Jessie. They must have been in the house.

But even as he hurried toward the house, Cade knew that was wrong. His grandfather would never allow himself to be pinned down.

"Where is my granddaughter?" Senora diViere demanded the moment Cade entered the front door. She held a rifle in her hands.

"She's safe. I left two men to look after her. Where are my grandfather and uncle?"

"I do not know," she said, suddenly angry. "They do not tell me what they do, where they go. They leave me here with this exploding stick"—she shook the rifle in Cade's direction, causing him to duck to one side—"and disappear. They are probably dead. They deserve to die. Where are the attackers?"

"They ran away."

"You call yourself an army officer and you let those desperadoes escape? It is no surprise you lost the war."

"I have to find my grandfather." Cade doubted that she would believe he considered her safety more important than capturing the attackers. "Holt and Ivan are bringing Pilar to the house. Until they get here, stay inside, keep your rifle loaded, and keep the door locked."

"Ivan will keep my granddaughter safe," Senora diViere said. "He is a gentleman."

Cade didn't attempt to point out that Ivan could shed his air of gentility in the blink of an eye.

Cade ran back to his horse. If the old man was okay, he'd go in search of the horses. Earl would know it would be impossible to get their cows to market without the remuda, but Cade didn't know what Earl thought he could do on foot.

An untutored child could follow the route taken by the herd. The horses hooves cut deep into the loose soil, their tightly packed bodies knocked down virtually everything in their path. Cade breathed a sigh of relief when his grandfather walked out of a thicket of mesquite, black chaparral, and acacia.

"They stole the horses," he said unnecessarily. "Give me your horse, and I'll go after them."

"Where's Uncle Jessie?" Cade asked.

"He went to see what they done to the cows. I

heard some shots in that direction before they showed up here."

"Get up behind me," Cade said. "We'll go after Jessie. I sent the boys after the horses."

His grandfather's face grew mottled with anger. "You think I'm too old and decrepit to do anything but sit in a rocking chair and suck my thumb."

"I think you're mean as a steer with a thorn in his nose, but we can't go after those horses riding double."

"I was going to leave you here."

"No doubt to hold Senora diViere's hand."

His grandfather almost laughed. "That's something I'd like to see."

"Well, I wouldn't. Now get up behind me. I'll take you back, then go find Jessie."

"I can walk." Earl started back toward the ranch. "I'm surprised you're not chasing after that girl instead of worrying about me."

"I must be crazy, but I *was* worried about you."

"I can take care of myself."

"And a handful of scoundrels stupid enough to think they could sneak up on you."

His grandfather's chest rose a little. "I didn't survive two wars by being stupid."

The old bastard's head was as hard as iron wood, but he wasn't stupid. "Since you don't need me, I'll go see if Pilar's reached the house yet."

"Two men aren't enough protection for her without you running off to check on her?"

"I want to know if Holt or Ivan saw anything on their way in."

"According to you, these fellas can do anything.

Surely they can follow a trail plain enough for a ch~~i~~
to see."

"You're right. Let's find Jessie."

❧

"Cade would probably have killed that man if his friends
hadn't tried to shoot Cade in the back," Pilar said.

"None of this would have happened if Laveau had
been here," her grandmother said.

Pilar had spent the last twenty minutes telling her
grandmother about the fight and how they'd gotten
Cade out of jail. Senora diViere had shown only mar-
ginal interest. She kept looking outside to make sure
Holt was still there. Ivan had gone off to help look for
the horses.

Pilar wondered where Cade had gone. Her grandmother said the attackers ran away when they heard
the shots, but she couldn't stop worrying. She was
certain Cade wouldn't stop until he found the horses.
Neither could she believe that after going to so much
trouble to steal the horses, the attackers would give
them up without a fight.

"I asked the major about Laveau," Pilar said.

As she expected, she caught her grandmother's
attention immediately. "Does he know Laveau? When
will he be coming home? Did anybody hurt him in
that war?"

"He doesn't know Laveau, but he knows of his
situation," Pilar explained. "Apparently, traitors are
despised by both sides."

"Laveau is not a traitor. He simply chooses the winning side."

Pilar had never doubted that her grandmother's loyalties lay with her family rather than any ideological considerations. "The major said Laveau may not come home for a long while yet."

"But he must. He must drive the squatters out. He must—"

"The major said every man in Texas will want to punish Laveau for changing sides."

"They cannot do that. He has a right to choose which side he wants."

"He could have in the beginning. It was changing sides in the middle of the war that was the problem. The major said even with the Union Army here, Laveau would never be safe. The major said—"

"*Sangre de Cristo!*" her grandmother swore. "I am a Cordoba. I cannot continue to live as a dog. I will die."

"He didn't say Laveau wouldn't come back," Pilar hastened to assure her. "He just said he would be in grave danger."

"From every man in Texas," her grandmother exclaimed. "Those infidels think they have the right to shoot my Laveau. Poor boy, he is not a brave man. He will not return."

Pilar was too shocked at her grandmother's words to respond. From the day he rode off to the war, her grandmother had spoken of Laveau as though he were the answer to every prayer. There was no problem that couldn't be fixed if Laveau were here, no injustice that couldn't be righted, no insult that couldn't be avenged.

"I'm sure he will come back," Pilar said. "He said so in his letters."

"That Wheeler boy and his friends, they come back, but Laveau, he does not return because he is afraid somebody will shoot him. Is that Wheeler boy afraid somebody will shoot him? No. He tries to get himself shot all the time, and all the time he escapes. What is he doing right now? Following those desperadoes so they can shoot at him again."

Pilar would have loved to explore this shocking shift in her grandmother's attitude, but she saw riders coming into the ranch yard. "They're back," she said as she hurried to the door.

Pilar rushed out to the porch, then stopped at the top of the steps. She wrapped her arms around the post to keep herself from running forward to meet them. Cade and his grandfather rode double. Jessie rode double with Ivan.

"Where are the others?" she asked. "Did anybody get hurt? Did you find the horses?"

"What are you standing about for, girl?" Earl Wheeler demanded as he slid to the ground. "Start cooking. You got nine hungry men to feed."

"She has a right to know what happened," Cade said.

"A right?" Earl squeaked.

"Nobody got hurt," Cade said, "and we found the horses. The boys are bringing them in now." He turned at the sound of an approaching horse. Rafe rode into the yard alone.

"We found the cows, too," Earl said, but Pilar had already turned her attention to Rafe. She could sense he had something important to tell Cade.

"Where've you been?" Cade asked.

"Getting me a squatter," Rafe said. "I only meant

to wing him, but the damned fool feinted to one side, and the bullet went through his lungs."

"I wanted to question him."

"I questioned him for you, but you're not going to like the answers."

"You can't trust a damned squatter farther than you can throw him," Earl Wheeler said.

"He said they attacked the ranch today because they thought we were still in prison. They wanted to take the horses and the steers we'd rounded up."

"I bet they just about messed their britches when they heard those shots," Earl said.

"He said they hadn't been making money like they hoped. Cattle aren't worth more than a couple dollars in Mexico because bandits have been stealing Texas cattle by the thousands and flooding the market. He said they were going to wait for Cortina to come north, then take all the cattle from both ranches and head to Mexico. He said they were going to burn the hacienda behind them."

"No!"

No one had noticed that Senora diViere stood in the doorway.

"You cannot let them burn my home," she cried, looking at Cade. "You must stop them."

"God almighty, woman!" Earl Wheeler exclaimed. "Why in tarnation should Cade want to do that?"

Senora diViere ignored Earl Wheeler. She stepped out onto the porch, moved toward Cade, her gaze focused on him. "You and your friends can drive them out," she said. "You are very brave. You are stronger and smarter than they are. They will run when they see you coming."

"There's more than twenty men on the place," Rafe said. "I doubt that a half dozen strangers will scare them much."

"What are ten times twenty squatters compared to seven men such as you?" Senora diViere said, her gaze never leaving Cade.

"You're crazy," Earl said. "You've been sitting in that room so long, mumbling to yourself, you've gone stark raving mad."

"Those men occupy a fortified position," Cade said. "You ought to wait until Laveau comes back. Maybe he can get the army—"

"It will be too late," Senora diViere said, her voice rising to a near scream. "You heard what that man said," she said, pointing to Rafe. "The cattle will be gone, the house burned. There will be nothing for the army to save."

"Sorry, ma'am, but Rafe is right. We don't have the men. Besides, why should I endanger myself to drive squatters off your ranch?" Cade said.

"To protect your own ranch. Once they take everything I have, they will turn on you."

"We can protect our own," Earl said.

"You've got a point, ma'am," Cade said, "but it's a big risk. I'd have to have a much better reason than that."

"I can offer you the best reason of all," Senora diViere said.

"What?" Cade asked.

"A wife. If you return my ranch, you can marry Pilar."

Seventeen

PILAR'S GRIP ON REALITY FRACTURED AND FELL INTO tinkling shards all around her. Her grandmother had offered her to Cade in return for driving the squatters from their ranch, had used her as a bargaining chip.

Seeing Cade look equally stunned made her feel better. He would refuse this incredible offer, and her grandmother would regret the panic that had caused her to make it.

"That's the most sensible idea you've ever had," Earl Wheeler said. "Don't know why I didn't think of it."

Her grandmother ignored Earl. "What do you say?" she asked Cade.

"You give him half the ranch and the house, and you've got yourself a deal," Earl said.

"The hacienda belongs to Laveau," the old woman said, directing a particularly hate-filled glare at Earl. "It has been the family home for four generations."

"He'll be just as happy with money. He'll never be a rancher."

Pilar couldn't understand why Cade didn't speak

up. There was no need to let his grandfather bargain for a deal neither of them wanted. She'd never known Cade to be speechless.

"Our custom is to give money to a daughter," Senora diViere said. "The son of the family—"

"You don't have any money," Earl said, interrupting her. "Cade will hold the ranch. Your boy will lose it. You people expect to give a dowry to get somebody to marry your girls, so consider half your land and the house her dowry."

"You are a foul, greedy old man," Senora diViere announced. "If I do not agree to your terms, will you take the land from me?"

"You don't have any land. There isn't a man in Texas who would deny my right to anything I can take from the squatters."

Cade continued to stand mute, listening to the two old people argue over their fates. This was unlike the Cade Pilar knew, unlike the man who was never at a loss to know what he wanted or how he meant to get it, the man who never once stepped back and let his grandfather make decisions for him, the man to whom other men looked for leadership.

"It is our rancho by law and by tradition," her grandmother announced. "Not even Texans would give it to you."

"Stop this!" Pilar finally managed to get her tongue to work. "This is crazy. Cade and I don't even like each other."

"Like is not necessary," her grandmother said. "Respect is all that is needed."

Pilar felt as if she were suffocating. Why wouldn't

her grandmother look at her? Why did Cade remain silent? "Tell them," she said, turning to him. "Tell them you don't want to marry me."

"But I do," Cade said. He spoke in a quiet, normal voice, just as though they were discussing something of no more importance than what vegetables to cook for supper. "Combining the ranches is a very good idea."

Pilar had been certain Cade would refuse, would treat the idea with scorn. But he hadn't. She had only to agree to the bargain, and she would be his wife.

The realization that this heretofore impossible eventuality was only a few steps from being reality was mind-numbing. As far back as she could remember, her grandmother had hated every Wheeler that ever drew breath. It was beyond the range of Pilar's imagination that her grandmother would consider marrying her to a Wheeler *for any reason*.

Earl Wheeler's feelings were just as vehement. Pilar was certain that only his desire for her land could account for his actions.

Cade's decision was more understandable. She knew that Cade found her attractive, probably even liked her. That was enough for most Texas men.

But what shocked Pilar, what caused her to go mute and virtually turn to stone, was the realization that she *wanted* to marry Cade, to be his wife. She couldn't say she loved him. She hadn't explored her emotional terrain enough to be able to say exactly what her feelings for him were, but she wanted to marry him. Of that she was quite certain.

"Then it's settled," Earl said. "We'll have the wedding as soon as we can get a preacher out here."

"We will have the wedding *after* we return to our hacienda," her grandmother said. "And we will have a priest. I will not have my granddaughter married off like a penniless provincial."

"She is penniless," Earl said.

"She is a diViere, and she will be married like one."

"Okay, but she gets married before we attack the ranch."

"After."

"Are you afraid Cade will be killed and she'll be left a widow?"

"We'll be married afterward," Cade said. "Only *if* I drive out the squatters."

Pilar couldn't fool herself that Cade was in a daze, that he didn't know what he was doing, or that he was letting his grandfather make decisions for him.

"Consider yourself lucky, girl," Earl said. "Every female who claps eyes on him wants a piece of my grandson. I bet thinking about going to bed with him gets you warm all over."

She felt swept along by events she couldn't control. She had to have some time to think. "I want to talk to my grandmother," she said.

"There's nothing to talk about," Earl said. "Everything's decided."

"No, it's not," Cade said. "Pilar hasn't agreed to anything."

"It's not up to her to agree," Earl said. "She's just a female."

Pilar pulled her grandmother into the house, down the short hall into her bedroom, and closed the door. She leaned against it as though by doing so she could keep out the madness swirling around her.

"Earl Wheeler is the lowest, most miserable crea-ture on the face of the earth," her grandmother fumed. "I wonder why God created him."

"Yet you want me to marry his grandson."

"The young one is better than the grandfather, but I do not intend for you to marry him. That would be worse than a thousand years in purgatory."

"But you just said—"

"You heard what the man said. The squatters plan to take the cattle and burn the hacienda. Laveau will not come back in time to prevent that. We will have nothing. We will be beggars."

"But Laveau—"

"Laveau is not a builder. He cannot create some-thing where there is nothing. We must save the rancho before it is too late."

"But I can't promise to marry Cade now, let him take back the rancho—maybe even get some of his friends killed—then refuse to marry him."

"Of course you can."

"That's not honorable."

"Do the Wheelers treat us with honor when they steal our land? We do not owe them honor."

"But Cade didn't steal anything."

"One Wheeler is like another."

Both Earl and Cade were strong, determined, capable, fearless. Natural leaders. But where Earl was stingy, mean-spirited, and greedy, Cade was honorable, dependable, and kind. He had always treated her fairly.

"I can't promise to marry Cade, knowing all the time I mean to renege on my promise."

"But you must. We will lose the rancho if you refuse."

Not a thought for Cade or herself, just the ranch. Their grandparents had more in common than either of them would admit. "We'll still have the land."

"The land is no good without cattle. The young Wheeler can drive out the squatters. He will do it for you. I can see it in his eyes. He wants you."

"That's all the more reason to refuse to make a promise I don't intend to fulfill."

"I do not understand why you hesitate."

"How do you think he'll feel if I refuse to marry him?"

"He's a Wheeler. He has no feelings."

"Have you forgotten he defended my honor in San Antonio?"

"Any man would have done as much."

"Not the man who was trying to haul me off."

"They are not men. They are animals."

"That's not the point."

"You are right. The point is your loyalty to your family."

"I am loyal to the family," Pilar protested. "I—"

"That loyalty demands that you make any sacrifice necessary. You do not consider yourself. Nor do you consider anyone outside the family."

"But this is a matter of honor."

Her grandmother reached out and grabbed Pilar by the arm. Her fingers curved into a claw, digging into her flesh. "Nothing is more honorable than preserving the family. It is your duty. Nothing must stop you. Nothing!"

The intensity of her grandmother's gaze unnerved Pilar. The violence of her feelings had transformed her well-preserved face into the mask of a driven, half-crazed creature. The red of her lips and the black of her brows made her powdered cheeks look hollow, like the skin of a dead person. The fierceness in her eyes made her seem like some predatory creature.

Pilar drew back from her grandmother as from a stranger.

"We could ask Cade to help us," Pilar said. "We can offer him a percentage of any cattle he manages to get to market. He plans to drive them to Missouri, where he can get ten times what they're worth in Texas." She found herself talking faster, trying by the force and rapidity of her words to sway her grandmother. "I'm sure his grandfather will agree. He doesn't like us any more than we like him. He's greedy for more land, but he could buy more with the money we'll pay him."

"That old man will not risk his grandson for some future reward," her grandmother said. "He agreed because he saw immediate gain. His grandson is the same."

"And what do you think they'll do when they find we've lied?"

"They can do nothing."

"They can run off our cattle and burn the hacienda."

"They would never do that!"

"I don't know what they'll do, but any man with enough nerve to openly take land from us isn't going to hesitate to take revenge if we cheat him."

Pilar was relieved to see that her grandmother was at least giving her arguments some thought. She wanted the rancho back, too, but there was only so much she could force herself to do. After his kindness to her, she

couldn't possibly treat Cade so badly. He would h．．
her, and she didn't think she could stand that.

"I will not give him cattle," her grandmother said.

"Then we have only two choices. First, I can actually marry him."

"No! I would kill myself."

"Or I can tell him that I would like to marry him, but that we don't know each other well enough. I can insist upon a period of time during which we can become acquainted, see if we're compatible."

"Why would he agree to such a thing?" her grandmother asked.

"Because he believes that a man and woman are equal, that they should share the decisions in their lives."

"A woman should concern herself with her children and keeping her husband happy. Everything else she should leave to him."

Without realizing it, her grandmother had just stated the reasons Pilar wanted to marry Cade rather than Manuel. "That's not the way Americans think, and we might as well take advantage of it."

"Will he not insist that you marry him before he drives the squatters out?"

"No. Once an idea starts to grow in Cade's head, he can't wait. I expect he's already working out a strategy to take the squatters by surprise."

"And if he does not?"

"Then we'll have to think of something else."

There was an abrupt silence when they rejoined the men. Cade looked so irritated, Pilar wondered what Earl had said. As usual, Rafe's expression was inscrutable.

"You ready to set the day, girl?" Earl asked.

My granddaughter is overcome by modesty," enora diViere said. "She finds herself unable to do this thing so quickly."

"You're not backing out, are you?" Earl demanded. "Because if you are—"

"If you'll let her talk, I expect you'll find out," Cade said.

Pilar threw Cade a grateful look, then turned away. She couldn't look him in the eye. She was about to do something unethical. She prayed he would turn her down.

"I haven't been thinking of marriage," Pilar began.

"That's a lie," Earl said. "You've been engaged to a fancy Mexican for I don't know how long."

"I don't think Manuel wishes to marry me any more than I wish to marry him."

"I didn't think your kind paid any attention to that."

"Gramps, will you let her talk?"

"Well, she won't get to it."

"She can't with you interrupting all the time."

"*I* could."

"Not everybody is as bullheaded as you."

"I never thought I'd see the day when you took her side against me."

"He did when he insisted she eat at the table," Rafe pointed out.

"Do you want me to gag him?" Cade asked Pilar.

"That'll be more than you can do," Earl said, dancing about like he was on a hot stove. "Ain't nobody getting the best of Earl Wheeler."

Pilar couldn't help smiling. If Cade could wrestle

full-grown steers to the ground, he could topple the old windbag in a second.

"We need time to find out if we like each other well enough to live together for the rest of our lives," Pilar said.

"You've had several weeks already," Earl said. "What more do you need?"

"With all the work he did, I hardly saw Cade," Pilar pointed out.

"You saw him at the table every day," Earl said. "I should think that would be more than enough."

"It would for any wife of yours," Senora diViere said.

"The idea is too new for me," Pilar said, sticking closely to her main point and hoping to head off a resumption of the battle between their grandparents. "Our families have been enemies all my life. I'm sure you taught Cade to hate all of us."

"But I didn't," Cade said.

"You kidnapped her," Senora diViere reminded him.

"Just having a bit of fun," Cade said. "I've never had to force any woman to my bed."

Pilar felt herself grow warm. The memory of the kisses they shared had kept her warm for two nights. The thought of sharing Cade's bed threatened to scald her.

"I am not interested in a litany of your conquests," her grandmother said.

"I didn't intend to give it. Now, if everyone will let Pilar finish."

"I have, essentially," Pilar said, pulling her mind from thoughts that made her feel far too warm. "I don't think we should make any promises before we can decide how we feel about each other."

"But you expect us to run off those scalawags while you sit around trying to make up your mind," Earl said.

Pilar decided Cade got his cleverness from his grandfather. The man might look old and feeble, but he didn't miss a trick.

"I'm not going to tell you what you should do," Pilar said.

"But you can't wait," her grandmother said, "or there won't be any cattle or hacienda for a dowry."

"Sounds like they're trying to bamboozle us," Earl said to his grandson.

"Maybe," Cade replied, "but I agree Pilar needs time to make her decision."

"What about the time *you* need to decide?" Earl asked.

"I already know what I want."

Pilar felt the heat rise again. Cade was looking at her in a way that made her feel as if he were undressing her. That had happened before, but never with a man she wanted to marry. She could picture herself married to Cade, and that picture caused every nerve in her body to sing.

Now that the shock of the proposal had worn off, Pilar experienced a resurgence of the feelings she'd experienced from time to time during the last few days. Only now they came at her all at once. And they all said the same thing.

She wanted to marry Cade.

Not because he was going to run the squatters off r ranch. Not because he was capable of turning both ranches into a very successful enterprise. Not because he was strong and big and handsome. Not because he was kind and thoughtful and treated her with respect.

Because she really liked him.

What she didn't understand, nor had she anticipated, was the physical attraction she felt for Cade. One minute she was feeling normal, and the next she felt as though she would explode from the force of feelings that were at once unfamiliar and frightening in their intensity. Her limbs started to feel weak, her muscles to quiver uncontrollably. Her stomach felt queasy.

Could this be the beginning of love, or was it simply lust?

Pilar didn't know, but she did know she didn't find the sensations enjoyable. If this was what love was all about, aristocrats were right to avoid affairs of the heart like a plague. Because that was exactly what it felt like.

⁓

"No man is going to be anxious to hang his brother-in-law," Owen said.

"You were just supposed to make up to her," Nate said. "Nobody ever said anything about marriage."

"She and her grandmother want their land back," Cade explained. "In exchange, I get half the ranch and a wife."

"She's not just a wife," Broc said. "She's beautiful, and I know what beautiful women can do."

"Nobody talks me into doing anything I don't want to do," Cade said. "Just consider it a business proposition."

"If you can look at that woman and consider her a business proposition, you're not human," Nate said.

Cade had been arguing with his friends since Rafe had told them of the conversation in the kitchen. All were dead set against this marriage.

"Cade probably jumped at the chance to get himself a beautiful wife on the strength of our work," Owen said. "He knows he can't get one any other way."

"When I commanded the troop, I made decisions based on how best to achieve our objectives. I didn't consider myself or any other man as an individual. I'm not commanding the troop anymore, so I'm deciding what's best for me. I want to be the most successful man in this part of Texas, and I'll do whatever it takes to get there. That's why I invited you to help me get this first herd to market. If you can't believe that I'm as firm as always in my desire to bring Laveau to justice, then maybe you'd better leave."

His gaze went from man to man, not leaving until each one met his gaze and signaled his acquiescence. He didn't want any reluctant followers. Retaking the diViere ranch wasn't going to be easy. He was certain there would be injuries. Or worse. He didn't want the men to think otherwise, but he meant to do it. This was a chance he could not turn down.

He'd hardly had time to get to know Pilar, but he liked her. She was spirited and energetic. And he could talk to her. That didn't sound like much, but he couldn't imagine a worse fate than being married to a woman without a thought in her head beyond the color and design of her next dress.

But there was much more to Pilar than brains and

energy. She was a fighter, a winner. She had been dealt rough blows, some bad enough to cause most women to cut and run, but she had stood her ground, fought back, and managed to make something fine and courageous out of tragedy. She had developed a sense of pride in doing whatever had to be done, a sense of self that enabled her to see herself as more than a pawn in the diViere family dynasty.

They wouldn't have love—she didn't believe in it and he didn't trust it—but Pilar would be loyal. Once she gave her word, it would be forever.

Women didn't last long in his family. His mother and grandmother had left Texas and their husbands, one because she couldn't stand Texas, the other because she couldn't stand Texas *or* her husband. Both had married intelligent, ambitious men, but both had married beneath themselves socially. His father had worked hard to give his wife the kind of life she expected, but his early death in a ranch accident had ended that hope. His grandfather had been pleased to see his daughter-in-law leave, had refused to let her take her six-year-old son with her. He'd said she wasn't going to turn his only grandson into a runny-nosed weakling. Apparently, his mother hadn't thought he was good enough even for that. She returned to Alabama, and he'd never heard from her again.

"Nobody's leaving," Holt told Cade. "None of us has enough money to make it out of Texas."

"But that doesn't mean I'm not against this marriage," Owen said. "When a man starts thinking about a wife, he forgets about his friends."

"But he's even better at remembering his responsibilities," Cade said. "And one of those responsibilities is to keep this ranch safe. I think we're in for an attack soon."

"Why?" Ivan asked.

"They can see we're settling in. Every time a legitimate rancher returns, it means greater danger to them. They've got to make a big push to run us off."

"When are you expecting it?" Nate asked.

"I don't know, but we're going to attack them first. Owen, I want you to come up with a plan for a defensive perimeter. I'll talk to Pilar about the layout of her ranch, then Rafe and I will come up with a plan of attack. Nate, I want you to do some reconnaissance. Learn anything you can about how many men they have, where they sleep, what they do, their weapons and supplies."

"And you want this in a few days?"

"Do your best. I've got an uneasy feeling we don't have very long." Cade knew that no one doubted his uneasy feelings. They'd proved accurate too many times.

"What about me?" Broc asked.

"I want you to ride into San Antonio and find me a half dozen cowhands. I'll pay thirty dollars a month, but they've got to be willing to work for nothing but their keep until I sell the herd. And they've got to be willing to fight. We'll meet up with rustlers and herd cutters along the trail."

"What if I can't get that many?"

"Ask around for ex-soldiers. You ought to find plenty of them. In the meantime, we'll drift the cattle north toward the river. I don't want to make it easy for Cortina to make off with them."

"What will you do about the diViere ran." Owen asked.

"I won't know until we take it. The squatters migh. have sold off everything already and be looking for their next spot, or they may be planning to stay."

"If so, they'll be desperate to hold on," Nate said.

"No more desperate than I am," Cade said. "And I have one big advantage they don't?"

"Your good looks?" Owen asked with a laugh.

"The six of you," Cade said, "along with Gramps and Uncle Jessie. I'd back the nine of us in any fight. Now I have to talk to Pilar and convince her to trust me."

"It might be easier to drive off the squatters," Holt said.

Eighteen

PILAR FIDGETED NERVOUSLY. SHE ATE HER DINNER
without tasting it. She talked without remembering
anything she said. She looked at people without seeing
them. She heard her own thoughts as though they
belonged to someone else. Cade had said he wanted
to talk with her after dinner. She had to tell him the
truth. She wasn't sure he would stick to his agreement
after that.

"You two had better have that talk," Holt said.
"You've been eyeing each other like two polecats
all evening."

Pilar pushed her chair back and got to her feet. "I have
to clear the table, put the food away, wash the dishes—"

"We can do that," Holt said.

"I won't have no man washing dishes in my house
when there's a woman about who can do it," Earl
growled.

"We spent four years washing up after ourselves,"
Holt said. "I don't suppose it will kill us to do it one
more time. Why don't you two take a walk or sit under
a tree?"

"What have they got to say that the rest of us [can't] hear?" Earl asked.

"A lot, I should hope," Holt replied.

Pilar allowed herself to be pushed toward the door. She did have a lot she didn't want Earl to hear.

"Don't pay any attention to my grandfather," Cade said. "He doesn't mean what he says."

"He means exactly what he says," Pilar contradicted. She was through with lies, half-truths, pretense. She wanted this marriage, but they had to start off on the right foot. If not, she'd be better off with Manuel. At least they knew to expect nothing of each other.

"Where are we going?" she asked when Cade led her down the steps and into the ranch yard.

"I thought we could talk down by the creek. It's nice to listen to the sound of running water."

They'd had a thunderstorm during dinner. The stream-bed would dry up in a matter of hours, but there would be water running now.

Pilar felt the earth soft under her feet. There was no breeze, and the moisture in the air hung cool and heavy as a cloud around her. She liked it. There was a softness to the air against her skin. She could almost hear the earth swelling, the plants drinking in every drop of moisture, tiny animals seeking out droplets on branches or tiny puddles in the cup formed by a dried leaf. The earth and all its creatures were desperate to store up every drop of life-giving fluid.

Just as she was desperate to preserve the small chance she had for happiness.

"We have a courtyard at home filled with trees and

rs, and a pool with brightly colored fish. We arly always sat outside after dinner."

She hadn't thought about her home recently—hadn't wanted to think of it in the hands of strangers—but tonight, with the prospect of being able to return soon, she couldn't stop thinking about it. For the first time in two years, she could allow herself to remember her home as it had been, to begin to think of all the things she would do when she returned.

"I liked it, especially in the evening. If the insects weren't too bad." The intrusion of reality often ruined things. She hoped it wouldn't ruin her future.

"You'll be able to enjoy it again very soon."

She looked forward to that. But first she had to talk to Cade.

They reached the edge of the creek where it wound its way between rocky outcroppings. Before them stretched a vista of endless flat plains covered with thickets of live oak, mesquite, post oak, prickly pear cactus, catclaw, black chaparral, and other thorny bushes and small trees. Beneath this canopy and on the plains to the south grew the grasses that nourished the thousands of cattle on which so many people pinned their hopes.

Cade found a flat rock along the edge of the stream just out of reach of the gently flowing water. A cactus grew along one edge, its prickly arms reaching out for any unwary passerby. Without warning, Cade lifted Pilar up onto the rock.

"Oh!"

Surprise squeezed the sound from her. She could think of nothing but the disturbing physical sensations

that centered around the places where Cade's
had touched her. His touch had turned his near.
into a tactile experience.

He stood a couple of paces away, breaking up a
small branch from a dead mesquite and tossing the
pieces into the steam to watch them float away. He
was so big, so powerful, so… She didn't know how to
say that his presence seemed to wrap around her. But
rather than hem her in, it freed her. The night held
many dangers, but she knew that Cade wouldn't let
them touch her.

"Everything seems so quiet and peaceful after a
rain," Cade said. "You could almost believe there was
no danger out here."

"There won't be once you drive out the squatters."

"There's always danger, especially to a rich man
with a beautiful wife."

She had never thought of herself in that way.

"Cortina isn't the only rustler out there. There are
Texans branding any cattle they find as fast as they can.
Once branded, the cows belong to them. Others are
running off whole herds."

"They won't bother your herds," she said.

"I'll have to keep one eye on them and one on
you." He moved a little closer, looked down at her,
and smiled. "I'd rather keep both eyes on you."

She wanted to ask him why. All her life she'd been
considered a valuable prize only for the wealth and
connections she represented. Cade had shown interest
in her when she was only a cook for his grandfather.
She hoped that at least part of the reason he had agreed
to marry her stemmed from the fact he liked her.

she couldn't let him make any kind of personal
mitment until she'd told him the truth. "I've
something to tell you." She looked at the toes
of her shoes peeping out from under the hem of her
gown. She didn't dare look up at him or at the sky
filled with dark clouds set into stark relief by a bright
moon. Driven on by winds she couldn't see, the
clouds boiled and churned, very much like her insides
right then.

"I'm sure we both have a lot to say to each other.
We haven't exactly been friends in the past."

"It's not about that. Well, maybe it is, but you
probably won't think so."

He turned and regarded her almost paternally. "Am
I supposed to understand that?"

"No. I'm not very good at explaining things.
Women in my family aren't supposed to have opinions. If we do, we aren't expected to express them."

"I'll listen."

"I know. That's one of the reasons it's so hard to
admit I've been misleading you."

His expression didn't change so much as harden.
She thought she would have preferred a scowl.

"Are you saying you're not going to marry me?"

"No. I do want to marry you. I didn't at first, but
I do now."

He cocked his head, regarding her as though he
didn't quite believe what she'd said. "Are you saying
you've fallen in love with me?"

She couldn't tell whether he would have greeted
that news with warmth or revulsion.

"No."

"You've never liked or trusted me. What makes you think you want to marry me?"

"You."

"Why?"

"Because of the way you treat me."

"I haven't done anything different from any-body else."

"You have, from the moment you arrived. Your grandfather treated me like a slave."

"Gramps would make a slave out of *me* if I let him."

"That's something else. You don't let people make decisions for you. You make them for yourself and get people to go along with your decisions even when they don't want to. Remember that first night, when you got your grandfather to let me sit at the table?"

"You cooked the food and paid for it. Who had a better right?"

"It had nothing to do with rights. And you talked to me, listened to me, helped when things got busy."

"I like getting to know the people around me. As for helping, we all learned to do that during the war."

"How many men do you think went home and reverted to their old ways?" she asked. "I'd say nearly all of them, but you didn't."

"And this is why you want to marry me?"

"Partly. You don't need me to tell you you're a nice-looking man. I'm sure women have been telling you that for years."

"Not as many as I would have liked."

She liked it when he joked with her. It made her feel closer to him, as if she was somebody he liked and enjoyed being with. He made her feel like a woman rather than an object; he had given her hope that her own girlish dreams might come true, that what her grandmother described as vulgar and ugly might be beautiful. But most important of all, he'd given her hope that her own feelings and desires might in some way determine her future.

"There's also another reason why I want to marry you. I haven't been engaged to you since I was six."

"Is Manuel that bad?"

"No, but no one ever asked me if I wanted to marry Manuel. I don't think you would have been surprised if I'd refused to marry you."

"You did refuse. You said we have to wait to see if we are compatible."

She couldn't help laughing. "That's not a refusal. It's really a yes."

"It didn't feel like it."

"You might be glad of that when you hear what I have to say."

"I can't imagine what you could say that would be so terrible."

"I could say that I distrusted you from the start, that I only pretended to like you so you would tell me anything you knew about Laveau."

"That's not so bad." He didn't look as if he believed it. His face was settling into a mask again.

"I could say I let you kiss me for the same reason."

He definitely didn't like that. His entire body stiffened.

"I could say I agreed to marry you to get our rancho back, that once my grandmother and I are back home, I plan to back out."

"If that's true, why should you tell me now?"

"Because my feelings for you have changed. I expected you to be like your grandfather, but you're not. You're willing to work hard for what you want, but you don't take all the credit for your success. You acknowledge debts and respect other people's talents even though you weren't raised that way. I could admire what you'd become, what you were able to do, without caring for you, but I started to like you. It's because I like you that I've got to get all the terrible things I've done out in the open so we can start over again."

"There's more?"

"Only one. In San Antonio, when I was supposed to be shopping, I went to ask Major Kramer about Laveau."

"You should have told me. I would have gone with you."

She didn't avoid his gaze now. She looked him straight in the eye. "You've been holding something back from me. I don't know what, but I've felt it from the first day."

His face had definitely turned to marble. "And what do you think I'm holding back?"

"I don't know, but the major said Texas was full of ex-Confederate soldiers who might try to kill Laveau, that he might not come home for years."

"He didn't tell you anything I couldn't have told you if you'd asked."

"But you didn't tell me. You made me think you didn't really care. He also said Laveau couldn't trust anybody, especially the men who'd served with him." Her gaze didn't waver as she looked at him. "You served with him. I didn't know if I could trust you. I was so unsure, I even considered leaving you in jail so you couldn't hurt Laveau when he came home."

Cade hadn't liked much of what Pilar said. She was obviously smart enough to figure out he would still be angry at her brother, but that didn't bother him so much as knowing she'd only pretended to like him to get information. Owen said Cade was too concerned with his duty to be a success with women. Now the one time he had put his interest in a woman before duty, she turned out to be using him.

"What made you change your mind?"

"A lot of things, but mostly because you risked trouble to help me. I couldn't let you rot in jail even if I'd known you were planning to shoot Laveau the moment you saw him."

Cade didn't know whether to be angry that she'd lied to him, embarrassed to have misjudged her intelligence so badly, or just disappointed that she wasn't attracted to him. He ended up being all three.

"Why didn't you just say you wanted to get your ranch back? We could have worked out a deal. My friends need all the money they can get. What do you say to a trade? We get your ranch back in exchange for all the cattle we can round up and brand in a month."

"You don't understand. I told you all this because I do want to marry you. How would you feel if, years later, you learned all this? You'd think our marriage was nothing but a calculated plan."

"Isn't that what people of your class do, marry for wealth and position regardless of feelings, hopes, or desires?"

"That's why I don't want to marry Manuel."

"So I'm looking like the better deal now." knew he was being unfair and hypocritical. He'd use Pilar, too. Only his goal was harder to defend. He intended to hang her brother.

He doubted that she really liked him very much, but she had been honest about her motives. His motives weren't pure, either. He didn't love her, though he admired her and had started to like her quite a lot. He enjoyed being with her. He did want her share of the diViere land and cows, but if he expected his marriage to be anything but a business deal of some kind, he'd better be honest with her. Or try to be.

"You haven't committed a terrible crime," he said. "At least, no worse than I did."

"What did you do?" She looked miserable. Confession might be good for the soul, but it was obviously hell on the spirits.

"I pretended to be interested in you because I wanted to know when Laveau was coming home. I haven't forgiven him for turning traitor. I wanted to beat him until I didn't feel angry anymore."

Then I meant to hang him. He didn't know what she would do if that happened; maybe he'd never have to face it. Laveau might never come home. He might even be dead. Cade hoped so. Then he wouldn't have to be the one to bring the bastard to justice.

"I don't intend to shoot him or encourage anyone else to shoot him. He knows the whereabouts of the man who betrayed my troop. A lot of men died as a result of that treachery."

He hadn't lied exactly. He *didn't* want to shoot

...u, and Laveau *did* have information about the
... who betrayed his troop—it was himself—but
...ch word out of Cade's mouth made him feel a little
more guilty than the last. And as much as he wanted to
marry Pilar, he knew his friends couldn't give up their
need for revenge. He didn't know what he would do
if he was caught between the two.

"My grandfather isn't the only one who's anxious
to increase the size of our ranch," Cade said. "Your
half of the rancho will more than double our holdings.
I'd be lying if I said I didn't want to be rich."

"I want that too," Pilar said. "I don't need to live
like my grandmother used to, but I dream about my soft
bed and how wonderful it was to live in the hacienda."

"It'll take a few years," Cade said, "but I plan to
have a big house in San Antonio. You'll have all
the clothes and jewels you could want. You'll be
invited everywhere."

"You forget my father and grandfather fought
for Mexico."

"That won't matter. You'll be the wife of a rich
man. People will want to be our friends."

"Is that so important?"

"I can't forget what your grandmother said about
me. A lot of other people said the same thing. I want
to make them eat their words."

But as soon as Cade said that, he realized it wasn't
true any longer. He didn't care what people said
about him, because he didn't accept their evaluation.
He was tired of war and hating, tired of feeling like a
thief. By marrying Pilar, in a sense he'd be returning
the land his family stole. He wanted to build, not

destroy. He wanted a family, not feuds. He
warm, happy life, and no one he knew deserv
any more than Pilar.

"Do you like me at all?" Pilar asked.

Her question surprised him. She wasn't a woman
who believed in love. Her social class followed strict
rules to secure social position and wealth. That didn't
allow room for passion, only cold calculation.

"Of course I like you. I thought I had made that
plain."

"We've both confessed to acting contrary to our
feelings for what we thought were good reasons.
Everything is different now. I need to know how you
really feel."

"Would you have asked that question of Manuel?"

She looked surprised. "No. The situation would
have been entirely different."

"How? You'd be his wife."

"We wouldn't expect to have any feelings for each
other. We share the same culture, the same social
system, the same religion, roles already defined for
us. We could go for days without meeting and know
exactly what the other was thinking. It's completely
different with us."

"How?"

"Your grandfather wants my land, but he scorns
me. My grandmother wants you to drive out the
squatters, but she wants me to renege on our agreement and marry Manuel. Laveau will hate both of us.
Everybody around us will try to drive us apart. If we
don't at least like and respect each other, the marriage
will be impossible. I've never known anybody more

...an my grandmother. Her husband did his ... at least Grandmother says he did—but they ... like strangers living under the same roof. They ...an't talk or spend time with each other. I don't want that to happen to me."

He hadn't viewed things in such a grim light, but there wasn't any question about his liking her. Even before Pilar's confession, he'd suspected that the old woman would not really give him Pilar. He couldn't see her throwing away thirty years of hatred so readily.

But he wanted Pilar, not for her land or her cows, but for herself. The part of him that admired Pilar and wanted to be equally honest about their marriage struggled against the part of him that demanded revenge. He felt like a heel, but he wanted Pilar too much to be honest. Doing so would mean he would lose her.

His brain said it would be better if he didn't care for her. Any warm feelings would die after they hanged Laveau. But another part of him wanted her to care about him, *needed* her to care. Somehow he'd figure out what to do about Laveau, but he had to have Pilar. He couldn't do without her.

Right now he had to convince Pilar he liked her. That shouldn't be hard. He didn't have to pretend. He reached out and took her hands in his. She didn't resist when he pulled her toward him. She slid off the rock, stood so close he could see the vein in the side of her neck throbbing with the rapid beat of her heart.

"I don't know when I stopped pretending, but it was long before we went to San Antonio." He remembered the walk by the river, the kisses they'd shared, the difficulty he had holding himself in check.

He pulled her closer until their bodies met, against chest.

He trailed his fingertip across her lower lip. It so very soft. "I can't imagine anyone ignoring you."

"It's a matter of honor with men like my father. A husband takes pains to demonstrate his indifference to his wife. Otherwise people might think she influenced his decisions, and that would be fatal to his prestige."

"Will you try to influence my decisions?"

"It depends on what you're deciding."

"Suppose I wanted to put my arms around you," he said as he slipped his arms around her waist.

"I wouldn't try to dissuade you."

"Even if I held you very tightly?" He pulled her to him until their bodies met from chest to thigh.

"You're not holding me too tightly now."

He couldn't see her expression clearly in the shadowed light filtering through the leaves of the live oak, but he felt the invitation of her body as it pressed against him, heard it in her voice. He could sense it in the electricity between their bodies. It was like heat lightning on a hot summer's night. Whatever her reasons for wanting him to like her, she was not dealing in half lies now.

There was just as much lightning coming from him. He'd never felt so keyed up. His body had begun to swell. But not even growing discomfort could draw his attention away from Pilar and his desire to kiss her soft lips. He'd spent far too much time during the last two nights thinking of the kisses they'd shared by the river.

He leaned down until their lips met. His memory

...nisled him. Her lips were incredibly soft, so ...weet, yielding, inviting. His gentle kiss deepened ... a hungry, greedy kiss which made no allowances ...r her inexperience. Rather, it yielded to the insistent need inside him, the need which she seemed to fan into a fierce flame. The intensity of this need, this urge to throw himself headlong into this novel experience, battled with his habit of control, with his personal requirement that everything he did have a specific, preplanned goal.

He broke the kiss, teetering on the edge, afraid he would fall into the abyss.

"Did I do something wrong?" she asked.

"No." He didn't want to admit that fear was at the root of his hesitation. "I didn't want to do anything that would frighten you."

"You didn't." She looked up at him, and a beam of moonlight found its way through the canopy overhead to illuminate her face so he could see her smile. "I like it. I don't understand why my grandmother should have told me I wouldn't."

"I think she was referring to something else."

"She said I wouldn't like anything my husband did." She stood on tiptoe, her face upturned, and it seemed the most natural thing in the world for Cade to drop his head and for their lips to meet in a deep, lingering kiss. Pilar returned his kiss, slipping her tongue between his teeth. Neither shy nor brazen, she seemed eager to enter fully into the experience.

Cade had never felt more than a physical response to any woman. It had taken him a little while before he realized his reaction to Pilar was quite different.

He told himself he ought to back up, pull hard on the reins, cut and run, but he couldn't stop himself from wanting to keep on kissing Pilar.

She didn't object when his hands left her waist and moved across her back. Nor when they moved over her shoulders or down her arms. She leaned closer to him, tightened her arms around his neck, pressed her breasts more firmly against his chest. Any desire to control himself deserted Cade. He could think of nothing but the woman in his arms, the throbbing need of his body. He pressed against her, knowing she must feel his hardness. The feel of her, the scent of her, the taste, had overpowered his senses. He no longer had any capacity to reason or to consider consequences.

He slipped his hand between them, covered one of her breasts.

Pilar's swift intake of breath caused him to hesitate. She pulled back, her chest heaving from her rapid breaths. "Is that one of the things husbands do to their wives?" she asked, inquiring, unsure.

"*With* their wives," Cade corrected. "Do you like it?" He didn't know if he could stop if she didn't.

"I don't know. My whole body feels strange."

"That's because kissing and being held in a man's arms are new to you."

"Do Americans do that much?"

"All the time." He had a hard time remembering that, though she lived in Texas, she had been brought up like a European.

"Do American women like it?"

"Yes." According to Owen, they craved it.

"Then let's try it again."

She sounded unsure but eager. Cade warned himself to remain in control. But as he put his arms around Pilar once more and covered her mouth with his, it was hard to remember any limits.

A moment later, Pilar pushed him away. "I hear something."

Somebody was coming in their direction, whistling so he wouldn't surprise anybody. Cade felt sudden, sharp embarrassment. If this had been a war situation, he would have been dead.

"It's one of the boys," Cade said.

"Is something wrong?"

"I doubt it. He's whistling."

Moments later, Owen rounded the sprawling branches of the live oak. He was smiling, trying to look nonchalant, but Cade noticed his sharp gaze taking in every detail of their position and expressions.

"I hate to break up this little tête-à-tête, but a rider just came by with a letter for Pilar. He says it's from her brother."

Nineteen

"YOU CANNOT MARRY A MAN WHO HATES YOUR BROTHER," Pilar's grandmother said.

"My father hated his brother. He said he was glad he died of diphtheria."

"His brother tried to steal his inheritance."

"That's not important now. What should I tell Laveau? He wants me to write him back immediately."

The rider had been happy to accept Cade's invitation to spend the night in the bunkhouse.

"You must tell him everything," her grandmother said. "He is your brother. You must be loyal to him."

"Of course I'm loyal, but what can I tell him that will be of any use?"

"That Cade Wheeler and his friends are here waiting for him."

"Cade hasn't made a secret of the fact that he's angry at Laveau for deserting, but he only wants Laveau to help him find the man who betrayed their troop. The major said any ex-Confederate soldier would want to see justice done."

"What is this Anglo justice?"

"He said they hang traitors."

Her grandmother lost color. "These bloodthirsty Americans cannot be satisfied with taking the life of my husband and my son."

"Cade doesn't want Laveau. He wants the traitor."

"Now they want my grandson, too," her grandmother said, ignoring her. "They will not have him. I will protect him with my life. You must tell Laveau that Cade and his friends are waiting to kill him. He must come at once with a great army and kill them all."

"Grandmother!" Pilar exclaimed, aghast. "How can you ask me to marry a man before supper and a few hours later ask me to tell my brother to kill him?"

"They killed my husband and my son," the old woman said, implacable hatred flashing in her eyes. "They stole our land and did nothing while squatters drove us out of our home."

"The war killed them, not Earl. And Cade has promised to get the hacienda back."

"We will not need him when Laveau comes with his army."

"If Laveau had an army, I'm sure he would have been here already."

Her grandmother appeared reluctant to give up her dream of such magnificent vengeance, but she was a realist. "What is this reconstruction he says is moving so slowly?"

"Cade says the Union Army is determined to make sure the freed slaves are treated fairly."

"We had no slaves. Why should we care about this army?"

"I think it's the army Laveau hoped would h[...] him get back our land."

"Then why is this army wasting its time on slaves? They are free, are they not? Our land is not free. They should help us."

"I think that's what Laveau wants them to do, but it doesn't appear that they agree."

"Why not? Is that not why he changed sides?"

"The major said no one trusts a traitor."

"This major, he is stupid."

"Maybe, but it sounds like Laveau's in trouble with both sides."

Her grandmother went into a tirade about Americans, which Pilar tried to ignore. The rider would leave first thing in the morning. She didn't have long to decide what to say to Laveau. She'd never been in such a quandary. Until today, she would have considered herself unshakably loyal to her family. Now she felt like a traitor herself because she kept thinking of Cade.

There really wasn't anything to tell Laveau beyond the fact that Cade was back, he and his friends were rounding up and branding their cattle, and he had promised to drive the squatters from their ranch.

She guessed it was the idea of being disloyal to Cade that bothered her, telling Laveau about him but not telling Cade about Laveau. She had taken a great chance confessing to Cade all her underhanded behavior and self-interested motives. She had insisted that they had to be honest with each other, had to like each other, feel some sort of bond and respect, or their marriage would be a terrible failure.

And Cade had spent at least half an hour convincing er his feelings were far from detached. She hoped they were warm enough to make him want to kiss her for the rest of their lives. She'd wanted to tell him that but couldn't bring herself to put it into words. She wondered if proper ladies felt as she did.

"There's nothing in this letter I can't show Cade," Pilar said to her grandmother.

"You would betray your brother!"

"He says Cade hates him and he's afraid to come home. Everybody knows that. He wants to know what Cade's doing. Everybody knows that, too. He doesn't tell me anything. I don't know where he is, how or if my letter will reach him. You have to start thinking about Cade differently. I can't have you hating my husband."

"I forbid you to marry him," her grandmother said. "We need him only to get the hacienda back."

"And what will you do if he refuses to hand it over until we're married?"

"You will tell him to go. You will say—"

Pilar's laugh was involuntary. "You've watched Earl Wheeler claw his way out of poverty for the last thirty years, and you still don't understand him. Cade is like his grandfather in that he will not give up anything he takes. He could put us out on the road, and there'd be no one to stop him."

"Laveau—"

"Laveau isn't here. If he does come back, he won't stand a chance against Cade."

"Where is your loyalty?"

"I'm loyal, but I'm not stupid. Laveau could never stand up to Cade. Now I've got to answer Laveau's letter. When I finish, I'll show my answer to Cade he won't think I'm trying to hide anything."

"I never thought my granddaughter would turn against her own family."

"There's something you'd better learn soon. Nobody betrays Cade Wheeler and gets away with it. I haven't agreed to marry him yet, but if I do, I will be his wife. If you don't want that, you'd better speak to him now. Maybe you can work out a deal where we can pay him in cattle."

"I will give up no cattle. They are mine."

"We don't have a whole lot of choices. If Cade agrees to get our rancho back, he'll expect payment. If I agree to marry him, there will be no going back. For either of us."

✦

"I don't think you ought to take her with us," Owen said. "Women are no good in battle."

"Normally I would agree with you," Cade said, "but she's the only one who's ever been inside the hacienda. Even with the extra men, we're going to need every advantage we can find."

During the last week they had spent their days rounding up and branding cattle, and their evenings trying to come up with a plan of attack. Broc had found six men—four ex-Confederates, one cowhand, and one with a reputation as a gunman.

"We've got thirteen men," Broc said.

"And they've got twenty," Cade reminded him.

"Don't forget me and Jessie," Earl Wheeler said.

"Somebody's got to stay here to protect our rear."

'Let one of your fancy soldiers do it," Earl said. I damned well ain't staying here when you go after them scallywags. I been holding them off for two years. I mean to kill at least one of the bastards."

It had taken all of Cade's persuasive talents to convince his grandfather that Jessie couldn't hold the ranch alone, that defending the ranch was a crucial part of their plan. But even now, Cade wasn't sure his grandfather wouldn't follow.

Cade had given the job of infiltrating the squatters to the gunman. If he could believe Bolin Bigelow, it had been no problem to stop at the hacienda for one night. He'd been questioned closely at first, but after that, he'd been free to wander about, observing things without hindrance.

What Cade had learned hadn't surprised him, but it would devastate Pilar to know what was going on in her home.

"They have beef every night," Bigelow said. "They take only the choicest pieces and leave the rest to rot or give it to the dog."

Cade wasn't pleased to learn about the dog.

"Then they drink themselves into a stupor," Bolin continued.

Bolin had been able to scout only a few of the buildings surrounding the hacienda. "They lock themselves in at night," Bolin said. "They might as well be in a fort."

Broc and Nate had argued for a daylight attack. Owen and Ivan said that was foolish. Holt said he didn't see any way they could win. Rafe said they should consider dynamite. Cade said Pilar and Senora diViere would rather the hacienda remain in the squatters' control than be destroyed. The discussion had deteriorated into arguments about one undesirable plan as opposed to another until Pilar dropped her bombshell.

"There's a tunnel into the hacienda." Every eye in the room swung instantly in her direction. "I've never actually been in it, but Laveau has. It was built in case of a Comanche attack."

"Where does it come out?" Cade asked.

"I don't know."

"Where does it begin?"

"In the floor of one of the stables."

"Describe the stable," Cade said.

"I can't, but I'm sure I'll know it when I see it."

Cade depended little on such assurances. He'd heard them before from experienced men.

"We can't build a battle plan around something we may not be able to find and which may not still be in working order," Owen said.

"I can find it," Pilar said confidently.

"The squatters could have discovered it," Broc said. "They've had two years to root around the place."

"Even if they have, we still might be able to use it," Cade said.

They finally settled on a night attack. Armed with whiskey laced with a sleep-inducing herb concoction prepared by Senora diViere, Bolin Bigelow and two others would get inside the hacienda for the night. The rest of them would have to find the tunnel or depend on Pilar to lead them inside the quickest way.

So after giving Bolin and his companions several

hours to get inside the hacienda and generously share their "found" whiskey, Cade and the rest of the men set out for the rancho. Earl had said he planned to hide in the brush.

"You don't have to worry none," he said to his brother as he prepared to leave Jessie with Senora diViere. "Anybody finding himself with that woman on his hands will turn tail faster than a wild bronco with a lasso in his face."

Having Pilar involved in the attack made the men jittery on the ride to the rancho. Cade felt uncomfortable because she had to ride across his lap. She'd never been allowed to ride a horse, not even sidesaddle. According to her grandmother, a lady traveled in a closed carriage or she stayed where she was.

Cade couldn't ride so many miles with Pilar's soft bottom pushing against him without the expected result. Pilar's confusion didn't help. Owen's caustic remarks—he had to know what was happening—only made things worse.

"We can always depend on Cade's total attention," Owen was telling Pilar. "Once we set out on a raid, nothing can dent his concentration."

Pilar couldn't like being told that Cade was impervious to her presence even when she was sitting in his lap. But thoughts of the upcoming battle weren't nearly powerful enough to take Cade's mind off Pilar completely or the feel of her bottom as it ceaselessly rubbed against his groin. He couldn't banish memories of holding her in his arms, the feel of her breasts as they pressed against him, of her body as it rubbed against his hardness. More than once he had to stifle a groan when she shifted her weight and it nearly sent him over the edge. He was enormously relieved when the dark shape of the hacienda came into view.

Even at night its two stories looked imposing, reminding Cade of the huge difference between the Wheeler and diViere families. The house appeared to be a large block with no windows or balconies to break up the facade, but Cade knew the hacienda was wrapped around an inner courtyard. The lack of outside windows on the ground floor was meant to protect the place from assault.

Cade could sense Pilar's excitement at seeing her home for the first time in two years.

"Owen, you and Rafe search the grounds for any guards. Look out for the dogs. Bolin says they'll do anything for food, so be generous with that meat. Leave one man here."

Cade and Pilar approached the empty stables from the side away from the house.

"I've never been in this part of the stable," Pilar said.

"It's the safest way to get in. No one can see us from the house."

Texas ranchers kept their riding horses in a corral or let them run loose, but the diViere stables were large enough to house more than two dozen horses for coaches and pleasure riding. A second courtyard was surrounded by workshops and storerooms, the contents of which had been dragged out and strewn across the courtyard.

"I'm glad my father didn't live to see this," Pilar said. "It would have broken his heart."

"Concentrate on remembering where to find the

tunnel," Cade said. "With nearly a dozen men wandering about the place in the dark, someone is bound to stumble into trouble before long."

"I don't recognize any of these stalls," Pilar said. "But I know I will remember it."

But a second circuit of the courtyard didn't yield any better results.

"There must be more stables," Pilar said. "It's not here."

"Time is running out. If we don't attack soon, it'll be too late."

"I know there are more stables. We just have to find them."

"Let's look on the other side of the shops."

Cade's instincts proved accurate, but a man lay asleep in front of one stall, the one Pilar pointed her finger at and whispered, "There it is. That's the one."

"Wait here," Cade said. He had to reach the man before he awoke and sounded the alarm, but the stable yard was in near stygian darkness. He practically had to drag his feet to keep from stumbling over debris he couldn't see. Once, he barely caught himself before falling. Pilar bumped into him. "I told you to wait."

"I'm afraid of the dark."

He'd spent so many years fighting at night, he'd forgotten that not everyone liked the dark. "Stay still before you stumble over something."

"You're the one who stumbled."

From the loud snores, Cade guessed the man had passed out. "Wait here," he whispered, then crept forward. Rather than risk an outcry, he stuck the man over the head with his pistol butt, then tied him

up and gagged him. The man came to jus...
dragged him to a post and tied him securely. ...
being drunk, the squatter's dark eyes blazed with ...
and hatred.

"If you try to sound an alarm, I'll have to kill you,..."
Cade warned. He turned around, and his heart jumped
into his throat. He didn't see Pilar. A quick survey of
the courtyard told him it was empty.

"It's here. I found it under the straw." Her voice
reached him as she emerged from a darkened doorway.

"Can you stay here while I bring the others?" he
asked.

"Yes." She sounded petrified.

"You'll be safe as long as you keep out of sight." He
glanced toward the man tied to the post, then handed
her a gun. "If he tries to escape, hit him with this. I'll
be back in a moment."

Cade threaded his way through the stables and out
into the open very quickly, but he knew that every
second would seem like ten times that long to Pilar.
He found the men and returned to find Pilar standing over the prisoner, her mouth set, her face white
with fear.

"You should have shot him," Owen said.

"We want to catch the squatters by surprise, not
give them warning," Cade said.

"I'll cut his throat," Rafe offered.

"We're taking them into San Antonio to jail," Cade
said. "Now let's see if this tunnel is still open."

Nothing about the tunnel reassured Cade. The
ladder had rotted and collapsed. They would have
to drop to the tunnel floor. He didn't know how

r end. *If* they could get to the
the tunnel first, lighted the
en Rafe and Broc lowered
He felt a momentary surge
body slowly slid down his, but
moment her feet hit the floor and she
away from him. He picked up the lantern and
started forward as, one by one, the men dropped into
the tunnel behind him.

Cade had been born and raised in open spaces,
and he hated the narrow confines of the tunnel.
The roof was so low it brushed against his back;
the sides squeezed his shoulders; the passage twisted
away before him into endless blackness and toward
unknown dangers. At one point the passage became
so constricted he had to crawl on his hands and knees.
At times he could barely fit his shoulders through the
narrow passage. He wondered how Ivan would get
his huge Polish frame through without getting stuck.
A very unpleasant damp, musty smell filled the tunnel.
Cobwebs, dancing in front of him like a forest of
lacework curtains, caused him to sneeze repeatedly.

"How far do we have to go?" The narrow confines
of the tunnel muffled the voice beyond recognition.

"I don't know, but I would guess about two hundred feet."

Whatever the actual distance, it was the longest of
Cade's life. His shoulder muscles hurt from crawling
on his forearms, supporting himself with one hand
and holding the lantern with the other. By the time
he reached the point where the tunnel widened and
turned upward, Cade's muscles were so cramped,

he had difficulty standing. There was only roo.
himself and Pilar to stand up.

There was no ladder. "You'll have to stand on m
shoulders," Cade said to Pilar.

"I don't know how."

"I'll stoop down. Just walk up me like I was a
ladder. Once you can reach the top, ease the door up
and tell me what you see."

Pilar placed a foot on his knee, braced herself
against the walls, and climbed up on his shoulders.

"I'm going to fall," she said when he started to
stand up.

"Keep yourself braced against the wall."

"Hurry up," the voice that proved to be Owen's
said. "We're dying in here."

"Can you reach the top?" Cade asked.

"Yes, but I can't lift the door," Pilar said.

"Push harder."

A moment passed.

"It won't budge."

Cade didn't know why he'd never considered
that the door might be under a piece of furniture.
Or nailed shut. They would have to back out of this
tunnel or die.

"Keep trying," he said to Pilar.

"I'm not strong enough."

She had to be. Owen had crawled out of the tunnel
and managed to stand up beside Cade, their bodies so
close together they could hardly take a deep breath at
the same time.

"Put one foot on my shoulder," Owen said.

She did.

e're going to bend down until you can put your
ds straight over your head," Cade said. "When we
and up, push against the door. Whatever you do,
don't let your arms bend."

It wasn't enough.

"Can you reach my knife?" Cade asked Owen.

"Yes."

"Get it and pass it up to Pilar. Maybe it's just
wedged shut from disuse," he told Pilar. "Push the
knife in any place you can, then we'll try pushing you
against the door again."

"Okay," Pilar said.

They bent down once again, then gradually inched
up into a standing position. Cade could hear Pilar
straining to keep her arms from bending, to keep the
pressure on the door. He heard her grunt and give up.

"Use the knife in a different place," Cade said.

They tried again with the same results.

"We've got to do something else," Owen said.

"Like what?"

"Back down the tunnel."

"We've come too far to give up."

They tried twice more. Just as Cade was certain
the last attempt had failed, they heard an exclamation
from Pilar.

"It's open," she whispered.

"What can you see?" Cade asked.

"The eyes of a very big dog about six inches from
my nose."

Twenty

PILAR FROZE AS SHE LOOKED INTO THE EYES OF THE dog. Its sheer size intimidated her. The soft growl deep in its throat terrified her.

"Speak to it," Cade said.

"What do I say?" How did one talk to a dog that obviously objected to strangers trying to sneak into its domain in the middle of the night?

"You can say anything as long as it sounds friendly."

"Hello," she said, feeling utterly foolish. "My name is Pilar. I used to live here. Do you think you could move so I could get out of this tunnel?"

She could feel the two shoulders beneath her feet shake slightly. Cade and Owen were laughing at her. The dog rose to its feet and stuck its nose into the opening. Pilar's instinct was to draw back, but she forced herself to remain still.

"This really is my house," Pilar said. "If you're good, I'll let you stay. We've got lots of room in the stables."

The growl died away, and the dog pushed its head inside the opening until he could have licked Pilar's cheek—or bitten her face. He sniffed repeatedly.

"I don't want to hurt you," Pilar said. "It's just those men I don't like. I bet they kick you when they're drunk."

"Stick your head out and see if there's anybody in the room," Cade said.

That was easy for Cade to say. He wasn't facing a hundred-and-fifty-pound canine. "Please move back," she said to the dog. "I need to see who's in the room."

She fully expected the dog to start growling again when she raised the door, but he didn't move, just kept watching her with big black eyes.

"I can't see anyone," she said, "but it's very dark."

"Open the door all the way and look around."

The dog remained where he was, ears perked, tail moving slowly from side to side. She managed to lower the door without any sound. "There's nobody here."

"Climb up. We've got to get out of this tunnel."

Pilar managed to pull herself up into the room. The dog backed up, then came forward and sniffed her dress.

"Let him smell your hand," Cade said as his head appeared above the opening in the floor.

Pilar extended her hand. The dog sniffed it; then his long tongue snaked out and he licked it.

"Looks like you've made a friend," Cade said as he pulled himself up into the room. "Let's hope he likes the rest of us."

He didn't. He started to growl and pinned his ears flat against his head when Owen's head appeared through the floor.

"Pet him," Cade said to Pilar. "Make him feel safe."

"I'm so scared my teeth are chattering, and you

want me to make a dog that weighs more than I do feel safe?"

Pilar was relieved to hear the growls gradually diminish. That was especially important, since the room was filling up with men.

"Where are we?" Cade asked.

"I don't know," Pilar said. After living in Earl Wheeler's small house, she felt foolish saying that, but there were more than forty rooms in the hacienda, less than half of them used by the family.

"With no windows and only one door," Cade observed, "I'd say this is a storeroom. The dog probably hid in here to get away from the men."

"I'm never going into a tunnel again," Nate announced as he poked his head into the room. "It's not right for a respectable man to have to crawl on his hands and knees in a hole in the ground."

"Keep your voice down," Cade hissed. "Someone could be outside the door."

"Then why haven't you cut his liver out?"

"I'll check around first," Cade said. "Be back in a minute."

Pilar decided she'd never have made a Night Rider. Waiting in the dark, remaining still for fear of making a betraying sound, unable to talk, wondering what was happening to Cade, wondering where the enemy was, what they'd do once the attack started, was too much suspense for her. She nearly sagged with relief when she heard Broc say, "I hear somebody coming."

Owen shielded the lantern as Cade slipped into the room.

"I found Bigelow. He says the men are scattered all

over the house, mostly in the bedrooms. We'll get the ones in the open first. If worse comes to worst, we can always starve out anybody who locks himself in a room. Move out together, but be especially careful not to make any sound. Nobody is to do anything until I give the signal."

"What do we do?" one of the ex-soldiers asked.

"Knock them out so they can't sound an alarm. Then tie them up and gag them."

"What do I do?" Pilar asked.

"Stay here. Your job was to find the tunnel. The rest is up to us."

"But I want to—"

"You can't help," Cade said. "If anybody wakes up, you'll be a target. What could we do if one of them grabbed you and used you for a shield?"

"You'd have to shoot them both," Rafe said.

Pilar's blood ran cold. She wasn't certain Rafe was joking.

One by one the men left the room on silent feet. When the last one disappeared through the doorway, Pilar felt abandoned. Instinctively she reached for the dog, patting his head to reassure herself. "They'll soon have every one of those squatters rounded up," she said to the dog. "Then nobody will ever kick you again."

The dog wagged his tail. The soft *thump-thump-thump* against the wall comforted her. When he pushed his head against her and licked her hand, she felt altogether better.

But as the minutes passed and the silence continued unbroken, her nerves grew taut. What was happening?

Why didn't she hear some sounds? Even a grunt would have been welcome. No, she didn't want any sounds. As long as it remained perfectly quiet, it meant Cade and the others were safe.

Pilar strained to hear even the slightest sound. Her heartbeat sounded unnaturally loud. She had to know what was happening. She started toward the doorway, then threw herself against the wall when she heard a shot and a loud exclamation.

The hacienda exploded into pandemonium. Men shouting in at least three different languages were drowned out by gunfire. She heard running footsteps, banging doors, splintering wood. Her need to know if Cade was safe drove her back to the doorway. As she opened it, a man hurtled through, nearly knocking her down. He seemed almost as frightened of her as she was of him. They recognized each other in the same instant. Clarence Odum was the man who'd tried to kidnap her in San Antonio.

"This is my lucky day. I wonder what your brave cavalier will do when he sees I've got his little whore."

Pilar tried to move out of his reach, but he was fast. And strong. His hand clamped around her wrist so tightly it was painful. She fought against him, but he brutally twisted her wrist. "Be good, and I just might let you live."

Pilar wasn't about to let him use her as a shield so he could kill Cade. She screamed as loudly as she could. He clamped his hand over her mouth, but she bit him and screamed again. He hit her so hard she lost her balance. As she fell, out of the corner of her eye she caught sight of grayish fur, a hurtling form. She heard

a shout. She hit the floor and rolled over in time to
see the dog on top of Odum, tearing at the arm Odum
had flung up to protect his throat.

She got to her feet and ran from the room.

It took her a moment to remember she was in
an unfamiliar part of the hacienda. She followed the
diminishing sounds of conflict until she reached a
doorway that gave access to the courtyard. She emerged
into the open and came to a halt, her gaze wide and
unbelieving, her mouth dropping open with shock.

The courtyard had been destroyed, trees cut down,
statues knocked over and broken, the small pool
empty of fish and water, the fountain dry. The ground
had been stomped flat and strewn with the refuse of
two years. Nausea rose into Pilar's throat.

Suddenly Cade was before her, reaching for her,
enfolding her in his arms. "I thought I heard you scream."

She didn't want to lift her head from his chest, to
pull her arms from around his waist. She wanted to
stay in the protective circle of his arms forever, but the
sounds of fighting still echoed around her.

"That man who tried to kidnap me in San Antonio
is in the storeroom. The dog attacked him."

Cade released her, drew his gun. "Stay here until I
get back."

Pilar couldn't move. Coming face-to-face with the
destruction of the home she'd dreamed of for two
years had drained all her energy.

The dog emerged from inside the room, looked
around, then came to her. He whined and thrust
his muzzle into her hand. She looked down, saw
the blood on her hand. She jerked her hand away,

looked for a wound on the dog before she realized he was unhurt.

This was Odum's blood.

"That's one squatter who won't kidnap any more women," Cade said when he rejoined Pilar. "That dog nearly tore his arm off. I'd better get Holt to look at him before he bleeds to death." He looked down at the dog still nuzzling Pilar's hand. "I don't know what that man did to that dog, but he paid for it tonight."

Silence had fallen over the hacienda. Small groups of men, their arms tightly bound behind them, some bleeding from wounds, appeared in the courtyard.

"It looks like the boys have everything under control," Cade said.

"What happened?" Pilar asked. "Everything was so quiet until I heard a shot."

"Ivan stumbled into a man leaning against a post. He shot him rather than using his knife. He said Poles never use a knife."

"Did anybody get hurt?"

"I don't know. We'll lock all the men in the stables for the night. Come with me."

"I want to stay here."

"I'm not letting you out of my sight until I'm certain there's nobody hiding in a cupboard or under a bed."

"The dog will protect me."

Cade turned his gaze to what had been the courtyard. "I don't want you to be alone when you see the rest of the house."

❧

Pilar watched the moon rise over the silhouette of the hacienda. The building looked huge and solid in the moonlight, dependable and permanent. She could remember as a little girl coming home from a visit, knowing her journey was at an end when the huge block of the house came into view. The house had represented rest, security, permanence, home.

"You've got to eat something," Cade said.

"I'm not hungry."

The men had butchered a steer and were roasting the meat over fires of mesquite wood. Not even that beguiling aroma tempted Pilar's appetite. She had the hacienda back again, but the home she had known was destroyed. The joyous return she'd looked forward to for years had turned into a wake.

"The men were hoping you would join them in their celebration. It isn't often we capture a virtually impregnable citadel without a casualty."

"Please tell them I'm sorry, but I'm not in the mood for celebrating."

"You knew things would be bad."

"I realize now it was stupid, but I imagined I would return to the home I left. This might as well be a place I've never seen." The dog nuzzled against her; she petted him in a purely reflex action. "I didn't realize they would destroy everything for the pleasure of it."

Pilar was glad Cade had insisted that she wait until he could go through the house with her. The story was the same in room after room. Destruction stared her in the face from every corner. The squatters hadn't been content to squander the food and wine. It was almost as though they knew they would only be able to hold the hacienda for a short time and were determined there wouldn't be anything for Pilar and her family to come back to.

"My grandmother will never survive this," she had told Cade. "The king of Spain gave this grant to her great-grandfather. Her grandfather built the first part of the hacienda and her father finished it. This rancho was her dowry. She loved it. Seeing what they have done will kill her."

Paintings had been slashed. Furniture had been gashed and broken. The floors were littered with the shards of broken china, ornaments, lamp globes. Carpets had been ripped or despoiled. Much to her surprise, the bedrooms had fared better. The mattresses and linens were ruined and would have to be burned, but the furnishings showed only minor abuse.

Laveau's clothes had disappeared. At least half of her grandmother's gowns had been ripped to shreds, but her own clothes had been left alone. She wondered if Odum had been hoping to capture her, or some other unfortunate woman who might wear them.

"I don't mean to sound ungrateful for what you did," she said to Cade. "It's just that—"

"You don't have to be grateful. I'm doing it as much for me as for you."

She didn't know why she didn't like hearing that. There was no pretense of love between them. Her only requirement was that they like each other. She wondered why she'd been ready to marry Manuel with no guarantees at all.

"The rancho is more than cows or land to me," she said. She moved away from him, walked toward a grove of pecan trees that grew along a dry wash. "It's the only home I've ever known."

He came toward her, took her hands in his. "I know it's a shock, but we can rebuild. The house is still here. It's functional."

"It was the needless destruction of something I loved, something that was beautiful."

"But it wasn't superficial beauty. It was beauty of character, of usefulness. This hacienda was a source of comfort and pleasure."

"I never thought of it like that."

"It has strength of character, just like you."

"I don't."

"You had to have it to admit you pretended to like me to get information about Laveau, to demand that we like each other before you would marry me, even though you couldn't get your ranch back without me."

"I don't want you to think I agreed to marry you for purely mercenary reasons."

"I don't. You wanted freedom, to be respected as a person. In return, you were willing to give me the comfort and pleasure of your body."

Pilar felt a muscle in the back of her neck jerk, her stomach do a quick somersault. She hadn't guessed that even under these circumstances their being together could give rise to a physical response in Cade. She recognized his look—the need, the naked hunger. For the first time, she realized this wasn't just sexual need or hunger. It was the need and hunger of a man who felt just as alone as she did, a man who felt people valued him only for what he could do for them, not for who he was.

She'd never seen him let his barriers down. He'd always been the one everyone else turned to. She'd never thought of how lonely that must be, always holding himself to a higher standard, never relaxing, never allowing himself the luxury of making a mistake. Never letting anyone see his doubt or uncertainty.

"Do you need the comfort and pleasure of my body? I know you want it," she said when he didn't respond, "but do you need it?"

It was an important distinction to her. She watched him struggle with himself. She wondered why it was so difficult for him to admit he needed her.

"Wheelers never admit that they need anyone."

"Neither did the diVicres, and look where it landed us. Maybe my grandmother should have married your grandfather."

Whatever else she'd meant to say was lost in Cade's crack of laughter. "They'd have killed each other."

"But my grandmother would never have left your grandfather. And your grandfather would never have lost the land. We wouldn't have been enemies."

"We couldn't be husband and wife."

"Am I that important to you? Do you need me even a little bit?"

"Yes."

"Why?" Nobody had never needed her.

"Ask me about ranching or fighting, and I know exactly what to say, but I'm not good at putting feelings into words," Cade said. "I never met a woman who affected me the way you do."

"What way is that?"

"Like I said, I can't put it into words." He pulled her into an embrace. "Surely you know I like kissing you."

Yes, she knew that. She wanted more, needed it, and Cade obliged. His mouth took hers in a hard, hungry kiss. Pilar wanted to be needed, too. And Cade's very solid presence answered that need in a way Manuel never could have.

But there was something different about tonight. She seemed to need him more than ever. Not his verbal assurances but his physical presence, his touch, his body's demonstration that she had a profound effect on him. In San Antonio the sensitivity of her breasts and the awareness of his swollen sex had made her uneasy. Tonight she wanted to press herself against him until she felt absorbed. A kind of tension, a kind of mystic understanding, began to hum between their two bodies, and they fed off each other.

Pilar didn't feel uneasy when Cade's hand slipped between their bodies and cupped her breast or when he ground his hardened body against her abdomen. She felt thrilled she was able to affect this strong man so dramatically, thrilled to have his need of her so palpably demonstrated.

What she hadn't anticipated, hadn't even suspected, was her need of him.

She had long since cataloged and memorized the list of reasons why she should marry Cade, why she *wanted* to marry him. Nowhere on her list did she find physical need, but she quickly realized that her need to be close to him was more than a need for physical safety. This was visceral, something so deeply imbedded in her that she didn't need to understand. Her body knew all that was necessary.

She heard herself moan softly when Cade's lips deserted her mouth to trail along her jaw and down the side of her neck to her shoulders. She moaned again when he delved inside her dress and she felt his callused fingers against the tender skin of her breast. Shivers of excitement chased each other up and down her spine. Nerve endings tingled. When Cade bent down and kissed the top of her breast, she thought she would simply melt and die.

When he lifted her breast free of her gown and took her nipple into his mouth, she was sure of it.

She tried to speak. She moved her lips, but the words wouldn't come. The effect was so incredibly powerful, she was hardly aware of his other hand as it moved down her side and over her bottom to press her hard against him. She flung her arms around his neck, clung to him, abandoned herself to needs she never knew she had. She kissed his neck, the top of his head, in a feverish attempt to reciprocate the intense pleasure he was giving her.

Cade raised her skirt and placed his hand on the naked flesh of her thigh. She responded with a gasp of surprise cut off by the convulsion that shook her body. Her legs went so weak she groped for support until she felt herself leaning against the rough bark of a pecan tree.

"Open for me," he said.

She didn't know what he meant until she felt his hand move between her legs. They immediately clamped together like a vise.

"Relax. I won't hurt you."

She hadn't thought he would. Her reaction had been involuntary. She had moved beyond her experience when he suckled her breast. This was beyond her imagination.

But not beyond her body's knowledge. Without her consciously doing anything, her muscles gradually relaxed and she felt herself move against a hand held flat against the most private part of her body. The need was great, the move instinctive. She didn't draw back even when he parted her flesh and she felt his finger enter her. The need grew stronger, her body's reaction more deliberate. Her body began to undulate in a slow, steady rhythm, driving Cade deeper inside, pulling away, then pushing against him once again.

She didn't understand it, couldn't control it. It was as though some primeval ritual buried deep in her subconscious had suddenly surfaced. She didn't know what she was doing, but she knew she couldn't stop. New feelings, new sensations radiated out from deep inside, making her feel weak yet giving her added strength to drive toward a goal she sensed rather than understood.

Her body moved against his hand in a steady rhythm that grew more rapid as the sensations engulfing her grew more powerful. Moan after soft moan escaped from her. She clung to Cade for support, certain she would collapse if she didn't.

She felt desperate to satisfy the need that saturated her body like an all-encompassing ache. Nothing else was important. She threw herself against Cade, calling his name, begging that he do something—she didn't know what—to release her from this delicious agony. But the more she wanted release, the tighter his bands wrapped around her.

Then when she thought she could stand no more, when she was certain she would release a cry that would reverberate through the night, her body twisting and jerking like a flag in the wind, she reached the peak of pleasure and tumbled over it into ecstasy. She fell back against the tree, completely limp.

Now she knew how she needed Cade. But the question still remained.

Did he need her?

❧

The trip back to the Wheeler ranch passed in a blur. Cade sent Bigelow and the other hired men to take the squatters to San Antonio. Nate, Rafe, and Ivan accompanied them to the outskirts of town, but Cade ordered them to stay well away in case Major Kramer was still there. Owen and Broc rode in front, entertaining each other with tales of other battles they'd fought. Holt, seemingly occupied with thoughts of his own, rode behind in contemplative silence. Cade had spent the first part of the trip helping Pilar accustom herself to riding sidesaddle. He continued giving her instructions, which she answered with a nod of her head. She couldn't stop thinking about the night before. She didn't know what had come over her.

She had wanted to see if they could get along, but she hadn't meant things to go that far.

"You've got to relax more in the saddle," Cade said. "You'll have blisters if you don't."

"I probably have them already."

She didn't mean to sound petulant. She was overwhelmed. And confused. And embarrassed. She was certain the men knew that something had happened between her and Cade. Owen's gaze told her he had no doubt what it was. Just knowing that made her feel hot all over.

Cade was in great spirits, planning what to do with the new land and herds. She couldn't tell whether his good mood was the result of a successful battle, the prospect of new wealth, or the evening spent with her. Since his attitude toward her seemed the same as ever, she doubted it was the latter.

He'd been kind and attentive, but never in a lovesick sort of way. She wouldn't have thought she wanted that, but she did want some outward sign that last night had meant something other than a release of physical tension. Then she remembered he hadn't achieved any release, that his attentions had all been for her, and she started feeling guilty for suspecting his motives. She was fortunate he wasn't as crabby as a bear. Her grandmother said men turned mean when their physical needs weren't met.

"I expected to see Gramps hiding in the bushes, waiting to see if we'd been wiped out," Cade said.

"He was sure you'd win," Pilar said. "I heard him tell Jessie there weren't enough scallywags in the whole state of Texas to beat you."

Cade chuckled. "I wish he'd say something like that to me."

"He's proud of you but too stubborn to admit it."

She knew he was pleased, and that made her feel

good. She liked doing things that pleased him, like last night. But it wasn't just for Cade. She liked it for herself.

Her grandmother had hinted at the nature of the physical requirements of being a wife and mother but always in the context of pain, forbearance, and the shameful lot of women. She'd said nothing about sheer ecstasy or the very strong desire to do it all over again.

Pilar wondered if she ought to be ashamed of her feelings. She wasn't, and she hoped Cade would take her back to the grove by the creek. She knew her grandmother would disapprove, but she was practically obligated to marry him now. And she did want to marry him. Unless she was badly mistaken, she was falling in love with him.

Earl Wheeler materialized out of a thicket of cat-claw and mesquite close to the ranch house. "Where's the rest of your band of thieves? Don't tell me you let them get killed."

Pilar thought she saw Cade flinch.

"They're taking the squatters to jail," Cade said. "They'll be back tomorrow."

"Then we're going to have a real celebration," Owen said, "so bring out all that whiskey you've been hiding."

"I'm not hiding no whiskey," Earl said. "If I was, I'd be drinking it myself."

"Don't worry. The boys are bringing some from town."

Earl fell in next to Owen, started drilling him on what had happened in the fight. Pilar could tell that Cade was hurt his grandfather didn't ask him.

She didn't understand how the old man could be so stupid. You'd think he'd know what was important to his grandson.

But it was too late to change Earl Wheeler. Pilar didn't know what forces had formed his character, but they'd been so harsh, he was incapable of showing the affection she was certain he felt for his grandson.

And that made her want to love Cade all the more. No one was more lonely than a man who thought he wasn't supposed to need anybody. She knew he needed her. He didn't know it yet, but she was sure he'd figure it out.

"How much do you want to tell your grandmother?" Cade asked. "How soon will she want to return to the hacienda?"

Pilar knew the answer without thinking. "Immediately." Pilar wanted to return immediately, too. And all of her dreams of returning home included Cade.

"That place isn't fit for occupation. Besides, two women can't live there by themselves."

Pilar couldn't suppress a smile. Cade wanted to go with her. He had to know that putting up with her grandmother was going to be horrible. Once she saw what had happened to the hacienda, she'd be so furious she'd lash out at everyone around her.

"I'd try to warn her gradually, but she'd know something was wrong. When do you think we'll go back?"

"Not for a few days at least."

They had ridden into the ranch yard. Much to her surprise, her grandmother came out on the porch and motioned impatiently for her to come to the house. Her grandmother was no more likely than Earl Wheeler to show emotion. Pilar waited for Cade to help her out of the saddle, but it was Owen who lifted her to the ground, a brittle smile on his face as he let her slide down his body.

Pilar was too startled to protest. Then her legs gave out from under her. By this time Cade had reached her side.

"I'd appreciate it if you'd unsaddle our horses," he said to Owen.

"Come on, boys," Earl said. "Jessie'll want to hear what happened."

Owen spun on his heel. "Good. I'll make sure I improve my part this time."

"Remind me never to ride a horse again," Pilar told Cade as she stumbled toward the porch. "My legs feel as if the bones have melted."

"You should ride some each day," Cade said.

"I'll be happy to ride if you'll take over the cooking."

"We'll see what we can work out."

Pilar was much too concerned with making her legs work to reply.

"Here, let me," Cade said. He picked her up, carried her up the steps, and set her down on the porch. Her legs felt shakier than before.

"Come inside," her grandmother said, then turned and went inside the house.

"Don't you want to know what happened?" Pilar asked.

"I have something more important to tell you."

"What could be more important than that?"

"Come inside, and I will tell you. You," she said, looking at Cade, "help your grandfather unsaddle his horse." She pushed Pilar inside the house and closed the door on Cade.

"Grandmother, that was rude. What could be so terribly important—"

"I got another letter from Laveau. He says he cannot come home because Cade and his friends are waiting to hang him."

Twenty-one

Pilar's hands shook so badly she could barely read the letter. Cade and his friends blamed Laveau for the betrayal, and they intended to hang him when he came home. Cade had lied to her.

"And you insisted upon showing him Laveau's letter and telling him what you wrote," her grandmother said bitterly.

"How could I have guessed?" The guilt nearly choked Pilar. She could have been responsible for her brother's death! "What are we going to do?"

"We will leave this evil house. As soon as I shake the dust of this place from my shoes, I will lay a curse on it that will last a hundred generations."

Pilar had no room in her thoughts for curses. She could only marvel that despite what she had learned, she still had feelings for Cade. Surely that was impossible. She had to be delirious. Mad.

"I packed your clothes as soon as I read the letter," her grandmother said. "We will go straight to the rancho."

"We can't," Pilar said, wrenched out of her thoughts. "It's—"

"Do you think I could spend another night under this roof?"

"There's no food, no one to prevent more squatters from coming in and forcing us out again."

"We will hire people."

"We don't have any money."

"Are you saying you want to stay in this house?"

"No, but I've seen what they did to the rancho. We can't return yet."

Her grandmother turned fearful. "What have they done to my house?"

Pilar had intended to postpone describing the horrific destruction she'd seen, but she decided now was the best time. By the time she'd finished, the old woman had lost so much color, looked so defeated Pilar wished she'd waited.

"They have destroyed my life," her grandmother said.

"They destroyed things. They didn't destroy us or our spirit," Pilar said. "We can start again. We can—"

"They have destroyed the irreplaceable," her grandmother said. "*Madre de Dios!* Why does God not strike these people dead?"

Pilar had wondered the same thing. Thinking what those men had done to her family made her hope they would be hanged. But the squatters had never pretended to be anything but what they were. Cade was the villain. He'd lied to her over and over again even after she'd confessed her own initial dishonesty. He'd taken advantage of her weakness to make her long for the physical pleasures he could give her. She would never have let him touch her if she'd known he was just waiting to hang Laveau.

She grabbed up the letter from where it had fallen to the floor. "I'll show him this letter," she said, her resolution formed. "I'll confront him with all his lies."

"No," her grandmother said. "You must not."

"Why? You just said you wanted to leave this house immediately."

"I let my emotions make me speak before I thought. You must keep pretending to like him."

"I can't do that!" Pilar protested, aghast.

Her grandmother took her by the shoulders and shook her. "You must. Laveau cannot come home for maybe a long time. We cannot leave the rancho unoccupied. We cannot live there alone."

"I'll find a way to hire some hands. I'll ask Broc. He found the ex-soldiers for Cade. He can—"

"We will let Cade and his friends restore us to our hacienda. Let them catch and brand our cows. Let him take them to market so we will have money. *Then* we throw him out and hire men to work for us. You will marry Manuel, and he will protect us until Laveau's army can bring him home."

"How can you ask me to pretend to like a man who has lied to me?"

"I ask because it is the only way we get our home back, the only way we leave this cursed place. Just pretend a little bit. He will be here and we will be at the hacienda. You will hardly see him."

"He'll be on our rancho, working with our cows."

"We do not keep cows in the hacienda," her grandmother said. "Nor is it my custom to invite hired hands inside."

Pilar doubted that Cade would think of himself as a

hired hand, nor did her grandmother understand that Pilar wasn't sure she could keep Cade at a distance. But she had to try. If she didn't, she might start liking him all over again.

❧

"What's wrong?" Cade asked Pilar. "You've been avoiding me all evening."

"I've been busy," she said without looking at him. "There's a lot to do after being gone."

"You're still upset about what the squatters did to the hacienda, aren't you?"

She looked up. "I thought my grandmother was going to be ill."

"It can be fixed. It will take time and money, but—"

"What you did... I mean, what the squatters did can never be fixed. I've been...*my grandmother and I* have been violated. Some things are irreplaceable. Once broken, they can never be mended."

She turned back to the work of clearing away after supper, but Cade had the definite impression she was not talking about the hacienda. Her whole attitude toward him had changed. She practically cringed when he touched her.

"There are so many cattle on that ranch, you can afford to strip the place bare and start all over again," Holt said.

"My grandmother doesn't want to start over again. She wants things to be like they were before the war."

"Nothing's like it was before the war," Holt said.

"Wait until your brother gets home," Ivan said. "I'm sure it'll soon be like old times."

"I don't know if Laveau will come home," Pilar said. She busied herself with scrubbing out the stubborn remains of baked beans from a pot. "He used to talk of starting a ranch in California." She looked up, tried to empty her face of any expression. "I wouldn't be surprised if he's out there already."

Cade reached out, gripped Ivan's shoulder to prevent an imprudent answer. "I'm sure he wouldn't go without seeing his family first. Besides, I doubt he has the money to buy a ranch."

"He's got—" Ivan began.

"He wouldn't leave without making sure you and your grandmother were safe," Cade cut in.

"We can take care of ourselves," Pilar said, again avoiding his gaze. "In fact, we want to return to the hacienda tomorrow."

"The place is nearly destroyed," Holt pointed out.

"You have no food," Cade reminded her.

"I'm sure you won't begrudge us some of your supplies. We don't need much."

"You can't live there unprotected," Cade said.

"You and your friends will be there rounding up cattle."

"We could be miles from the hacienda."

"I'm sure no one will bother us. Besides, I planned to ask Owen if he would stay at the hacienda at night."

"Did I hear my name mentioned?" Owen asked, breaking off an argument he'd been having with Earl and Jessie Wheeler over some tales about mutual relatives.

"I was telling Cade my grandmother and I want to move back to the hacienda tomorrow."

"Good riddance," Earl said. "I can't wait to get shut of that old woman."

"You can't go without someone to protect you," Owen said.

"Hell, people need protection *from* that woman," Earl Wheeler said.

"Will you stay at the hacienda with us?" Pilar asked Owen. "Now that Cade has all those other men, he won't need you."

Holt laughed. "How does it feel to be replaced so easily?" he asked Owen.

"I didn't mean that," Pilar said, embarrassed. "I meant—"

"I'll be delighted to move to your hacienda," Owen said, looking at Cade rather than Pilar. "I'll stay *very* close so no one will harm you."

"You won't have to do that," Cade said. "We're all moving to the hacienda."

Cade was surprised at his own words. He'd been planning to use the Wheeler ranch as a base, but it was more sensible to use the diViere rancho instead. It was bigger and had more room for the extra men. They would be closer to their work, and they could protect the land better.

"I'm sure I can provide enough protection," Owen said.

"I don't want you to move to the hacienda, Cade," Pilar said. "This is your home. I wouldn't ask you to leave."

"I won't be leaving my old home as much as going

to my new one," Cade said, trying to understand what had gotten into Pilar. It had to be something her grandmother had said since their return. He could almost believe she knew he wanted to hang her brother. But she couldn't. If she did, he was certain the old woman would have attacked him with the kitchen knife by now.

"I'm not moving to that damn place," Earl said.

"Good," Cade said. "It won't do to leave this place unattended."

"Since you can cook, you'd better stay with him," Pilar said. "He'll starve otherwise."

"I survived two years before you got here," Earl said.

"Only because you're too mean to die."

The only things normal about this evening were Earl and Pilar taking verbal shots at each other, and Owen trying to insinuate himself into Pilar's good graces.

Cade didn't bother denying the tide of jealousy that rose up in him like bile, but he didn't understand the reason for it. He knew women liked Owen's handsome face and sweet talk, but Pilar had practically agreed to marry him. They got along, and each would give the other what they needed. And he knew from Pilar's response to him the previous evening that her nature was as passionate as his own.

They were perfect for each other.

But something was wrong.

What he felt for Pilar was more than liking, more than lust, more than satisfaction at acquiring an exceptional bride. He was very fond of her, and it was important to him that she return his feeling. Last night he'd felt she did. Tonight he didn't feel any warmth at all.

Never trust feelings. Even people you love can turn against you.

What better example could he want than his own mother? No, feelings weren't dependable. People put their loyalties where it was to their advantage.

But loyalty wasn't enough. He and his grandfather were loyal to each other, but there wasn't enough warmth in that relationship. Something inside him cried out for the kind of deep, unshakable loyalty—should he call it love?—he'd seen in some of the married couples who'd given his troop shelter during the war. It was obvious their feelings went beyond being able to get along together. Some women looked at their husbands with something akin to worship in their eyes.

He wanted that for himself.

He'd seen the way those men looked at their wives. Women of mature years and full bodies, women who'd lost the bloom of youth long ago. Women worn down by years of bearing too many children and working too hard. Yet when those men looked at their wives, they saw and valued the beauty of what was within, not the shell visible to the world. Those men could face the future knowing that neither age nor familiarity could wither the affection in their hearts or diminish the warmth of companionship.

Cade wanted that for himself, too.

He wasn't sure he believed in love—he was certain he couldn't trust it if he did—but he wanted devotion. He was tired of the cold emptiness inside. Pilar had given him a hint of what it could be like if two people really cared for each other. Having gotten a taste, he wanted more.

"Why don't we go for a walk?" Cade asked Pilar.

"I haven't finished," Pilar said.

"Owen's dying to be helpful. Let him finish up."

"I didn't come here to wash dishes," Owen said.

"There aren't many," Holt said. "Let them go." He winked at Pilar. "A woman needs to talk about moving to a new house."

"Don't see any need myself," Earl said. "You just load all their junk in the wagon and cart it over there."

"Your grandfather's right," Pilar said.

Earl looked at Pilar as though she'd turned into a rattler, coiled and ready to strike. "That gal has something up her sleeve," he said. "She's never agreed with me in her life."

"Even you can be right once," Pilar said.

"Don't trust her," Earl said. "She's acting like her grandma now."

"I really do need to talk to you," Cade said to Pilar.

She hesitated before nodding agreement, then walked out of the room and the house without waiting for him. Something was definitely wrong.

She turned to face him in the middle of the ranch yard. "What do you want to talk about?"

"I wanted to discuss your moving back to the hacienda, but first I'd like to know what happened to you between the time we got back here and when I came in for supper."

She looked defiant. "I don't know what you mean."

"You're mad about something. What did your grandmother say?"

"Don't blame everything on my grandmother."

"I wouldn't except you went into her room one person and came out another. As your future husband, I think I have a right to know what she said."

Pilar broke eye contact, then turned back toward the house. "We discussed this proposed marriage between us," she said, still avoiding looking at him. "And the fact that you want half of the ranch as my dowry."

"Plus the hacienda."

"Grandmother thinks that's too much."

"Okay. What do you think is a reasonable dowry? Keep in mind that I'll be doing the work for the whole ranch until Laveau comes home."

Her head jerked up and she spun to him. Not even the darkness could hide the anger in her face. She turned and took a few steps away from him. "It doesn't matter." She stopped and pivoted to face him again. "I've decided we will never get along. I can't marry you."

Cade was stunned. He hadn't anticipated anything like this, especially after last night. She was going back on their deal after he'd done his part. She had turned out to be less honorable than he'd thought.

What he didn't want her to see—what he wanted to deny to himself—was his hurt and panic. He wasn't sure he could explain the hurt. He didn't love Pilar, but he sure did like her a lot. Maybe it was his pride at being turned down. Maybe he was hurt because he liked her and she didn't like him.

Unfortunately, he knew exactly why he felt panicked. Something very special had started to develop between them, something he'd realized he wanted desperately. He knew that if he let it go now, he'd never get it back again.

"What caused you to change your mind? You gave a very different impression last night."

"I should apologize for—"

"I don't want your apology. I want to know why you changed your mind."

"I thought I could marry you, but it would never work," she said, facing him squarely this time. "There's too much animosity between our families. You only have to listen to your grandfather—"

"What you mean to say is you got what you wanted, and now you're trying to back out of the deal. Is that an example of the honesty and trust you were talking about a few nights ago?"

Once again he saw hot anger flash in her eyes like javelins of fire, but she quickly hooded her eyes. He didn't know what had happened, but he knew she wasn't telling the truth. Her grandmother had told her something that made her furious. What he didn't understand was why she thought she had to keep it to herself.

"My grandmother and I have decided to offer you a new agreement. If you'll round up and brand all our cows, we'll give you a portion of any money you get for those you manage to take to market."

"And if I don't get any to market?"

"You will. Nobody can stop you. You're too smart."

"If I'm so smart and unstoppable, why don't you want to marry me? I sound like exactly the kind of husband you would want."

"I don't want to talk about it anymore."

"I do."

"It won't change anything. Grandmother and I will—"

"We can talk about this after we get settled at the hacienda."

"I don't want you at the hacienda. I don't see any reason—"

"Understand this. I go to the hacienda or I don't touch one cow on your place. I don't protect you from more squatters and I don't protect your herds from Cortina. But I'm not going to let you decide. You'd probably try to hire your own men without realizing that any men you hired would be in an even better position to take advantage of you than the squatters."

"I'm not stupid. I wouldn't—"

"You're not experienced. I am. I'll round up and brand your cattle. And I'll take as many to market next spring as I can. In the meantime, I mean to find out what has caused you to change your mind. You're lying about something."

"You don't want me to lie to you, but you can lie to me and expect me never to question a word you say."

"What are you talking about? When have I lied?"

He nearly stumbled over the last words. He had lied to her every time he talked about Laveau, and he had to keep on lying.

He'd taken an oath.

The anger that flared in her eyes this time didn't fade. She turned away and started back to the house. "It doesn't matter. All that matters is I will never be your wife."

Cade had never liked Senora diViere, but he felt sorry for her as she gazed at the destruction of what had once been her home.

"Wait until we can clear a room for you," Cade said.

The old woman ignored him. She walked through the barren space that had once been her courtyard with the same dazed look he'd seen on some of the young soldiers after their first battle.

"Do you want me to ask Holt to see to her?" he asked Pilar.

"Leave her alone," she said fiercely. "Can't you see she's suffering?"

"That's why I want Holt to check on her."

"Just leave us alone."

"Maybe I will when you tell me what's eating you. Now I've got to speak to Holt."

But even as Cade explained his worries about Senora diViere, he couldn't stop thinking about Pilar. Her attitude toward him was worse than ever. He'd thought at first that she'd been angry because he'd insisted they wait until the men returned from San Antonio. But she'd been spitting angry all day, getting madder the closer they came to the hacienda. She'd stopped trying to talk him into going back long before they reached halfway.

"Where do you want us to bed down tonight?" Rafe asked.

"Anywhere inside the hacienda," Cade said. "Owen's worked out a schedule for guard duty. I don't think anyone will attack the house, but we can't be sure."

"The horses?"

"Hobble them so they'll stay close. Put the mares in the stables."

Cade spent the next half hour arranging the defense of the hacienda. After that, he talked with Rafe about the roundup. Rafe never said much, but Cade had learned almost from the beginning that Rafe knew as much about ranching as he did. The other men had thrown themselves into the work of clearing rubbish from the rooms. They pitched stuff into the courtyard from both floors.

"Where is Pilar?" he asked Holt, who appeared to be in charge of the cleanup.

"Somewhere in the house," he said. "Ivan offered to make sure all the rooms are safe."

Cade tended to forget that Ivan had been trained as an engineer by the Polish army.

"There's nothing wrong with this house," Holt said.

"I think Ivan just wanted to reassure Senora diViere. She's not taking this very well."

"I heard Pilar say she wanted her grandmother to lie down," Holt said.

Cade remembered the room Pilar said had belonged to her grandmother. It had been spared much damage, but he hoped Owen had thought to remove the clothes that had been cut up and strewn over the floor. That might be too much for the old woman.

He found Pilar coaxing her grandmother to lie down on a bed that had been covered with blankets brought from the Wheeler ranch. The dog lay in the corner, watching everything Pilar did.

"Is your grandmother okay?" Cade asked.

"No, she's not, but she will be better once she gets some rest. Ask the men to be quiet."

"They have to clear places to sleep."

"Why can't they sleep outside? You said you did it all the time during the war."

"It doesn't make sense to have all these beds and not use them."

She looked angry, but apparently realized his words were reasonable.

"Have they cleared your room?" he asked.

"Yes. I've got them working on Laveau's bedroom now. I'll use it for a sitting room so Grandmother won't have to go downstairs."

"You can't use that room."

"Why not?"

"Because I'm going to use it for my bedroom."

"But it's next to mine."

"I know."

Twenty-two

PILAR WAS SO ANGRY SHE COULD BARELY CONTROL herself. While she made her grandmother as comfortable as possible, she planned her argument. The idea of Cade occupying Laveau's room was an insult she could not bear.

When she went looking for Cade, she found him in Laveau's room. The spacious chamber had traditionally been the bedroom of the head of the family. It was twice the size of any other bedroom except the one she occupied, the traditional bedroom of the don's wife. A door connected the two rooms.

"You can't stay in this room," she said the moment she stepped inside.

"It isn't that bad."

"This is Laveau's room. I don't see how you can sleep here with a clear conscience."

"I promise not to dirty his mattress." He frowned. "I'll probably buy him a new one."

"That's not what I meant."

"Then what do you mean?" Cade said, turning on her with a suddenness that caused her to catch her breath. "You've been fuming about something for the last few days. It's time you got it out of your system."

"How dare you say something like that when…" She choked off the words, remembering her promise to her grandmother.

"When what?" Cade demanded. He grabbed her by the shoulder when she tried to turn away. "You're not leaving. You're almost angry enough to tell me what's bothering you."

"That's not it. It's just that—"

"Don't lie to me."

Her face went white. "I can't believe that you, of all people, would say that to me. You've lied to me from the start. Even after I bared my soul, you kept right on lying."

"What are you talking about?"

"You know."

"No, I don't."

"Liar."

He shook her so violently she almost bit her tongue. "Tell me what you're talking about!"

She tried to hold back by thinking of the money they needed to survive, the independence it would give them, but she failed. His betrayal loomed larger than money or independence. She had been on the point of giving him her heart, doing what her grandmother said no properly reared lady would ever do—falling in love. She'd betrayed her class, her heritage, her family, and all for a man who had no more integrity than the squatters he'd driven out.

"I'm talking about your blaming Laveau for the people dying in your troop. I'm talking about your using me to find out when he's coming home so you can hang him."

Cade seemed to freeze. All the passion went out of him. "You got another letter from him."

"Yes."

"Tell me what he said."

She began reading the letter to him, but before she reached the last sentences, he cut her off with anger such as she'd never seen flaming in his eyes. "Laveau diViere betrayed the troop he had ridden with for three years. He led a Union Army detachment to the farm where we were sleeping. We were surrounded. Twenty-four men were shot down like ducks on a pond. Eleven of us swore an oath on the sword of Nate's dead brother that we wouldn't rest until he was brought to justice, but only seven survived the war."

"I don't believe you. Laveau would never do anything like that."

The words were hardly out of her mouth when his fingers closed around her wrist in a painfully tight grip and he practically dragged her from the room. He headed out and down the stairs so fast she had to run to keep up. "Owen!" he shouted. "Get the boys together. Pilar has something to say to them."

"I don't want to talk to your friends," she said, trying to pull back, but her strength was as nothing against Cade's.

"Maybe not, but they have something to say to you."

She stopped fighting him. This was not the Cade she knew. There was nothing soft or forgiving about him. Nor was there anything false. The rage that poured off him like rainwater was pure and hot.

Whatever the men were going to tell her, it wouldn't be that Cade had lied.

"I don't want to go down there," she said as he pulled her down the steps.

"Once you've heard what the boys have to say, you'll want to hide in your room for the rest of your life." They reached the bottom of the stairs and he turned to her. "But you've got too much character, too much innate honesty for that. Your loyalty is misplaced, but you're not a weakling."

"What's wrong with being loyal to my brother?"

Cade didn't answer. The men had gathered, their expressions ranging from curiosity to amusement.

"Are we here to arbitrate a marital spat?" Holt asked.

"*Premarital*," Owen said, "or have we missed something?"

"Pilar's grandmother got a letter from Laveau."

Pilar was shocked to see the instantaneous change that came over the men at the mention of her brother's name. They looked as coldly furious as Cade.

"Laveau says he didn't betray our troop, that we're blaming him for what another man did because I want to steal the diViere ranch. He says we were so successful at turning everybody against him, he had to desert to save his life."

Pilar closed her ears to the string of curses that erupted from Nate. His rage squeezed his words until they were barely understandable.

"My brother died in that raid," he managed to say. "He was only sixteen. Mama said I had to take care of him, so I always made him sleep next to me. I told him to get up, that Cade thought we ought to move into the barn. I got up and rolled up my blankets, but he didn't move. Do you know what he said? '*I feel all warm and safe.*' Those were the last words he uttered." His voice broke, and he covered his eyes with his hand. "They shot him right where he lay. If Cade hadn't dragged me into the barn, they'd have killed me, too."

Pilar felt sorry for Nate, but that didn't prove Laveau was the one who'd betrayed them.

"I used to be an actor," Broc said. "I was born into it, grew up with it. It was my life. My mother often told me, 'Your face is your fortune, Son. Take care of it.'" He turned the scarred side of his face toward Pilar. "One of the soldiers put a gun to my head, would have shot me where I lay if I hadn't moved. There are times when I wish he'd been a little quicker on the trigger." He pulled up his shirt to disclose another scar. "He shot me as I tried to crawl away. I was going in the wrong direction. There was so much blood in my eyes, I couldn't see."

Pilar tried to break Cade's hold. She didn't want to hear any more.

"They killed a young girl," Owen said. "I'd only known her a few hours, but she was beautiful and eager for the war to be over so she could explore life. She treated us like heroes, white knights on big black horses. She was running from the orchard toward the house, her laughter floating on the air. I wanted to go after her, but Cade said I wasn't good enough for her. I argued with him, turned to call to her. I saw her stumble before I heard the shot. They killed her because she was with me."

"But that doesn't prove that Laveau did it," she protested.

"I thought he was my friend," Ivan said. "I told him about the money I'd saved, where I hid it. After the attack, it was gone. And so was Laveau."

"That still doesn't—"

"The only man missing was Laveau, and he was the only one who knew where the money was."

"He escaped," Pilar said, desperate to believe they blamed her brother unfairly.

"He had time to take everything with him," Cade said, "his horse, his saddlebags, his guns and ammunition. Later we discovered that no one had seen him since we'd reached the farm."

"But that doesn't mean—"

"We had set a guard," Cade said. "He could only have been approached by a friend. He was stabbed to death. We found the hoofprints of Laveau's horse next to his body, hoofprints that led away from the farm."

"What about you?" Pilar demanded, turning angrily to Rafe. "Don't you have some horror story to torture my dreams?"

Rafe just stared back at her.

"I didn't lose anyone," Holt said, "but I spent four years trying to piece together the broken bodies of boys who should have been courting their first girl, not trying to kill each other. I can't imagine what kind of man would lift his hand to kill one of his friends so the enemy could massacre the rest."

"But you don't know…" She couldn't finish the sentence. The faces around her told her what she could no longer deny.

"It couldn't have been anyone else," Cade said.

"So you're just going to hang him," she cried.

"We'll give him a chance to speak for himself," Cade said.

Pilar's laugh was harsh. "You've already judged him. Why go through the mockery of a trial?"

"He took my brother's life for no reason," Nate said. "But I won't have it said we did the same."

"He didn't kill your brother," Pilar protested.

"He killed those men just as surely as if he'd held the gun himself," Cade said. "We rode with him. We knew him. We trusted him."

Pilar jerked her wrist from Cade's slackened grip, turned, and ran up the stairs, away from the angry faces, the accusing words she could no longer deny. She ran into her grandmother's bedroom and threw herself on the bed sobbing.

"What is wrong?" Her grandmother didn't sound as though she'd been sleeping.

"It's Laveau," she said.

Her grandmother sat up abruptly. "Has he come? They have not hurt him, have they? If they touch—"

"He won't come. He betrayed his friends," she told her grandmother through her tears.

"If you dare say such a thing of your brother again, I will slap you."

"Then go downstairs and ask Cade."

"I will not believe anything a Wheeler says."

"Are you going to disbelieve the rest of them— Broc, Nate, Ivan?"

"Ivan would not say such a thing of your brother."

"Ivan said Laveau stole his money."

"You will not believe such lies. Somebody else stole that money, and Cade Wheeler wants to blame poor Laveau."

"Laveau was the only one who knew where he kept it. It couldn't have been anyone else."

"If you believe—"

"I don't want to believe them. I tried not to, but Laveau was the only one missing after the raid. He had taken his horse and everything with him. He couldn't have gotten away unless he left before the attack. They were surrounded."

"I do not—"

"You can't keep denying it. Laveau is a traitor, and his treason caused twenty-four men to die. Your beloved, infallible grandson is practically a killer." She tried to cry some more, but all the tears had dried up. She couldn't cry for Laveau, herself, her grandmother, or the death of another dream. "I should have known something was wrong when Major Kramer told me Yankees despised a traitor, too. Now I see what kind of traitor he meant—the worst kind, the kind who betrays his friends."

"Stop it!" her grandmother said. "It is not treason to turn your back on a man who steals land from your family."

"It's not only Cade. It's all those other men. Did you know—"

"I will not listen to anything they say. It is all lies. Laveau would not do such a thing."

Pilar didn't try to argue. Once her grandmother made up her mind, nothing could change it.

"Even if he did those things, it would change

nothing. He is your brother. You owe loyalty only to him. You must help him against these men."

Pilar couldn't argue that Laveau was her brother or that she would always want to protect him, but she couldn't accept the rest. "How can you expect me to help him after what he did?"

"They were not family. It does not matter."

Pilar sat up, looked hard at her grandmother. The old woman's face was set, implacable.

"He's my brother. I can't change that," Pilar said with less heat than she felt, "but he's destroyed any feeling I had for him. He has no honor, Grandmother. What's to keep him from betraying us?"

"He would never do that."

"Hasn't he already? He didn't come home even though he knew we needed him. Now he asks me to betray the men who did help us."

"They are hired hands," her grandmother said. "We owe them nothing."

"They were not *hired*. We haven't paid them anything because we can't. They knew that and helped us anyway. Doesn't that mean anything to you?"

"Nothing is more important than family."

"Not even honesty, loyalty, integrity?"

Her grandmother fixed her with an eagle eye. "Would you betray your brother to those men down there?"

She didn't have to search for an answer to that question. "No, I wouldn't."

"There, you have your answer. We will use them as long as we can. When we no longer need them, we will send them away. Now leave me. I need to rest.

Though I doubt I will be able to close my eyes with all that noise. Please ask them to be quiet."

"They're cleaning up *our* home, Grandmother. I wouldn't think of it."

❧

The week had gone by in a flurry of activity for Cade. The men rode out at dawn each day to round up and brand cattle. Ivan and one other man stayed at the hacienda to guard against a second attack and to help with the cleanup. Ivan was only a tolerable cowhand, but he was a superb engineer. He had already planned several changes that would make life more comfortable once they had money to pay for them.

Though he wanted more than anything to stay at the hacienda, Cade left with the other men. As the man who would marry the daughter of the house, the role of leadership fell naturally to him. He had not told the men that Pilar had changed her mind because he hoped to change it back again. His reticence also postponed some uncomfortable questions for which he had no answers.

"When is the wedding day?" Owen asked as they neared the hacienda after a particularly grueling day. The squatters had preferred to kill younger animals, so the older ones had just gotten bigger, stronger, and meaner. Every muscle in Cade's body ached. He couldn't wait to sell these steers for slaughter. It would be just retribution for what they'd done to him.

"We'd have to go to San Antonio for a priest," Cade said, "and there's too much work to do to take that much time off."

"I'd have thought you'd be so anxious to get to the marriage bed, you'd have been willing to forgo a couple days wrestling steers."

"To wrestle with my wife?" Cade said, adding what he knew Owen had intentionally left unsaid.

"Sounds better than steers to me," Broc said with a grin.

"Me, too," Cade said, "but she's not too happy with me right now. You do remember that we forced her to accept that her brother is a murdering traitor."

"It's the truth," Nate said.

"That doesn't change the fact that he's her brother. It'll be better to give her some time."

"And give you time to break your neck trying to personally subdue every steer on the place," Holt said.

Bigelow and one of the other men were good cowhands, so Cade used them to help him drive the cows out of the brush. They ended every day covered in scratches and deep gouges Holt had to treat.

"I can't ask anybody to do what I'm not willing to do myself."

Cade knew he was working himself to exhaustion out of guilt for having lied to Pilar. Her defeated look made him feel even more ashamed. He had nothing to do with Laveau's being a traitor, but he felt responsible for Pilar's misery. After all, he was the one who'd forced the knowledge on her, the one who'd broken her trust.

Cade went in search of Pilar as soon as he unsaddled his horse. She had just started dinner. She had insisted that she continue to cook. She looked dismayed to see him back so early. She was obviously feeling guilty for what Laveau had done. She could talk to the men only with great difficulty.

"Supper won't be ready for more than an hour," she said.

"I know."

She turned away. "Then you'd better go away and let me cook."

"I can help."

"I don't need help."

"What you mean is you don't want my help." Cade tried to restrain himself, but it didn't work. It was time to face the issue squarely.

"Look, Cade, we've been over this before."

"Not really. You won't talk to me."

"Can you blame me?"

"Yes. I didn't do anything."

"But you want to."

"No, I don't *want* to, but I must. For the sake of the men who died."

"They're dead, Cade. You can't help them now."

"So I should let Laveau go unpunished, leave him free to betray other people?"

Pilar turned away from the pot she was stirring. "I've accepted that Laveau betrayed your troop. Surely you don't expect me to help you find him."

"I had hoped you would."

"He's my brother, Cade. I can't do that."

"Why not? He's a traitor."

"He hasn't betrayed me."

"He hasn't helped you, either."

"He can't, with you and your friends here."

"Believe me, he'd be more than happy to kill us,

too. Then there wouldn't be anyone who knows of his treachery."

"A whole lot of Union soldiers know."

"They don't care. They probably didn't even know his name."

"Major Kramer knew."

"All I'm asking you to do is let me know if he writes again, if he's intending to come back."

She turned away from him. "I can't do that. I won't write back to him, but I won't help you catch him, either."

"I thought you were more honorable than that."

"Honor!" The word exploded from her, and she whipped around to face him, brandishing a large wooden spoon as a weapon. "How can you speak to me of honor when you've lied to me from the day you got here?"

"You broke your promise to marry me."

"You shouldn't care about that. You don't love me, and I don't love you. We'll pay you for your work. You won't go away empty-handed."

"I'm not talking about that."

"You can't expect me to marry a man who would use me to help him hang my brother. What kind of woman do you think I am?"

He could hardly have less chance of marrying Pilar than he had now, but it was time to be completely honest. "I can only excuse myself because I didn't believe you could ever love me. You've always hated me."

"No, I didn't. I liked you."

"Even after I kidnapped you?"

"*Because* you kidnapped me." She smiled. "That

was the most exciting day of my life. You were very handsome and so very daring. And you made everybody so mad."

"Including my grandfather."

"Did you like me then, even a little?"

"You were beyond my reach. Liking you would have been a sacrilege."

"Yet you kidnapped me."

Now it was his turn to grin. "That was my way to thumb my nose at people who thought I was white trash."

He forced himself to tell the truth. "I'm tired of people looking down on me. I figured if I married a real lady, I wouldn't be a social outcast anymore."

"Whatever put such a preposterous notion in your head?"

"You've never been at the bottom of the hill looking up. You don't know what it's like to know the people at the top have pulled the steps up behind them so you can't follow."

"My grandmother is Spanish, not Mexican. My father and grandfather were French. They fought on the losing side in two Texas wars. I'm as much of an outcast as you."

She thought their situations were similar. She didn't understand. "That's only one of my reasons for wanting to marry you."

"One? What were the others?"

She wouldn't believe him, not after what he'd already said, but he had to tell her. He didn't want to look back years from now and think things might have been different if he'd only told her everything.

"I really like you. It has nothing to do with your looks, your family, or your ranch. I just like *you*. You're not afraid to speak your mind." He chuckled. "My grandfather has certainly learned that. That shows courage, and I admire courage. You didn't give up when the squatters drove you out. You weren't too proud to do what you had to do to survive."

"You sound like you're recruiting a soldier, not choosing a wife."

Did she want him to talk about the clarity of her eyes, the sheen of her hair, her perfect teeth? Owen said women liked that, but he thought it sounded like he was choosing a broodmare rather than a wife.

"Then maybe you should marry Owen. He'll give you all the flowery compliments you could want."

"I don't like Owen, not the way I would if I wanted to marry him."

"Do you like me that way?"

She kept stirring that pot of beans. They ought to have been reduced to mush by now. "It doesn't matter what I feel. You don't like me that way."

"But I do. That's what I've been trying to tell you."

"If you mean that all this talk about my good qualities was supposed to convince me you were in love with me, why didn't you say so?" she said.

"I didn't think people in your class believed in love."

"They don't, but I thought you did."

"Not if it's what my mother and grandmother felt for their husbands. Your class is probably very wise to avoid it," he said.

"Will you stop saying *your class*? It makes me feel like I'm different from regular people."

"You are."

"No, I'm not. I laugh and cry just like anyone else. I get hungry, sleepy, suffer pain and heart-ache just like anyone else. I get lonely, frightened, bewildered—"

He closed the space between them so swiftly he didn't even remember the movement. He turned her around so quickly some of the liquid from the spoon spattered across his shirt.

"You don't have to be lonely or frightened. I won't ever leave you. I wouldn't let anything hurt you."

She tried to turn away. "You can't prevent things like that."

He turned her back around, gripped her shoulders hard. "Yes, I can. I can do anything as long as it's for you. I'll drive every squatter out of the county, out of the state if I have to. I'll build a wall around the haci-enda so high no one will ever climb over it. I won't let you out of my sight. I'll---"

She laughed, but it wasn't a happy sound. "The people we love the most are always the ones who hurt us the most."

"I won't hurt you. I won't love you. I won't let you love me. I'll—"

"You don't understand, do you?"

"What don't I understand? Tell me. I'm not stupid. I'll figure it out."

"I already love you."

He vaguely remembered some story from the Bible about someone being turned into a pillar of salt. That was how he felt now. Petrified. Immobile. "But you're not supposed to."

"I know. Grandmother is constantly telling me I won't act like a proper young lady."

"Forget your grandmother. Do you really love me?"

"I can't forget my grandmother for the very reason I do love you. I also love my brother. What you want to do to Laveau would drive a wedge between us forever."

"Forget Laveau. Forget everybody. Just think about us. I don't know if I love you—I'm not sure I'm capable of love—but I do know I feel like I'll bust if I don't have you." He pulled her closer. "I can hardly sleep for wanting you. When I do sleep, I dream of holding you, kissing you, making love to you."

"Cade, stop. We shouldn't—"

"I've never met a woman I really wanted except you. You're becoming an obsession. I even think about you when we're branding. Holt says I'll get myself killed one day."

"You've got to be careful."

"Then say you'll marry me. I'll go crazy if you don't."

He'd never let himself go before, never admitted his feelings or how strong they were. Now that he had, he felt carried away by them. No promise seemed unreasonable, no sacrifice too extreme if only Pilar would promise to marry him.

"Cade, please—"

He kissed her. He couldn't hold off any longer. The pressure had been building until it was nearly unbearable. Seeing her every morning and evening, having her within reach and not being able to touch her was driving him wild. The longer he went without being close to her, being able to touch her, hold her, kiss her, the greater his need to do just that.

His kisses were desperate, nothing
trolled person he wanted to be. And th
resisted him, the more desperate he becam
she loved him. She *had* to marry him. If he c
keep kissing her until—

Without warning, her resistance collapsed.
returned his kisses with a fervor that caused his tem
perature to spike upward faster than dandelion seeds in
a stiff wind. He loved Pilar! She loved him! The last
vestige of control, the last ounce of restraint, fell from
him like an old skin, and he emerged new into a world
that offered new hope.

He wanted to immerse himself in an orgy of unrestrained feeling. He wanted to kiss Pilar until her lips
felt bruised, hold her until their bodies melded, make
love to her until they were drained of all energy. It
didn't matter that they were in the kitchen. It didn't
matter that his friends were just outside. He wanted to
shout, to tell the world. He wanted to—

He didn't hear the knock or the soft voice until
Pilar pushed hard against him. He turned to find a
very uncomfortable looking Holt standing in the
kitchen doorway.

"I don't like to interrupt," he said, "but there's a
man here who says his name is Manuel. He says he's
come to marry Pilar."

ike the con-
more she
She said
uld just

She

venty-three

"YOU CANNOT MARRY THAT MAN," HER GRANDMOTHER said. "I will not allow it."

Pilar and her grandmother had conducted a running argument as Pilar sorted through things that had been damaged by the squatters. Her grandmother wanted to save everything, have it repaired or rebuilt. Pilar saw no point in spending time and money they didn't have to repair useless relics of the past.

"I wore that mantilla for my first communion," her grandmother said when Pilar tossed aside a ruined scrap of lace.

"It can't be repaired."

"I want to keep it."

"No one can use it again."

"Your daughter—"

"It's so old-fashioned no one would wear it. Besides, black is miserably hot."

Pilar had yet to discover why her clothes had been spared while those of her grandmother had been largely destroyed. Everything would be used for rags or cut into squares to make quilts like those at the

Wheeler ranch. Her grandmother considered them beneath her, but they had a kind of hardy character, a simplicity and utility Pilar found appealing. Under normal circumstances, she wouldn't have altered the character of the hacienda, but with so much destroyed, she didn't mean to return to the heavy, dark, humorless style favored by her grandmother. She wanted more openness, more simplicity. She intended to ask Ivan if he could cut new windows. She wanted more light in the rooms.

"I don't know what's come over you," her grandmother said. "You never used to be so willful or disrespectful."

"I didn't know any other way. Now I do. I intend to use the money we earn to make sure we're safe, not fill this huge hacienda with useless, expensive ornaments that can be destroyed by anybody who breaks in."

"That'll be for Laveau to decide. And your husband."

The three days since Manuel had arrived had been the worst of Pilar's life.

She should have been thankful for his arrival. She had let her emotions overcome her common sense to the point that she had been on the verge of agreeing to marry Cade. She had gotten herself in hand since then, but her feelings hadn't changed. She still loved Cade. Having confessed it to him made it easier to confess it to herself.

But she couldn't marry him.

"I don't intend to be ruled by my husband like you and my mother were. I will not be kept in the dark about the rancho."

"It will become your husband's upon your marriage."

"That part of the contract will have to be changed."

"Manuel would never agree."

"Then I won't marry him."

"You cannot ask such a thing of him. It would insult his manhood."

"It wouldn't insult Cade's manhood."

"Pilar, you cannot marry that man."

"I've said I won't, but neither will I make myself a slave to Manuel. Either I have control of my property, or he can find himself another wife."

"This is Cade Wheeler's doing. He has filled your head with foolish ideas to make you dissatisfied with a proper husband."

"The only foolish idea Cade put in my head is that I have a mind, thoughts, desires of my own—that I have a right to have them considered."

"Your husband will do so."

"When did your husband ever consider your wishes?"

"It is a man's right to decide for his family."

"Then let Manuel find himself a weak-willed female."

"It is those Wheelers," her grandmother said again. "You would never have talked like this before the war."

"Before the war I wasn't allowed to want anything unless some man told me to want it. When Laveau ran off, I had to learn to manage on my own. When the squatters came, I had to learn to cook and put up with an old man who didn't like anything I did. And I had to do it by myself because you refused to come out of that room *for two whole years*. It was horribly lonely, but I learned one very valuable lesson. I can survive on my own. If Manuel wants to marry me, he'll have to do it on my terms."

She had meant to subdue her rebellious will, forget she loved Cade more than anything on earth, and be a good wife to Manuel. But her grandmother asked too much. She would give up her body because it was required. She would try to learn to respect her husband. But she would not go back to being property.

"No decent man will marry you under those terms," her grandmother said.

"I don't need a husband."

"You need one to run the ranch."

"What I can't do, Cade will do for me. Maybe I'll talk to him about combining our herds. I'm sure he would agree. Cade wants to become rich."

"I command you to have nothing to do with that man."

"He doesn't ignore me or think I'm an idiot. When I ask him to show me the records, he will. I think I should learn to ride. It would be good to know more about day-to-day activities. You can oversee the household. I'm not very interested in that anyway."

"Pilar diViere! Have you gone mad?"

"Maybe, but I don't care. I like it."

"All of this about letting Cade Wheeler work our herd is nonsense. Once we have money, I refuse to let him set foot in my house."

Pilar didn't know what came over her, but it happened so fast she couldn't stop it. "Then we'll divide the hacienda in half."

"What are you talking about?"

"I'll build a wall right through the middle. If

Laveau comes home and tries to take it down, I'll fight you both."

"I hope you're not talking about me." Manuel had stuck his head in the door.

Her grandmother broke into smiles and moved to welcome Manuel. "Pilar is making very foolish pronouncements. I depend on you to talk some sense into her."

Manuel's swaggering into the room like he had a right to be there set Pilar's back up. For four years she hadn't heard a word from him. He claimed he'd been fully occupied protecting his own ranch from bandits and rogue soldiers and hadn't been aware of her situation. Yet he'd showed up little more than a week after Cade had driven the squatters out.

"What has my very beautiful future wife said that could upset her estimable grandmother?"

"She is talking about riding horses and learning to round up cows."

"I was telling my grandmother I didn't mean to give up control of my property upon my marriage."

"But that is most unusual," Manuel said, his expression stiffening. "In fact, it is unheard of."

"I'm a most unusual woman."

She heard a low rumble from the dog's throat. Much to her grandmother's fury, she had named him Wheeler. *Because he's big and coarse,* her grandmother had said. The dog didn't like Manuel. The feeling was mutual.

"She says she means to hire Cade Wheeler to be her foreman."

"I intend to give him a percentage of the income in

exchange for his work," Pilar said. "Maybe once learned all he can teach me, I'll do it myself."

"What about what I can teach you?"

"I don't know if I can depend on you, Manuel. I needed you badly during these last four years, but you never came or so much as sent a message."

"I explained that—"

"I would really be much better off marrying Cade. Don't you think that would be a good idea?"

"You cannot marry a man who would hang your brother," Manuel said.

"Yes, that is a difficulty, but Cade thinks we can find a way around it."

"You have talked about such a thing?"

"You'd be horrified if you knew the things we've talked about."

"This is not proper."

"No, but neither is being driven out of your house nor coming back to near total destruction. Quiet, Wheeler, I can hardly hear myself think."

"I hate that dog," her grandmother said for the hundredth time. "He is a big, smelly mongrel."

"I keep him because he protected me from Clarence Odum. Did you know Cade went to jail because he protected me from Odum?" she asked Manuel.

"I do not understand her," Manuel said to Senora diViere. "She has changed so much."

"Everything has changed, Manuel, but I still need a husband. I will marry you, but the contract must be changed so that I retain control of my dowry."

"But that is impossible. It cannot be done."

"Then I won't marry you."

"But you must marry someone," her grandmother said.

"Then I guess I'll have to marry Cade."

"I forbid it!" her grandmother declared so loudly Wheeler turned his big head in the old woman's direction.

"Then talk some sense into Manuel. In the meantime, I've got to start supper."

"Why do we still eat at this uncivilized hour?" Manuel asked. "And why do you persist in calling it supper rather than dinner?"

"We eat at this hour because the men need to eat before they go to bed. I call it supper because that's the kind of food I cook."

She left the room, closing the door behind her so quickly she left Wheeler inside. A sharp bark brought the error to her attention. She opened the door to let him out.

"I wouldn't want to stay in there either. I have to do something about Manuel. Maybe he should live on his ranch in Mexico while I live here."

How could anybody think she would prefer living with Manuel rather than Cade? It wasn't that Manuel was so terrible—well, he was, but it had to be expected of anyone raised as he had been—but Cade was simply so much better.

But it would do her no good to dwell on Cade's superiority. Or on anything about Cade. She couldn't marry the man who wanted to hang her brother.

"You ought to be glad you're a dog," she said to Wheeler. "You don't have to get married."

"It can't be that bad," Holt said. He'd rounded the corner without her seeing him.

Pilar blushed. She still couldn't get used to every-body knowing her business.

"It is when you don't have any choice," she said.

"You have a choice."

"Are you saying I should marry the man who intends to hang my brother?"

"No. I'm just saying you have a choice."

"I'd prefer a better one."

Wheeler let out a bark and lumbered off down the breezeway. That meant Cade was coming. He was nearly equal to Pilar in Wheeler's affections.

"You've got the best one there is," Holt said. "Now I need to see your grandmother. I don't like the sound of her cough."

Pilar decided her grandmother coughed because it brought Holt and Ivan to her side with Manuel not far behind. She'd never had so much attention in her whole life.

Pilar would have preferred to stay out of sight until Cade passed, but it was time to stop acting like a child. If she intended to ask Cade to work her ranch, she had to get used to seeing him, being around him, spending time with him.

The plan to hire Cade had popped out of her mouth because she was angry with Manuel. It made good business sense, but she didn't know if she could do it. When Cade came out of one of the rooms, with Wheeler gamboling at his heels, she realized she couldn't. She might hire him to do the work, but she would have to lock herself in when he came to the hacienda. Otherwise, just being around him, being close enough to reach out and touch him, might be nough to cause her to break her marriage vows. She didn't want to marry Manuel, but if she did, she had every intention of being faithful.

Cade hesitated when he saw her, then strode forward with purpose. He clearly had something he wanted to say. Pilar decided to speak first. She didn't trust him not to say something that would undermine what little self-control she had left.

"I've been looking for you," she said. "I have a business proposition to offer you." She had definitely caught him off guard.

"Drop the word *business,* and I'm all ears."

She refused to be seduced by his smile. He'd lost most of his sense of humor sometime during the war, but traces of it surfaced now and again.

"My grandmother and I need someone to manage our herd. You'll know the ranch well by the time you've finished the roundup. We'll offer you a percentage of every cow you sell if you'll take care of them along with your own."

"What about Manuel?"

"I'm going to retain control of my property."

Cade laughed. She didn't like the sound. "He won't agree to that."

"Then I won't marry him."

She shouldn't have said that. His attitude changed abruptly. She saw hope spring into his eyes. "Then who will you marry?"

"With you taking care of my herds, I won't need to marry anyone."

"My friends won't stay long. They only came to earn money for a grubstake."

"I trust you to hire anybody you need. I'll offer you half of the profits after all wages and expenses have been paid."

"That's very generous."

"You're very good. Now I have to go. Think about it and let me know."

She hurried away before he could stop her. At least that was what she thought until she realized he hadn't tried to stop her. She wasn't at all sure she liked that.

Nate and Broc stopped her before she reached the kitchen.

"We've seen signs of somebody hanging around the ranch," Nate said.

Was it more squatters or Cortina's bandits from across the Rio Grande? "Did you tell Cade?" she said. "He'll know what to do if it's bandits."

"It's not bandits," Broc said.

"Or it's only one bandit," Nate said.

Something in the tone of Nate's voice made her feel uneasy. "Why hasn't Cade said anything?"

"Because he's in love with you."

She felt heat suffuse her entire body.

"Why should that stop him?"

Wheeler whined impatiently. He knew she'd been headed toward the kitchen. He always got something to eat when she cooked.

"Because we think it may be your brother."

Pilar's emotions nearly overwhelmed her. She felt relief that Laveau was safe and joy that he might be coming home. At the same moment, she feared for his safety. And she felt angry at Laveau for deserting and making it impossible for her to marry the only man she could love. Angry at Cade and all his friends for their determination to hang Laveau. But she was determined that she would show none of these feelings. She couldn't help Laveau if his enemies could read her like a book.

"Why are you telling me this?"

"We expect he'll try to contact you," Broc said.

"Not as long as you're here. He knows what you want to do to him."

"He has no idea what I'd like to do to him," Nate said, hatred in his voice. "If he did, he wouldn't come within a thousand miles of this place."

"I'm sorry," Pilar said. "If I could do anything—"

"You can," Nate said. "Let us know if he tries to contact you."

"It may not be Laveau."

"It doesn't really matter who this man is," Nate said. "Sooner or later Laveau will try to contact you, and we want you to let us know."

"So you can hang him?"

"Men who were our friends died because of him," Broc said.

"My brother died because of him," Nate said. "Do you know what that's like?"

"No, but if you have your way, I will."

That seemed to give them both pause, but just for a moment.

"He's a traitor," Nate said. "He has to die."

"I hope it's not Laveau," Pilar said. "But if it is, I will not help you catch him. Whatever he did, he's my brother."

"You're honor bound to help us," Nate said.

"I'm honor bound to protect my family." She tried to move past them, but Broc blocked her patch.

"People have to live by rules," he said. "If they don't, society will crumble."

"Do you call fighting a war a rule that society must live by?" she shot back. "Wars cost me my father and grandfather. They took your friends, Nate's brother. And now they're threatening to take my brother. As far as I'm concerned, society has already crumbled and fallen apart."

"Cade's holding it together for you."

"No, he's not. He's on your side. Now let me pass."

They let her pass, but Nate's voice stopped her before she had gone far.

"What he did was the act of a coward," he said, speaking softly. "He traded his honor and integrity for a few acres of land. He has to pay."

Pilar hurried away, not wanting to hear any more. She was afraid that Nate was right. And she was even more afraid that Cade would be the one to bring Laveau to justice.

⁓

"You shouldn't have said anything to her," Cade told Nate. "How is she supposed to react when you ask her to help catch her brother?"

"I know he'll try to contact her," Nate said.

"We don't know it's Laveau, we don't know he'll contact her, and I can promise you she won't say a word if he does."

"You took the same vow we did," Broc said.

"Pilar didn't."

"But you've got to help."

"Not by trying to force Pilar to turn on her own brother. I never had a brother, so I don't know how I would feel in her position, but I doubt you'd have turned on your brother, Nate."

"My brother would have let himself be tortured before he turned traitor."

"And you'd have let yourself be tortured before you betrayed him."

"It's not the same," Nate said.

"You can't expect Pilar to see it that way."

"But I expect you to."

"She's not going to marry me, Nate. Get this through your head. I have no influence over her."

"She can't mean to marry that stuffed quail who's been strutting around here the last few days."

"If you mean Manuel, yes." Cade smiled grimly. "But she doesn't mean to give up control of one bit of her dowry. She's offered us fifty percent of the profits after expenses if we'll manage her herd along with mine."

"Manuel will never go for that."

"Then she says she won't marry him."

"That means you—"

"That means there are two men she won't marry. I'm still at the top of the list."

"You can still try to convince her to help us."

"No. And don't remind me of my vow."

"You're not backing out, are you?" Broc asked.

"No. If I find Laveau, I'll do everything I can to capture him. Those men were my responsibility. I failed them."

"Nobody holds you responsible," Broc said. "If you hadn't warned us, we'd all be dead."

Knowing that didn't help Cade. It never had. "I need to find Pilar to tell her we've accepted her offer."

He hadn't seen her since supper. He suspected she was hiding from him. He returned to his room to give her time to get over being upset. She would have to return to her room eventually. He would hear her. He'd talk to her then.

As the minutes began to weigh heavily on his mind, he found himself thinking more about himself than Pilar. It was ironic that he was in this room, sleeping in the bed occupied by the heads of the diViere household for three generations, the Cordobas before that. Cade Wheeler, the poor white whose family hailed from the hills of Virginia, the man so far removed from them that no diViere would talk to him. And yet he had come close to marrying the daughter of the family and coming into possession of half of everything they had.

You had to laugh at the twists of fate that could turn men's lives upside down and inside out until nothing was recognizable. He hadn't done anything special to get here. He'd just been luckier than the other guy. Even when his side hadn't won, he'd won. He'd come within a hairbreadth of getting everything he'd ever wanted, and it had been denied him by a matter of principle.

Ironic. He was the man who didn't believe in love, who never expected it, didn't want it, and now it was the only thing he wanted. Was he in love? He still didn't know. He told himself he didn't believe in love, but his reasons had nothing to do with money.

They had to do with a little boy being abandoned by a mother who didn't want him, who said he belonged with the cactus and the heat and the wild longhorns, a mother who in all the intervening years had never once bothered to contact him to see if he was alive.

He had been afraid to believe in love after that. Sometimes he wanted to, sometimes he even tried to convince himself it was possible, but so far he hadn't succeeded. He had been willing to do without when the least likely woman in the world had changed everything.

The faint sound of a door closing interrupted his thoughts, caused him to flinch. Pilar had entered her bedroom. He felt conflicting impulses—to go in immediately, to put it off until tomorrow. Nothing he could say would change anything. He was already half-undressed. He'd probably be better off going to bed.

But the need to see her, talk to her, be near her never left him. He hadn't accepted her decision to marry Manuel. He wasn't an expert at love like Owen, but he didn't have to be a genius to see she didn't feel about Manuel the way she felt about him. She didn't follow him with her eyes, yet avoided talking to him. She didn't want to know everything about his day, yet pretend her feelings for him were dead.

It was time he stopped pretending, too. He'd held back out of pride, out of uncertainty about his feelings. He still wasn't sure what he did feel, but he knew he wanted Pilar to be his wife. He also knew he didn't give a snap of his fingers about her money or anything else.

He walked over to the door that joined their two rooms and opened it before he had time to change his mind.

Twenty-four

AT THE SOUND OF THE DOOR OPENING, PILAR SWUNG around, not knowing what to expect. The sight of Cade stepping into her bedroom in just his pants sent the blood thrumming through her veins. He shouldn't be there. She had already changed for bed. She would ask Ivan to nail the door shut. She wouldn't be able to sleep knowing that Cade could enter her bedroom at any moment.

She backed away, keeping the large bed between them.

"Nate told me what he said. I came to apologize."

"That wasn't necessary."

"I wanted to do it anyway."

They just stood there, too far apart and yet much too close. She wondered all over again how her grandmother could think she could prefer Manuel. His presence didn't make her heart beat faster, her breath become shallow, or her body grow tense. His nearness didn't reach out and encompass her as though it were the natural way things should be. She didn't feel energized by his presence. She wasn't drawn to him b an invisible force almost too strong to resist. She didn't think about him nearly every moment she was awake.

She didn't long to have him look in her direction, didn't wait breathlessly to see him smile when he caught sight of her, wouldn't listen eagerly when he spoke. More importantly, she didn't long for him to hold her close, to kiss her, to tell her that he loved her. She would have been upset if he had. She was upset that Cade hadn't.

"Do you think that man is Laveau?" she asked.

"There's no way to tell. He seems to know the area, but anybody living here would know it better than Nate and Broc."

"Does he know it as well as you?"

"Better."

She felt something heavy hit the bottom of her stomach. "Then you think it's Laveau."

He was reluctant to answer, but he didn't try to be evasive. "Yes."

"I won't help you catch him. You can't expect me to."

"I don't." He emerged from the shadows that lurked in the corners of the room and came into the sphere of light provided by her lone candle. The clear view of his half-naked body caused her belly to tighten.

"But you said—"

"I felt guilty, responsible for the deaths of my men. I was trying to use you to help ease my conscience. That was wrong. I'm sorry I wasn't smart enough to see that from the beginning."

The sense of relief astounded her. She'd had no

idea she'd been so upset thinking he'd hate her for not helping.

"Nate and the others don't feel the same."

"It'll be hard at first, but they won't blame you."

"Are you sure you don't blame me?" She stepped closer. She wanted to look into his eyes, make sure she could believe his answer.

"I couldn't turn against my grandfather, cantankerous, bullheaded know-it-all that he is. War changes the rules. Its lessons are brutal, impossible to forget. Afterward it's hard to change back to the way things were."

"I can never go back."

"Then why are you marrying Manuel? Why can't you marry me?"

He stepped forward, and she moved back.

"I can't marry a man who wants to hang my brother."

"So you're going to marry a man you don't even like."

"I like Manuel."

He moved closer, and she backed around a chair. "No, you don't. You don't look at him when he's in the same room. You stay as far away from him as possible. Hell, you don't even talk to him when you can help it. How are you going to have a decent marriage with this man?"

"That's not your concern. All you have to know—"

He moved so quickly she couldn't stay out of his reach. When he gripped her by the arms, she glanced around to see if Wheeler would come to her defense, but the dog had gone to sleep on the hearth. He trusted Cade. So much for the intuition of a dog.

"It is my concern," Cade said.

"Why?"

"Because I care about you."

"You don't care about anything but the land and the cows," Pilar said, throwing at him the fear she'd harbored for so long, that no one could care for her without caring for her possessions even more.

"That's not true," he said.

"Even when you were lying to me?"

That caused him to pause but not stop. "Even then. I always liked you."

"Not me, but what I represented. You said yourself that running off with me was just a way to thumb your nose at my family."

"It was also a way to discover you were human, made of warm flesh and blood, not the heartless doll I saw through a window or in a carriage."

"You watched me through my window?" He couldn't have. That would have meant he had somehow gotten onto their property.

"Your *vaqueros* were too well-fed. It was easy to slip into the thickets at night."

"But those were the pranks of a boy. We're adults now, and we're talking about the rest of our lives."

"That's all the more reason you shouldn't spend it with a man who disgusts you."

It was useless to pretend. "Manuel and I have been betrothed since we were children. This is the way it's done in my family."

"So you're going to allow your grandmother to trade you off like a piece of property just like your class has always done with women?"

"I'm not giving up my property."

"You might as well. Anybody who works for you will take orders from Manuel."

"He won't be here. He'll live on his ranch in Mexico."

"And he agreed to that?"

She hoped he wouldn't. "I haven't told him yet."

His grip on her arms tightened. "Pilar, don't sell yourself to a man you don't love."

"I thought you said you didn't believe in love, that people *of my class* didn't know what it was."

"That's no reason to marry a man who disgusts you so much you can't stand to live in the same country with him. If you must marry somebody, marry me. At least I love you."

The word hit her with the force of a lightning bolt. Did he mean what he said, or was this just another lie to help him get what he wanted?

She fought off the birth of hope. Cade didn't believe in love, for him or for her. Yet hope would not be held down. Ever since she could remember, she'd wanted to be loved for herself. No one had ever made her feel that way, including her grandmother or Laveau. She wasn't sure any man could, but surely the least likely would be Cade Wheeler.

Cade's words appeared to have affected himself no less profoundly. Her grandmother would have said he looked as if he'd seen a ghost. She would say he'd just realized he'd made a promise he couldn't keep, and his conscience was pinching him.

"Do you know what you just said?"

"Yes." He still looked as if he'd swallowed something that had caught in his throat.

"You don't believe in love," she said.

"I know."

"Did you believe me when I said I loved you?"

"I don't know."

"Why not?"

"No woman has ever loved a Wheeler enough to stay with him."

"If I married you, I'd never leave no matter what. Do you believe that?"

He didn't answer.

He didn't believe her. How could she expect him to when his own mother had walked out on him?

"We should never have met. The worst thing we could have done was fall in love," she said.

"Why?"

"Because neither one of us believes in love, yet we want it so badly we're willing to make bargains with the devil."

"I don't know if what I feel is really love, but I know it has nothing to do with cows, land, or this hacienda. I'd want to marry you if you came to me barefoot."

"Do you mean if I walked up to your grandfather's ranch and said I had no land, no cows, no hacienda, you'd still want to marry me?"

"Yes."

He meant it. She didn't know if he *really* meant it, deep down where true desires hide, but he thought he meant it.

"Do you love me enough to give up this hacienda and come live with me and my grandfather?"

Even though she'd been promised to Manuel, she'd always pictured herself living in the hacienda with her husband and family. The roots that bound her to her family's past and traditions were so strong, she had never considered severing them. And she knew that moving to the Wheeler ranch would mean cutting herself off from her family.

That thought frightened her. She had never been cut adrift. Even when she'd been driven from her home, she had her grandmother, who never ceased to invoke the past when the uncertainties of the present became too great. And in an odd sort of way, Earl Wheeler supported that vision. He complained about her grandmother, never said anything nice about her, considered all her pretensions hogwash, yet moved out of his own house, his own bedroom, and never once demanded it back.

"I would be very frightened and unsure of myself, but as long as I could feel your love, I would do it," she said.

She expected more conversation, more attempts to figure out what had gone wrong between them. But Cade had apparently finished with words. He took her into his arms and began to kiss her with the hunger of a man long denied everything essential for the continuance of life. Pilar knew she should resist, that yielding to temptation would only make it harder to step back later, but she couldn't help herself. Nothing had ever felt so good. All of the tension of the last few days melted away and she dissolved into his embrace, willing to let him do whatever he wanted as long as he did it with her.

She didn't understand how simply being held in his arms, being kissed, could infuse her with such energy. She felt the fatigue of the day fall away like a discarded cloak. She wanted to kiss Cade as hard as he kissed her. She wanted to hold him as tightly, press herself against him until she felt absorbed, become so much a part of him that they could never be separated again. She couldn't explain this need to feel attached to him, but it seemed vital to her very existence. She didn't know how she could think of living without him. He was as necessary as the air she breathed.

"I think I've always wanted you," Cade said, "but I wouldn't let myself think about it. It seemed too impossible."

"I never dreamed about you until you ran off with me. Then I dreamed about you all the time. I told myself I was dreaming of some duke or noble warrior—I even gave them names—but they always ended up being you."

"The women in my dreams were faceless. Or maybe they were all you." They had worked themselves over to the bed. Cade sat down and pulled Pilar into his lap. "But they haven't been faceless for a long time."

She took his face in her hands and kissed him on the nose and eyes. She kissed him all over until he started to laugh. That goaded her into redoubling her efforts. Cade laughed so hard he fell back on the bed, pulling her over on top of him.

"What is so funny?" she asked.

"I don't know. It's like there's a big bubble of happiness inside me I can't keep down. Have you ever felt that way?"

"No, but it sounds wonderful."

He pulled her down and kissed her soundly. "It feels wonderful, too."

A quick body movement, and she found herself on her back with Cade's face looming over her, his elbows resting on either side of her.

"No fair," she said through her laughter. "You're stronger than I am."

"I want to see your face, but the light was behind you." He indicated the single candle.

"But I can't see your face."

"You're prettier than I am."

"Who told you that?"

"I have a mirror."

"Well, it's wrong. You're the most handsome man I've ever met."

"Just my luck. Fall in love with a woman, and she goes stark raving mad."

Pilar punched him. "I'm not mad," she said, though she didn't care what he said about her as long as he prefaced it by saying he loved her. "You are handsome. Any woman would tell you so."

"Unfortunately for my ego, none have. But that doesn't matter as long as you think I'm handsome."

"I do." She pulled him down so she could kiss him.

She liked the weight of him pressed down on her. It made her feel more connected, more protected. She didn't like to admit that was so important to her, but after living for so long in perpetual fear, it was wonderful to know that Cade was there, that he wouldn't let anything happen to her.

And it was absolutely wonderful to be so important in a man's eyes.

For too long she was important only for what she represented. She was criticized, chastised, cloistered, her wants ignored, her opinions rejected, her compliance taken for granted. To be thought beautiful, to be cherished for herself alone…well, that was more than she could fathom.

"You should be surrounded by a thousand candles," Cade said.

She laughed. "I'd faint from the heat."

"I could sit and look at you for hours."

"I'd rather you spend the time kissing me." She pushed him over and rolled onto her side. "It's not fair. The light is still behind you."

"I have memorized every part of your face." He closed his eyes. "I see you as clearly as before."

Pilar closed her eyes and was delighted to discover she could visualize Cade's face. She would never be without him again.

Keeping his eyes closed, Cade started to kiss her again, but he quickly deserted her lips for her neck and the top of her shoulder. The feel of his lips sent shivers racing up and down her spine. Her grandmother said a gentleman only kissed a lady's hand.

But why would she have assumed that Cade would stay within any limits outlined by her grandmother?

Cade's lips had wandered to the tops of her breasts, and her thoughts catapulted back to that night outside the hacienda. Just thinking about it caused her body to quiver. She had dreamed of it nearly every night since, more than once waking to find her body covered with a film of moisture. Cade's kisses were making her so hot she felt like pulling off her clothes to keep from fainting.

Cade took care of that. He reached inside her gown,

freed one breast, and took the nipple into his mouth. Pilar thought she would rise up from the bed. It seemed impossible that such a small part of her body could have such a powerful effect on the rest of it. She felt as though every inch of her had been transformed into pulses and nerves. Even the material of her gown touching her body had a sensuous feel about it. She felt so alive, so intensely, acutely aware of every part of her, that she felt unable to concentrate on anything.

She didn't want it to stop.

She wanted to consume Cade's body just as he consumed hers, but she was powerless to divert his attention from her breasts. He tortured one nipple with his teeth and tongue while he lightly pinched the other between his fingers. She ran her fingers through his hair, digging her nails into his scalp as the sensations rocking her body caused her to arch off the bed. She pushed against his shoulders, struggled to escape the sweet torture, hoping he would never let her go.

During one of the times her body rose off the bed, Cade pulled her nightgown down to her waist. The feel of the night air on her moist nipples caused them to turned marble hard. But Cade didn't notice. He was too busy kissing the curve of each rib.

And sliding her nightgown under her hips until she lay naked before him.

The suddenness of it startled her. It seemed only moments ago that he had stepped through the door into her room, much too short a time for her to have allowed him to undress her. Yet she lay before him, her body entirely exposed.

"You're beautiful," he whispered, "even more beautiful than I imagined."

She didn't feel beautiful. She felt awkward. All her life she'd been told that personal modesty was the supreme virtue, that no part of her body could ever be exposed to a man's gaze. She'd been forced to conceal herself behind doors, curtains, even traveling in a stifling closed carriage. She had always been forced to remain out of sight when strangers came to the house. She loved Cade, but the change was too great, too abrupt. The heat that had warmed her body began to fade. She felt herself grow stiff, begin to withdraw.

"Are you cold?"

She didn't know how to explain what she felt, so she nodded her head.

He pulled a sheet over her body and leaned on his elbow. "I went too fast."

She felt him begin to pull away, and that stopped her withdrawal. She didn't want him to leave. She needed his presence, his touch, the reaffirmation she was beautiful, that *he loved her*. She reached up and cupped his cheek in her palm. "Hold me, and I won't be cold."

He put his arms around her and pulled her close. She put her hand against his chest, pushed her fingers through the sprinkling of light brown hair in the center. She nuzzled his neck as he gently placed kiss after kiss in her hair.

"Take off the rest of your clothes and get under the sheet with me."

She didn't know where she'd found the courage to say that. She just knew she wanted to feel as close to him as possible.

"Are you sure?"

"Yes."

The cold returned when he withdrew from her, but it was the cold of separation, not of fear. It didn't last long. Cade could hardly have removed his pants more quickly if he'd used magic. He opened his arms to her, and she moved quickly into his embrace. The feel of his bare skin against hers restored the heat to her body. The evidence of his arousal, freed from restraint and pressing insistently against her thigh, turned up the heat in her. "Hold me close."

"I'm afraid I'll hurt you."

He was already holding her tight, but it wasn't enough. She placed his hand on her back and pushed her body against his entire length, but that still didn't give her the feeling she wanted. She felt herself growing more agitated as she sought a closer joining with him.

Cade's hand moved down her back, over her bottom, across her thigh, and between her legs. Instinctively she drew back, opened to him. She heard herself moan softly when his finger entered her, felt her body tense as he gently stroked her. Yet even as the waves of pleasure began to lap at the edges of her senses, as the heat coiled in her belly began to loosen and spread throughout her body, she knew this wasn't enough. It was wonderful, exciting, and her body yearned for more, but somehow it wasn't enough.

Gradually the waves of pleasure overcame the sense of incompleteness, rendering her incapable of feeling anything but the sweet agony that made every part of her ache deliciously. She moaned softly, breathing hard, as if she were running a race. Then with a suddenness that caught her by surprise, the sweet ache crested into intense pleasure and flowed through her like water cascading over a fall.

Pilar collapsed against the bed, her muscles spent, her breath slowing. Gradually her sense of being connected to the external world returned and she realized Cade was above her, entering her again, but this time she had to stretch to accommodate him. She heard him gasp softly as he entered her fully, heard her answering moan.

She had found all that was missing.

She felt joined with Cade. She felt complete.

Now, as the currents of pleasure began to pulse in her body, she sensed the same feelings building in Cade. When she moaned or gasped for air, she heard him do the same. The knowledge that she could give him as much pleasure as he gave her awakened a new sense of power in her. She was no longer merely the recipient, no longer waiting for a male to make her complete. She was a partner, equally capable of reducing Cade to the same state of uncontrolled, mindless, nerveless ecstasy she had enjoyed only moments earlier.

She joined eagerly in the building of the passion that united their bodies more deeply in its spiral with each passing moment. She clung to him, moved with him, covered his face with kisses. She wanted to become part of him, to feel absorbed by him, wrapped in his embrace, protected from the world by him. As the pulse of shared passion coiled through them, she achieved a feeling of oneness that answered all her longings.

And with that came the peak, complete surrender,

a falling open and away. But she had fallen into Cade's arms, and that was where she wanted to stay.

❧

Pilar had made the most momentous decision of her life. She would marry Cade. She didn't know what she would do about Laveau, but somehow she would find an answer. Maybe she would ride out and find him, convince him it was better to go away and never come back. She could send him half the income from the ranch.

She had awakened to find herself in Cade's arms. The initial shock had given way to indescribable happiness, a feeling of peace and well-being unlike anything she had ever known. Everything felt right, all her doubts resolved, all her worries pushed aside. Everything would be okay as long as she loved Cade and he loved her. She was certain that would last forever.

"You've got to go back to your own room," she told him.

"Why?"

"Because my grandmother might come in here any minute."

"That will be a good time to tell her you're not going to marry Manuel."

"There will never be a good time for that. Now move. I've got to start breakfast, or your friends will be banging on my door as well."

She pushed him through the door into his room, laughing so loudly she feared her grandmother would hear. She thought of checking on her but decided against it. She was already late.

She had herself under control by the time the men came to the table, but she found it nearly impossible to contain her emotions once Cade entered the room. Owen noticed it immediately. "Do I notice a thaw in the atmosphere?" he asked, his gaze focusing on Pilar.

"We've decided to call a truce," Cade said. "Some things take time to figure out."

"And just when did you decide this? It wasn't by chance after we all went to bed, was it?"

"I can't say," Pilar said, "not being aware of when you go to bed. Would you like more coffee?"

"You haven't come to any secret agreements, have you?" Nate asked.

"We've come to no agreements you need to know about," Cade said. "Now if you boys have finished eating, we have cows to brand."

Cade had managed to be the last to leave the room. "I love you," he whispered before he left. "Always remember that."

She hadn't thought of anything else all morning. In fact, she was so preoccupied, she was late with her grandmother's breakfast. Her grandmother had clung to the same habits for her entire life. The world around her might go to pieces, but she expected her part of it to stay the same. Pilar put her grandmother's breakfast on a tray and hurried upstairs with Wheeler at her heels.

Her grandmother opened the door before she could knock twice. She pulled Pilar into the room so quickly she nearly closed the door on the dog.

"Bring more food. Laveau is here, and he has eaten nothing since yesterday."

Twenty-five

PILAR'S BREATH CAUGHT IN HER THROAT. SHE WAS relieved to see Laveau. She had been afraid she would never see him again. Yet she knew his return would destroy any chance for peace between the two families.

Laveau grabbed the tray from her. "How do you expect our grandmother to survive on so little, especially when you don't bring it until nearly noon?"

Her reaction was immediate and unmistakable. She resented his arrogance, felt anger that he spoke to her as though she were a servant. She swallowed her anger. She hadn't been hiding out for the last several days, as he had, most likely hungry and miserably uncomfortable. She hadn't been afraid for her life. He had a right to be upset.

She held out her arms and walked toward her brother. "I'm so glad you're home. Grandmother and I have been praying for your return."

Laveau ignored her welcome, concentrating on eating his grandmother's breakfast as quickly as he could stuff it into his mouth. "Bring me some more food. When I've eaten, I'll tell you what you have to do."

"When did you get here? How did you get in without anybody seeing you?"

"I said get me something to eat!" he hissed. "Can't you hear, or has Cade's treating you like some kind of princess given you an exaggerated sense of your importance?"

Pilar had never really known Laveau well. The lives of men and women in the diViere household converged only at meals and social events, when men consumed most of the attention and dominated all conversation, but Laveau had never shouted at her. He'd ignored her, but even in that, there had been a sense of family, of belonging, of the way things were.

Laveau seemed to have forgotten that.

"I can hear you quite well, and I imagine Ivan will hear you, too."

"Is that fool here?"

"Do you call him a fool because he trusted you enough to tell you where he hid his money?"

"If I hadn't taken it, someone else would have. The fool kept it in the bottom of his portmanteau."

"He thought you were his friend."

"I needed money. The army didn't pay us. Half the time we didn't have anything to eat that we didn't steal."

"You must have eaten quite well."

"War changes men."

"I'm sure it does, but it doesn't turn them all into thieves."

Why was she fighting with her brother? She should be overjoyed he was safe. She should want to celebrate, tell the whole world…but she couldn't. She couldn't tell anyone.

"What have you done to her?" Laveau said, turning to his grandmother. "She never used to act like this."

Pilar's sympathy froze under the coldness of her brother's scorn. "I never before had been left alone to run a ranch, driven out of my home and forced to learn to cook for a foul-tempered old man to keep from starving. The war changed me, too."

"I'll damned well change you right back."

"I suppose this is where the part about being treated like a princess comes in. What did you tell him?" she asked her grandmother.

"She told me that you'd agreed to marry Cade Wheeler and give him half this rancho."

"Grandmother wanted me to pretend I was going to marry him so he would drive out the squatters."

"What was wrong with that?"

"I don't like lying."

"It's not lying if it's Wheelers."

"What's happened to you? You were never like this before."

"You change when you discover a man wants to kill you. When you come home to find him sleeping in your bed and preparing to marry your sister, you don't know who you can trust."

"You can trust me."

Immediately she felt guilty for uttering those words. While he'd been sneaking into the hacienda last light, she'd been making love to Cade. While Laveau was waiting for food, she was making up her mind to marry Cade. Now she was thrown back into the same quandary she thought she'd escaped.

"You can prove that by helping me kill Cade."

"What!" The word exploded from her, driven by shock and fear.

"He says Cade and the others have taken a vow to kill him," her grandmother said.

"They want justice," Pilar said. "Cade is an honorable man."

"That shows how little you know your future husband."

"He would never betray his friends," she said.

"I didn't have any choice. I had to do something that would convince the Union I wasn't a spy."

"So you stole your best friend's money and watched twenty-four of your fellow soldiers die."

"I was miles away when it happened."

"How can you admit what you've done without being overcome by shame?"

"Shame? Do you think I gave a damn for any of those men? I'd have sacrificed every one of them to see Cade dead. Curse that man! He always did have all the luck."

"I think his good fortune comes from hard work, attention to detail, and the ability to inspire confidence in those working with him."

"I don't care what you call it as long as you help me kill him."

"I can't. I won't."

"But you must," her grandmother said. "Only then will Laveau be safe."

Pilar had been shocked that Laveau could casually consider killing anybody, but she was stunned that her grandmother could feel the same way.

"There are seven men who want to see you face justice."

"They'll leave once Cade's dead."

"They'll be even more determined to hang you."

"I'll kill them all first."

"The land isn't worth the lives of so many men, and I don't believe you care about it that much. I've heard you say it's more than you could look after."

"It was my land," her grandmother said. "It came to your grandfather with my marriage. It belongs to us."

Pilar couldn't argue that, she didn't want to, but it hardly seemed reason enough to warrant so many people dying.

"I can't help you kill Cade," she said. "I wouldn't know how to begin. I wouldn't do it if I did."

"Then you're a traitor."

"I've made no promises to go back on. I've betrayed no one. No one has died because of me."

"Don't you have any family loyalty?"

"Don't you preach loyalty to me. I'm not the one who ran off and left two women to fend for themselves. I'm not the one who slunk around, hiding in bushes, afraid for his life, while somebody else protected his grandmother and sister."

"They would have killed me if I had returned."

"They're angry, but I think I could talk them out of it."

"You know nothing about them."

"I have worked with them for the past several weeks. They're all hardworking, honorable men. I like them."

"They'd all like to kill me."

"Then I suggest you leave."

Her words shocked her as much as they obviously shocked her brother and grandmother.

"This is your brother," her grandmother said. "You owe him your loyalty and your allegiance."

Pilar could no longer accept this blind, reasonless loyalty, especially when doing so would result in evil. "I am loyal to him but will not help him commit murder. I could never look myself in the face again."

"It is your duty. You must support your family in everything."

"I support my family, but—"

"There can be no exceptions," her grandmother said.

"You're either for me or against me," Laveau said.

Pilar had never expected that Laveau would draw such a line, but she couldn't do as he asked.

"If you leave, I'll send you half of everything we earn," she told him. "I've asked Cade to manage the herd for us. He will sell—"

"You've done what!"

"I had to hire somebody. He's a good rancher. He's honest, dependable, and—"

"You sound like you're in love with him."

She wouldn't have given herself away if his accusation hadn't been so unexpected. She knew her flush was undeniable. "Yes, I am in love with him."

Laveau's face went cold and hard. She saw the hate-filled expression of a man she didn't know. "You greedy little bitch! You've probably been plotting all along to marry him and keep the whole ranch for yourself. You probably knew I was here and sent somebody to warn Cade. Now you're keeping me here until he arrives."

"Don't be ridiculous," she said, barely able to collect her thoughts in the face of his spewing hatred.

"How is it being ridiculous to suspect my sister when she's going to marry the man who wants to kill me?"

He came toward her, his expression so violent she almost believed he would kill her. Wheeler was between them in an instant, teeth bared, a growl deep in his throat.

"I'd be careful if I were you. He nearly killed the last man who tried to hurt me."

"I'll kill him first."

Pilar stepped forward to protect Wheeler. "Your quarrel is with me, not the dog."

"Now that you are here, we can tell Cade to go," their grandmother said to Laveau.

"You don't understand," Laveau shouted. "He means to kill me. I can't stay unless he's dead."

"Then leave before the men come back this evening," Pilar said.

He looked like he didn't believe her words. "You would throw your own brother out?"

"Stay if you wish."

"You've got to help me—"

"No! I won't help Cade find you, but I will have no part in your harming even one of these men. I have no money, but I will prepare some food."

"Harlot!"

"Think what you want of me. I don't care anymore."

❧

"There's nobody else in the house now," Pilar said to

Laveau. "You must go. Now. Ivan may return any minute."

She had led him through a storeroom to a door that opened out on what had been the kitchen garden. Little remained of the trees and vines that had once flourished there, but it offered Laveau a means of escape.

"I could kill him."

"You'd have every man in the area on your trail," Pilar said. "Cade would see to it."

Laveau cursed long and hard. He wasn't even grateful when Pilar gave him the last pieces of their grandmother's jewelry.

"This is not enough."

"It's all we have."

Pilar was thankful that Ivan was working on the other side of the stables. She was equally thankful that Manuel had decided to ride out with Cade. Laveau made no attempt to keep his voice down.

"I'll come back, and I'll get even with you and your lover."

Pilar couldn't tell him Cade wasn't her lover because he was. "I hope you will come back. Maybe in a few years Cade and the others will forget."

"*I* won't forget, and I'll make sure I shoot that dog."

Pilar said nothing. She was certain it must be hard for Laveau to be driven out of his own home knowing his most hated enemy was welcome.

"Write me as soon as you get settled," Pilar said.

"So you can tell Cade where to find me?"

"Cade knows I will not do that. I can't send you any money if I don't know where you are."

"When can I expect money?"

"Cade said he'd take the first herd to market in the spring."

She listened to him complain that he didn't know how he'd live until then. She didn't say anything because she didn't know what to say. She watched him look around carefully and then make a run for the nearest sheltering trees. They swallowed him up, and she saw him no more.

She felt guilty that the most prominent emotion she felt was relief. She turned back toward the hacienda. She looked up at the huge building and wondered how she could have thought that coming back here would be the answer to everything.

She thought of the promises she and Cade had made to each other, that they could turn their backs on all this and live at the Wheeler ranch without regret. She wished it were possible. She had been a fool to make love to Cade, a fool to think it would change anything.

She still couldn't marry him.

In that same instant she knew something else as well.

❧

"I'm not going to marry you," she said to Manuel. "I want you to return to Mexico immediately."

Manuel looked from Pilar to her grandmother and back. "You don't mean what you're saying. You're just upset Laveau has had to run away because that man—"

"This has nothing to do with Laveau. If I can't marry the one man I want to marry, I won't marry anyone at all."

"You must stop her," Manuel said to her grandmother. "She can't do this."

"I have talked to her and talked to her. She refuses to change her mind."

"I have a signed contract."

"I didn't sign it," Pilar said.

"I will make you. I will—"

He had approached her as he argued, his voice rising with his anger. But as he got close to Pilar, he found himself facing a large dog rather than a helpless woman. A loud bark caused him to jump back.

It also brought Cade into the room.

"What's going on?"

"I've just told Manuel I'm not going to marry him. I've asked him to return to his home immediately."

"What are you waiting for?" Cade asked.

"I cannot be dismissed like this. I—"

"Take your choice. Leave under your own power, or I'll *dismiss* you right through the window. And if you don't move out of the way in a hurry, you'll get hit by your own luggage."

As angry as Manuel was, no one had any doubt that Cade would be as good as his word. Gathering what little dignity he had left, Manuel marched to the door.

"I will vacate this house within the hour."

"Make it half an hour," Cade said.

Manuel slammed the door behind him.

"I hope you are satisfied with yourself." Her grandmother almost stuttered, obviously caught between the desire to pour out her anger at Pilar and her aversion to saying anything in front of Cade.

"I'm not satisfied with anything that's happened for as long as I can remember, but refusing to marry

Manuel was the best for him as well as me. I would have made him a horrible wife."

"It is not for a woman to judge these things. It is for a man to decide——" her grandmother began.

"We've been over this before. I've changed," Pilar said.

"It is your fault," Senora diViere said, turning on Cade. "She never was like this before you came back."

"If I encouraged her to think for herself, I'm glad. Nobody in your family ever thought of her as anything but a poker chip."

"That was my life. It is good enough for her."

"It wasn't nearly good enough for you," Cade said. "According to my grandfather, you are worth two of your husband."

Pilar's surprise at Cade's remark didn't compare to her grandmother's. It left her speechless.

Cade took Pilar's hand, pulled her toward the door. "We have to talk."

Pilar felt her spirits plummet. She knew that after last night, Cade believed she had decided to marry him. She had, but Laveau's arrival had shown her the futility of her decision. She had tried to ignore the problem, had wanted to believe Cade's assurances that they could think of something, but nothing but the death of her brother or her lover could eliminate the hatred between the two men.

"She has nothing to say to you. I forbid you to speak to him. I want him out of the hacienda immediately. Every calamity that has befallen our family is the fault of his family."

"I do have some things to say to Cade, but I can

say them in front of you, Grandmother." Pilar tried to gather her thoughts, say what she had to say.

"If I could have foreseen what would happen, I would have left your grandfather's house the day you arrived. I would have camped in the forest. I would have thrown myself on the mercy of the citizens of San Antonio. I would never have risked falling in love with you. But I didn't know, and I did fall in love with you."

"Pilar! How can you say such a thing?"

She ignored her grandmother. She would have years to face the old woman's recriminations. "You did much more for me than you will ever know. You made me a whole person. No matter what happens, I will always be grateful to you for that."

"A person who turns against her brother and has no respect for her elders."

"I thought being in love, being loved, was enough to enable us to ignore the world, but I was wrong. The world doesn't pay heed to love. Greed and ambition, hatred and revenge demand all the attention."

"We don't have to let it," Cade said.

"You already have. You took a vow to hang my brother for what he did, but I can't be the wife of a man who would hang my brother any more than I could be the widow of a man killed by my brother."

"Laveau won't—"

"This is not about you or Laveau anymore. It's about me, what I want, what I *need*. Last night I made you a promise I thought I could keep. I'm sorry, but I was wrong."

"Pilar, you can't—"

"What promise?"

"Before that, I asked you to round up and sell the cattle for us. I thought I could endure seeing you from time to time, working with you, but I can't do that, either. You must take your friends and go. I'll ask Bolin Bigelow if he'll work for me."

The paralysis that had held Cade motionless fell away and he surged forward. Pilar tried to avoid him, but there was no possibility of resistance. He swept her into his arms. "I'm not going to let you do this."

"You can't stop me."

"This is my happiness you're talking about, not just yours."

"You couldn't be happy married to a wife who was miserable."

"I'd be even more miserable not being married to you."

"I forbid you to talk in this manner," her grandmother said.

Cade ignored her and kissed Pilar ruthlessly. Her grandmother's outraged screech had no effect on him. "You can't deny that you love me."

"I don't. I never will, but I won't marry you."

Cade seemed to freeze. "You really mean that, don't you?"

"Yes."

He released her and stepped back. "Your brother isn't worth the sacrifice of my happiness. He most certainly isn't worth the sacrifice of yours. I won't let you do this."

"You can't stop me."

"Yes, I can. I don't know how just yet, but I will

figure it out. Laveau diViere is a liar, a traitor, and a thief." He ignored another shrill protest from her grandmother. "I won't let him spoil your life."

"If he's so vile, why should you want to marry his sister?"

"Because you're as wonderful as he is vile. Know this, Pilar diViere, you are going to be my wife. And you're going to *want* to be married to me."

He turned and stalked out of the room.

"I wish Laveau had shot him."

"No, you don't, Grandmother. Because then I would have had to kill Laveau."

❧

Pilar lay awake, too restless to sleep, her brain in constant turmoil with questions she'd asked herself a hundred times only to discover they had no answers. The last three days had passed with agonizing slowness. Cade refused to leave the ranch regardless of what she or her grandmother said. When she asked why he ignored her, he said only that he was waiting for her to come to her senses. His friends were equally uncommunicative.

Even Owen, who usually was quite happy to put a spoke in Cade's wheel, had cast his lot firmly with his cousin. "You're wrong" was all she could get out of him.

Holt wasn't much better. "It's stupid to be loyal to someone just because you share the same parents."

Nate and Broc avoided her. Rafe rarely spoke. Ivan refused to talk about anything except how to put indoor plumbing in the hacienda.

"They would go if you did not cook for them," her grandmother said.

"They would simply do their own cooking."

Her grandmother didn't understand men who would prepare their own food, but then her grandmother didn't understand anything about a man like Cade. Pilar decided she must not understand him very well herself. She had begged him to go, pleaded with him. He'd said he'd leave when she didn't love him any longer. Her reply that he'd have to stay forever elicited "That's exactly what I mean to do" from him.

He had to go, but she didn't want him to.

Frustrated, she sat up in bed. Silence reigned in the hacienda except for the soft breathing of Wheeler asleep in the corner. She got out of bed and went over to the window. She didn't know why she was so restless tonight. It was almost as though she could feel something about to happen. She kept telling herself she was being foolish, that Cade was sleeping next door with more than a dozen men scattered through the hacienda. They were armed and prepared for any attack. It would take a small army to break into the hacienda. Yet the feeling that Cade was in danger would not leave her.

She felt her lips curve in a rueful smile. The only person in danger would be anyone foolish enough to attack Cade. He was big, powerful, and according to his friends, the best hand-to-hand brawler of the group.

That wasn't the only kind of hand-to-hand encounter he was good at.

Pilar felt herself grow warm with the memory of their lovemaking. She had comforted herself by reliving every kiss, every moment of ecstasy, but each time left her longing for more, having to fight harder to convince herself she couldn't marry Cade, that she shouldn't simply open the door between their rooms and go to him.

She'd hoped he would come to her, but she knew he was too honorable to use her body against her. She was thankful he had such firm principles. She doubted she could have held out against him.

She looked out the window. The night seemed perfectly designed for skulduggery. The full moon hid itself behind dark clouds that scurried across the black sky, almost as though racing ahead of some pursuing enemy. The leaves of the trees remained deathly still, rendering sounds louder, more ominous. The inky blackness under the trees could have shielded the entire army of the devil.

Pilar chided herself for being so foolish. She hadn't behaved this irrationally since the night the squatters attacked the hacienda. It had been wakefulness then that had enabled her and her grandmother to escape.

Could her wakefulness again be a harbinger of danger? Should she wake Cade and warm him?

She didn't have to turn her head to visualize the door between their rooms. It would be so simple to walk over, open it, warn Cade.

Warn him of what? That she had premonitions of danger? He'd think she was crazy or making an excuse to get into his bed. She forced herself to put the door out of her mind. She *would not* go through all the arguments again why she couldn't marry Cade. She *would not* go through all the reasons she couldn't go into his room and let him make love to her. She *would not* recount all the reasons Cade was at least a hundred times a better choice to manage her herds than Bolin Bigelow. She *would not* attempt to remind herself of why she would go mad if she had to see him, talk to him, be near him for as much as one month and not be able to make love to him. Going over the same territory was making her so irritable she was jumpy.

She opened the window to let some of the night air cool her fevered body. Her grandmother believed night air contained dangerous miasmas that harmed the constitution. Pilar wondered if there was something in the night air that could unsettle the mind. The air tonight seemed thick and sinister. She told herself she was imagining things, that one night's air was much the same as any other night's. Maybe a storm was brewing.

She closed the window and turned back to her bed, determined to put the premonitions out of her head. But getting back into bed did nothing to remove them. She still had the feeling that something was going to happen to Cade. She lay there for a while— she had no idea how long—her hands folded across her chest, eyes closed, her body straight and rigid. She *would* go back to sleep. She *would* stop imagining that sinister persons lurked outside the hacienda.

Finally she could stand it no longer. She threw the covers aside and got out of bed. Regardless of how ridiculous it seemed, she wouldn't be able to go to sleep until she satisfied herself that Cade was sleeping soundly in his bed. She wouldn't wake him up, just ease the door open, listen for his breathing, then get back into her own bed reassured and able to go to sleep.

She crossed the room on tiptoe, eased the door open, and stared into the blackness that filled the room. She could barely make out the bed against the wall and the shape of Cade's body. He was sleeping on his side, turned toward the window and away from the door. He moved restlessly, flinging his arms, jerking at the covers as he turned on his other side.

She struggled for a moment with the desire to get closer to him, to stand for just a few minutes looking at him, drinking in the feeling of completeness that only he could give her. She finally began to back away. She knew that if she crossed the room, she would stay for the rest of the night.

She backed through the doorway. Just as she reached out to pull the door shut, her ears caught the faint sound of a door opening. Thinking it was her own door, she was prepared to jump back into her room and into her bed when she saw a rectangle of light open on the far side of Cade's bedroom. Framed in the light was the outline of a man with a knife in his hand.

Twenty-six

BEDEVILED BY A DREAM IN WHICH HE WAS PURSUED BY a dozen gun-toting rustlers, Cade tossed restlessly on the verge of wakefulness. A scream brought him out of his fitful slumber as a sense of impending danger caused him to roll to the far side of the bed.

In the same instant that he realized Pilar was in his room, a knife plunged into the mattress where he had lain half an instant before. His attention was riveted on the dark form hovering next to the bed. He could barely make out Pilar's shape as she raced across the room to get between him and his attacker. It was incredible that she would do such a thing. She could be killed.

But even as he got his feet under him and prepared to launch himself across the bed, the intruder pushed Pilar to the floor. "It's Laveau," she cried as she lost her balance. "He means to kill you."

Cade struck Laveau with the full force of his body, and they went down together. Cade located the knife as it opened a cut across his ribs. Forcing himself to ignore the pain, he twisted about, using his weight to pin Laveau to the floor, struggling to get a grip on his knife hand before he could strike again. He caught Laveau's wrist just as it swung a second time, but not before the point of the knife entered the flesh of his upper arm. Muttering curses at the pain, Cade gripped Laveau's hand in both of his and broke his wrist.

He heard the bones snap—it sounded like the breaking of small, dry twigs—before Laveau's scream of pain shattered what was left of the night's quiet.

Light suddenly illuminated the darkness. Pilar had struck a match.

"The boys have been waiting for a chance to get their hands on you," Cade said, attempting to get to his feet. He slipped and fell, reached out, and found the floor covered with something warm and wet. His own blood. Suddenly reminded of the pain, he put his hand to his side, felt warm blood as it soaked through his nightshirt to coat his hand.

"You broke my hand," Laveau wailed.

"I preferred that to having a knife in my heart."

"The others will be up here in a moment," Pilar warned. "Get away while you can."

"How am I supposed to survive with a broken hand?"

Pilar pushed her brother toward the door. "Go. Please. Before they find you."

"Stop," Cade said. He reached under the pillow for the gun he always kept at his side. Just as his fingers closed around the gun, Pilar threw her body across his arm.

"Run," she screamed at her brother, "or they'll kill you!"

"Let go of my arm," Cade said.

"I won't let you kill Laveau. I can't." She turned to look at Laveau. "Go, you idiot! Can't you hear them coming?"

Before Cade could free his arm from Pilar's grip, Laveau seemed to come to his senses, become aware of the danger. He darted through the door into Pilar's room moments before Rafe charged through the bedroom door.

"What's going on?"

"It's Laveau," Cade said. "He tried to kill me. He ran into Pilar's room."

Pilar couldn't be sure, but she thought she heard something hit the ground outside. She hoped Laveau had jumped from her window. The risk of a broken leg was better than the certainty of a broken neck.

Rafe darted through the door between the rooms as sounds of running feet and shouts of alarm sounded from all corners of the hacienda. In no time at all the room was crowded, the light of three lanterns exposing the knife wound in Cade's side.

"He cut you," Owen said.

"He has a knife," Cade said, getting to his feet slowly.

"He must have jumped from the window," Rafe said when he returned to the room. "Come on. If we hurry, maybe we can catch him."

"I'll get my bag," Holt said. "You need stitches."

The room emptied as quickly as it had filled. Cade turned to Pilar. "You let him escape. You held my arm until he got away."

"I couldn't let you kill him."

"I wasn't going to kill him. I was just going to—"

"Hold him so your friends could kill him. That's pretty much the same to me, Cade."

"He's a traitor, Pilar. He's responsible for the deaths of innocent men."

"I know, and I accept that he must pay his debt, but I can't let you be the one to collect it."

"But you won't marry me. It doesn't make any difference."

"I can't stop loving you. That's what makes the difference."

"But you don't love me enough to marry me."

"I want to marry you more than anything in the world, but I can't, knowing sooner or later you'll be responsible for my brother's death. I understand why you feel you've got to do this. Please understand why I can't."

"The war—"

"The war is over. It's time for people to rebuild their lives. I'm sure there were many terrible things that happened, but if you can't let go of them, you'll never be happy."

"I can't let go of this. If you had known the men—"

"But I didn't. I'll never be able to feel any different."

The choice before Cade was simple. Hold on to his need for revenge and lose his chance for happiness or give up his pursuit of Laveau and marry the only woman he could ever love. But he couldn't turn his back on his dead comrades any more than he could give up Pilar.

There had to be a compromise. He had to be able to find it and convince her to accept it. In that moment he knew what it was.

"Come here."

She came gradually into the light of the single candle.

"I'll make you a promise. I will not pursue Laveau, but if he falls into my hands, I can't in all honor let him go. I'll turn him over to a sheriff or some other law officer and do my best to see he gets a fair trial. I'll do my best to convince my friends to do the same. But if I do that, you'll have to make me a promise."

"What?"

"If I should happen to be the one responsible for turning Laveau over to the authorities and he is judged guilty and hanged, you will not hold me responsible for his death. You will have to be able to accept the fact that his actions determined his fate."

She didn't move, not even by the flicker of an eyelash. He waited, his breath suspended, knowing that the rest of his life would depend on the next words she uttered. As the moment stretched into more and more moments, he began to fear he'd asked too much of her. But he couldn't ask less. He was honor bound to fight for justice for his men. There was no one else to do it for them. If it meant he had to sacrifice his happiness, he had no choice.

Pilar's shoulders sagged. Her face relaxed into a very slow smile. "Yes," she said. "I would very much like to be your wife."

They were still clutched in a fierce embrace when Holt returned.

"Let me borrow him for a minute. If you want to marry him, he's going to need all the blood he has left."

∽✦∾

Cade and Pilar felt like two castaways caught in the eye of a storm. Cade's friends had shouted at him, and Pilar's grandmother had done everything but take a hairbrush to Pilar, but no one could make them change their minds. Nobody was willing to accept their compromise. They all felt they had been betrayed. The rancor of Cade's friends had been particularly hard on him. Nate was so angry he had threatened to go after Laveau himself. Owen's attack had been just as sharp until Rafe spoke up.

"Cade doesn't owe you the rest of his life," he'd said, cutting Owen off in the middle of a particularly acrimonious diatribe. "He saved your lives in Virginia, and he's giving all of us the means to start fresh. He's fulfilled his duty as our leader."

"The hell he has!" Owen shouted.

"He's put limits on it," Rafe said, "limits determined by his personal need for happiness, his need to put the war and all its immorality behind him. The fate of this country depends on people like Cade and Pilar being able to work toward a future that's better than the past. We all have our individual ghosts we need to put to rest—hanging Laveau or whatever else it may be—but knowing that Cade has made the compromises necessary to create new hope and a new life should encourage you to do the same when your time comes. Now if you can't accept his compromise, I say you ought to get the hell out and leave him alone."

Rafe's speech, the longest anyone had ever heard him make, had forced his friends to reexamine their feelings about what Cade had done. It was clear that the vow that had bound them together would never again be their all-consuming obsession.

"That's as it should be," Rafe had said before retreating into silence.

The only person who seemed pleased was Cade's grandfather.

"It's about time you got sensible," he said to his grandson. "No point in letting all that land go begging over a bunch of dead men."

Senora diViere refused to come out of her room while Earl was in the hacienda. Her temper had become so volatile, Pilar was tempted to ask the old curmudgeon to move in just to give her relief from her grandmother's continual anger. Now that she was going to be his daughter-in-law, he didn't find so much wrong with her.

"It's amazing how the prospect of wealth can improve a person's character," Cade said to his grandfather.

"Don't get smart with me," Earl said. "You'll have to work for your money. Her steers are as wild as bejesus."

Cade had to listen to his grandfather's plans for ways to take the quickest advantage of the diViere land and herds. Pilar had to endure her grandmother's lamentations that the Wheelers would rob them of everything they had. She swore she would go live with Laveau as soon as she knew where he'd settled. Earl said he hoped she didn't change her mind. "Just her being here is enough to turn a baby's milk sour." He winked at Cade. "I expect you'll be welcoming your first son come summer."

"Or daughter," Pilar said.

"Wheelers don't have no daughters," Earl said proudly.

"Things have changed, Gramps," Cade said. "I think it's time you had a great-granddaughter."

Cade teased his grandfather so much the old man threatened to return permanently to the Wheeler ranch, but he changed his mind when Senora diViere said she wouldn't leave her room until he left the hacienda.

"It's my Christian duty to spare you from having to face that woman across the supper table every night," he told Cade.

To escape the overheated emotions swirling around them, each evening after supper was over, Cade and Pilar would sneak away by themselves to a small hill they'd discovered overlooking the valley where the San Antonio River made its way to the Gulf of Mexico. There they could concentrate on their love and each other. They didn't do a lot of talking.

"I'm sorry about my grandfather," Cade said. "He's really not as bad as he seems."

"My grandmother is worse than she seems. She really hates you."

"Maybe she'll change after your first son is born."

"She'll say Laveau's son should have been born first."

"I don't care as long as you continue to love me."

"I'll never stop."

"You don't regret it, do you?" he asked a few moments later.

"I'll never regret marrying you."

"Not even though it means you'll be estranged from your grandmother?"

"I love my grandmother, but I can't live my life for her. I want to live it with you."

"And all those great-grandsons we're going to give her."

"Them, too, but it's you I love. It's always been you. There's never been anybody else."

"Poor Manuel. I feel sorry for him."

"Don't. He'll marry some meek girl who'll think he's a god. She'll devote herself to pleasing him and making him feel he's the most important man in the world. He'll love it."

"That doesn't sound half bad. Do you know any girls who might like to devote their lives to pleasing me?"

Pilar punched him. "You look at another woman, and I'll scratch her eyes out."

"Mine, too?"

"No. I want you to be able to see what a wonderful choice you made."

Cade's laughter started as a low rumble and grew in volume until he was really quite loud. "I could be blind and still know you were perfect. Dangerous, but still perfect."

Epilogue

LAVEAU REMAINED CONCEALED IN THE TREES, HIS broken hand splinted and useless at his side, a pair of binoculars in the other. The longer he watched, the more his rage grew. The festivities of Pilar and Cade's wedding had spilled outside the hacienda. He was too far away to hear the music, but he could easily make out Cade and Pilar as they danced. He recognized the faces of the men who encouraged them with boisterous shouts accompanied by smiles and laughter. He didn't recognize everyone, but he knew some of the guests to be neighboring ranchers, some important people from San Antonio. Everybody had turned out to welcome Cade home and celebrate his wedding.

Laveau's curses were pithy and continuous.

Cade not only had all the diViere land, he had the diViere heiress. The Wheeler triumph was complete. They had taken everything. It didn't matter to Laveau that he technically still owned half of the rancho. He wasn't free to enter it. He might as well have been an outcast. With a last withering curse, he put his binoculars into their case and melted back into the thicket where his horse waited.

It took considerable effort, caused some pain, and elicited a lot more curses, but he managed to hoist himself into the saddle. Being careful to avoid low-hanging limbs and thorny branches, he worked his way out of the thicket and headed south.

"I'll be back," he vowed.

He wouldn't rest until he'd finished what the Union soldiers had begun—the complete destruction of the Night Riders. He reserved special vengeance for his sister.

No one betrayed Laveau diViere.

About the Author

Leigh Greenwood is the award-winning author of over fifty books, many of which have appeared on the *USA Today* bestseller list. Leigh lives in Charlotte, North Carolina. Please visit his website at www.leigh-greenwood.com.

Read on for a sneak peek of the second book in the
Men of Legend series by New York Times
bestselling author Linda Broday

the HEART of a TEXAS COWBOY

North Texas
Spring 1876

SOME OLD WIVES SOMEWHERE PROBABLY SAID THAT
blood on a wedding day forewarned of things to
come. But he didn't have any patience for curses or
omens today. Becky Golden was the only girl he'd
ever loved. They were perfect for each other.

Nothing would stop him from making a future
with her. Nothing.

Houston Legend sucked a drop of blood from the
thumb he'd cut on a piece of shattered coffee cup.
"Great," he muttered. He'd probably get blood on
the highfalutin ascot he was trying to tie. One good
thing—it was black.

"Houston, get a move on. You're going to be late

for your wedding." His brother's bellow was louder than a snorting, snot-slinging steer on the rampage. The huge stone house that served as headquarters for the famous Lone Star Ranch picked up his voice and bounced it around the walls.

"Hold your horses!" Houston Legend fumbled with the fancy neckpiece that his beautiful bride-to-be had insisted he wear.

The bedroom door flung open and his younger brother Sam poked his head in. "What's the holdup?"

"This damn tie. For two cents I'd wear my normal clothes." Houston shot a longing glance at his comfortable trousers and shirt on the bed. He seldom wore a neckpiece and when he did, it was a simple western tie. "This isn't me. I think it's called an ascot or some such nonsense, but with this thingamajig on, the only ass in the room is me."

Sam strode forward. "You can do anything once, big brother. Becky wants her wedding perfect and you're gonna give it to her. Let me see it."

With a flick of his wrists, Sam had the silk neckpiece tied in nothing flat. "Where's your stickpin?"

Houston handed him the diamond pin. "You're not wearing your sheriff's badge."

"Not on duty." Sam reached for the black cutaway coat and held it for Houston. "Besides, it ruins the look of my suit."

A former Texas Ranger, Sam had given up the job when he married Sierra Hunt and adopted an orphaned boy two months ago. Sam was now sheriff of Lost Point, Texas—a place that until recently had been an outlaw haven. The town was an hour's ride from the Lone Star, so that made their pa happy. Stoker had said if Sam couldn't live on the ranch, he wanted him nearby. Houston was glad he hadn't gone far. He liked having his brother around.

"Shouldn't need the badge today. At least I hope not." Houston nodded and shot him a grin. "Were you nervous when you and Sierra tied the knot? My hands are shaking."

"Mine shook too the day I wed Sierra." Sam shot him a narrowed glance. "Becky's the right one, isn't she? I mean you don't have any doubts or anything."

Houston paused for a moment in thought. Although they'd grown up together on different ranches, he knew the exact second he'd fallen hard. Becky was ten and Houston had been twelve. It was right after they'd buried his mother. Although he protested, his father made him go to a barn dance at the Golden ranch. She wore a blue dress that seemed woven from his dreams and the soft lantern light shining on her hair reminded him of daffodils. He knew right then that there would never be another girl for him. Lord, how his heart pounded when he took her in his arms. Becky pushed away the dark shadows of his life with rays of sunshine. He'd known then that she was his one true love for all eternity, and he still knew it now.

"She's the one," Houston assured him.

"I wish Mother was alive to see you," Sam said quietly. "You'd make her proud." He wandered to the window and pushed the curtain aside. "I wonder if Luke will show up."

With one last glance in the mirror, Houston turned. "Hope so. I miss him, you know. I really like having our outlaw brother in the family—it's easier than having a lawman like you, anyway."

Sam moved from the window and flicked off a piece of lint from Houston's shoulder.

Houston slapped his hand. "Stop it. You're not Mother."

Paying him no mind, Sam straightened the ascot. "I worry about Luke out there all alone, searching for the man who framed him for murder. He needs us."

"It's what he chose," Houston reminded him.

Music drifted upstairs from the piano they'd lugged outside for the ceremony. Both bolted from the room. Houston would never hear the end of it if he kept Becky waiting at the altar.

A few minutes later, he pushed through the door and stepped onto the wide porch. Though this was a ranch, it was so large that it was more like a town, complete with a mercantile, school, telegraph office, and its own doctor. The early May afternoon was beautiful with sun splashing onto rooftops and white-washed buildings.

Everything was perfect, and not a cloud in the sky.

He and Sam strode to stand next to the preacher they'd brought all the way from Squaw Valley, the nearest town with a church. Overhead, the Texas flag fluttered in the breeze and the sun caught on the huge bronze star that hung suspended twenty feet away. The brilliant rays passed through the cutouts in each star point, creating a beautiful image at Houston's feet.

Reverend Smith fought a sudden gust of wind that sent his long red hair tumbling, blocking his vision. Remaining ramrod straight, he calmly parted the copper strands in the center like a curtain and peered out. Houston covered his mouth to keep from laughing.

The pianist launched into the wedding march and all eyes turned. Houston's tongue glued to the roof of his mouth. Becky was truly a vision with her golden hair hanging in ringlets from the crown of her head.

How had he landed such a breathtaking woman? Must've been fate. She slowly made her way to his side and took Houston's hand. Crazy with love for her, he stared into her soft brown eyes and squeezed her palm. He mouthed, "I love you for all of eternity."

The sound of a horse whickering outside caught his attention. Guests had been arriving all day. When he glanced up, he spotted his brother Luke, standing apart from the rest next to his black gelding. He'd made it after all. Their gazes met and he nodded to Houston. Houston nodded back, happier than he'd ever been in his life.

Just as the good reverend opened his mouth to speak, a single shot rang out. It happened so fast, no one had time to react. As if in a daze, Houston heard Becky cry out, watched her collapse. He caught her in his arms before she hit the ground.

Blood oozed from a hole in her chest and stained her beautiful blue dress.

Two

CHAOS ENSUED. GUESTS SCREAMED. SOME DROPPED onto their bellies while others ran for cover. Mothers shielded their children with their bodies.

In shock, Houston stared as Luke whirled and fired faster than a man could breathe, aiming toward the corner of the house. Sam leaped over bodies, racing to capture the shooter.

Shrugging off his coat, Houston placed it over his bride. Her eyes were open and filled with pain. A gurgling came from her throat, freezing Houston's heart.

"Someone get Doc Jenkins!" he shouted as he focused on his bride. "Dearest, hold on. Doc will be here in a minute. He'll fix you up and you'll be fine. Just don't go to sleep. Please don't close your eyes. Look at me and don't close them."

Houston's hand trembled when he brushed her hair back from her face. This couldn't happen to the woman he loved.

She had to live. They had so much happiness ahead of them.

Please, God, don't take her. Take me instead.

The gurgling worsened. She went limp as life drained from her body.

Doc Jenkins knelt beside him and felt for a pulse. Sadly, he shook his head.

How long Houston held her to him, he didn't know. His father knelt beside him. "Son, you have to let her go. Becky is gone. You can't do anything else for her. Let us take her into the house."

"I can't, Pa."

"Yes, you can. Just let her go."

"I love her." The deafening cry that sprang from Houston's mouth sounded like it came from some wild animal. He met his father's stricken gaze. "Why? Why did this happen to Becky of all people?"

"I don't know, son." Stoker laid an arm across Houston's shoulders. "We're going to find out though; you can damn sure bet on that."

"I hope they catch the bastard and that he's alive."

"I only know Luke's bullet struck him. I haven't heard how bad it is."

"Good that they caught him. I hope he doesn't bite the dust before I can talk to him." Houston would do a damn sight more than talk. He'd rip the man apart piece by piece and take deep satisfaction in the pain he inflicted.

"Houston, let these men have her so they can take her into the house, away from curious eyes," Stoker said gently.

Houston slowly released his grip.

Fighting crushing pain, Houston watched as men carried his love into the Lone Star headquarters and out of sight. Nothing made sense. How could Becky be dead? He accepted his father's hand and put weight on legs that seemed made of wood.

Only one thing penetrated the shock and horror—he'd lost the love of his life, and someone would pay. He'd take great pleasure in making sure the murdering bastard never hurt another woman. He knew ways to get the shooter to talk.

Oh yeah, lots of ways, and all of them very painful.

♠

How much time had passed Houston couldn't venture a guess although something told him it must've been quite a while. He sat next to Becky's cold body in the dim parlor. Seeing her on the sofa so silent and still, he couldn't believe she was dead. Piercing pain ripped through him and he had to force himself to breathe. He was glad someone had pulled the thick drapes that blocked out most of the sunlight. The dim shadows let him grieve in private. He just wanted to be left alone in the darkness of his soul.

In the shadows, he could pretend it was all a dream and she'd wake up. Sobs erupted around him, reminding him that he wasn't alone as he wished, but he paid them no heed. He was lost in a thick haze, where little thought could penetrate. Though he felt sympathetic mourners touch his back, he didn't turn to acknowledge them.

Why couldn't they leave him be with the woman he loved?

He unclenched his fist and stared at the bloody veil he gripped. He couldn't let go of the last thing his bride had worn.

Wailing echoed through the walls of the huge house that was still filled with wedding guests. He'd briefly spoken to Becky's parents but they, like him, were grief-stricken and in shock.

How the hell had this happened? How could the love of his life lie stone dead? It couldn't be possible. Houston still felt the weight of her in his arms as she fell. Still heard the gurgle as life drained from her body. Still smelled the stench of death.

How would he be able to live without his Becky?

Stoker Legend pressed a glass of whiskey into his hand. "Drink this. It'll brace you for what you have to do."

Houston took the offering but didn't drink. "Why, Pa? Why did someone have to shoot her? She never hurt a fly, nor spoke ill of anyone."

"I don't know, son." Stoker dropped heavily into the chair next to Houston. "But you can damn well bet we'll find out, even if we have to rip the killer apart."

"Sam and Luke really caught him? There's no mistake?" Houston's thoughts were so muddled. Words refused to penetrate his brain or maybe they were rebelling like him, refusing to believe what had happened.

"Yes, your brothers did get the bastard. Doc Jenkins is treating the wound where Luke shot him." Stoker emptied his glass in one gulp.

Houston stared down at the bloody veil.

Becky was gone and he didn't know how he could live without her.

Daylight had begun to fade and Houston still sat with Becky in the parlor. The room was quiet and he had such a frightening stillness inside. Houston gripped the glass of whiskey but had yet to take a sip. He hadn't heard his father leave.

Maybe when the bullet took Becky's life, it had taken his hearing too.

Footsteps sounded on the hardwood floor and Sam sat next to him. "Luke and I locked the murdering varmint in the basement, where no one would hear him yell. Doc removed the bullet without benefit of anything for pain."

"Did the sorry bastard say why he did it?" Houston met Sam's eyes. "I hope you waited for me."

"We did, but he's saying plenty without prodding. He says Becky belonged to him, and he couldn't let you have her."

"She wouldn't let some cur dog think he had a chance in hell at her heart." Becky wasn't that sort of woman.

She would've made a wonderful mother for their children. The house he'd built for her just past the schoolhouse would sit empty forever.

The cry that tore from Houston's throat made a sound he'd never heard before. Rage built higher and higher until he shot to his feet hurled the still-untouched whiskey glass against the wall. It shattered, sending shards everywhere and amber liquid running down the expensive wallpaper like tears. "I want to hear that from his lips, see his eyes. I want to taste his fear. I want him to choke when I put my hands around his damn throat."

Full of blinding fury, Houston stuffed Becky's wedding veil into his pocket and stormed from the room with Sam trailing behind. The crack of his boot heels against the floor sounded like rifle shots all the way down to the basement door off the kitchen.

In seconds, Houston stood over the rotten bastard who'd viciously stolen his bride. He recognized him from the handful of times he'd seen the man on the Golden Ranch. Ernie Newman lay on a blanket on the dirt floor with Luke guarding from a nearby crate.

Cold, sullen eyes glared up.

Overcome with a rage unlike anything he'd ever felt, he grabbed Newman by the shirtfront, lifting him off his feet with one hand. Houston slammed a fist into the man's face.

When he drew back to hit him again, Luke grabbed his arm. "Beating him senseless won't change the facts, brother."

Houston flung the man back to the blanket. "You're lucky my brothers are here or I'd kill you. I want answers and I'll know if you're lying. For each lie, I'll hit you again."

Hate flashed from Newman's eyes as he dragged his sleeve across his bloody mouth.

"How well did you know Becky?" Houston yelled.

"She always came to me when she needed her horse saddled or the wagon hitched. Then she came to find me just to talk. No woman ever gave me the time of day until I met her."

"Prove it."

"Whatever you want, *Mr. Legend*. I watched from a window when you gave her a ring and asked her father for her hand," Newman spat. "I watched it all. She was having a child—mine."

"You're a lying sack of shit!"

"We planned to run off together but she couldn't do that to her parents. She knew it would've killed them. Doc Jenkins can provide proof of the babe."

Houston turned to Sam. "Bring Doc down here. We'll find out the truth."

Sam nodded and left. Houston leaned against the basement wall to wait. He cast daggers at Becky's killer. No one spoke—not Luke, Houston, or Ernie. It didn't take long for Sam to return.

"What can I do for you, Houston?" Doc asked.

Houston shoved away from the wall. "Tell me about Becky. Tell me she wasn't with child."

"I can't do that." Doc glanced at Newman. "Becky came to me with her secret, begging me not to tell you or her parents. I urged her to come clean, but she said she couldn't. I'm sorry, son." Doc hesitated a moment, torn by whatever he saw on Houston's face, turned, and climbed the stairs to the kitchen without another word.

The air left Houston. It was true. Everything Newman said. Houston wanted to pound something. Anger sat thick and bitter on his tongue.

"Why in hell would she agree to marry me, then?" Houston thundered. He grabbed Newman and slammed his fist into the bastard's jaw. "Why?"

Newman's cold eyes glittered. "Becky was desperate for a name for the babe and her parents wouldn't let her marry me. I wasn't good enough for their daughter. And apparently Becky shared their views.

We had a terrible fight this morning. She told me you could better provide for the babe and, when it came, she would tell you it came early."

"So I was nothing but a means to an end?"

"You get the picture. For a smart man, you're really slow, *Mr. Legend*."

God, Houston's stomach revolted, sending bile into his mouth.

Stupid.

Stupid.

Stupid.

He tightened his hands around the man's throat. "Why did you have to kill her? And the babe. It was your flesh and blood, you worthless bastard." Houston could kind of understand the deception and Becky's desperation to some degree. But putting a bullet in her—she hadn't deserved that, no matter what she'd done.

Newman gasped for breath. "If I couldn't have her, no one would. You Legends, with your power and land, think you can have whatever you want. I showed you. Killing her was the only way."

"The only way?" Houston's yell sprang from the hole left deep inside that nothing would ever fill.

"I wanted you to live in hell. When you came to call, you always walked by me like I was some bug crawling on the damn ground. I was beneath the powerful Houston Legend!" Newman shouted.

Houston pushed his face into the man's. It was possible he could've slighted Ernie Newman without even knowing it. On visits to the Golden's, Houston's mind had been on Becky and stealing a kiss not on making friends with the hands. Still he didn't think he was ever rude.

"You did this for what? Revenge?"

"In part. I did love Becky, but she wanted what I couldn't give. I hated you and wanted you to suffer." Newman clawed at Houston's hands.

Something glittered, catching Houston's attention. He released Newman's throat to grab his hand.

On the bastard's little finger winked the family heirloom Becky always wore.

Memories danced around Houston's fury. Becky had said the ring had belonged to her great-grandmother. When it disappeared from her hand, he bought her claim of losing it but noticed how she avoided his eyes. Loving her, he'd silenced the whispers in his head.

A guttural sound of pain sprang from Houston's mouth. He was such a fool. When he kissed her, how could he not have felt her pulling back?

But—he had. He'd simply blocked it. Truth was, she'd sidestepped his kisses and dodged passionate embraces. Most times she'd distracted him with teasing conversation. He'd put down her reluctance to shyness and not wanting to make a show of affection. How could he have been so blind? She'd never once spoken words of love.

The truth hit him.

Becky had never loved him.

"God have mercy on your poor, pitiful, pathetic soul." Houston hurled Newman away and stalked to the stairs. He never wanted to see the man's face again.

From this moment on, he'd never speak Becky's

name or allow it to be spoken in his presence. He'd never trust *love* again.

Houston jerked the bloody veil from his pocket. Wadding it into a ball, he dropped it to the dirt floor and climbed the stairs.

❧

Dawn splashed through the windows of Houston's bedroom. Staggering, he rose from the chair where he'd sat all night. He unbuttoned his blood-soaked shirt and launched it into a corner, frowning at the red stains on his skin. Pouring water from a pitcher into a porcelain bowl, he scrubbed away every trace of Becky. His chest was raw by the time he finished.

In the early morning quiet, Houston forced back memories that crowded his mind. Too many, and all brought jagged pain. He strode to the dresser drawer, selected a clean shirt, and thrust his arms into the sleeves.

Betrayal still shook him to the core.

Last night, he'd helped carry Becky's casket and load it into a wagon for the journey home. People would wonder at his cold distance and refusal to accompany her parents. Let them.

A low knock sounded at the door. "It's open," he barked.

His brothers entered. Sam spoke. "We were worried."

"I'm fine. You can head right back out. I'm in a hell of a mood."

"You wouldn't be normal if you weren't," Luke replied.

"But you're still here." Houston buttoned his shirt and tucked it into his pants.

Sam dropped into a chair in the corner. "We have a suggestion."

"I don't need coddling like some child, Sam. Go tend to your wife and son." Houston put on his hat and snatched his gun belt from the bedpost. "I'm not going to blow my brains out. Just need to be alone. Alone as in *by myself*." He gave them a pointed glare.

"Sierra and Hector are still asleep." Sam folded his arms. "We want to help. You're in shock."

"Yeah, well, I'll live." Somehow or another.

"A good hard ride up to the ridge is what you need."

Damn, Sam wasn't giving up. Houston let out a long sigh. Much as he loved his little brother, Sam's mothering irritated the hell out of him.

"Fresh air is exactly what you need." Luke threw in his two cents. "Besides, I want to talk to you both about something."

"I'm in no mood for this. I just want to be alone." Houston's patience hung by a thread.

Sam sighed and softened his voice. "Remember where we went when our baby brother, William Travis, and Mother died? When Pa dove headfirst into a bottle and couldn't remember he had two scared boys who needed him? When Pa started gambling recklessly? Each time we sought comfort on the ridge above the Red River. It'll help you now."

At last, Houston threw up his hands. "You win." He did need to clear the smell of blood and betrayal from his nostrils, and he'd go crazy if he stayed here listening to his brother's yacking at him. Somehow, he'd pry the worst day of his life from his head.

Houston buckled his gun belt and strapped it on. Reaching for his hat, he strode to the corral with them, where they saddled their horses. A short time later, he galloped with Sam and Luke across raw, uneven ground, letting the wind blow Becky from his mind.

After riding full-out for five miles, Houston reined to a stop on the high bluff overlooking the mighty Red. The water was as murky as his thoughts, and moved just as fast. The hard truth of loving Becky was the part that hurt the most. While he'd been giving his whole heart and soul to her, she'd been slipping around with another man.

Dammit to hell!

He dismounted and sat, letting his feet dangle off the cliff edge. Sam and Luke dropped down on either side of him. No one spoke for a long while. The quiet was good.

Finally, Houston shot Luke a glance. His brother had a thousand-dollar price on his head for robbery and the murder of federal judge, Edgar Percival. The tangled mess of Luke's life was even worse than Houston's.

Maybe talking about someone else's problems would take Houston's mind off his. "You said you wanted to talk about something, Luke."

"My problem is a name taken from one of Beadle's dime novels—Ned Sweeney. The man using it is the one who really murdered Judge Percival." Luke swung to stare into the distance. "Find him and I clear mys of that. Ever hear of anyone going by that name?"

"Nope." Houston absently watched the water below. Had Becky ever truly cared for him, or had she just pretended all these years? He wished he could talk to her once more. He'd ask why she hadn't been honest with him. Why she hadn't been able to tell him about Newman. And why she'd let him fall so deeply in love with her.

"I never heard the name mentioned," Sam said. "How do you know he's the murderer?"

With his thumb and forefinger, Luke pulled his hat lower on his forehead. "I ran into a man, Joe Calderon, down in San Antone, and he told me Ned Sweeney is the one who pulled the trigger. I tried to get Joe to tell the sheriff but he said Ned would kill him."

"Somehow, somewhere, you crossed paths with this killer before," Houston said.

Luke sent a stone zinging out into the water below. "Must've. But don't know where."

"Can you trust this Joe guy?" Sam asked. "He might've fed you a load of bull."

"I've had a few dealings with him. He's always been honest," Luke said.

"How can we help?" Houston asked.

"You and Sam can get access to things I can't. I thought if you could send out some telegrams to different people and see if they've heard of anyone using the name Ned Sweeney, we might find a clear direction for me to go." Luke paused. "I won't ask you for more than you feel comfortable with."

"We'll be glad to help, won't we, Sam?" The ⸱eels in Houston's brain were already turning. A might just calm him down. He was angry, and it would feel good to haul off and hit something. Anything.

"I've still got ties to the Texas Rangers and my old boss, Captain O'Reilly," Sam said.

Luke threw three stones down below in rapid succession. "Thanks. Like I said, you have access to people and places I can never have."

"Turnabout is fair play." Houston laid a hand on his outlaw brother's shoulder. They wouldn't have caught Becky's killer if not for Luke. "We couldn't have whipped Felix Bardo and that outlaw mess that had dug in over at Lost Point without you. Your ability to fit in with them and gain their trust saved the people of that town. You made this part of Texas safer. Sam sure wouldn't be here either if you hadn't cut him down so fast after Bardo hung him."

They owed Luke a hell of a lot more than a few telegrams.

"Sierra's and my wedding sure wouldn't have happened. Felix Bardo would've killed her and certainly meant to," Sam said quietly. "I'll be glad to help in any way."

"Appreciate it." Luke seemed lost in thought. Something more was bothering his brother, but Houston knew better than to ask. One thing Houston had learned about Luke was that you didn't push him. Anyone who tried found themselves full of regrets. "What are you going to do now, Houston?" Luke asked.

"Go on like I always have."

"That's no damn plan," Sam hollered. "You're going to have to deal with what happened sooner or later."

"Sam, it's my problem and I'll handle it," Houston grated out. "Now, if you don't mind, I've got some thinking to do."

"Fine." Sam rose. "By the way, you might like to know that Ernie Newman is gone. Pa and some of the ranch hands have carted him to Fort Worth to stand trial."

"I hope he swings for what he did." Houston wouldn't waste one ounce of pity on him.

Luke got to his feet. "I'm leaving at first light. Don't let this gnaw on you, Houston. A man only has so much flesh. Take it from me."

An ache filled Houston's chest, a space he'd thought couldn't hold any more pain. He didn't know what it was like to be hunted like Luke. He'd always known the safety of the ranch. But after yesterday, he knew death could always find him, no matter where he was.

"When you're out there, don't forget you're a Legend, even if you refused to take the name. And that you have a home and people who care for you," Houston reminded him gruffly.

They had an unbreakable bond.

They were brothers.

They were Legends.

Houston watched his brothers mount up and gallop off. His thoughts turned back to Becky. As much as he'd tried to prevent it, she *would* gnaw on him.

It would take a lifetime to forget the woman who'd ruined him.

Three

IN THE YEAR FOLLOWING THE SHOOTING, HOUSTON threw himself into work with a vengeance, trying to forget Becky and her stinging betrayal. His heart was nothing more than a piece of raw meat that had been stomped and left in the hot sun to wither. He knew he'd let himself descend into darkness, but it was there he found solace…and escape.

Though he tried to resist, he lost the battle, and most nights found him hugging a bottle of whiskey. He turned a blind eye to the looks Stoker, Sam, and sometimes Luke gave him when he briefly swung by. When they said anything, he snapped that he was doing his best.

On a Monday morning in May, Houston pored over the books in the office of Lone Star headquarters and frowned at the figures. The tally didn't make sense. They were four thousand dollars down from where they had been last week. Sure, the ranch had been in trouble for a while, but the steady decline had turned into a free fall off a cliff.

And if he didn't know why, he didn't know how to stop it.

Long-term trouble was coming from the size of their ever-increasing herd and not enough grazing land, even with four hundred eighty thousand acres. Though they'd had a little rain, this year had brought a drought, and the cattle were starving. A ranch in North Texas was always between hay and grass anyway, never flush with either. Simply the hard truth. The only solution for the cattle surge that would bring a little relief was taking two thousand head or more up the Great Western Trail to Dodge City. He'd already given the hands the order to start rounding them up and branding them. He hadn't told Stoker yet. Didn't want an argument.

Having almost a hundred employees to pay didn't help. In addition to the cowboys, they had to support and look after the new schoolteacher, Doc Jenkins, and Jim Wheeler, who operated the telegraph. They also went halves on stocking merchandise for the mercantile, but the store owner kept nearly all the profits.

Houston rubbed his bleary eyes and glanced up as his father entered. His pa didn't appear in any better shape than Houston. His pale-green eyes were bloodshot and his clothes had been slept in, if he'd slept at all. Stoker Legend gave a deep sigh and slumped into the leather chair opposite the desk.

The ladies around the ranch would say Stoker Legend was a handsome man for fifty-eight years old. Only a smattering of silver streaked his dark hair and he didn't have an ounce of fat on his tall frame. Stoker was a man who'd lived hard and carved out the famous Lone Star spread from nothing. He'd cut his teeth on men who'd tried to take his land, and had made plenty of enemies along the way. Not that he gave a damn about any of that. Today, he looked exhausted.

Stoker sighed again.

"Something bothering you, Pa?"

"Had poker games all weekend, but last night's lasted until dawn."

Houston chuckled. "Pa, everyone in the whole blame state knows about your poker games. They're legendary. That must be why you look like you've been dragged behind a horse. I take it there was a good bit of drinking involved?"

"Can't play cards without it, son. The two just go together." Stoker ran a finger along the edge of the desk. "I won a few. Lost a few. There's something I've got to tell you, son."

"Start at the beginning and let it fly," Houston advised. "That's what you'd tell me."

Stoker rose and stared out the window. "It's about… Perhaps I can shed some light on the problem with those books you've been studying."

Houston's stomach clenched. This sounded worse than losing a couple of hands of poker with friends. "The ranch is in a pretty tight bind right now, but tell me how much you lost and we'll cover it. I take it that's where the huge deficit in the books went."

They couldn't take many more losses like that. How many times was Stoker going to wager his life's work away?

"It is." Stoker gave a curt nod. "But that's only a small corner of the problem. The truth is… The ranch has been cut in half. Yours, Sam's, and Luke's—your legacies have shrunk considerably."

Everything inside Houston stilled: his heart, his breathing, his ability to swallow. He couldn't stop anger from flaring. "What do you mean cut in half? What have you done, Pa?"

"It's gone."

"What's gone? Are you talking about land, money, or what?" Houston slammed the receipts register closed. He dreaded telling his brothers their father had finally lost it all.

"You know how I have a standing poker game every Saturday night."

For Stoker to repeat himself meant he couldn't even bear to say the words.

"Quit stalling, Pa. Yes, for as long as I can recall, you, Max Golden, and Kern Smith have cut loose on Saturday nights. You lost half the ranch to them?" That might not be so bad. They were longtime friends. Maybe Houston could persuade them to let the wager go for a drunken mistake and they'd all have a good laugh. After all, they were reasonable men. Kern's wife once came to ask that Stoker return money they needed for ranch expenses.

"Not exactly." Stoker looked away. "We had another rancher join us. New to the area. Name's Till Boone. He bought the spread adjoining ours to the south that's lain idle for thirty years. Till now owns two hundred forty thousand acres of our ranch where it adjoins his."

"Damn it, Pa! That's where all the grass is. What were you thinking?"

Stoker plowed his fingers through his thick hair. "I had a little too much bourbon."

"Pa, you promised to slow down."

His father whirled and leaned over the desk, pointing his finger. "I don't need a lecture from you. I will when *you* will. The main thing is that we can fix this."

"How? I've never known you not to honor all your debts, even the ones made when you were soused. I can't believe this." He didn't see a way in hell of keeping the ranch together. None whatsoever. What was he going to tell Sam? Or Luke, who'd just started to feel a part of the family?

Fire flashed from Stoker's bloodshot eyes. "There's only one way and it'll be up to you. I need you in on this, Houston."

Fury crawled up Houston's spine. "So I'm supposed to fix the mess you've made?"

"You're the only one who can, son."

"Stop talking in riddles, Pa, and get on with it." Houston could barely contain his fury. He didn't like having hard feelings for his father, but for Stoker to expect him to fix a stupid blunder like this stretched their relationship to the breaking point.

"Till Boone's daughter needs a husband. Boone said if you'll marry his Lara, he'll forgive my foolish wager. And we can keep the land."

"What? This is your idea of fixing things?" Houston exploded in a single word: "*NO!*" He leaped to his feet so fast it sent his chair toppling. "You're crazy to even think I'd consider this."

Houston couldn't marry again. He hadn't slept a full night since his first disastrous wedding and only whiskey could silence his demons. He carried festering wounds that hadn't even begun to scab over, and to ask him to marry another would throw him right back into that pit with no way to crawl out. He hadn't been able to trust Becky and he'd known her forever. How could he bind himself to a perfect stranger and not expect more of the same?

"Boone gave us twenty-four hours to think about it." Stoker crossed the space to him and laid a hand on his shoulder. "I know it's asking a lot."

"Hell yeah, it's asking a lot. How about asking me to give up the rest of my life? Asking me to live with a stranger, sleep in the same bed, pretend to care for someone sitting across from me at the supper table? The answer is no. And all that aside, I leave on the cattle drive in three weeks. I don't have time to deal with this." Houston shrugged out from under Stoker's hand. He strode for the door, putting some distance between them before he hauled off and hit his father.

"There's more." Stoker's words stopped him in his tracks.

With narrowed eyes, Houston whirled. "How much worse can it be? What else is Boone wanting? The marriage license signed in blood? Tacking my hide to the barn door? What?"

"His daughter, Lara, has a child. A little girl. In return for giving us back the land, Boone is asking you to give her child a name and raise the girl as your daughter."

The air left Houston in a big whoosh. This was like

Becky all over again. She had needed a name for *her* child. Was he never to be anything more than a tool for someone to use for their own ends? What about his wants? His longings?

Becky had wanted to foist Ernie Newman's child off on him. He wondered if he would've known, if he'd have seen the man's resemblance in the babe. Would it have mattered, he wondered? He'd loved Becky so fully and completely. If she'd survived, would he have forgiven her and have a child he loved as his own even now?

And what of *this* girl's innocent babe?

Houston's brother Luke came to mind. He'd been raised a bastard child and it had turned him into an outlaw. People had called him the devil's spawn. What would the slurs do to an innocent girl? Could Houston live with people calling her and her baby all manner of names, looking down on them, when he could have done something about it?

"How old is the child?" Houston asked quietly.

"A babe…not quite a year."

Houston met Stoker's green gaze. "The child's father is dead?"

"He will be when Boone finds the bastard. He forced himself on Lara. The babe needs a real father. She can never know the truth of her birth."

Damn! Stoker had him over a barrel, and he knew it. First there was the land, and then this. And Houston would be the bastard of the year if he didn't help a woman in trouble.

"Boone needs an answer quick, Houston."

Everyone needed something and right away. What

about his need for a heart that wasn't scarred and pitted? "You'll have your answer in the morning. Until then, give me some space."

Houston had lots of thinking to do and a hefty decision to make.

All Lara Boone needed was his name. He could do that much. Couldn't he?

No one said he had to love her. Or sleep beside her. Or share secrets with her.

Besides, what else did he have to look forward to in his life? Pretending he cared, pretending pain didn't rip through him every time he breathed—pretending he lived.

❧

Dawn rose on Tuesday with a whisper and Houston had not once closed his eyes. A fist gripped his heart as he got to his feet on the bluff overlooking the mighty Red. Stone-cold sober, he'd spent the night gazing up at the star-studded sky. There alone he'd made up his mind about what he had to do.

For years he'd envied Sam, who lived his life as he wanted. Houston had resented him for always riding off to chase adventure as a Texas Ranger. For always leaving big brother with the obligation to run the ranch and try to corral Stoker.

Just once, Houston wanted to see what it was like to wake up to snow-covered mountain peaks. Just once he wanted to taste the salty ocean air. And just once he wanted to get on a ship and sail to some faraway place.

When he was a boy, he'd entertained notions of riding the Butterfield Overland Mail stage all the way to the California gold fields. He'd wanted to pan for gold and put his feet in the Pacific Ocean.

But after his mother died and Stoker took to drink and gambling, Houston had been forced to quash those dreams of adventure. Because he was the oldest. Because Sam had washed his hands of the ranch. Because someone had to stay behind. That someone was Houston.

Hell!

Others' wishes *always* seemed more important than his.

When would it be *his* turn? Would it ever?

❧

The Lone Star was beginning to wake up when he reined in at the corral.

As he dismounted, the day's brand-new rays bounced off the huge bronze star that hung next to the headquarters, suspended by heavy chains between two poles.

"I should've slept under that blasted star," Houston muttered. A local legend said a man would learn his true worth if he slept under the Texas star. Of course, no one knew for sure what that meant, exactly. The "Texas star" could refer to the bronze one, the ones overhead, or to the Lone Star Ranch itself. Sam had talked about sleeping on the ground beneath this bronze star to see if that would help him, but then he'd found his worth deep in the depths of Sierra's blue eyes.

Maybe one day Houston would find his worth and know the man he was. If he lived long enough.

As he strolled toward headquarters for breakfast,

two ranch hands hoisted the Texas flag up the tall pole that stood at a corner of the two-story, white-stone house. He stopped for a moment to watch the breeze unfurl the fabric, the banner that sported one large star. His chest swelled with pride. His father had told him that he'd lost his father and every one of his brothers in the Texas War of Independence. They, plus thousands of other men, had died so Houston, Sam, and Luke could live free.

Even though he yearned to see other places in the world for a spell, he had no desire to live out all his days anywhere but here. This was his home, his roots. He loved this wild state and the land where he'd been born and lived his whole life. He'd do anything to keep the ranch in one piece.

Even take a wife sight unseen.

With long strides, Houston entered the house and went straight to the kitchen. Stoker silently glanced up. His father's eyes held the question that his tongue would not ask.

Houston gave him a curt nod and poured a cup of coffee from the granite pot sitting on the table. "I've made my decision, Pa. But before I tell you, I want to say that this is the last damn time I'm bailing you out of anything."

Stoker's face flushed as he snapped, "I'm not a boy in knee britches. I'm your father, dammit."

"Then act like one," Houston snapped back, and took his seat. He lifted his cup for a sip of hot brew. It warmed the outside but did nothing to melt the layer of ice inside his chest. "I don't intend to have this conversation ever again."

Silence spun between them as fragile as a piece of handblown glass.

Finally, Houston spoke. "I'll marry Lara Boone and give her baby daughter my name. I'll raise her as a Legend." He paused then added, "But only if you put this ranch in all our names, and sign over the land you wagered to me and my brothers."

Stoker's face darkened. "Those are your terms?"

"They are. I don't think they're unreasonable."

His father studied his coffee cup for a minute. "I'll agree—if you tell no one, and I'm still the boss."

"Deal. I'll put aside my life for Lara Boone." Houston finished his coffee and set down the cup. "If anyone ever speaks ill of her child, they'll answer to my fists."

"And to mine," Stoker said firmly, slamming his hand down on the table, jarring the coffeepot. "One thing I won't abide is someone being mean and spiteful to a child. I know I've hurt Luke real bad, and damn, that tears into me. If I'd known he was my son, I'd have claimed him in a heartbeat. I can only imagine the names people called him. But they're not going to do that to Lara's child if I have anything to say about it."

At least they were in agreement on this. But the hot words Houston had spoken sat on his tongue like a sour persimmon. To have to fix another one of his father's careless mistakes stuck in his craw. In Houston's almost thirty years, he'd never once had his father apologize for anything. And Stoker sure didn't look like he was going to start now.

Releasing a loud sigh of frustration, Houston rose

and sauntered toward the door. "You'll let Boone know?" he asked without turning.

"I'll send a message," Stoker replied.

"The sooner I get this over with the better."